Th Frozen Pirate

William Clark Russell

Solis Press

ALSO BY WILLIAM CLARK RUSSELL AND
PUBLISHED BY SOLIS PRESS

The Wreck of the "Grosvenor"

List, Ye Landsmen!

Sailors' Language: A Collection of Sea-terms and their Definitions

A Nightmare of the Doldrums

ALL THESE TITLES ARE AVAILABLE FROM AMAZON

Publisher's Note

Caution: this book contains words that are offensive. The book was first published in 1877 when such language was not thought of as being unacceptable. However, rather than censor or bowdlerize the book we have reproduced it in full.

ISBN: 978-1-910146-04-0

Published by Solis Press, PO Box 482
Tunbridge Wells TN2 9QT, Kent, England

Web: www.solispress.com I *Twitter*: @SolisPress

Contents

Chapter I.
The Storm

THE *Laughing Mary* was a light ship, as sailors term a vessel that stands high upon the water, having discharged her cargo at Callao, from which port we were proceeding in ballast to Cape Town, South Africa, there to call for orders. Our run to within a few parallels of the latitude of the Horn had been extremely pleasant; the proverbial mildness of the Pacific Ocean was in the mellow sweetness of the wind and in the gentle undulations of the silver-laced swell; but scarce had we passed the height of forty-nine degrees when the weather grew sullen and dark, a heavy bank of clouds of a livid hue rose in the north-east, and the wind came and went in small guns, the gusts venting themselves in dreary moans, insomuch that our oldest hands confessed they had never heard blasts more portentous.

The gale came on with some lightning and several claps of thunder and heavy rain. Though it was but two o'clock in the afternoon, the air was so dusky that the men had to feel for the ropes; and when the first of the tempest stormed down upon us the appearance of the sea was uncommonly terrible, being swept and mangled into boiling froth in the north-east quarter, whilst all about us and in the south-west it lay in a sort of swollen huddle of shadows, glooming into the darkness of the sky without offering the smallest glimpse of the horizon.

In a few minutes the hurricane struck us. We had bared the brig down to the close-reefed main-topsail; yet, though we were dead before the outfly, its first blow rent the fragment of sail as if it were formed of smoke, and in an instant it disappeared, flashing over the bows like a scattering of torn paper, leaving nothing but the bolt-ropes behind. The bursting of the topsail was like the explosion of a large cannon. In a breath the brig was smothered with froth torn up in huge clouds, and hurled over and ahead of her in vast quivering bodies that filled the wind with a dismal twilight of their own, in which nothing was visible but their terrific speeding. Through these slinging, soft, and singing masses of spume drove the rain in horizontal steel-like lines, which gleamed in the lightning stroke as though indeed they were barbed weapons of bright metal, darted by armies of invisible spirits raving out their war cries as they chased us.

The storm made a loud thunder in the sky, and this tremendous utterance dominated without subduing the many screaming, hissing, shrieking, and hooting noises raised in the rigging and about the decks, and the wild, seething, weltering sound of the sea, maddened by the gale and struggling in its enormous passion under the first choking and iron grip of the hurricane's hand.

I had used the ocean for above ten years, but never had I encountered anything suddener or fiercer in the form of weather than this. Though the wind blew from the tropics it was as cruel in bitterness as frost. Yet there was neither snow nor hail, only rain that seemed to pass like a knife through the head if you showed your face to it for a second. It was necessary to bring the brig to the wind before the sea rose. The helm was put down, and without a rag of canvas on her she came round; but when she brought the hurricane fair abeam, I thought it was all over with us. She lay down to it until her bulwarks were under water, and the sheer-poles in the rigging above the rail hidden.

In this posture she hung so long that Captain Rosy, the master, bawled to me to tell the carpenter to stand by to cut away the topmast rigging. But the *Laughing Mary*, as the brig was called, was a buoyant ship and lightly sparred, and presently bringing the sea on the bow, through our seizing a small tarpaulin in the weather main shrouds, she erected her masts afresh, like some sentient creature pricking its ears for the affray, and with that showed herself game and made indifferently good weather of it.

But though the first rage of the storm was terrible enough, its fierceness did not come to its height till about one o'clock in the middle watch. Long before then the sea had grown mountainous, and the dance of our eggshell of a brig upon it was sickening and affrighting. The heads of the Andean peaks of black water looked tall enough to brush the lowering soot of the heavens with the blue and yellow phosphoric fires which sparkled ghastly amid the bursting froth. Bodies of foam flew like the flashings of pale sheet-lightning through our rigging and over us, and a dreadful roaring of mighty surges in mad career, and battling as they ran, rose out of the sea to deepen yet the thunderous bellowing of the hurricane on high.

No man could show himself on deck and preserve his life. Between the rails it was waist high, and this water, converted by the motions of the brig into a wild torrent, had its volume perpetually maintained by ton-loads of sea falling in dull and pounding crashes over the bows on to the forecastle. There was nothing to be done but secure the helm and await the issue below, for, if we were to be drowned, it would make a more easy foundering to go down dry and warm in the cabin, than to perish half-frozen and already nearly strangled by the bitter cold and flooded tempest on deck.

There was Captain Rosy; there was myself, by name Paul Rodney, mate of the brig; and there were the remaining seven of a crew, including the carpenter. We sat in the cabin, one of us from time to time clawing his way up the ladder to peer through the companion, and we looked at one another with the melancholy of malefactors waiting to be called from their cells for the last jaunt to Tyburn.

"May God have mercy upon us!" cries the carpenter. "There must be an earthquake inside this storm. Something more than wind is going to the making of these seas. Hear that, now! naught less than a forty-foot chuck-up could ha' ended in that souse, mates."

"A man can die but once," says Captain Rosy, "and he'll not perish the quicker for looking at his end with a stout heart;" and with that he put his hand into the locker on which he had been sitting and pulled out a jar of whisky, which, after putting his lips to it and keeping them glued there whilst you could have counted twenty, he handed to me, and so it went round, coming back to him empty.

I often have the sight of that cabin in my mind's eye; and it was not long afterwards that it would visit me as such a vision of comfort, I would with a grateful heart have accepted it with tenfold darker conditions of danger, had it been possible to exchange my situation for it. A lantern hung from a beam, and swung violently to the rolling and pitching of the brig. The alternations of its light put twenty different meanings, one after another, into the settled dismal and rueful expressions in the faces of my companions. We were clad in warm clothes, and the steam rose from the damp in our coats and trousers like vapour from wet straw. The drink mottled some of our faces, but the spirituous tincture only imparted a quality of irony to the melancholy of our visages, as if our mournfulness were not wholly sincere, when, God knows, our hearts were taken up with counting the minutes when we should find ourselves bursting for want of breath under water.

Thus it continued till daybreak, all which time we strove to encourage one another as best we could, sometimes with words, sometimes with putting the bottle about. It was impossible for any of us at any moment to show more than our noses above the companion; and even at that you needed the utmost caution, for the decks being full of water, it was necessary to await the lurch of the vessel before moving the slide or cover to the companion, else you stood to drown the cabin.

Being exceedingly anxious, for the brig lay unwatched, I looked forth on one occasion longer than the others chose to venture, and beheld the most extravagant scene of raging commotion it could enter the brain of man to imagine. The night was as black as the bottom of a well; but the prodigious swelling and flinging of white waters hove a faintness upon the air that was in its way a dim light, by which it was just possible to distinguish the reeling masts to the height of the tops, and to observe the figure of the brig springing black and trembling out of the head of a surge that had broken over and smothered her as in a cauldron, and to note the shapes of the nearer liquid acclivities as they bore down upon our weather bow, catching the brig fair under the bluff, and so sloping her that she seemed to stand end on, and so heeling her that the sea would wash to the height of the main hatch. Indeed, had she been loaded, and therefore deep, she could not have lived an hour in that hollow and frightful ocean; but having nothing in her but ballast she was like a bladder, and swung up the surges and blew away to leeward like an empty cask.

When the dawn broke something of its midnight fury went out of the gale. The carpenter made shift to sound the well, and to our great satisfaction found but little water, only as much as we had a right to suppose she would take in above. But it was impossible to stand at the pumps, so we returned to the cabin and brewed some cold punch and did what we could to keep our spirits hearty. By noon the wind had weakened yet, but the sea still ran very heavily, and the sky was uncommonly thick with piles of dusky, yellowish, hurrying clouds; and though we could fairly reckon upon our position, the atmosphere was so nipping it was difficult to persuade ourselves that Cape Horn was not close aboard.

We could now work the pumps, and a short spell freed the brig. We got up a new main-topsail and bent it, and, setting the reefed foresail, put the vessel before the wind, and away she ran, chased by the swollen seas. Thus we continued till by dead reckoning we calculated that we were about thirty leagues south of the parallel of the Horn, and in longitude eighty-seven degrees west. We then boarded our larboard tacks and brought the brig as close to the wind as it was proper to lay her for a progress that should not be wholly leeway; but four hours after we had handled the braces the gale, that had not veered two points since it first came on to blow, stormed up again into its first fury; and the morning of the 1st of July, *anno* 1801, found the *Laughing Mary* passionately labouring in the midst of an enraged Cape Horn sea, her jibboom and fore top-gallant mast gone, her ballast shifted, so that her posture even in a calm would have exhibited her with her starboard channels under, and her decks swept by enormous surges, which, fetching her larboard bilge dreadful blows, thundered in mighty green masses over her.

Chapter II.
The Iceberg

THE loss of the spars I have named was no great matter, nor were we to be intimidated by such weather as was to be expected off Cape Horn. For what sailor entering this icy and tempestuous tract of waters but knows that here he must expect to find Nature in her most violent moods, crueller and more unreckonable than a mad woman, who one moment looks with a silent sinister sullenness upon you, and the next is shrieking with devilish laughter as she makes as if to spring upon you?

But there was an inveteracy in the gale which had driven us down to this part that bore heavily upon our spirits. It was impossible to trim the ballast. We dared not veer so as to bring the ship on the other tack. And the slope of the decks, added to the fierce wild motions of the fabric, made our situation as unendurable as that of one who should be confined in a cask and sent rolling downhill. It was impossible to light a fire, and we could not therefore dress our food or obtain a warm drink. The cold was beyond language severe. The rigging was glazed with ice, and great pendants of the silvery brilliance of crystal hung from the yards, bowsprit, and catheads, whilst the sails were frozen to the hardness of granite, and lay like sheets of iron rolled up in gaskets of steel. We had no means of drying our clothes, nor were we able so to move as by exercise we might keep ourselves warm. Never once did the sun shine to give us the encouragement of his glorious beam. Hour after hour found us amid the same distracting scene: the tall olive-coloured seas hurling out their rage in foam as they roared towards us in ranges of dissolving cliffs; the wind screaming and whistling through our grey and frozen rigging; the water washing in floods about our decks, with the ends of the running gear snaking about in the torrent, and the live stock lying drowned and stiff in their coops and pen near the caboose.

With helm lashed and yards pointed to the wind thus we lay, thus we drifted, steadily trending with the send of each giant surge further and deeper into the icy regions of the south-west, helpless, foreboding, disconsolate.

It was the night of the fourth day of the month. The crew were forward in the forecastle, and I knew not if any man was on deck saving myself. In truth, there was no place in which a watch could be kept, if it were not in the companion hatch. Such was the violence with which the seas broke over the brig that it was at the risk of his life a man crawled the distance betwixt the forecastle and the quarter-deck. It had been as thick as mud all day, and now upon this flying gloom of haze, sleet, and spray had descended the blackness of the night.

I stood in the companion as in a sentry-box, with my eyes just above the cover. Nothing was to be seen but sheets of ghostly white water sweeping up the blackness on the vessel's lee, or breaking and boiling to windward. It was sheer blind chaos to the sight, and you might have supposed that the brig was in the midst of some enormous vaporous turmoil, so illusive and indefinable were the shadows of the storm-tormented night—one block of blackness melting into another, with sometimes an extraordinary faintness of light speeding along the dark sky like to the dim reflection of a lanthorn flinging its radiance from afar, which no doubt must have been the reflection of some particular bright and extensive bed of foam upon a sooty belly on high, hanging lower than the other clouds. I say, you might have thought yourself in the midst of some hellish conflict of vapour but for the substantial thunder of the surges upon the vessel and the shriek of the slung masses of water flying like cannon balls between the masts.

After a long and eager look round into the obscurity, semi-lucent with froth, I went below for a mouthful of spirits and a bite of supper, the hour being eight bells in the second dog watch as we say, that is, eight o'clock in the evening. The captain and carpenter were in the cabin. Upon the swing-tray over the table were a piece of corned beef, some biscuit, and a bottle of hollands.

"Nothing to be seen, I suppose, Rodney?" says the captain.

"Nothing," I answered. "She looks well up, and that's all that can be said."

"I've been hove to under bare poles more than once in my time," said the carpenter, "but never through so long a stretch. I doubt if you'll find many vessels to look up to it as this here *Laughing Mary* does."

"The loss of hamper forward will make her the more weatherly," says Captain Rosy. "But we're in an ugly part of the globe. When bad sailors die they're sent here, I reckon. The worst nautical sinner can't be hove to long off the Horn without coming out of it with a purged soul. He must start afresh to deserve further punishment."

"Well, here's a breeze that can't go on blowing much longer," cries the carpenter. "The place it comes from must give out soon, unless a new trade wind's got fixed into a whole gale for this here ocean."

"What southing do you allow our drift will be giving us, captain?" I asked, munching a piece of beef.

"All four mile an hour," he answered. "If this goes on I shall look to make some discoveries. The Antarctic circle won't be far off presently, and since you're a scholar, Rodney, I'll leave you to describe what's inside of it, though boil me if I don't have the naming of the tallest land; for, d'ye see, I've a mind to be known after I'm dead, and there's nothing like your signature on a mountain to be remembered by."

He grinned and put his hand out for the bottle, and after a pull passed it to the carpenter. I guessed by his jocosity that he had already been making somewhat free; for although I love a bold face put upon a difficulty, ours was a situation in which only a tipsy man could find food for merriment.

At this instant we were startled by a wild and fearful shout on deck. It sounded high above the sweeping and seething of the wind and the hissing of the lashed waters, and it penetrated the planks with a note that gave it an inexpressible character of anguish.

"A man washed overboard!" bawled the carpenter, springing to his feet.

"No!" cried I, for my younger and shrewder ear had caught a note in the cry that persuaded me it was not as the carpenter said; and in an instant the three of us jumped up the ladder and gained the deck.

The moment I was in the gale the same affrighted cry rang down along the wind from some man forward: *For God's sake tumble up before we are upon it!*

"What do you see?" I roared, sending my voice, trumpet-fashion, through my hands; for as to my own and the sight of Captain Rosy and the carpenter, why, it was like being struck blind to come on a sudden out of the lighted cabin into the black night.

Any reply that might have been attempted was choked out by the dive of the brig's head into a sea, which furiously flooded her forecastle and came washing aft like milk in the darkness till it was up to our knees.

"See there!" suddenly roared the carpenter.

"Where, man, where?" bawled the captain.

But in this brief time my sight had grown used to the night, and I saw the object before the carpenter could answer. It lay on our lee beam, but how far off no man could have told in that black thickness. It stood against the darkness and hung out a dim complexion of light, or rather of pallidness, that was not light—not to be described by the pen. It was like a small hill of snow, and looked as snow does or the foam of the sea in darkness, and it came and went with our soaring and sinking.

"Ice!" I shouted to the captain.

"I see it!" he answered, in a voice that satisfied me the consternation he was under had settled the fumes of the spirits out of his head. "We must drive her clear at all risks."

There was no need to call the men. To the second cry that had been raised by one among them who had come out of the forecastle and seen the berg, they had tumbled up as sailors will when they jump for their lives; and now they came staggering, splashing, crawling aft to us, for the lamp in the cabin made a sheen in the companion hatch, and they could see us as we stood there.

"Men," cried Captain Rosy, "yonder's a gravestone for our carcases if we are not lively! Cast the helm adrift!" (we steered by a tiller). "Two hands stand by it. Forward, some of ye, and loose the stay-foresail, and show the head of it."

The fellows hung in the wind. I could not wonder. The bowsprit had been sprung when the jibboom was wrenched from the cap by the fall of the top-gallant-mast; it still had to bear the weight of the heavy spritsail yard, and the drag of the staysail might carry the spar overboard with the men upon it. Yet it was our best chance; the one sail most speedily released and hoisted, the one that would pay the brig's head off quickest, and the only fragment that promised to stand.

"Jump!" roared the captain, in a passion of hurry. "Great thunder! 'tis close aboard! You'll leave me no sea room for veering if you delay an instant."

"Follow me who will!" I cried out; "and others stand by ready to hoist away."

Thus speaking—for there seemed to my mind a surer promise of death in hesitation at this supreme moment than in twenty such risks as laying out on the bowsprit signified—I made for the lee of the weather bulwarks, and blindly hauled myself forward by such pins and gear as came to my hands. A man might spend his life on the ocean and never have to deal with such a passage as this. It was not the bitter cold only, though perhaps of its full fierceness the wildness of my feelings did not suffer me to be sensible; it was the pouring of volumes of water upon me from over the rail, often tumbling upon my head with such weight as nearly to beat the breath out of my body and sink me to the deck; it was the frenzy excited in me by the tremendous obligation of despatch and my retardment by the washing seas, the violent motions of the brig, the encumbrance of gear and deck furniture adrift and sweeping here and there, and the sense that the vessel might be grinding her bows against the iceberg before I should be able to reach the bowsprit. All this it was that filled me with a kind of madness, by the sheer force of which alone I was enabled to reach the forecastle, for had I gone to my duty coldly, without agitation of spirits, my heart must have failed me before I had measured half the length of the brig.

I got on to the bowsprit nearly stifled by the showering of the seas, holding an open knife between my teeth, half dazed by the prodigious motion of the light brig, which, at this extreme end of her, was to be felt to the full height of its extravagance. At every plunge I expected to be buried, and every moment I was prepared to be torn from my hold. It was a fearful time; the falling off of the brig into the trough—and never was I in a hollower and more swelling sea—her falling off, I say, in the act of veering might end us out of hand by the rolling of a surge over us big enough to crush the vessel down fathoms out of sight; and then there was that horrible heap of faint whiteness leaping out of the dense blackness of the sky, gathering a more visible sharpness of outline with every liquid heave that forked us high into the flying night with shrieking rigging and boiling decks.

Commending myself to God, for I was now to let go with my hands, I pulled the knife from my teeth, and feeling for the gaskets or lines which bound the sail to the spar, I cut and hacked as fast as I could ply my arms. In a flash the gale, whipping into a liberated fold of the canvas, blew the whole sail out; the bowsprit reeled and quivered under me; I danced off it with incredible despatch, shouting to the men to hoist away. The head of the staysail mounted in thunder, and the slatting of its folds and the thrashing of its sheet was like the rattling of heavy field-pieces whisked at full gallop over a stony road.

"High enough!" I bawled, guessing enough was shown, for I could not see. "Get a drag upon the sheet, lads, and then aft with you for your lives!"

Scarce had I let forth my breath in this cry when I heard the blast as of a gun, and knew by that the sail was gone; an instant after wash came a mountainous sea sheer over the weather bulwarks fair betwixt the fore and main rigging; but happily, standing near the fore shrouds, I was holding on with both hands to the topsail halliards whilst calling to the men, so that being under the rail, which broke the blow of the sea, and holding on too, no mischief befell me, only that for about twenty seconds I stood in a horrible fury and smother of frothing water, hearing nothing, seeing nothing, with every faculty in me so numbed and dulled by the wet, cold, and horror of our situation, that I knew not whether in that space of time I was in the least degree sensible of what had happened or what might befall.

The water leaving the deck, I rallied, though half-drowned, and staggered aft, and found the helm deserted, nor could I see any signs of my companions. I rushed to the tiller, and putting my whole weight and force to it, drove it up to windward and secured it by a turn of its own rope; for ice or no ice—and for the moment I was so blinded by the wet that I could not see the berg—my madness now was to get the brig before the sea and out of the trough, advised by every instinct in me that such another surge as that which had rolled over her must send her to the bottom in less time than it would take a man to cry "O God!"

A figure came out of the blackness on the lee side of the deck.

"Who is that?" said he. It was Captain Rosy.

I answered.

"What, Rodney! alive?" cried he. "I think I have been struck insensible."

Two more figures came crawling aft. Then two more. They were the carpenter and three seamen.

I cried out, "Who was at the helm when that sea was shipped?"

A man answered, "Me, Thomas Jobling."

"Where's your mate?" I asked; and it seemed to me that I was the only man who had his senses full just then.

"He was washed forward along with me," he replied.

Now a fifth man joined us, but before I could question him as to the others, the captain, with a scream like an epileptic's cry, shrieked, "It's all over with us! We are upon it!"

I looked and perceived the iceberg to be within a musket-shot, whence it was clear that it had been closer to us when first sighted than the blackness of the night would suffer us to distinguish. In a time like this at sea events throng so fast they come in a heap, and even if the intelligence were not confounded by the uproar and peril, if indeed it were as placid as in any time of perfect security, it could not possibly take note of one-tenth that happens.

I confess that, for my part, I was very nearly paralysed by the nearness of the iceberg, and by the cry of the captain, and by the perception that there was nothing to be done. That which I best recollect is the appearance of the mass of ice lying solidly, like a little island, upon the seas which roared in creaming waters about it. Every blow of the black and arching surge was reverberated in a dull hollow tremble back to the ear through the hissing flight of the gale. The frozen body was not taller than our mastheads, yet it showed like a mountain hanging over us as the brig was flung swirling into the deep Pacific hollow, leaving us staring upwards out of the instant's stagnation of the trough with lips set breathlessly and with dying eyes. It put a kind of film of faint light outside the lines of its own shape, and this served to magnify it, and it showed spectrally in the darkness as though it reflected some visionary light that came neither from the sea nor the sky. These points I recollect; likewise the maddening and maddened motion of our vessel, sliding towards it down one midnight declivity to another.

All other features were swallowed up in the agony of the time. One monstrous swing the brig gave, like to some doomed creature's last delirious struggle; the bowsprit caught the ice and snapped with the noise of a great tree crackling in fire. I could hear the masts breaking overhead—the crash and blows of spars and yards torn down and striking the hull; above all the grating of the vessel, that was now head on to the sea and swept by the billows, broadside on, along the sharp and murderous projections. Two monster seas tumbled over the bows, floated me off my legs, and dashed me against the tiller, to which I clung. I heard no cries. I regained my feet, clinging with a death-grip to the tiller, and, seeing no one near me, tried to holloa, to know if any man were living, but could not make my voice sound.

The fearful grating noise ceased on a sudden, and the faintness of the berg loomed upon the starboard bow. We had been hurled clear of it and were to leeward; but what was our condition? I tried to shout again, but to no purpose; and was in the act of quitting the tiller to go forward when I was struck over the brows by something from aloft—a block, as I believe—and fell senseless upon the deck.

Chapter III.
I Lose My Companions

I LAY for a long while insensible; and that I should have recovered my mind instead of dying in that swoon I must ever account as the greatest wonder of a life that has not been wanting in the marvellous. I had no sooner sat up than all that had happened and my present situation instantly came to me. My hair was stiff with ice; there was no more feeling in my hands than had they been of stone; my clothes weighed upon me like a suit of armour, so inflexibly hard were they frozen. Yet I got upon my legs, and found that I could stand and walk, and that life flowed warm in my veins, for all that I had been lying motionless for an hour or more, laved by water that would have become ice had it been still.

It was intensely dark; the binnacle lamp was extinguished, and the light in the cabin burned too dimly to throw the faintest colour upon the hatchway. One thing I quickly noticed, that the gale had broken and blew no more than a fresh breeze. The sea still ran very high, but though every surge continued to hurl its head of snow, and the heavens to resemble ink from contrast with the passage, as it seemed, close under them of these pallid bodies, there was less spite in its wash, less fury in its blow. The multitudinous roaring of the heaving blackness had sobered into a hard and sullen growling, a sound as of thunder among mountains heard in a valley.

The brig pitched and rolled heavily. Much of the buoyancy of her earlier dance was gone out of her. Nevertheless, I could not persuade myself that this sluggishness was altogether due to the water she had taken in. It was wonderful, however, that she should still be afloat. No man could have heard the rending and grating of her side against the ice without supposing that every plank in it was being torn out.

Finding that I had the use of my voice, I holloaed as loudly as I could, but no human note responded. Three or four times I shouted, giving some of the people their names, but in vain. Father of mercy! I thought, what has come to pass? Is it possible that all my companions have been washed overboard? Certainly, five men at least were living before we fouled the ice. And again I cried out, "Is there any one alive?" looking wildly along the black decks, and putting so much force into my voice with the consternation that the thought of my being alone raised in me, that I had like to have burst a blood-vessel.

My loneliness was more terrible to me than any other condition of my situation. It was dreadful to be standing, nearly dead with cold, in utter darkness, upon the flooded decks of a hull wallowing miserably amid the black hollows and eager foaming peaks of the labouring sea, convinced that she was slowly filling, and that at any moment she might go down with me; it was dreadful, I say, to be thus placed, and to feel that I was in the heart of the rudest, most desolate space of sea in the world, into which the commerce of the earth dispatched but few ships all the year round. But no feature of my lamentable situation so affrighted me, so worked upon the passions of my mind, as my loneliness. Oh, for one companion, even one only, to make me an echo for mine own speech! Nay, God Himself, the merciful Father of all, even He seemed not! The blackness lay like a pall upon the deep, and upon my soul. Misery and horror were within that shadow, and beyond it nothing that my spirit could look up to!

I stood for some moments as one stunned, and then my manhood— trained to some purpose by the usage of the sea—reasserted itself; and maybe I also got some slender comfort from observing that, dull and heavy as was the motion of the brig, there was yet the buoyancy of vitality in her manner of mounting the seas, and that, after all, her case might not be so desperate as was threatened by the way in which she had been torn and precipitated past the iceberg. At moments when she plunged the whiteness of the water creaming upon the surges on either hand threw out a phantom light of sufficient power to enable me to see that the forward part of the brig was littered with wreckage, which served to a certain extent as a breakwater by preventing the seas, which washed on to the forecastle, from cascading with their former violence aft; also that the whole length of the main and top masts lay upon the larboard rail and over the side, held in that position by the gear, attached to them. This was all that I could distinguish, and of this only the most elusive glimpse was to be had.

Feeling as though the very marrow in my bones were frozen, I crawled to the companion and, pulling open the door, descended. The lamp in the companion burnt faintly. There was a clock fixed to a beam over the table; my eyes directly sought it, and found the time twenty minutes after ten. This signified that I had ten or eleven hours of darkness before me!

I took down the lamp, trimmed it, and went to the lazarette hatch at the after end of the cabin. Here were kept the stores for the crew. I lifted the hatch and listened, and could hear the water in the hold gurgling and rushing with every lift of the brig's bows; and I could not question from the volume of water which the sound indicated that the vessel was steadily taking it in, but not rapidly. I swallowed half a pannikin of the hollands for the sake of the warmth and life of the draught, and entering my cabin, put on thick dry stockings, first, chafing my feet till I felt the blood in them; and I then, with a seaman's dispatch, shifted the rest of my apparel, and cannot express how greatly I was comforted by the change, though the jacket and trousers I put on were still damp with the soaking of previous days. To render myself as waterproof as possible—for it was the wet clothes against the skin that made the cold so cruel—I took from the captain's cabin a stout cloak and threw it over me, enveloping my head, which I had cased in a warm fur cap, with the hood of it; and thus equipped I lighted a small hand-lantern that was used on dark nights for heaving the log, that is, for showing how the sand runs in the glass, and carried it on deck.

The lantern made the scene a dead, grave-like black outside its little circle of illumination; nevertheless its rays suffered me to guess at the picture of ruin the decks offered. The main mast was snapped three or four feet above the deck, and the stump of it showed as jagged and barbed as a wild beast's teeth. But I now noticed that the weight of the hamper being on the larboard side, balanced the list the vessel took from her shifted ballast, and that she floated on a level keel with her bows fair at the sea, whence I concluded that a sort of sea-anchor had been formed ahead of her by the wreckage, and that it held her in that posture, otherwise she must certainly have fallen into the trough.

I moved with extreme caution, casting the lantern light before me, sometimes starting at a sound that resembled a groan, then stopping to steady myself during some particular wild leap of the hull; until, coming abreast of the main hatch, the rays of the lantern struck upon a man's body, which, on my bringing the flame to his face, proved to be Captain Rosy. There was a wound over his right brow; and as if that had not sufficed to slay him, the fall of the masts had in some wonderful manner whipped a rope several times round his body, binding his arms and encircling his throat so tightly, that no executioner could have gone more artistically to work to pinion and choke a man.

Under a mass of rigging in the larboard scuppers lay two bodies, as I could just faintly discern; it was impossible to put the lantern close enough to either one of them to distinguish his face, nor had I the strength even if I had possessed the weapons to extricate them, for they lay under a whole body of shrouds, complicated by a mass of other gear, against which leaned a portion of the caboose. I viewed them long enough to satisfy my mind that they were dead, and then with a heart of lead turned away.

I crossed to the starboard side, where the deck was comparatively clear, and found the body of a seaman named Abraham Wise near the fore-hatch. This man had probably been stunned and drowned by the sea that filled the deck after I loosed the staysail. These were all of our people that I could find; the others I supposed had been washed by the water or knocked by the falling spars overboard.

I returned to the quarter-deck, and sat down in the companion way for the shelter of it and to think. No language that I have command of could put before you the horror that possessed me as I sat meditating upon my situation and recalling the faces of the dead. The wind was rapidly falling, and with it the sea, but the motion of the brig continued very heavy, a large swell having been set running by the long, fierce gale that was gone; and there being no uproar of tempest in the sky to confound the senses, I could hear a hundred harsh and melancholy groaning and straining sounds rising from the hull, with now and again a mighty blow as from some spar or lump of ice alongside, weighty enough, you would have supposed, to stave the ship. But though the *Laughing Mary* was not a new vessel, she was one of the stoutest of her kind ever launched, built mainly of oak and put together by an honest artificer. Nevertheless her continuing to float in her miserably torn and mangled condition was so great a miracle, that, spite of my poor shipmates having perished and my own state being as hopeless as the sky was starless, I could not but consider that God's hand was very visible in this business.

I will not pretend to remember how I passed the hours till the dawn came. I recollect of frequently stepping below to lift the hatch of the lazarette, to judge by the sound of the quantity of water in the vessel. That she was filling I knew well, yet not leaking so rapidly but that, had our crew been preserved, we might easily have kept her free, and made shift to rig up jury masts and haul us as best we could out of these desolate parallels. There was, however, nothing to be done till the day broke. I had noticed the jolly-boat bottom up near the starboard gangway, and so far as I could make out by throwing the dull lantern light upon her she was sound; but I could not have launched her without seeing what I was doing, and even had I managed this, she stood to be swamped and I to be drowned. And, in sober truth, so horrible was the prospect of going adrift in her without preparing for the adventure with oars, sail, mast, provisions, and water—most of which, by the lamplight only, were not to be come at amid the hideous muddle of wreckage—that sooner than face it I was perfectly satisfied to take my chance of the hulk sinking with me in her before the sun rose.

Chapter IV.
I Quit the Wreck

THE east grew pale and grey at last. The sea rolled black as the night from it, with a rounded smooth-backed swell; the wind was spent; only a small air, still from the north-east, stirred. There were a few stars dying out in the dark west; the atmosphere was clear, and when the sun rose I knew he would turn the sable pall overhead into blueness.

The hull lay very deep. I had at one time, during the black hours, struck into a mournful calculation, and reckoned that the brig would float some two or three hours after sunrise; but when the glorious beam flashed out at last, and transformed the ashen hue of dawn into a cerulean brilliance and a deep of rolling sapphire, I started with sudden terror to observe how close the covering-board sat upon the water, and how the head of every swell ran past as high as the bulwark rail.

Yet for a few moments I stood contemplating the scene of ruin. It was visible now to its most trifling detail. The foremast was gone smooth off at the deck; it lay over the starboard bow; and the topmast floated ahead of the hull, held by the gear. Many feet of bulwarks were crushed level; the pumps had vanished; the caboose was gone! A completer nautical ruin I had never viewed.

One extraordinary stroke I quickly detected. The jolly-boat had lain stowed in the long-boat; it was thus we carried those boats, the little one lying snugly enough in the other. The sea that had flooded our decks had floated the jolly-boat out of the long-boat, and swept it bottom up to the gangway where it lay, as though God's mercy designed it should be preserved for my use; for, not long after it had been floated out, the brig struck the berg, the masts fell—and there lay the long-boat crushed into staves!

This signal and surprising intervention filled my heart with thankfulness, though my spirits sank again at the sight of my poor drowned shipmates. But, unless I had a mind to join them, it was necessary I should speedily bestir myself. So after a minute's reflection I whipped out my knife, and cutting a couple of blocks away from the raffle on deck, I rove a line through them, and so made a tackle, by the help of which I turned the jolly-boat over; I then with a handspike prised her nose to the gangway, secured a bunch of rope on either side her to act as fenders or buffers when she should be launched and lying alongside, ran her midway out by the tackle, and, attaching a line to a ring-bolt in her bow, shoved her over the side, and she fell with a splash, shipping scarce a hatful of water.

I found her mast and sail—the sail furled to the mast, as it was used to lie in her—close against the stump of the mainmast; but though I sought with all the diligence that hurry would permit for her rudder, I nowhere saw it, but I met with an oar that had belonged to the other boat, and this with the mast and sail I dropped into her, the swell lifting her up to my hand when the blue fold swung past.

My next business was to victual her. I ran to the cabin, but the lazarette was full of water, and none of the provisions in it to be come at. I thereupon ransacked the cabin, and found a whole Dutch cheese, a piece of raw pork, half a ham, eight or ten biscuits, some candles, a tinder-box, several lemons, a little bag of flower, and thirteen bottles of beer. These things I rolled up in a cloth and placed them in the boat, then took from the captain's locker four jars of spirits, two of which I emptied that I might fill them with fresh water. I also took with me from the captain's cabin a small boat compass.

The heavy, sluggish, sodden movement of the hull advised me to make haste. She was now barely lifting to the swell that came brimming in broad liquid blue brows to her stem. It seemed as though another ton of water would sink her; and if the swell fell over her bows and filled the decks, down she would go. I had a small parcel of guineas in my chest, and was about to fetch this money, when a sort of staggering sensation in the upward slide of the hull gave me a fright, and, watching my chance, I jumped into the boat and cast the line that held her adrift.

The sun was an hour above the horizon. The sea was a deep blue, heaving very slowly, though you felt the weight of the mighty ocean in every fold; and eastwards, the shoulders of the swell, catching the glorious reflection of the sun, hurled the splendour along, till all that quarter of the sea looked to be a mass of leaping dazzle. Upon the eastern sea-line lay a range of white clouds, compact as the chalk cliffs of Dover; threads, crescents, feather-shapes of vapour of the daintiest sort, shot with pearly lustre, floated overhead very high. It was in truth a fair and pleasant morning—of an icy coldness indeed, but the air being dry, its shrewdness was endurable. Yet was it a brightness to fill me with anguish by obliging me to reflect how it would have been with us had it dawned yesterday instead of to-day. My companions would have been alive, and yonder sinking ruined fabric a trim ship capable of bearing us stoutly into warm seas and to our homes at last.

I threw the oar over the stern of the boat to keep her near to the brig, not so much because I desired to see the last of her, as because of the shrinking of my soul within me from the thought of heading in my loneliness into those prodigious leagues of ocean which lay stretched under the sky. Whilst the hull floated she was something to hold on to, so to say, something for the eye amid the vastness of water to rest upon, something to take out of the insufferable feeling of solitude the poisonous sting of conviction.

But her end was at hand. I had risen to step the boat's mast, and was standing and grasping it whilst I directed a slow look round the horizon in God knows what vain hope of beholding a sail, when my eye coming to the brig, I observed that she was sinking. She went down very slowly; there was a horrible gurgling sound of water rushing into her, and her main deck blew up with a loud clap or blast of noise. I could follow the line of her bulwarks fluctuating and waving in the clear dark blue when she was some feet under. A number of whirlpools spun round over her, but the slowness of her foundering was solemnly marked by the gradual descent of the ruins of masts and yards which were attached to the hull by their rigging, and which she dragged down with her. On a sudden, when the last fragment of mast had disappeared, and when the hollows of the whirlpools were flattening to the level surface of the sea, up rose a body, with a sort of leap. It was the sailor that had lain drowned on the starboard side of the forward deck. Being frozen stiff he rose in the posture in which he had expired, that is, with his arms extended; so that, when he jumped to the surface, he came with his hands lifted up to heaven, and thus he stayed a minute, sustained by the eddies which also revolved him.

The shock occasioned by this melancholy object was so great, it came near to causing me to swoon. He sank when the water ceased to twist him, and I was unspeakingly thankful to see him vanish, for his posture had all the horror of a spectral appeal, and such was the state of my mind that imagination might quickly have worked the apparition, had it lingered, into an instrument for the unsettling of my reason.

I rose from the seat on to which I had sunk and loosed the sail, and hauling the sheet aft, put the oar over the stern, and brought the little craft's head to an easterly course. The draught of air was extremely weak, and scarce furnished impulse enough to the sail to raise a bubble alongside. The boat was about fifteen feet long; she would be but a small boat for summer pleasuring in English July lake-waters, yet here was I in her in the heart of a vast ocean, many leagues south and west of the stormiest, most inhospitable point of land in the world, with distances before me almost infinite for such a boat as this to measure ere I could heave a civilized coast or a habitable island into view!

At the start I had a mind to steer north-west and blow, as the wind would suffer, into the South Sea, where perchance I might meet a whaler or a Southseaman from New Holland; but my heart sank at the prospect of the leagues of water which rolled between me and the islands and the western American seaboard. Indeed I understood that my only hope of deliverance lay in being picked up; and that, though by heading east I should be clinging to the stormy parts, I was more likely to meet with a ship hereabouts than by sailing into the great desolation of the north-west. The burden of my loneliness weighed down upon me so crushingly that I cannot but consider my senses must have been somewhat dulled by suffering, for had they been active to their old accustomed height, I am persuaded my heart must have broken and that I should have died of grief.

Faintly as the wind blew, it speedily wafted me out of sight of the floating relics of the wreck, and then all was bare, bald, swelling sea and empearled sky, darkening in lagoons of azure down to the soft mountainous masses of white vapour lying like the coast of a continent on the larboard horizon. But one living thing there was besides myself: a grey-breasted albatross, of a princely width of pinion. I had not observed it till the hull went down, and then, lifting my eyes with involuntary sympathy in the direction pointed to by the upraised arms of the sailor, I observed the great royal bird hanging like a shape of marble directly over the frothing eddies. It was as though the spirit of the deep had taken form in the substance of the noblest of all the fowls of its dominions, and, poised on tremorless wings, was surveying with the cold curiosity of an intelligence empty of human emotion the destruction of one of those fabrics whose unequal contests and repeated triumphs had provoked its haughty surprise. The bird quitted the spot of the wreck after a while and followed me. Its eyes had the sparkling blood-red gleam of rubies. It was as silent as a phantom, and with arched neck and motionless plumes seemed to watch me with an earnestness that presently grew insufferable. So far from finding any comfort of companionship in the creature, methought if it did not speedily break from the motionless posture in which it rested on its seat of air, and remove its piercing gaze, it would end in crazing me. I felt a sudden rage, and, jumping up, shouted and shook my fist at it. This frightened the thing. It uttered a strange salt cry—the very note of a gust of wind splitting upon a rope—flapped its wings, and after a turn or two sailed away into the north.

I watched it till its figure melted into the blue atmosphere, and then sank trembling into the sternsheets of the boat.

Chapter V.
I Sight a White Coast

Four days did I pass in that little open boat.

The first day was fine, till sunset; it then blew fresh from the north-west, and I was obliged to keep the boat before the wind. The next day was dark and turbulent, with heavy falls of snow and a high swell from the north, and the wind a small gale. On the third day the sun shone, and it was a fair day, but horribly cold, and I saw two icebergs like clouds upon the far western sea-line. There followed a cruel night of clouded skies, sleet, and snow, and a very troubled sea; and then broke the fourth day, as softly brilliant as an English May day, but cold—great God, how cold!

Thus might I epitomize this passage; and I do so to spare you the weariness of a relation of uneventful suffering.

In those four days I mainly ran before the wind, and in this way drove many leagues south, though whenever a chance offered I hauled my sheet for the east. I know not, I am sure, how the boat lived. I might pretend it was due to my clever management—I do not say I had no share in my own preservation, but to God belongs all the praise.

In the blackness of the first night the sea boiled all about me. The boat leapt into hollows in which the sail slapped the mast. One look behind me at the high dark curl of the oncoming surge had so affrighted me that I never durst turn my head again lest the sight should deprive me of the nerve to hold the oar with which I steered. I sat as squarely as the task of steering would suffer, trusting that if a sea should tumble over the stern my back would serve as a breakwater, and save the boat from being swamped. The whole sail was on her, and I could not help myself; for it would have been certain death to quit the steering oar for an instant. It was this that saved me, perhaps; for the boat blew along with such prodigious speed, running to the height of a sea as though she meant to dart from that eminence into the air, that the slope of each following surge swung like a pendulum under her, and though her sail was becalmed in the trough, her momentum was so great that she was speeding up the acclivity and catching the whole weight of the wind afresh before there was time for her to lose way.

I was nearly dead with cold and misery when the morning came, but the sparkling sun and the blue sky cheered me, and as wind and sea fell with the soaring of the orb, I was enabled to flatten aft the sheet and let the boat steer herself whilst I beat my arms about for warmth and broke my fast. When I look back I wonder that I should have taken any pains to live. That it is possible for the human mind at any period of its existence to be absolutely hopeless I do not believe; but I can very honestly say that when I gazed round upon the enormous sea I was in, and considered the size of my boat, the quantity of my provisions, and my distance (even if I was heading that way) from the nearest point of land, I was not sensible of the faintest stirring of hope, and viewed myself as a dead man.

No bird came near me. Once I spied the back of a great black fish about a quarter of a mile off. The wetness of it caught the sunshine and reflected it like a mirror of polished steel, and the flash was so brilliant it might have passed for a bed of white fire floating on the blue heavings. But nothing more that was living did I meet, and such was the vastness of the sea over which my little keel glided, in the midst of which I sat abandoned by the angels, that for utter loneliness I might have been the very last of the human race.

When the third night came down with sullen blasts sweeping into a steady storming of wind, that swung a strong melancholy howl through the gloom, it found me so weak with cold, watching, and anxiety, and the want of space wherein to rid my limbs of the painful cramp which weighted them with an insupportable leaden sensation, that I had barely power to control the boat with the oar. I pined for sleep; one hour of slumber would, I felt, give me new life, but I durst not close my eyes. The boat was sweeping through the dark and seething seas, and her course had to be that of an arrow, or she would capsize and be smothered in a breath.

Maybe I fell something delirious, for I had many strange and frightful fancies. Indeed I doubt not it was the spirit of madness—that is certainly tonical when small—which furnished strength enough to my arm to steer with. It was like the action of a powerful cordial in my blood, and the very horrors it fed my brain with were an animation to my physical qualities. The gale became a voice; it cried out my name, and every shout of it past my ear had the sound of the word 'Despair!' I witnessed the forms of huge phantoms flying over the boat; I watched the beating of their giant wings of shadow and heard the thunder of their laughter as they fled ahead, leaving scores of like monstrous shapes to follow. There was a faint lightning of phosphor in the creaming heads of the ebon surges, and my sick imagination twisted that pallid complexion into the dim reflection of the lamps of illuminated pavilions at the bottom of the sea; mystic palaces of green marble, radiant cities in the measureless kingdoms of the ocean gods. I had a fancy of roofs of pearl below, turrets of milk-white coral, pavements of rainbow lustre like to the shootings and dartings of the hues of shells inclined and trembled to the sun. I thought I could behold the movements of shapes as indeterminable as the forms which swarm in dreams, human brows crowned with gold, the cold round emerald eyes of fish, the creamy breasts of women, large outlines slowly floating upwards, making a deeper blackness upon the blackness like the dye of the electric storm upon the velvet bosom of midnight. Often would I shrink from side to side, starting from a fancied apparition leaping into terrible being out of some hurling block of liquid obscurity.

Once a light shone upon the masthead. At any other time I should have known this to be a St. Elmo's fire, a corposant, the *ignis fatuus* of the deep, and hailed it with a seaman's faith in its promise of gentle weather. But to my distempered fancy it was a lanthorn hung up by a spirit hand; I traced the dusky curve of an arm and observed the busy twitching of visionary fingers by the rays of the ghostly light; the outline of a large face of a bland and sorrowful expression, pallid as any foam-flake whirling past, came into the sphere of those graveyard rays. I shrieked and shut my eyes, and when I looked again the light was gone.

Long before daybreak I was exhausted. Mercifully, the wind was scant; the stars shone very gloriously; on high sparkled the Cross of the southern world. A benign influence seemed to steal into me out of its silver shining; the craze fell from me, and I wept.

Shortly afterwards, worn out by three days and nights of suffering, I fell into a deep sleep, and when I awoke my eyes opened right upon the blinding sun.

This was the morning of the fourth day. I was without a watch. By the height of the sun I reckoned the hour to be ten. I threw a languid glance at the compass and found the boat's head pointing north-west; she fell off and came to, being without governance, and was scarcely sailing therefore. The wind was west, a very light breeze, just enough to put a bright twinkling into the long, smooth folds of the wide and weighty swell that was rolling up from the north-east. I tried to stand, but was so benumbed that many minutes passed before I had the use of my legs. Brightly as the sun shone there was no more warmth in his light than you find in a moon-beam on a frosty night, and the bite in the air was like the pang of ice itself pressed against the cheek. My right hand suffered most; I had fallen asleep clasping the loom of the steering oar, and when I awoke my fingers still gripped it, so that, on withdrawing them, they remained curved like talons, and I believed I had lost their use, and even reckoned they would snap off and so set up a mortification, till by much diligent rubbing I grew sensible of a small glow which, increasing, ended in rendering the joints supple.

I stood up to take a view of the horizon, and the first sight that met my eye forced a cry from me. Extending the whole length of the south-west seaboard lay what I took to be a line of white coast melting at either extremity into the blue airy distance. Even at the low elevation of the boat my eye seemed to measure thirty miles of it. It was not white as chalk is; there was something of a crystalline complexion upon the face of its solidity. It was too far off to enable me to remark its outline; yet on straining my sight—the atmosphere being very exquisitely clear—I thought I could distinguish the projections of peaks, of rounded slopes, and aerial angularities in places which, in the refractive lens of the air, looked, with their hue of glassy azure, like the loom of high land behind the coastal line.

The notion that it was ice came into my head after the first prospect of it; and then I returned to my earlier belief that it was land. Methought if it were ice, it must be the borderland of the Antarctic circle, the limits of the unfrozen ocean, for it was incredible that so mighty a body could signify less than the capes and terraces of a continent of ice glazing the circumference of the pole for leagues and leagues; but then I also knew that, though first the brig and then my boat had been for days steadily blown south, I was still to the north of the South Shetland parallels, and many degrees therefore removed from the polar barrier. Hence I concluded that what I saw was land, and that the peculiar crystal shining of it was caused by the snow that covered it.

But what land? Some large island that had been missed by the explorers and left uncharted? I put a picture of the map of this part of the world before my mind's eye, and fell to an earnest consideration of it, but could recollect of no land hereabouts, unless indeed we had been wildly wrong in our reckoning aboard the brig, and I in the boat had been driven four or five times the distance I had calculated—things not to be entertained.

Yet even as a mere break in the frightful and enduring continuity of the sea-line—even as something that was not sea nor sky nor the cold silent and mocking illusion of clouds—it took a character of blessedness in my eyes; my gaze hung upon it joyously, and my heart swelled with a new impulse of life in my breast. It would be strange, I thought, if on approaching it something to promise me deliverance from this dreadful situation did not offer itself—some whaler or trader at anchor, signs of habitation and of the presence of men, nay, even a single hut to serve as a refuge from the pitiless cold, the stormy waters, the black, lonely, delirious watches of the night, till help should heave into view with the white canvas of a ship.

I put the boat's head before the wind, and steered with one hand whilst I got some breakfast with the other. I thanked God for the brightness of the day and for the sight of that strange white line of land, that went in glimmering blobs of faintness to the trembling horizon where the southern end of it died out. The swell rose full and brimming ahead, rolling in sapphire hills out of the north-east, as I have said, whence I inferred that that extremity of the land did not extend very much further than I could see it, otherwise there could not have been so much weight of water as I found in the heaving.

The breeze blew lightly and was the weaker for my running before it; but the little line of froth that slipped past either side the boat gave me to know that the speed would not be less than four miles in the hour; and as I reckoned the land to be but a few leagues distant, I calculated upon being ashore some little while before sundown.

In this way two hours passed. By this time the features of the coast were tolerably distinct. Yet I was puzzled. There was a peculiar sheen all about the irregular sky-line; a kind of pearly whitening, as it were, of the heavens beyond, like to the effect produced by the rising of a very delicate soft mist melting from a mountain's brow into the air. This dismayed me. Still I cried to myself, 'It must be land! All that whiteness is snow, and the luminous tinge above it is the reflection of the glaring sunshine thrown upwards from the dazzle. It cannot be ice! 'tis too mighty a barrier. Surely no single iceberg ever reached to the prodigious proportions of that coast. And it cannot be an assemblage of bergs, for there is no break—it is leagues of solid conformation. Oh yes, it is land, sure enough! some island whose tops and seaboard are covered with snow. But what of that? It may be populated all the same. Are the northern kingdoms of Europe bare of life because of the winter rigours?' And then thought to myself, if that island have natives, I would rather encounter them as the savages of an ice-bound country than as the inhabitants of a land of sunshine and spices and radiant vegetation; for it is the denizens of the most gloriously fair ocean seats in the world who are man-eaters; not the Patagonian, giant though he be, nor the blubber-fed anatomies of the ice-climes.

Thus I sought to reassure and comfort myself. Meanwhile my boat sailed quietly along, running up and down the smooth and foamless hills of water very buoyantly, and the sun slided into the north-west sky and darted a reddening beam upon the coast towards which I steered.

Chapter VI.
An Island of Ice

I HAD to approach the coast within two miles before I could satisfy my mind of its nature, and then all doubt left me.

It was *ice!* a mighty crescent of it—as was now in a measure gatherable, floating upon the dark blue waters like the new moon upon the field of the sky.

For a great while I had struggled with my misgivings, so tyrannically will hope lord it even over conviction itself, until it was impossible for me to any longer mistake. And then, when I knew it to be ice, I asked myself what other thing I expected it should prove, seeing that this ocean had been plentifully navigated since Cook's time and no land discovered where I was; and I called myself a fool and cursed the hope that had cheated me, and, in short, gave way to a violent outburst of passion, and was indeed so wild with grief and rage that, had my ecstasy been but a very little greater, I must have jumped overboard, so great was my loathing of life then, and the horror the sight of the ice filled me with.

Indeed, you cannot conceive how shocking to me was the appearance of that great gleaming length of white desolation. On the deck of a stout ship sailing safely past it I should have found the scene magnificent, I doubt not; for the sun, being low with westering, shone redly, and the range of ice stood in a kind of gold atmosphere which gave an extraordinary richness to the shadowings of its rocks and peaks, and a particular fullness of mellow whiteness to its lustrous parts, softening the dazzle into an airy tenderness of brightness, so that the whole mass shone out with the blandness visible in a glorious star. But its main beauty lay in those features by which I knew it to be ice—I mean in a vast surprising variety of forms, such as steeples, towers, columns, pyramids, ruins as it might be of temples, grotesque shapes as of mighty statues, left unfinished by the hands of Titans, domes as of cathedrals, castellated heights, fragments of ramparts, and the like. These features lay in groups, as if veritably the line of coast were dotted with gatherings of royal mansions and remains of imperial magnificence, all of white marble, yet with a glassy tincture as though the material owned something of a Parian quality.

I had to come within two miles, as I have said, before these elegancies broke upon me, so deceptively did their delicacy of outlines mingle with the dark blue softness beyond. In places the coast ran up to a height of two or three hundred feet, in others it sloped down to twenty feet. For some miles it was like the face of a cliff, a sheer abrupt, with scarce a scar upon its front, staring with a wild bald look over the frosty beautiful blue of that afternoon sea. Here and there it projected a forefoot, some white and massive rock, upon which the swell of the ocean burst in thunder, and flew to almost the height of the cliff in a very great and glorious fury of foam. In other parts, where I suspected a sort of beach, there was the silver tremble of surf; but in the main, the heave coming out of the north-east, the folds swept the base of the ice without froth.

I say again, beheld in the red sunshine, that line of ice, resembling a coast of marble defining the liquid junction of the swelling folds of sapphire below and the moist violet of the eastern sky beyond and over it, crowned at points with delicate imitations of princely habitations, would have offered a noble and magnificent spectacle to a mind at ease; but to my eyes its enchantments were killed by the horror I felt. It was a lonely, hideous waste, rendered the more shocking by the consideration that the whole vast range was formed of blocks of frozen water which warmth would dissolve; that it was a country as solid as rock and as unsubstantial as a cloud, to be shunned by the mariner as though it was Death's own pavilion, the estate and mansion of the grisly spectre, and creating round about it as supreme a desolation and loneliness of ocean as that which reigned in its own white stillness.

Though I held the boat's head for it I was at a loss—in so much confusion of mind that I knew not what to do. I did not doubt by the character of the swell that its limits in the north-east extended only to the sensible horizon; in other words, that its extremity there would not be above five miles distant, though to what latitude its southern arm did curve was not to be conjectured.

Should I steer north and seek to go clear of it? Somehow, the presence of this similitude of land made the sea appear as enormous as space itself. Whilst it was all clear horizon the immensity of the deep was in a measure limited to the vision by its cincture. But this ice-line gave the eye something to measure with, and when I looked at those leagues of frozen shore my spirits sank into deepest dejection at the thought of the vastness of the waters in whose heart I floated in my little boat.

However, I resolved at last to land if landing was possible. I could stretch my limbs, recruit myself by exercise, and might even make shift to obtain a night's rest. I stood in desperate need of sleep, but there was no repose to be had in the boat. I durst not lie down in her; if nature overcame me and I fell asleep in a sitting posture, I might wake to find the boat capsized and myself drowning. This consideration resolved me, and by this time being within half a mile of the coast, I ran my eye carefully along it to observe a safe nook for my boat to enter and myself to land in.

Though for a great distance, as I have said, the front of the cliff, and where it was highest too, was a sheer fall, coming like the side of a house to the water, that part of the island towards which my boat's head was pointed sloped down and continued in a low shore, with hummocks of ice upon it at irregular intervals, to where it died out in the northeast. I now saw that this part had a broken appearance as if it had been violently rent from a mainland of ice; also, to my approach, many ledges projecting into the sea stole into view. There were ravines and gorges, and almost on a line with the boat's head was an assemblage of those delicate glass-like counterfeits of spires, towers, and the like, of which I have spoken, standing just beyond a brow whose declivity fell very easily to the water.

To make you see the picture as I have it in my mind would be beyond my art; it is not in the pen—not in the brush either, I should think—to convey even a tolerable portraiture of the ruggedness, the fairy grouping, the shelves, hollows, crags, terraces, precipices, and beach of this kingdom of ice, where its frontal line broke away from the smooth face of the tall reaches, and ran with a ploughed, scarred, and serrated countenance northwards.

Very happily I had insensibly steered for perhaps the safest spot that I could have lighted on; this was formed of a large projection of rock, standing aslant, so that the swell rolled past it without breaking. The rock made a sort of cove, towards which I sailed in full confidence that the water there would be smooth. Nor was I deceived, for I saw that the rock acted as a breakwater, whose stilling influence was felt a good way beyond it. I thereupon steered for the starboard of this rock, and when I was within it found the heave of the sea dwindled to a scarce perceptible undulation, whereupon I lowered my sail, and, standing to the oar, sculled the boat to a low lump of ice, on to which I stepped.

My first business was to secure the boat; this I did by inserting the mast into a deep, thin crevice in the ice and making the painter fast to it as to a pole. The sun was now very low, and would soon be gone. The cold was extreme, yet I did not suffer from it as in the boat. There is a quality in snow which it would be ridiculous to speak of as *warmth*; yet, as you may observe after a heavy fall ashore on top of a black frost, it seems to have a power of blunting the sharp edge of the cold, and the snow on this shore of ice being very abundant, though frozen as hard as the ice itself, appeared to mitigate the intolerable rigour I had languished under upon the water, in the brig and afterwards. This might also be owing to the dryness of the cold.

Having secured the boat I beat my hands heartily upon my breast, and fell to pacing a little level of ice whilst I considered what I should do. The coast—I cannot but speak of this frozen territory as land—went in a gentle slope behind me to the height of about thirty feet; the ground was greatly broken with rocks and boulders and sharp points, whence I suspected many fissures in which the snow might not be so hard but that I might sink deep enough to be smothered. I saw no cave nor hollow that I could make a bedroom of, and the improved circulation of my blood giving me spirits enough to resolve quickly, I made up my mind to use my boat as a bed.

So I went to work. I took the oar and jammed it into such another crevice as the mast stood in, and to it I secured the boat by another line. This moored her very safely. There was as good promise of a fair quiet night as I might count upon in these treacherous latitudes; the haven in which the boat lay was sheltered and the water almost still, and this I reckoned would hold whilst the breeze hung northerly and the swell rolled from the north-east. I spread the sail over the seats, which served as beams for the support of this little ceiling of canvas, and enough of it remained to supply me with a pillow and to cover my legs. I fell to this work whilst there was light, and when I had prepared my habitation, I took a bottle of ale and a handful of victuals ashore and made my supper, walking briskly whilst I ate and drank.

I caught myself sometimes looking yearningly towards the brow of the slope, as though from that eminence I should gain an extensive prospect of the sea and perhaps behold a ship; but I wanted the courage to climb, chiefly because I was afraid of tumbling into a hole and miserably perishing, and likewise because I shrank from the idea of being overtaken up there by the darkness. There was a kind of companionship in the boat, the support of which I should lose if I left her.

The going of the sun was attended by so much glory that the whole weight of my situation and the pressure of my solitude did not come upon me until his light was gone. The swell ran athwart his mirroring in lines of molten gold; the sky was a sheet of scarlet fire where he was, paling zenithwards into an ardent orange. The splendour tipped the frozen coast with points of ruby flame which sparkled and throbbed like sentinel beacons along the white and silent range. The low thunder of far-off hills of water bursting against the projections rolled sulkily down upon the weak wind. Just beyond the edge of the slope, about a third of a mile to the north of my little haven, stood an assemblage of exquisitely airy outlines—configurations such as I have described; their crystalline nature stole out to the lustrous colouring of the glowing west, and they had the appearance of tinted glass of several dyes of red, the delicate fibres being deep of hue, the stouter ones pale; and never did the highest moon of human invention reach to anything more glorious and dainty, more sweetly simulative of the arts of a fairy-like imagination than yonder cluster of icy fabrics, fashioned, as it entered my head to conceive, as pavilions by the hands of the spirits of the frozen world, and gilt and painted by the beams of the setting sun.

But all this wild and unreal beauty melted away to the oncoming of the dusk; and when the sun was gone and the twilight had put a new quality of bleakness into the air, when the sea rolled in a welter of dark shadows, one sombre fold shouldering another—a very swarming of restless giant phantoms—when the shining of the stars low down in the unfathomable obscurity of the north and south quarters gave to the ocean in those directions a frightful immensity of surface, making you feel as though you viewed the scene from the centre of the firmament, and were gazing down the spangled slopes of infinity—oh, *then* it was that the full spirit of the solitude of this pale and silent seat of ice took possession of me. I found a meaning I had not before caught in the complaining murmur of the night breeze blowing in small gusts along the rocky shore, and in the deep organ-like tremulous *hum* of the swell thundering miles distant on the northward-pointing cliffs. This was a note I had missed whilst the sun shone. Perhaps my senses were sharpened by the darkness. It mingled with the booming of the bursts of water on this side the range, and gave me to know that the northward extremity of the island did not extend so far as I had supposed from my view of it in the boat. Yet I could also suppose that the beat of the swell formed a mighty cannonading capable of making itself heard afar, and the ice, being resonant, with many smooth if not polished tracts upon it, readily transmitted the sound, yes, though the cause of it lay as far off as the horizon.

I will not say that my loneliness frightened me, but it subdued my heart with a weight as if it were something sensible, and filled me with a sort of consternation that was full of awe. The moon was up, but the rocks hid the side of the sea she rode over, and her face was not to be viewed from where I was until she had marched two-thirds of her path to the meridian. The coast ran away on either hand in cold motionless blocks of pallor, which further on fell (by deception of the sheen of the stars) into a kind of twisting and snaking glimmer, and you followed it into an extraordinarily elusive faintness that was neither light nor colour in the liquid gloom, long after the sight had outrun the visibility of the range. At intervals I was startled by sounds, sometimes sullen, like a muffled subterranean explosion, sometimes sharp, like a quick splintering of an iron-hard substance. These noises, I presently gathered, were made by the ice stretching and cracking in fifty different directions. The mass was so vast and substantial you could not but think of it as a country with its foot resting upon the bed of the sea. 'Twas a folly of my nerves no doubt, yet it added to my consternation to reflect that this solid territory, reverberating the repelled blows of the ocean swell, was as much afloat as my boat, and so much less actual than my boat that, could it be towed a few degrees further north, it would melt into pouring waters and vanish as utterly with its little cities of columns, steeples, and minarets as a wreath of steam upon the air.

This gave a spirit-like character to it in my dismayed inquiring eyes which was greatly increased by the vagueness it took from the dusk. It was such a scene, methought, as the souls of seamen drowned in these seas might flock to and haunt. The white and icy spell upon it wrought in familiar things. The stars looking down upon me over the edge of the cliffs were like the eyes of shapes (easy to fashion out of the darkness) kneeling up there and peering at the human intruder who was pacing his narrow floor of ice for warmth. The deceit of the shadows proportioned the blanched ruggedness of the cliff's face on the north side into heads and bodies of monsters. I beheld a giant, from his waist up, leaning his cheek upon his arm; a great cross with a burlesque figure, as of a friar, kneeling near it; a mighty helmet with a white plume curled; the shadowy conformation of a huge couchant beast, with a hundred other such unsubstantial prodigies. Had the moon shone in the west I dare say I should have witnessed a score more such things, for the snow was like white paper, on which the clear black shadows of the ice-rocks could not but have cast the likeness of many startling phantasies.

I sought to calm my mind by considering my position, and to divert my thoughts from the star-wrought apparitions of the broken slopes I asked myself what should be my plans, what my chance for delivering myself from this unparalleled situation. At this distance of time I cannot precisely tell how long the provisions I had brought from the foundered brig were calculated to last me, but I am sure I had not a week's supply. This, then, made it plain that my business was not to linger here, but to push into the ocean afresh as speedily as possible, for to my mind nothing in life was clearer than that my only chance lay in my falling in with a ship. Yet how did my heart sink when I reflected upon the mighty breast of sea in which I was forlornly to seek for succour! My eyes went to the squab black outline of the boat, and the littleness of her sent a shudder through me. It is true she had nobly carried me through some fierce weather, yet at the expense of many leagues of southing, of a deeper penetration into the solitary wilds of the polar waters.

However, I was sensible that I was depressed, melancholy, and under a continued consternation, something of which the morning sun might dissipate, so that I should be able to take a heartier view of my woeful plight. So after a good look seawards and at the heavens to satisfy myself on the subject of the weather, and after a careful inspection of the moorings of the boat, I entered her, feeling very sure that, if a sea set in from the west or south and tumbled her, the motion would quickly arouse me; and getting under the roof of sail, with my legs along the bottom and my back against the stem, which I had bolstered with the slack of the canvas, I commended myself to God, folded my arms, and went to sleep.

Chapter VII.
I am Startled by a Discovery

IN this uneasy posture, despite the intense cold, I continued to sleep soundly during the greater part of the night. I was awakened by a horrid dream of some giant shape stalking down the slope of ice to seize and devour me, and sat up trembling with horror that was not a little increased by my inability to recollect myself, and by my therefore conceiving the canvas that covered me to be the groping of the ogre's hand over my face.

I pushed the sail away and stood up, but had instantly to sit again, my legs being terribly cramped. A drink of spirits helped me; my blood presently flowed with briskness.

The moon was in the west; she hung large, red, and distorted, and shed no light save her reflection that waved in the sea under her like several lengths of undulating red-hot wire. My haven was still very tranquil—the boat lay calm; but there was a deeper tone in the booming sound of the distant surf, and a more menacing note in the echoing of the blows of the swell along this side of the coast, whence I concluded that, despite the fairness of the weather, the heave of the deep had, whilst I slept, gathered a greater weight, which might signify stormy winds not very many leagues away.

The pale stare of the heights of ice at that red and shapeless disc was shocking. "Oh," I cried aloud, as I had once cried before, "but for one, even but for one, companion to speak to!"

I had no mind to lie down again. The cold indeed was cruelly sharp, and the smoke sped from my mouth with every breath as though I held a tobacco pipe betwixt my teeth. I got upon the ice and stepped about it quickly, darting searching glances into the gloom to left and right of the setting moon; but all lay bare, bleak, and black. I pulled off my stout gloves with the hope of getting my fingers to tingle by handling the snow; but it was frozen so hard I could not scrape up with my nails as much as a half-dozen of flakes would make. What I got I dissolved in my mouth and found it brackish; however, I suspected it would be sweeter and perhaps not so stonily frozen higher up, where there was less chance of the salt spray mingling with it, and I resolved when the light came to fill my empty beer-bottles as with salt or pounded sugar for use hereafter—that is, if it should prove sweet; as to melting it, I had indeed a tinder-box and the means of obtaining fire, but no fuel.

It seemed as if the night had only just descended, so tardy was the dawn. Outside the slanting wall of ice that made my haven the swell swept past in a gurgling, bubbling, drowning sound, dismal and ghastly, as though in truth some such ogre as the monster I had dreamt of lay suffocating there. I welcomed the cold colouring of the east as if it had been a ship, and watched the stars dying and the frozen shore darkening to the dim and sifting dawn behind it, against which the outline of the cliffs ran in a broken streak of ink. The rising of the sun gave me fresh life. The ice flashed out of its slatish hue into a radiant white, the ocean changed into a rich blue that seemed as violet under the paler azure of the heavens; but I could now see that the swell was heavier than I had suspected from the echo of its remote roaring in the north. It ran steadily out of the north-east. This was miserable to see, for the line of its running was directly my course, and if I committed myself to it in that little boat, the impulse of the long and swinging folds could not but set me steadily southwards, unless a breeze sprang up in that quarter to blow me towards the sun. There was a small current of air stirring, a mere trickle of wind from the north-west.

I made up my mind to climb as high as I could, taking the oar with me to serve as a pole, that I might view the ice and the ocean round about and form a judgment of the weather by the aspect of the sky, of which only the western part was visible from my low strand. But first I must break my fast. I remember bitterly lamenting the lack of means to make a fire, that I might obtain a warm meal and a hot drink and dry my gloves, coat, and breeches, to which the damp of the salt clung tenaciously. Had this ice been land, though the most desolate, gloomy, repulsive spot in the world, I had surely found something that would burn.

I sat in the boat to eat, and whilst thus occupied pondered over this great field of ice, and wondered how so mighty a berg should travel in such compacted bulk so far north—that is, so far north from the seat of its creation. Now leisurely and curiously observing it, it seemed to me that the north part of it, from much about the spot where my boat lay, was formed of a chain of icebergs knitted one to another in a consolidated range of irregular low steeps. The beautiful appearances of spires, towers, and the like seemed as if they had been formed by an upheaval, as of an earthquake, of splinters and bodies of the frozen stuff; for, so far as it was possible for me to see from the low shore, wherever these radiant and lovely figures were assembled I noticed great rents, spacious chasms, narrow and tortuous ravines. Certain appearances, however, caused me to suspect that this island was steadily decaying, and that, large as it still was, it had been many times vaster when it broke away from the continent about the Pole. Naturally, as it progressed northwards it would dissolve, and the cracking and thunderous noises I had heard in the night, sounds very audible now when I gave them my attention—sometimes a hollow distant rumbling as of some great body dislodged and set rolling far off, sometimes an inwards roaring crack or blast of noise like the report of a cannon fired deep down—advised me that the work of dissolution was perpetually progressing, and that this prodigious island which appeared to barricade the horizon might in a few months be dwindled into half a score of rapidly dissolving bergs.

My slender repast ended, I pulled the oar out of the crevice, and found it would make me a good pole to probe my way with and support myself by up the slope. The boat was now held by the mast, which I shook and found very firm. I put an empty beer-bottle in my pocket, meaning to see if I could fill it, if the snow above was sweet enough to be well-tasted, and then with a final look at the boat I started.

The slope was extremely craggy. Blocks of ice lay about, some on top of the others, like the stones of which the pyramids are built; the white glare of the snow caused these stones at a little distance to appear flat— that is, by merging them into and blending them with the soft brilliance of the background; and I had sometimes to warily walk fifty or sixty paces round these blocks to come at a part of the slope that was smooth.

I speedily found, however, that there was no danger of my being buried by stepping into a hollow full of snow; for the same hardness was everywhere, the snow, whether one or twenty feet deep, offering as solid a surface as the bare ice. This encouraged me to step out, and I began to move with some spirit; the exercise was as good as a fire, and before I was half-way up I was as warm as ever I had been in my life.

I had come to a stand to fetch a breath, and was moving on afresh, when, having taken not half a dozen steps, I spied the figure of a man. He was in a sitting posture, his back against a rock that had concealed him. His head was bowed, and his knees drawn up to a level with his chin, and his naked hands were clasped upon his legs. His attitude was that of a person lost in thought, very easy and calm.

I stopped as if I had been shot through the heart. Had it been a bear, or a sea-lion, or any creature which my mind could instantly have associated with this white and stirless desolation, I might have been startled indeed; but no such amazement could have possessed me as I now felt. It never entered into my head to doubt that he was alive, so natural was his attitude, as of one lost in a mood of tender melancholy.

I stood staring at him, myself motionless, for some minutes, too greatly astonished and thunder-struck to note more than that he was a man. Then I looked about me to see if he had companions or for some signs of a habitation, but the ice was everywhere naked. I fixed my eyes on him again. His hair was above a foot long, black as ink, and the blacker maybe for the contrast of the snow. His beard and mustachios, which were also of this raven hue, fell to his girdle. He wore a great yellow flapping hat, such as was in fashion among the Spaniards and buccaneers of the South Sea; but over his ears, for the warmth of the protection, were squares of flannel, secured by a very fine red silk handkerchief knotted under his beard, and this, with his hair and pale cheeks and black shaggy eyebrows, gave him a terrible and ghastly appearance. From his shoulders hung a rich thick cloak lined with red, and the legs to the height of the knees were encased in large boots.

I continued surveying him with my heart beating fast. Every instant I expected to see him turn his head and start to behold me. My emotions were too tumultuous to analyse, yet I believe I was more frightened than gladdened by the sight of a fellow-creature, though not long before I had sighed bitterly for some one to speak to. I looked around again, prepared to find another one like him taking stock of me from behind a rock, and then ventured to approach him by a few steps the better to see him. He had certainly a frightful face. It was not only the length of his coal-black hair and beard; it was the hue of his skin, a greenish ashen colour, an unspeakably hideous complexion, sharpened on the one hand by the red handkerchief over his ears and on the other by the dazzle of the snow. Then, again, there was the extreme strangeness of his costume.

I coughed loudly, holding my pole in readiness for whatever might befall, but he did not stir; I then holloaed, and was answered by the echoes of my own voice among the rocks. His stillness persuaded me he was in one of those deep slumbers which fall upon a man in frozen places, for I could not persuade myself he was dead, so living was his posture.

This will not do, thought I; so I went close to him and peered into his face.

His eyes were fixed; they resembled glass painted as eyes, the colours faded. He had a broad belt round his waist, and the hilt of a kind of cutlass peeped from under his cloak. Otherwise he was unarmed. I thought he breathed, and seemed to see a movement in his breast, and I took him by the shoulder; but in the hurry of my feelings I exerted more strength than I was sensible of. I pushed him with the violence of sudden trepidation; my hand slipped off his shoulder, and he fell on his side, exactly as a statue would, preserving his posture as though, like a statue, he had been chiselled out of marble or stone.

I started back frightened by his fall, in which my fears found a sort of life; but it was soon clear to me his rigidity was that of a man frozen to death. His very hair and beard stood stiff, as before, as though they were some exquisite counterfeit in ebony. Perfectly satisfied that he was dead, I stepped round to the other side of him, and set him up as I had found him. He was as heavy as if he had been alive, and when I put his back to the rock his posture was exactly as it had been, that of one deeply meditating.

Who had this man been in life? How had he fallen into this pass? How long had he been dead there, seated as I saw him?

These were speculations not to be resolved by conjecture. On looking at the rock against which he leaned and observing its curvature, it seemed to me that it had formed part of a cave, or of some large, deep hole of ice; and this I was sure must have been the case, for it is certain that, had this body remained long unsheltered, it must have been hidden by the snow.

I concluded then that the unhappy man had been cast away upon this ice whilst it was under bleaker heights than these parallels, and that he had crawled into a hollow, and perished in that melancholic sitting posture. But in what year had his fate come upon him? I had made several voyages into distant places in my time and seen a great variety of people; but I had never met any man habited as that body. He had the appearance of a Spanish or French cut-throat of the middle of last century, and of earlier times yet; for it may be known to you that the buccaneers of the Spanish Main and the South Sea were great lovers of finery; they had a strange theatrical taste in their choice of costumes, which, as you will suppose, they had abundant opportunities for gratifying out of the many rich and glittering wardrobes that fell into their hands; and this man, I say, with his large fine hat, handsome cloak and boots, coupled with the villainous cast of his countenance and the frightful appearance his long hair gave him, rendered him to my notions the completest figure that could be imagined of one of those rogues who earned their living as pirates.

Thinking I might find something on his person to acquaint me with his story or that would furnish me with some idea of the date of his being cast away, I pulled his cloak aside and searched his pockets. His legs were thickly cased in two or three pairs of breeches, the outer pair being of a dark green cloth. He also wore a handsome red waistcoat, laced, and a stout coat of a kind of frieze. In his coat pocket I found a silver tobacco-box, a small glass flask fitted with a silver band and half full of an amber-coloured liquor, hard froze; and in his waistcoat pocket a gold watch, shaped like an apple, the back curiously chased and inlaid with jewels of several kinds, forming a small letter M. The hands pointed to twenty minutes after three. A key of a strange shape and a number of seals, trinkets, and the like, were attached to the watch.

These things, together with a knife, a key, a thick plain silver ring, and some Spanish pieces in gold and silver were what I found on this man. There was nothing to tell me who he was nor how long he had been on the island.

The searching him was the most disagreeable job I ever undertook in my life. His iron-like rigidity made him seem to resist me, and the swaying of his back against the rock to the motions of my hand was so full of life that twice I quitted him, frightened by it. On touching his naked hand by accident I discovered that the flesh of it moved upon the bones as you pull a glove off and on. I had had enough of him, and walked away feeling sick. If he had companions, and they were like him, I did not want to see them, unless it was that I might satisfy my curiosity as to the time they had been here. I determined, however, on my way back to take his cloak, which would make me a comfortable rug in the boat, and also the watch, flask, and tobacco-box; for if I was drowned they could but go to the bottom of the sea, which was their certain destination if I left them in his pockets; and if I came off with them, then the money they would bring me must somewhat lighten the loss of my clothes and property in the brig.

I pushed onwards, stepping warily and probing cautiously at every step, and earnestly peering about me, for after such a sight as that dead man I was never to know what new wonder I might stumble upon. About a quarter of a mile on my left—that is, on my left whilst I kept my face to the slope—there was the appearance of a ravine not discernible from where the boat lay. When I was within twenty feet of the summit of the cliff, the acclivity continuing gentle to the very brow, but much broken, as I have said, I noticed this hollow, and more particularly a small collection of ice-forms, not nearly so large as the other groups of this kind, but most dainty and lovely nevertheless. They showed as the heads of trees might to my ascent, and when I had got a little higher I observed that they were formed upon the hither side of the hollow, as though the convulsion which had wrought that chasm had tossed up those exquisite caprices of ice. However, I was too eager to view the prospect from the top of the cliff to suffer my admiration to detain me; in a few minutes I had gained the brow, and, clambering on to a mass of rock, I sent my gaze around.

Chapter VIII.
The Frozen Schooner

I FOUND myself on the summit of a kind of table-land; vast bodies of ice, every block weighing hundreds and perhaps thousands of tons lay scattered over it; yet for the space of a mile or so the character was that of flatness. Southwards the range went upwards to a coastal front of some hundred feet, with a huddle of peaks and strange configurations behind soaring to an elevation from the sea-line of two or three hundred feet. Northwards the range sloped gradually, with such a shelving of its hinder part that I could catch a glimpse of a little space of the blue sea that way. From this I perceived that whatever thickness and surface of ice lay southwards, in the north it was attenuated to the shape of a wedge, so that its extreme breadth where it projected its cape or extremity would not exceed a musket shot.

A companion might have qualified in my mind something of the sense of prodigious loneliness and desolation inspired by that huge picture of dazzling uneven whiteness, blotting out the whole of the south-east ocean, rolling in hills of blinding brilliance into the blue heavens, and curving and dying out into an airy film of silvery-azure radiance leagues away down in the south-west. But to my solitary eye the spectacle was an amazing and confounding one.

If I had not seen the tract of dark blue water in the north-east, I might have imagined that this island stretched as far into the east and north as it did in the south and west. And one thing I quickly enough understood: that if I wanted to behold the ocean on the east side of the ice I should have to journey the breadth of the range, which here, where I was, might mean one or five miles, for the blocks and lumps hid the view, and how far off the edge of the cliffs on the other side might be I could not therefore gather. This was not to be dreamt of, and therefore to this extent my climb had been useless.

Being on the top of the range now, I could plainly hear the noises of the splitting and internal convulsions of this vast formation. The sounds are not describable. Sometimes they seemed like the explosions of guns, sometimes like the growlings and mutterings of huge fierce beasts, sometimes like smart single echoless blasts of thunder; and sometimes you heard a singular sort of hissing or snarling, such as iron makes when speeding over ice, only when this noise happened the volume of it was so great that the atmosphere trembled upon the ear with it. It was impossible to fix the direction of these sounds, the island was full of them; and always sullenly booming upon the breeze was the voice of the ocean swell bursting in foam against the ice-coast that confronted it.

You may talk of the solitude of a Selkirk, but surely the spirit of loneliness in him could not rival the unutterable emotion of solitariness that filled my mind as I sent my gaze over those miles of frozen stirless whiteness. He had the sight of fair pastures, of trees making a twinkling twilight on the sward, of grassy savannahs and pleasant slopes of hills; the air was illuminated by the glorious plumage of flying birds; the bleat of goats broke the stillness in the valleys; there was a golden regale for his eye, and his other senses were gratified with the perfumes of rich flowers and engaging concerts among the trembling leaves. Above all, there was the soothing warmth of a delicious climate. But out upon those heaped and spreading plains of snow nothing stirred, if it were not once that I was startled by a loud report, and spied a rock about half a mile away slide down the edge of the flat cliff and tumble into the sea. Nothing stirred, I say; there was an affrighting solemnity of motionlessness everywhere. The countenance of this plain glared like a great dead face at the sky; neither sympathy, nor fancy, no, not the utmost forces of the imagination, could witness expression in it. Its unmeaningness was ghastly, and the ghastlier for the greatness of its bald and lifeless stare.

I turned my eyes seawards; haply it was the whiteness that gave the ocean the extraordinarily rich dye I found in it. The expanse went in flowing folds of violet into the nethermost heavens, and though God knows what extent of horizon I surveyed, the line of it, as clear as glass, ran without the faintest flaw to amuse my heart with even an instant's hope.

There was more weight, however, in the wind than I had supposed. It blew from the west of north, and was an exquisitely frosty wind, despite the quarter whence it came. It swept in moans among the rocks, and there were tones in it that recalled the stormy mutterings we had heard in the blasts which came upon the brig before the storm boiled down upon her. But my imagination was now so tight-strung as to be unwholesomely and unnaturally responsive to impulses and influences which at another time I had not noticed. There were a few heavy clouds in the north-east, so steam-like that methought they borrowed their complexion from the snow on the island's cape there. I was pretty sure, however, that there was wind behind them, for if the roll of the ocean did not signify heavy weather near to, then what else it betokened I could not imagine.

I cannot express to you how the very soul within me shrank from putting to sea in the little boat. There was no longer the support of the excitement and terror of escaping from a sinking vessel. I stood upon an island as solid as land, and the very sense of security it imparted rendered the boat an object of terror, and the obligation upon me to launch into yonder mighty space as frightful as a sentence of death. Yet I could not but consider that it would be equally shocking to me to be locked up in this slowly crumbling body of ice—nay, tenfold more shocking, and that, if I had to choose between the boat and this hideous solitude and sure starvation, I would cheerfully accept fifty times over again the perils of a navigation in my tiny ark.

This reflection comforted me somewhat, and whilst I thus mused I remained standing with my eyes upon the little group of fanciful fanes and spires of ice on the edge of the abrupt hollow. I had been too preoccupied to take close notice; on a sudden I started, amazed by an appearance too exquisitely perfect to be credible. The sun shone with a fine white frosty brilliance in the north-east; some of these spikes and figures of ice reflected the radiance in several colours. In places where they were wind-swept of their snow and showed the naked ice, the hues were wondrously splendid, and, mingling upon the sight, formed a kind of airy, rainbow-like veil that complicated the whole congregation of white shaft and many-tinctured spire, the marble column, the alabaster steeple into a confused but most surprisingly dainty and shining scene.

It was whilst looking at this that my eye traced, a little distance beyond, the form of a ship's spars and rigging. Through the labyrinth of the ice outlines I clearly made out two masts, with two square yards on the foremast, the rigging perfect so far as it went, for the figuration showed no more than half the height of the masts, the lower parts being apparently hidden behind the edge of the hollow. I have said that this coast to the north abounded in many groups of beautiful fantastic shapes, suggesting a great variety of objects, as the forms of clouds do, but nothing perfect; but here now was something in ice that could not have been completer, more symmetrical, more faultlessly proportioned had it been the work of an artist. I walked close to it and a little way around so as to obtain a clearer view, and then getting a fair sight of the appearance I halted again, transfixed with amazement.

The fabric appeared as if formed of frosted glass. The masts had a good rake, and with a seaman's eye I took notice of the furniture, observing the shrouds, stays, backstays, braces to be perfect. Nay, as though the spirit artist of this fragile glittering pageant had resolved to omit no detail to complete the illusion, there stood a vane at the masthead, shining like a tongue of ice against the soft blue of the sky. Come, thought I, recovering from my wonder, there is more in this than it is possible for me to guess by staring from a distance; so, striking my pole into the snow, I made carefully towards the edge of the hollow.

The gradual unfolding of the picture prepared my mind for what I could not see till the brink was reached; then, looking down, I beheld a schooner-rigged vessel lying in a sort of cradle of ice, stern-on to the sea. A man bulked out with frozen snow, so as to make his shape as great as a bear, leaned upon the rail with a slight upwards inclination of his head, as though he were in the act of looking fully up to hail me. His posture was even more lifelike than that of the man under the rock, but his garment of snow robbed him of that reality of vitality which had startled me in the other, and the instant I saw him I knew him to be dead. He was the only figure visible. The whole body of the vessel was frosted by the snow into the glassy aspect of the spars and rigging, and the sunshine striking down made a beautiful prismatic picture of the silent ship.

She was a very old craft. The snow had moulded itself upon her and enlarged without spoiling her form. I found her age in the structure of her bows, the headboards of which curved very low round to the top of the stem, forming a kind of well there, the after-part of which was framed by the forecastle bulkhead, after the fashion of ship-building in vogue in the reign of Anne and the first two Georges. Her topmasts were standing, but her jib-boom was rigged in. I could find no other evidence of her people having snugged her for these winter quarters, in which she had been manifestly lying for years and years. I traced the outlines of six small cannons covered with snow, but resting with clean-sculptured forms in their white coats; a considerable piece of ordnance aft, and several petararoes or swivel-pieces upon the after-bulwark rails. Gaffs and booms were in their places, and the sails furled upon them. The figuration of the main hatch showed a small square, and there was a companion or hatch-cover abaft the mainmast. There was no trace of a boat. She had a flush or level deck from the well in the bows to a fathom or so past the main-shrouds; it was then broken by a short poop-deck, which went in a great spring or rise to the stern, that was after the pink style, very narrow and tall.

Though I write this description coldly, let it not be supposed that I was not violently agitated and astonished almost into the belief that what I beheld was a mere vision, a phenomenon. The sight of the body I examined did not nearly so greatly astound me as the spectacle of this ice-locked schooner. It was easy to account for the presence of a dead man. My own situation, indeed, sufficiently solved the riddle of that corpse. But the ship, perfect in all respects, was like a stroke of magic. She lay with a slight list or inclination to larboard, but on the whole tolerably upright, owing to the corpulence of her bilge. The hollow or ravine that formed her bed went with a sharp incline under her stern to the sea, which was visible from the top of the cliffs here through the split in the rocks. The shelving of the ice put the wash of the ocean at a distance of a few hundred feet from the schooner; but I calculated that the vessel's actual elevation above the water-line, supposing you to measure it with a plummet up and down, did not exceed twenty feet, if so much, the hollow in which she rested being above twenty feet deep.

It was very evident that the schooner had in years gone by got embayed in this ice when it was far to the southward, and had in course of time been built up in it by floating masses. For how old the ice about the poles may be who can tell? In those sunless worlds the frozen continents may well possess the antiquity of the land. And who shall name the monarch who filled the throne of Britain when this vast field broke away from the main and started on its stealthy navigation sunwards?

Chapter IX.
I Lose my Boat

I LINGERED, I daresay, above twenty minutes contemplating this singular crystal fossil of a ship, and considering whether I should go down to her and ransack her for whatever might answer my turn. But she looked so darkly secret under her white garb, and there was something so terrible in the aspect of the motionless snow-clad sentinel who leaned upon the rail, that my heart failed me, and I very easily persuaded myself to believe that, first, it would take me longer to penetrate and search her than it was proper I should be away from the boat; that, second, it was scarce to be supposed her crew had left any provisions in her, or that, if stores there were, they would be fit to eat; and that, finally, my boat was so small it would be rash to put into her any the most trifling matter that was not essential to the preservation of my life.

So, concluding to have nothing to do with the ghostly sparkling fabric, I started for the body under the rock, and with some pain and staggering, the ice being very jagged, lumpish, and deceitful to the tread, arrived at it.

Nothing but the desire to possess the fine warm cloak could have tempted me to handle or even to cast my eye upon the dead man again. I found myself more scared by him now than at first. His attitude was so lifelike that, though I knew him to be a corpse, had he risen on a sudden the surprise of it could hardly have shocked me more than the astonishment his posture raised. As a skeleton he could not have so chilled and awed me; but so well preserved was his flesh by the cold, that it was hard to persuade myself he was not breathing, and that, though he feigned to be gazing downwards, he was not secretly observing me.

His beard was frozen as hard as a bush, and it crackled unpleasantly to the movement of my hands, which I was obliged to force under it to unhook the silver chain that confined the cloak about his neck. I felt like a thief, and stole a glance over either shoulder as though, forsooth, some strangely clad companion of his should be creeping upon me unawares. Then, thought I, since I have the cloak I may as well take the watch, flask, and tobacco-box, as I had before resolved; and so I dipped my hand into his pockets, and without another glance at his fierce still face made for the boat.

I now noticed for the first time, so overwhelmingly had my discoveries occupied my attention, that the wind had freshened and was blowing briskly and piercingly. When I had first started upon the ascent of the slope, the wind had merely wrinkled the swell as the large bodies ran;

but those wrinkles had become little seas, which flashed into foam after a short race, and the whole surface of the ocean was a brilliant blue tremble. I came to a halt to view the north-east sky before the brow of the rocks hid it, and saw that clouds were congregating there, and some of them blowing up to where the sun hung, these resembling in shape and colour the compact puff of the first discharge of a cannon before the smoke spreads on the air. What should I do? I sank into a miserable perplexity. If it was going to blow what good could attend my departure from this island? It was an adverse wind, and when it freshened I could not choose but run before it, and that would drive me clean away from the direction I required to steer in. Yet if I was to wait upon the weather, for how long should I be kept a prisoner in this horrid place? True, a southerly wind might spring up to-morrow, but it might be otherwise, or come in a hard gale; and if I faltered now I might go on hesitating, and then my provisions would give out, and God alone knows how it would end with me. Besides, the presence of the two bodies made the island fearful to my imagination, and nature clamoured in me to be gone, a summons my judgment could not resist, for reason often misleads, but instincts never.

I fell again to my downward march and looked towards my boat— that is to say, I looked towards the part of the ice where the little haven in which she lay had been, and I found both boat and haven gone!

I rubbed my eyes and stared again. Tush, thought I, I am deceived by the ice. I glanced at the slope behind to keep me to my bearings, and once more sought the haven; but the rock that had formed it was gone, the blue swell rolled brimming past the line of shore there, and my eye following the swing of a fold, I saw the boat about three cables length distant out upon the water, swinging steadily away into the south, and showing and disappearing with the heave.

The dead man's cloak fell from my arm; I uttered a cry of anguish; I clasped my hands and lifted them to God, and looked up to Him. I was for kicking off my boots and plunging into the water, but, mad as I was, I was not so mad as that; and mad I should have been to attempt it, for I could not swim twenty strokes, and had I been the stoutest swimmer that ever breasted the salt spray, the cold must speedily put an end to my misery.

What was to be done? Nothing! I could only look idly at the receding boat with reeling brain. The full blast of the wind was upon her, and helping the driving action of the billows. I perceived that she was irrecoverable, and yet I stood watching, watching, watching! my head burning with the surgings of twenty impracticable schemes. I cast myself down and wept, stood up afresh and looked at the boat, then cried to God for help and mercy, bringing my hands to my throbbing temples, and in that posture straining my eyes at the fast vanishing structure. She was the only hope I had—my sole chance. My little stock of provisions was in her—oh, what was I to do?

Though I was at some distance from the place where what I have called my haven had been, there was no need for me to approach it to understand how my misfortune had come about. It was likely enough that the very crevice in which I had jammed the mast to secure the boat by was a deep crack that the increased swell had wholly split, so that the mast had tumbled when the rock floated away and liberated the boat.

The horror that this white and frightful scene of desolation had at the beginning filled me with was renewed with such violence when I saw that my boat was lost, and I was to be a prisoner on the death-haunted waste, that I fell down in a sort of swoon, like one partly stunned, and had any person come along and seen me he would have thought me as dead as the body on the hill or the corpse that kept its dismal look-out from the deck of the schooner.

My senses presently returning, I got up, and the rock upon which I stood being level, I fell to pacing it with my hands locked behind me, my head sunk, lost in thought. The wind was steadily freshening; it split with a howling noise upon the ice-crags and unequal surfaces, and spun with a hollow note past my ear; and the thunder of the breakers on the other side of the island was deepening its tone. The sea was lifting and whitening; something of mistiness had grown up over the horizon that made a blue dullness of the junction of the elements there; but though a few clouds out of the collection of vapour in the north-east had floated to the zenith and were sailing down the south-west heaven, the azure remained pure and the sun very frostily white and sparkling.

I am writing a strange story with the utmost candour, and trust that the reader will not judge me severely for my confession of weakness, or consider me as wanting in the stuff out of which the hardy seaman is made for owning to having shed tears and been stunned by the loss of my little boat and slender stock of food. You will say, "It is not in the power of the dead to hurt a man; what more pitiful and harmless than a poor unburied corpse?" I answer, "True," and declare that of the two bodies, as dead men, I was not afraid; but this mass of frozen solitude was about them, and they took a frightful character from it; they communicated an element of death to the desolation of the snow-clad island; their presence made a principality of it for the souls of dead sailors, and into their lifelike stillness it put its own supernatural spirit of loneliness; so that to my imagination, disordered by suffering and exposure, this melancholy region appeared a scene without parallel on the face of the globe, a place of doom and madness, as dreadful and wild as the highest mood of the poet could reach up to.

49

By this time the boat was out of sight. I looked and looked, but she was gone. Then came my good angel to my help and put some courage into me. "After all," thought I, "what do I dread? Death! it can but come to that. It is not long ago that Captain Rosy cried to me, "*A man can die but once. He'll not perish the quicker for contemplating his end with a stout heart.*" He that so spoke is dead. The worst is over for him. Were he a babe resting upon his mother's breast he could not sleep more soundly, be more tenderly lulled, nor be freer from such anguish as now afflicts me who cling to life, as if this—this," I cried, looking around me, "were a paradise of warmth and beauty. I must be a man, ask God for courage to meet whatever may betide, and stoutly endure what cannot be evaded."

Do not smile at the simple thoughts of a poor castaway sailor. I hold them still to be good reasoning, and had my flesh been as strong as my spirit they had availed, I don't doubt. But I was chilled to the marrow; the mere knowing that there was nothing to eat sharpened my appetite, and I felt as if I had not tasted food for a week; and here then were physical conditions which broke ruinously into philosophy and staggered religious trust.

My mind went to the schooner, yet I felt an extraordinary recoil within me when I thought of seeking an asylum in her. I had the figure of her before my fancy, viewed the form of the man on her deck, and the idea of penetrating her dark interior and seeking shelter in a fabric that time and frost and death had wrought into a black mystery was dreadful to me. Nor was this all. It seemed like the very last expression of despair to board that stirless frame; to make a dwelling-place, without prospect of deliverance, in that hollow of ice; to become in one sense as dead as her lonely mariner, yet preserve all the sensibility of the living to a condition he was as unconscious of as the ice that enclosed him.

It must be done nevertheless, thought I; I shall certainly perish from exposure if I linger here; besides, how do I know but that I may discover in that ship some means of escaping from the island? Assuredly there was plenty of material in her for the building of a boat, if I could meet with tools. Or possibly I might find a boat under hatches, for it was common for vessels of her class and in her time to stow their pinnaces in the hold, and, when the necessity for using them arose, to hoist them out and tow them astern.

These reflections somewhat heartened me, and also let me add that the steady mounting of the wind into a small gale served to reconcile me, not indeed to the loss of my boat, but to my detention; for though there might be a miserable languishing end for me here, I could not but believe that there was certain death, too, out there in that high swell and in those sharpening peaks of water off whose foaming heads the wind was blowing the spray. By which I mean the boat could not have plyed in such a wind; she must have run, and by running have carried me into the stormier regions of the south, where, even if she had lived, I must speedily have starved for victuals and perished of cold.

Hope lives like a spark amid the very blackest embers of despondency. Twenty minutes before I had awakened from a sort of swoon and was overwhelmed with misery; and now here was I taking a collected view of my situation, even to the extent of being willing to believe that on the whole it was perhaps as well that I should have been hindered from putting to sea in my little eggshell. So at every step we rebel at the shadowy conducting of the hand of God; yet from every stage we arrive at we look back and know the road we have travelled to be the right one though we start afresh mutinously. Lord, what patience hast Thou!

I turned my back upon the clamorous ocean and started to ascend the slope once more. When I reached the brow of the cliffs I observed that the clouds had lost their fleeciness and taken a slatish tinge, were moving fast and crowding up the sky, insomuch that the sun was leaping from one edge to another and darting a keen and frosty light upon the scene. The wind was bitterly cold, and screamed shrilly in my ears when I met the full tide of it. The change was sudden, but it did not surprise me. I knew these seas, and that our English April is not more capricious than the weather in them, only that here the sunny smile, though sparkling, is frostier than the kiss of death, and brief as the flight of a musket-ball, whilst the frowns are black, savage, and lasting.

I bore the dead man's cloak on my arm and helped myself along with the oar, and presently arrived at the brink of the slope in whose hollow lay the ship as in a cup. The wind made a noisy howling in her rigging, but the tackling was frozen so iron hard that not a rope stirred, and the vane at the masthead was as motionless as any of the adjacent steeples or pillars of ice. My heart was dismayed again by the figure of the man. He was more dreadful than the other because of the size to which the frozen snow upon his head, trunk, and limbs had swelled him; and the half-rise of his face was particularly startling, as if he were in the very act of running his gaze softly upwards. That he should have died in that easy leaning posture was strange; however, I supposed, and no doubt rightly, that he had been seized with a sudden faintness, and had leaned upon the rail and so expired. The cold would quickly make him rigid and likewise preserve him, and thus he might have been leaning, contemplating the ice of the cliffs, for years and years!

A wild and dreadful thing for one in my condition to light on and be forced to think of.

My heart, as I have said, sank in me again at the sight of him, and fear and awe and superstition so worked upon my spirits that I stood irresolute, and would have gone back had there been any place to return to. I plucked up after a little, and, rolling up the cloak into a compact bundle, flung it with all my strength to the vessel, and it fell cleverly just within the rail. Then gripping the oar I started on the descent.

The depth was not great nor the declivity sharp; but the surface was formed of blocks of ice, like the collections of big stones you sometimes encounter on the sides of mountains near the base; and I had again and again to fetch a compass so as to gain a smaller block down which to drop, till I was close to the vessel, and here the snow had piled and frozen into a smooth face.

The ship lay with a list or inclination to larboard. I had come down to her on her starboard side. She had small channels with long plates, but her list, on my side, hove them somewhat high, beyond my reach, and I perceived that to get aboard I must seek an entrance on the larboard hand. This was not hard to arrive at; indeed, I had but to walk round her, under her bows. She was so coated with hard snow I could see nothing of her timbers, and was therefore unable to guess at the condition of the hull. She had a most absurd swelling bilge, and her buttocks, viewed on a line with her rudder, doubtless presented the exact appearance of an apple. She was sunk in snow to some planks above the garboard-streak, but her lines forward were fine, making her almost wedge-shaped, though the flair of her bows was great, so that she swelled up like a balloon to the catheads. She had something of the look of the barca-longas of half a century ago—that is, half a century ago from the date of my adventure; but that which, in sober truth, a man would have taken her to be was a vessel formed of snow, sparred and rigged with glass-like frosted ice, the artistic caprice of the genius or spirit of this white and melancholy scene, who, to complete the mocking illusion, had fashioned the figure of a man to stand on deck with a human face toughened into an idle eternal contemplation.

On the larboard hand the ice pressed close against the vessel's side, some pieces rising to the height of her wash-streak. The face of the hollow was precipitous here, full of cracks and flaws and sharp projections. Indeed, had the breadth of the island been as it was at the extremity I might have counted upon the first violent commotion of the sea snapping this part of the ice, and converting the northern part of the body into a separate berg.

I climbed without difficulty into the fore-chains, the snow being so hard that my feet and hands made not the least impression on it, and somewhat warily—feeling the government of a peculiar awe, mounting into a sort of terror indeed—stood awhile peering over the rail of the bulwarks; then entered the ship. I ran my eyes swiftly here and there, for indeed I did not know what might steal or leap into view. Let it be remembered that I was a sailor, with the superstitious feelings of my calling in me, and though I do not know that I actually believed in ghosts and apparitions and spectrums, yet I felt as if I did; particularly upon the deck of this silent ship, rendered spirit-like by the grave of ice in which she lay and by the long years (as I could not doubt) during which she had thus rested. Hence, when I slipped off the bulwark on to the deck and viewed the ghastly, white, lonely scene, I felt for the moment as if this strange discovery of mine was not to be exhausted of its wonders and terrors by the mere existence of the ship—in other words, that I must expect something of the supernatural to enter into this icy sepulchre, and be prepared for sights more marvellous and terrifying than frozen corpses.

So I stood looking forward and aft, very swiftly, and in a way I dare say that a spectator would have thought laughable enough; nor was my imagination soothed by the clear, harping, ringing sounds of the wind seething through the frozen rigging where the masts rose above the shelter of the sides of the hollow.

Presently, getting the better of my perturbation, I walked aft, and, stepping on to the poop-deck, fell to an examination of the companion or covering of the after-hatch, which, as I have elsewhere said, was covered with snow.

Chapter X.
Another Startling Discovery

THIS hatch formed the entrance to the cabin, and there was no other road to it that I could see. If I wanted to use it I must first scrape away the snow; but unhappily I had left my knife in the boat, and was without any instrument that would serve me to scrape with. I thought of breaking the beer-bottle that was in my pocket and scratching with a piece of the glass; but before doing this it occurred to me to search the body on the starboard side.

I approached him as if he were alive and murderously fierce, and I own I did not like to touch him. He resembled the figure of a giant moulded in snow. In life he must have been six feet and a half tall. The snow had bloated him, and though he leaned he stood as high as I, who was of a tolerable stature. The snow was on his beard and moustaches and on his hair; but these features were merged and compacted into the snow on his coat, and as his cap came low and was covered with snow too, he, with the little fragment of countenance that remained, the flesh whereof had the colour and toughness of the skin of a drum that has been well beaten, submitted as terrible an object as mortal sight ever rested on. I say I did not like to touch him, and one reason was I feared he would tumble; and though I know not why I should have dreaded this, yet the apprehension of it so worked in me that for some time it held me idly staring at him.

But I could not enter the cabin without first scraping the snow from the companion door; and the cold, after I had stood a few moments inactive, was so bitter as to set me craving for shelter. So I put my hand upon the body, and discovered it, as I might have foreseen, frozen to the hardness of steel. His coat—if I may call that a coat which resembled a robe of snow—fell to within a few inches of the deck. Steadying the body with one hand, I heartily tweaked the coat with the other, hoping thus to rupture the ice upon it; in doing which I slipped and fell on my back, and in falling gave a convulsive kick which, striking the feet of the figure, dislodged them from their frozen hold of the deck, and down it fell with a mighty bang alongside of me, and with a loud crackling noise, like the rending of a sheet of silk.

I was not hurt, and sprang to my feet with the alacrity of fright, and looking at the body saw that it had managed by its fall much better than my hands could have compassed; for the snow shroud was cracked and crumpled, slabs of it had broken away leaving the cloth of the coat visible, and what best pleased me was the sight of the end of a hanger forking out from the skirt of the coat.

Yet to come at it so as to draw the blade from its scabbard required an intolerable exertion of strength. The clothes on this body were indeed like a suit of mail. I never could have believed that frost served cloth so. At last I managed to pull the coat clear of the hilt of the hanger; the blade was stuck, but after I had tugged a bit it slipped out, and I found it a good piece of steel.

The corpse was habited in jackboots, a coat of coarse thick cloth lined with flannel, under this a kind of blouse or doublet of red cloth, confined by a belt with leathern loops for pistols. His apparel gave me no clue to the age he belonged to; it was no better, indeed, than a sort of masquerading attire, as though the fashions of more than one country, and perhaps of more than one age, had gone to the habiting of him. He looked a burly, immense creature, as he lay upon the deck in the same bent attitude in which he had stood at the rail, and so dreadful was his face, with a singular diabolical expression of leering malice, caused by the lids of his eyes being half closed, that having taken one peep I had no mind to repeat it, though I was above ten minutes wrestling with his cloak and hanger before I had the weapon fairly in my hand.

I walked to the companion and fell to scraping the snow away from it. 'Twas like scratching at mortar between bricks. But I worked hard, and presently, with the point of the hanger, felt the crevice 'twixt the door and its jamb, after which it was not long before I had carved the door out of its plate of ice and snow.

The wind was now blowing a fresh gale, and the howling aloft was extremely melancholy and dismal. I could not see the ocean, but I heard it thundering with a hollow roaring note; and the sharp reports and distant sullen crashing noises, with nearer convulsions within the ice, were very frequent.

My labour warmed me, but it also increased my hunger. While I hacked and scraped at the snow I was considering whether I should come across anything fit to eat in the ship, and if not what I was to do. Here was a vessel assuredly not less than fifty or sixty years old, and even supposing she was almost new when she fell in with the ice, the date of her disaster would still carry her back half a century; so that—and certainly there was much in the appearance of the body on the rocks to warrant the conjecture—she would have been thus sepulchred and fossilized for fifty years!

What, then, in the form of provisions proper for human food, such as even a famine-driven stomach could deal with, was I likely to find in her? Would not her crew have eaten her bare, devoured the very heart out of her, before they perished?

55

These thoughts weighed heavily in me, but I toiled on nevertheless, and having cleared the door of the snow that bound it, I prized it apart with the hanger and then dragged at it; but the snow on the deck would not let it open far, and as there was room for me to squeeze through, I did not stop to scrape the obstruction away.

A flight of steps sank into the darkness of the interior, and a cold strange smell floated up, with something of a dry earthiness of flavour and a mingling of leather and timber. I fell back a pace to let something of this smell exhale before I ventured into an atmosphere that had been hermetically bottled by the ice in that cabin since the hour when this little door was last closed. Superstition was active in me again, and when I peered into the blackness at the bottom of the hatch I felt as might a schoolboy on the threshold of a haunted room in which he is to be locked up as a punishment.

I put my foot on the ladder and descended very slowly indeed, my inclination being strong the other way, and I kept on looking downwards in a state of ridiculous fright as though at any moment I should be seized by the leg; being in too much confusion of mind to consider that it was impossible anything living could be below, whilst a ghostly shadow could not catch hold of me so as to cause me to feel its grasp. But then if fear could reason, it would cease to be fear.

On reaching the bottom I remained standing close against the ladder, striving to see into what manner of place I was arrived. The glare of the whiteness of the decks and rocks hung upon my eyes like a kind of blindness charged with fires of several colours, and I could not obtain the faintest glimpse of any part of this interior outside the sphere of the little square of hazy light which lay upon the deck at the foot of the steps. The darkness, indeed, was so deep that I concluded this was no more than a narrow well formed of bulkheads, and that the cabin was beyond, and led to by a door in the bulkhead.

To test this conjecture I extended my arms in a groping posture and stepped a pace forward, feeling to right and left, till, having gone five or six paces from the ladder, my fingers touched something cold, and feeling it, I passed my hand down what I instantly knew by the projection of the nose and the roughness of hair on the upper lip to be a human face!

A little reflection might have prepared me for this, but I had not reflected, at least in this direction, and was therefore not prepared; and the horrible thrill of that black chill contact went in an agony through my nerves, and I burst into a violent perspiration.

I backed away with all my hair astir, and then shot up the ladder as if the devil had been behind me; and when I reached the deck I was trembling so violently that I had to lean against the companion lest my knees should give way. Never in all my time had I received such a fright as this; but then I had gone to it in a fright, and was exactly in the state of mind to be terrified out of my senses. My soul had been rendered sick and weak within me by mental and corporeal suffering; my loneliness, too, was dreadful, and the wilder and more scaring too for this my unhappy association with the dead; the shrieking in the rigging was like the tongue given by endless packs of hunting phantom wolves, and the growling and cracking noises of the ice in all directions would have made one coming new to this desolate scene suppose that the island of ice was full of fierce beasts.

But needs must when Old Nick drives; I had either to find courage to enter the schooner and search her, and so stand to come across the means to prolong my life, and perhaps procure my deliverance, or perish of famine and frost on deck.

The companion door was small, and being scarce more than ajar I was not surprised that only a very faint light entered by it. If the top were removed I doubted not I should be able to get a view of the cabin, enough to show me where the windows or port-holes were. So I went to work with the hanger again, insensibly obtaining a little stock of courage from the mere brandishing of it. In half an hour I had chipped and cut away the ice round the companion, and then found it to be one of those old-fashioned clumsy hatch-covers formerly used in certain kinds of Dutch ships—namely, a box with a shoulder-shaped lid. This lid, though heavy, and fitting with a tongue, I managed to unship, on which the full square of the hatch lay open to the sky.

The light gave me heart. Once more I descended. After a few moments the bewildering dazzle of the snow faded off my sight, and I could see very distinctly.

The cabin was a small room. The forward part lay in shadow, but I could distinguish the outline of the mainmast amidships of the bulkhead there. In the centre of this cabin was a small square table supported by iron pins, that pierced through stanchions in such a manner that the table could at will be raised to the ceiling, and there left for the conveniency of space.

At this table, seated upon short quaintly-wrought benches, and immediately facing each other, were two men. They were incomparably more lifelike than the frozen figures. The one whose back was upon the hatchway ladder, being the man whose face I had stroked, sat upright, in the posture of a person about to start up, both hands upon the rim of the table, and his countenance raised as if, in a sudden terror and agony of death, he had darted a look to God. So inimitably expressive of life was his attitude, that though I knew him to be a frozen body as perished as if he had died with Adam or Noah, I was sensible of a breathless wonder in me that the affrighted start with which he seemed to be rising from the table was not continued—that, in short, he did not spring to his feet with the cry that you seemed to *hear* in his posture.

The other figure lay over the table with his face buried in his arms. He wore no covering to his head, which was bald, yet his hair on either side was plentiful and lay upon his arms, and his beard fluffing up about his buried face gave him an uncommon shaggy appearance. The other had on a round fur cap with lappets for the ears. His body was muffled in a thick ash-coloured coat; his hair was also abundant, curling long and black down his back; his cheeks were smooth manifestly through nature rather than the razor, and the ends of a small black moustache were twisted up to his eyes. These were the only occupants of the cabin, which their presence rendered terribly ghastly and strange.

There was perhaps something in keeping with the icy spell of death upon this vessel in the figure of the man who was bowed over the table, for he looked as though he slept; but the other mocked the view with a *spectrum* of the fever and passion of life. You would have sworn he had beheld the skeleton hand of the Shadow reaching out of the dimness for him; that he had started back with a curse and cry of horror, and expired in the very agony of his affrighted recoil.

The interior was extremely plain: the bulkheads of a mahogany colour, the decks bare, and nothing in the form of an ornament saving a silver crucifix hanging by a nail to the trunk of the mainmast, and a cage with a frozen bird of gorgeous plumage suspended to the bulkhead near the hatch. A small lanthorn of an old pattern dangled over the table, and I noticed that it contained two or three inches of candle. Abaft the hatchway was a door on the starboard side which I opened, and found a narrow dark passage. I could not pierce it with my eye beyond a few feet; but perceiving within this range the outline of a little door, I concluded that here were the berths in which the master and his mates slept. There was nothing to be done in the dark, and I bitterly lamented that I had left my tinder-box and flint in the boat, for then I could have lighted the candle in the lanthorn.

"Perhaps," thought I, "one of those figures may have a tinder-box upon him."

Custom was now somewhat hardening me; moreover I was spurred on by mortal anxiety to discover if there was any kind of food to be met with in the vessel. So I stepped up to the figure whose face I had touched, and felt in his pockets; but neither on him nor on the other did I find what I wanted, though I was not a little astonished to discover in the pockets of the occupants of so small and humble a ship as this schooner a fine gold watch as rich as the one I had brought away from the man on the rocks, and more elegant in shape, a gold snuff-box set with diamonds, several rings of beauty and value lying loose in the breeches pocket of the man whose face was hidden, a handful of Spanish pieces in gold, handkerchiefs of fine silk, and other articles, as if indeed these fellows had been overhauling a parcel of booty, and then carelessly returned the contents to their pockets.

But what I needed was the means of obtaining a light, so, after casting about, I thought I would search the body on deck, and went to it, and to my great satisfaction discovered what I wanted in the first pocket I dipped my hand into, though I had to rip open the mouth of it away from the snow with the hanger.

I returned to the cabin and lighted the candle, and carried the lanthorn into the black passage or corridor. There were four small doors, belonging to as many berths; I opened the first, and entered a compartment that smelt so intolerably stale and fusty that I had to come into the passage again and fetch a few breaths to humour my nose to the odour. As in the cabin, however, so here I found this noxiousness of air was not caused by putrefaction or any tainting qualities of a vegetable or animal kind, but by the deadness of the pent-up air itself, as the foulness of bilge-water is owing to its being imprisoned from air in the bottom of the hold.

I held up the lanthorn and looked about me. A glance or two satisfied me that I was in a room that had been appropriated to the steward and his mates. A number of dark objects, which on inspection I found to be hams, were stowed snugly away in battens under the ceiling or upper-deck; a cask half full of flour stood in a corner; near it lay a large coarse sack in which was a quantity of biscuit, a piece of which I bit and found it as hard as flint and tasteless, but not in the least degree mouldy. There were four shelves running athwartships full of glass, knives and forks, dishes, and so forth, some of the glass very choice and elegant, and many of the dishes and plates also very fine, fit for the greatest nobleman's table. Under the lower shelf, on the deck, lay a sack of what I believed to be black stones until, after turning one or two of them about, it came upon me that they were, or had been, I should say, potatoes.

Not to tease you with too many particulars under this head, let me briefly say that in this larder or steward's room I found among other things several cheeses, a quantity of candles, a great earthenware pot full of pease, several pounds of tobacco, about thirty lemons, along with two small casks and three or four jars, manifestly of spirits, but of what kind I could not tell. I took a stout sharp knife from one of the shelves, and pulling down one of the hams tried to cut it, but I might as well have striven to slice a piece of marble. I attempted next to cut a cheese, but this was frozen as hard as the ham. The lemons, candles, and tobacco had the same astonishing quality of stoniness, and nothing yielded to the touch but the flour. I laid hold of one of the jars, and thought to pull the stopper out, but it was frozen hard in the hole it fitted, and I was five minutes hammering it loose. When it was out I inserted a steel—used for the sharpening of knives—and found the contents solid ice, nor was there the faintest smell to tell me what the spirit or wine was.

Never before did plenty offer itself in so mocking a shape. It was the very irony of abundance—substantial ghostliness and a Barmecide's feast to my aching stomach.

But there was biscuit not unconquerable by teeth used to the fare of the sea life, and picking up a whole one, I sat me down on the edge of a cask and fell a-munching. One reflection, however, comforted me, namely, that this petrifaction by freezing had kept the victuals sweet. I was sure there was little here that might not be thawed into relishable and nourishing food and drink by a good fire. The sight of these stores took such a weight off my mind that no felon reprieved from death could feel more elated than I. My forebodings had come to nought in this regard, and here for the moment my grateful spirits were content to stop.

Chapter XI.
I Make Further Discoveries

So long as I moved about and worked I did not feel the cold; but if I stood or sat for a couple of minutes I felt the nip of it in my very marrow. Yet, fierce as the cold was here, it was impossible it could be comparable with the rigours of the parts in which this schooner had originally got locked up in the ice. No doubt if I died on deck my body would be frozen as stiff as the figure on the rocks; but, though it was very conceivable that I might perish of cold in the cabin by sitting still, I was sure the temperature below had not the severity to stonify me to the granite of the men at the table.

Still, though a greater degree of cold—cold as killing as if the world had fallen sunless—did unquestionably exist in those latitudes whence this ice with the schooner in its hug had floated, it was so bitterly bleak in this interior that 'twas scarce imaginable it could be colder elsewhere; and as I rose from the cask shuddering to the heart with the frosty motionless atmosphere, my mind naturally went to the consideration of a fire by which I might sit and toast myself.

I put a bunch of candles in my pocket—they were as hard as a parcel of marline-spikes—and took the lanthorn into the passage and inspected the next room. Here was a cot hung up by hooks, and a large black chest stood in cleats upon the deck; some clothes dangled from pins in the bulkhead, and upon a kind of tray fixed upon short legs and serving as a shelf were a miscellaneous bundle of boots, laced waistcoats, three-corner hats, a couple of swords, three or four pistols, and other objects not very readily distinguishable by the candle-light. There was a port which I tried to open, but found it so hard frozen I should need a handspike to start it. There were three cabins besides this; the last cabin, that is the one in the stern, being the biggest of the lot. Each had its cot, and each also had its own special muddle and litter of boxes, clothes, firearms, swords, and the like.

Indeed, by this time I was beginning to see how it was. The suspicion that the watches and jewellery I had discovered on the bodies of the men had excited was now confirmed, and I was satisfied that this schooner had been a pirate or buccaneer, of what nationality I could not yet divine—methought Spanish from the costume of the first figure I had encountered; and I was also convinced by the brief glance I directed at the things in the cabin, particularly the wearing apparel, and the make and appearance of the firearms, that she must have been in this position for upwards of fifty years.

The thought awed me greatly: *twenty years before I was born* those two men were sitting dead in the cabin!—he on deck was keeping his blind and silent look-out; he on the rocks with his hands locked upon his knees sat sunk in blank and frozen contemplation!

Every cabin had its port, and there were ports in the vessel's side opposite; but on reflection I considered that the cabin would be the warmer for their remaining closed, and so I came away and entered the great cabin afresh, bent on exploring the forward part.

I must tell you that the mainmast, piercing the upper deck, came down close against the bulkhead that formed the forward wall of the cabin, and on approaching this partition, the daylight being broad enough now that the hatch lay open on top, I remarked a sliding door on the larboard side of the mast. I put my shoulder to it and very easily ran it along its grooves, and then found myself in the way of a direct communication with all the fore portion of the schooner. The arrangement indeed was so odd that I suspected a piratical device in this uncommon method of opening out at will the whole range of deck. The air here was as vile as in the cabins, and I had to wait a bit.

On entering I discovered a little compartment with racks on either hand filled with small-arms. I afterwards counted a hundred and thirteen muskets, blunderbusses, and fusils, all of an antique kind, whilst the sides of the vessel were hung with pistols great and little, boarding-pikes, cutlasses, hangers, and other sorts of sword. This armoury was a sight to set me walking very cautiously, for it was not likely that powder should be wanting in a ship thus equipped; and where was it stowed?

There was another sliding door in the forward partition; it stood open, and I passed through it into what I immediately saw was the cook-house. I turned the lanthorn about, and discovered every convenience for dressing food. The furnaces were of brick and the oven was a great one— great, I mean, for the size of the vessel. There were pots, pans, and kettles in plenty, a dresser with drawers, dishes of tin and earthenware, a Dutch clock—in short, such an equipment of kitchen furniture as you would not expect to find in the galley of an Indiaman built to carry two or three hundred passengers. About half a chaldron of small coal lay heaped in a wooden angular fence fitted to the ship's side, for the sight of which I thanked God. I held the lanthorn to the furnace, and observed a crooked chimney rising to the deck and passing through it. The mouth or head of it was no doubt covered by the snow, for I had not noticed any such object in the survey I had taken of the vessel above. Strange, I thought, that these men should have frozen to death with the material in the ship for keeping a fire going. But then my whole discovery I regarded as one of those secrets of the deep which defy the utmost imagination and experience of man to explain them. Enough that here was a schooner which had been interred in a sepulchre of ice, as I might rationally conclude, for near half a century, that there were dead men in her who looked to have been frozen to death, that she was apparently stored with miscellaneous booty, that she was powerfully armed for a craft of her size, and had manifestly gone crowded with men. All this was plain, and I say it was enough for me. If she had papers they were to be met with presently; otherwise, conjecture would be mere imbecility in the face of those white and frost-bound countenances and iron silent lips.

I thrust back another sliding door and entered the ship's forecastle. The ceiling, as I choose to call the upper deck, was lined with hammocks, and the floor was covered with chests, bedding, clothes, and I know not what else. The ringing of the wind on high did not disturb the stillness, and I cannot convey the impression produced on my mind by this extraordinary scene of confusion beheld amid the silence of that tomblike interior. I stood in the doorway, not having the courage to venture further. For all I knew many of those hammocks might be tenanted; for as this kind of bed expresses by its curvature the rounded shape of a seaman, whether it be empty or not, so it is impossible by merely looking to know whether it is occupied or vacant. The dismalness of the prospect was of course vastly exaggerated by the feeble light of the candle, which, swaying in my hand, flung a swarming of shadows upon the scene, through which the hammocks glimmered wan and melancholy.

I came away in a fright, sliding the door to in my hurry with a bang that fetched a groaning echo out of the hold. If this ship were haunted, the forecastle would be the abode of the spirits!

Before I could make a fire the chimney must be cleared. Among the furniture in the arms-room were a number of spade-headed spears; the spade as wide as the length of a man's thumb, and about a foot long, mounted on light thin wood. Armed with one of these weapons, the like of which is to be met with among certain South American tribes, I passed into the cabin to proceed on deck; but though I knew the two figures were there, the coming upon them afresh struck me with as much astonishment and alarm as if I had not before seen them. The man starting from the table confronted me on this entrance, and I stopped dead to that astounding living posture of terror, even recoiling, as though he were alive indeed, and was jumping up from the table in his amazement at my apparition.

The brilliance of the snow was very striking after the dusk of the interiors I had been penetrating. The glare seemed like a blaze of white sunshine; yet it was the dazzle of the ice and nothing more for the sun was hidden; the fairness of the morning was passed; the sky was lead-coloured down to the ocean line, with a quantity of smoke-brown scud flying along it. The change had been rapid, as it always is hereabouts. The wind screamed with a piercing whistling sound through the frozen rigging, splitting in wails and bounding in a roar upon the adamantine peaks and rocks; the cracking of the ice was loud, continuous, and mighty startling; and these sounds, combined with the thundering of the sea and the fierce hissing of its rushing yeast, gave the weather the character of a storm, though as yet it was no more than a fresh gale.

However, though it was frightful to be alone in this frozen vault, with no other society than that of the dead, not even a seafowl to put life into the scene, I could not but feel that, be my prospects what they might, for the moment I was safe—that is to say, I was immeasurably securer than ever I could have been in the boat, which, when I had emerged into this stormy sound and realized the sea that was running outside, I instantly thought of with a shudder. Had the rock, I mused, not fallen and liberated the boat, where should I be now? Perhaps floating, a corpse, fathoms deep under water, or, if alive, then flying before this gale into the south, ever widening the distance betwixt me and all chance of my deliverance, and every hour gauging more deeply the horrible cold of the pole. Indeed I began to understand that I had been mercifully diverted from courting a hideous fate, and my spirits rose with the emotion of gratitude and hope that attends upon preservation.

I speedily spied the chimney, which showed a head of two feet above the deck, and made short work of the snow that was frozen in it, as nothing could have been fitter to cut ice with than the spade-shaped weapon I carried. This done, I returned to the cook-room, and with a butcher's axe that hung against the bulkhead I knocked away one of the boards that confined the coal, split it into small pieces, and in a short time had kindled a good fire. One does not need the experience of being cast away upon an iceberg to understand the comfort of a fire. I had a mind to be prodigal, and threw a good deal of coals into the furnace, and presently had a noble blaze. The heat was exquisite. I pulled a little bench, after the pattern of those on which the men sat in the cabin, to the fire, and, with outstretched legs and arms, thawed out of me the frost that had lain taut in my flesh ever since the wreck of the *Laughing Mary*. When I was thoroughly warm and comforted I took the lanthorn and went aft to the steward's room, and brought thence a cheese, a ham, some biscuit, and one of the jars of spirits, all which I carried to the cook-room, and placed the whole of them in the oven. I was extremely hungry and thirsty, and the warmth and cheerfulness of the fire set me yearning for a hot meal. But how was I to make a bowl without fresh water? I went on deck and scratched up some snow, but the salt in it gave it a sickly taste, and I was not only certain it would spoil and make disgusting whatever

I mixed it with or cooked in it, but it stood as a drink to disorder my stomach and bring on an illness. So, thought I to myself, there must be fresh water about—casks enough in the hold, I dare say; but the hold was not to be entered and explored without labour and difficulty, and I was weary and famished, and in no temper for hard work.

In all ships it is the custom to carry one or more casks called scuttlebutts on deck, into which fresh water is pumped for the use of the crew. I stepped along looking earnestly at the several shapes of guns, coils of rigging, hatchways, and the like, upon which the snow lay thick and solid, sometimes preserving the mould of the object it covered, sometimes distorting and exaggerating it into an unrecognizable outline, but perceived nothing that answered to the shape of a cask. At last I came to the well in the head, passed the forecastle deck, and on looking down spied among other shapes three bulged and bulky forms. I seemed by instinct to know that these were the scuttlebutts and went for the chopper, with which I returned and got into this hollow, that was four or five feet deep. The snow had the hardness of iron; it took me a quarter of an hour of severe labour to make sure of the character of the bulky thing I wrought at, and then it proved to be a cask. Whatever might be its contents it was not empty, but I was pretty nigh spent by the time I had knocked off the iron bands and beaten out staves enough to enable me to get at the frozen body within. There were three-quarters of a cask full. It was sparkling clear ice, and chipping off a piece and sucking it, I found it to be very sweet fresh water. Thus was my labour rewarded.

I cut off as much as, when dissolved, would make a couple of gallons, but stayed a minute to regain my breath and take a view of this well or hollow before going aft. It was formed of the great open head-timbers of the schooner curving up to the stem, and by the forecastle deck ending like a cuddy front. I scraped at this front and removed enough snow to exhibit a portion of a window. It was by this window I supposed that the forecastle was lighted. Out of this well forked the bowsprit, with the spritsail yard braced fore and aft. The whole fabric close to looked more like glass than at a distance, owing to the million crystalline sparkles of the ice-like snow that coated the structure from the vane at the masthead to the keel.

Well, I clambered on to the forecastle deck and returned to the cook-room with my piece of ice, struck as I went along by the sudden comfortable quality of life the gushing of the black smoke out of the chimney put into the ship, and how, indeed, it seemed to soften as if by magic the savage wildness and haggard austerity and gale-swept loneliness of the white rocks and peaks. It was extremely disagreeable and disconcerting to me to have to pass the ghastly occupants of the cabin every time I went in and out; and I made up my mind to get them on deck when I felt equal to the work, and cover them up there. The slanting posture of the one was a sort of fierce rebuke; the sleeping attitude of the other was a dark and sullen enjoinment of silence. I never passed them without a quick beat of the heart and shortened breathing; and the more I looked at them the keener became the superstitious alarm they excited.

The fire burned brightly, and its ruddy glow was sweet as human companionship. I put the ice into a saucepan and set it upon the fire, and then pulling the cheese and ham out of the oven found them warm and thawed. On smelling to the mouth of the jar I discovered its contents to be brandy.[1] Only about an inch deep of it was melted. I poured this into a pannikin and took a sup, and a finer drop of spirits I never swallowed in all my life; its elegant perfume proved it amazingly choice and old. I fetched a lemon and some sugar and speedily prepared a small smoking bowl of punch. The ham cut readily; I fried a couple of stout rashers, and fell to the heartiest and most delicious repast I ever sat down to. At any time there is something fragrant and appetizing in the smell of fried ham; conceive then the relish that the appetite of a starved, half-frozen, shipwrecked man would find in it! The cheese was extremely good, and was as sound as if it had been made a week ago. Indeed, the preservative virtues of the cold struck me with astonishment. Here was I making a fine meal off stores which in all probability had lain in this ship fifty years, and they ate as choicely as like food of a similar quality ashore. Possibly some of these days science may devise a means for keeping the stores of a ship frozen, which would be as great a blessing as could befall the mariner, and a sure remedy for the scurvy, for then as much fresh meat might be carried as salt, besides other articles of a perishable kind.

[1] I can give the reader no better idea of the cold of the latitudes in which this schooner had lain, than by speaking of the brandy as being frozen. This may have happened through its having lost twenty or thirty per cent. of its Strength.—P. R.

Chapter XII.
A Lonely Night

I HAD a pipe of my own in my pocket; I fetched a small block of the black tobacco that was in the pantry, and, with some trouble, for it was as hard and dry as glass, chipped off a bowlful and fell a-puffing with all the satisfaction of a hardened lover of tobacco who has long been denied his favourite relish. The punch diffused a pleasing glow through my frame, the tobacco was lulling, the heat of the fire very soothing, the hearty meal I had eaten had also marvellously invigorated me, so that I found my mind in a posture to justly and rationally consider my condition, and to reason out such probabilities as seemed to be attached to it.

First of all I reflected that by the usual operation of natural laws this vast seat of "thrilling and thick-ribbed ice" in which the schooner lay bound was steadily travelling to the northward, where in due course it would dissolve, though that would not happen yet. But as it advanced so would it carry me nearer to the pathways of ships using these seas, and any day might disclose a sail near enough to observe such signals of smoke or flag as I might best contrive. But supposing no opportunity of this kind to offer, then I ought to be able to find in the vessel materials fit for the construction of a boat, if, indeed, I met not with a pinnace of her own stowed under the main-hatch, for there was certainly no boat on deck. Nay, my meditations even carried me further: this was the winter season of the southern hemisphere, but presently the sun would be coming my way, whilst the ice, on the other hand, floated towards him; if by the wreck and dissolution of the island the schooner was not crushed, she must be released, in which case, providing she was tight—and my brief inspection of her bottom showed nothing wrong with her that was visible through the shroud of snow—I should have a stout ship under me in which I would be able to lie hove to, or even make shift to sail her if the breeze came from the south, and thus take my chance of being sighted and discovered.

Much, I had almost said everything, depended on the quantity of provisions I should find in here and particularly on the stock of coal, for I feared I must perish if I had not a fire. But there was the hold to be explored yet; the navigation of these waters must have been anticipated by the men of the schooner, who were sure to make handsome provision for the cold—and the surer if, as I fancied, they were Spaniards. Certainly they might have exhausted their stock of coal, but I could not persuade myself of this, since the heap in the corner of the cook-room somehow or other was suggestive of a store behind.

I knew not yet whether more of the crew lay in the forecastle, but so far I had encountered four men only. If these were all, then I had a right to believe, grounding my fancy on the absence of boats, that most of the company had quitted the ship, and this they would have done early—a supposition that promised me a fair discovery of stores. Herein lay my hope; if I could prolong my life for three or four months, then, if the ice was not all gone, it would have advanced far north, serving me as a ship and putting me in the way of delivering myself, either by the sight of a sail, or by the schooner floating free, or by my construction of a boat.

Thus I sat musing, as I venture to think, in a clearheaded way. Yet all the same I could not glance around without feeling as if I was bewitched. The red shining of the furnace ruddily gilded the cook-house; through the after-sliding door went the passage to the cabin in blackness; the storming of the wind was subdued into a strange moaning and complaining; often through the body of the ship came the thrill of a sudden explosion; and haunting all was the sense of the dead men just without, the frozen desolation of the island, the mighty world of waters in which it lay. No! you can think of no isolation comparable to this; and I tremble as I review it, for under the thought of the enormous loneliness of that time my spirit must ever sink and break down.

It was melancholy to be without time, so I pulled out the gold watch I had taken from the man on the rocks and wound it up, and guessing at the hour, set the hands at half-past four. The watch ticked bravely. It was indeed a noble piece of mechanism, very costly and glorious with its jewels, and more than a hint as to the character of this schooner; and had there been nothing else to judge by I should still have sworn to her by this watch.

My pipe being emptied, I threw some more coals into the furnace, and putting a candle in the lanthorn went aft to take another view of the little cabins, in one of which I resolved to sleep, for though the cook-room would have served me best whilst the fire burned, I reckoned upon it making a colder habitation when the furnace was black than those small compartments in the stern. The cold on deck gushed down so bitingly through the open companion-hatch that I was fain to close it. I mounted the steps, and with much ado shipped the cover and shut the door, by which of course the great cabin, as I call the room in which the two men were, was plunged in darkness; but the cold was not tolerable, and the parcels of candles in the larder rendered me indifferent to the gloom.

On entering the passage in which were the doors of the berths, I noticed an object that had before escaped my observation—I mean a small trap-hatch, no bigger than a manhole, with a ring for lifting it, midway down the lane. I suspected this to be the entrance to the lazarette, and putting both hands to the ring pulled the hatch up. I sniffed cautiously, fearing foul air, and then sinking the lanthorn by the length of my arm I peered down, and observed the outlines of casks, bales, cases of white wood, chests, and so forth. I dropped through the hole on to a cask, which left me my head and shoulders above the deck, and then with the utmost caution stooped and threw the lanthorn light around me. But the casks were not powder-barrels, which perhaps a little reflection might have led me to suspect, since it was not to be supposed that any man would stow his powder in the lazarette.

As I was in the way of settling my misgivings touching the stock of food in the schooner, I resolved to push through with this business at once, and fetching the chopper went to work upon these barrels and chests; and very briefly I will tell you what I found. First, I dealt with a tierce that proved full of salt beef. There was a whole row of these tierces, and one sufficed to express the nature of the rest; there were upwards of thirty barrels of pork; one canvas bale I ripped open was full of hams, and of these bales I counted half a score. The white cases held biscuit. There were several sacks of pease, a number of barrels of flour, cases of candles, cheeses, a quantity of tobacco, not to mention a variety of jars of several shapes, some of which I afterwards found to contain marmalade and succadoes of different kinds. On knocking the head off one cask I found it held a frozen body, that by the light of the lanthorn looked as black as ink; I chipped off a bit, sucked it, and found it wine.

I was so transported by the sight of this wonderful plenty that I fell upon my knees in an outburst of gratitude and gave hearty thanks to God for His mercy. There was no further need for me to dismally wonder whether I was to starve or no; supposing the provisions sweet, here was food enough to last me three or four years. I was so overjoyed and withal curious that I forgot all about the time, and flourishing the chopper made the round of the lazarette, sampling its freight by individual instances, so that by the time I was tired I had enlarged the list I have given, by discoveries of brandy, beer, oatmeal, oil, lemons, tongues, vinegar, rum, and eight or ten other matters, all stowed very bunglingly, and in so many different kinds of casks, cases, jars, and other vessels as disposed me to believe that several piratical rummagings must have gone to the creation of this handsome and plentiful stock of good things.

Well, thought I, even if there be no more coal in the ship than what lies in the cook-house, enough fuel is here in the shape of casks, boxes, and the like to thaw me provisions for six months, besides what I may come across in the hold, along with the hammocks, bedding, boxes, and so forth in the forecastle, all which would be good to feed my fire with. This was a most comforting reflection, and I recollect springing out through the lazarette hatch with as spirited a caper as ever I had cut at any time in my life.

I replaced the hatch-cover, and having resolved upon the aftmost of the four cabins as my bedroom, entered it to see what kind of accommodation it would yield me. I hung up the lanthorn and looked into the cot, that was slung athwartships, and spied a couple of rugs, or blankets, which I pulled out, having no fancy to lie under them. The deck was like an old clothes' shop, or the wardrobe of a travelling troop of actors. From the confusion in this and the ajoining cabins, I concluded that there had been a rush at the last, a wild overhauling and flinging about of clothes for articles of more value hidden amongst them. But just as likely as not the disorder merely indicated the slovenly indifference of plunderers to the fruits of a pillage that had overstocked them.

The first garment I picked up was a cloak of a sort of silk material, richly furred and lined; all the buttons but one had been cut off, and that which remained was silver. I spread it in the cot, as it was a soft thing to lie upon. Then I picked up a coat of the fashion you will see in Hogarth's engravings; the coat collar a broad fold, and the cuffs to the elbow. This was as good as a rug, and I put it into the cot with the other. I inspected others of the articles on the deck, and among them recollect a gold-laced waistcoat of green velvet, two or three pairs of high-heeled shoes, a woman's yellow sacque, several frizzled wigs, silk stockings, pumps—in fine the contents of the trunks of some dandy passengers, long since gathered to their forefathers no doubt, even if the gentlemen of this schooner had not then and there walked them overboard or split their windpipes. But, to be honest, I cannot remember a third of what lay tumbled upon the deck or hung against the bulkhead. So far as my knowledge of costume went, every article pointed to the date which I had fixed upon for this vessel.

I swept the huddle of things with my foot into a corner, and lifting the lids of the boxes saw more clothes, some books, a collection of small-arms, a couple of quadrants, and sundry rolls of paper which proved to be charts of the islands of the Antilles and the western South American coast, very ill-digested. There were no papers of any kind to determine the vessel's character, nor journal to acquaint me with her story.

I was tired in my limbs rather than sleepy, and went to the cook-room to warm myself at the fire and get me some supper, meaning to sit there till the fire died out and then go to rest; but when I put my knife to the ham I found it as hard frozen as when I had first met with it; so with the cheese; and this though there had been a fire burning for hours! I put the things into the oven to thaw as before, and sitting down fell very pensive over this severity of cold, which had power to freeze within a yard or two of the furnace. To be sure the fire by my absence had shrunk, and the sliding door being open admitted the cold of the cabin; but the consideration was, how was I to resist the killing enfoldment of this atmosphere? I had slept in the boat, it is true, and was none the worse; and now I was under shelter, with the heat of a plentiful bellyful of meat and liquor to warm me; but if wine and ham and cheese froze in an air in which a fire had been burning, why not I in my sleep, when there was no fire, and life beat weakly, as it does in slumber? Those figures in the cabin were dismal warnings and assurances; they had been men perhaps stouter and heartier in their day than ever I was, but they had been frozen into stony images nevertheless, under cover too, with the materials to make a fire, and as much strong waters in their lazarette as would serve their schooner to float in.

Well, thought I, after a spell of melancholy thinking, if I *am* to perish of cold, there's an end; it is preordained, and it is as easy as drowning, anyhow, and better than hanging; and with that I pulled out the ham and found it soft enough to cut, finding philosophy (which, as the French cynic says, triumphs over past and future ills) not so hard because somehow I did not myself then particularly feel the cold—I mean, I was not certainly suffering here from that pain of frost which I had felt in the open boat.

Having heartily supped, I brewed a pint of punch, and, charging my pipe, sat smoking with my feet against the furnace. It was after eight o'clock by the watch I was wearing. I knew by the humming noise that it was blowing a gale of wind outside, and from time to time the decks rattled to a heavy discharge of hail. All sounds were naturally much subdued to my ear by the ship lying in a hollow, and I being in her with the hatches closed; but this very faintness of uproar formed of itself a quality of mystery very pat to the ghastliness of my surroundings. It was like the notes of an elfin storm of necromantic imagination; it was hollow, weak, and terrifying; and it and the thunder of the seas commingling, together with the rumbling blasts and shocks of splitting ice, disjointed as by an earthquake, loaded the inward silence with unearthly tones, which my lonely and quickened imagination readily furnished with syllables. The lanthorn diffused but a small light, and the flickering of the fire made a movement of shadows about me. I was separated from the great cabin where the figures were by the little arms-room only, and the passage to it ran there in blackness.

It strangely and importunately entered my head to conceive, that though those men were frozen and stirless they were not dead as corpses are, but as a stream whose current, checked by ice, will flow when the ice is melted. Might not life in them be suspended by the cold, not ended? There is vitality in the seed though it lies a dead thing in the hand. Those men are corpses to my eye; but said I to myself, they may have the principles of life in them, which heat might call into being. Putrefaction is a natural law, but it is balked by frost, and just as decay is hindered by cold, might not the property of life be left unaffected in a body, though it should be numbed in a marble form for fifty years?

This was a terrible fancy to possess a man situated as I was, and it so worked in me that again and again I caught myself looking first forward, then aft, as though, Heaven help me! my secret instincts foreboded that at any moment I should behold some form from the forecastle, or one of those figures in the cabin, stalking in, and coming to my side and silently seating himself. I pshaw'd and pish'd, and querulously asked of myself what manner of English sailor was I to suffer such womanly terrors to visit me; but it would not do; I could not smoke; a coldness of the heart fell upon me, and set me trembling above any sort of shivers which the frost of the air had chased through me; and presently a hollow creak sounding out of the hold, caused by some movement of the bed of ice on which the vessel lay, I was seized with a panic terror and sprang to my feet, and, lanthorn in hand, made for the companion-ladder, with a prayer in me for the sight of a star!

I durst not look at the figures, but, setting the light down at the foot of the ladder, squeezed through the companion-door on to the deck. My fear was a fever in its way, and I did not feel the cold. There was no star to be seen, but the whiteness of the ice was flung out in a wild strange glare by the blackness of the sky, and made a light of its own. It was the most savage and terrible picture of solitude the invention of man could reach to, yet I blessed it for the relief it gave to my ghost-enkindled imagination. No squall was then passing; the rocks rose up on either hand in a ghastly glimmer to the ebony of the heavens; the gale swept overhead in a wild, mad blending of whistlings, roarings, and cryings in many keys, falling on a sudden into a doleful wailing, then rising in a breath to the full fury of its concert; the sea thundered like the cannonading of an electric storm, and you would have said that the rending and crackling noises of the ice were responses to the crashing blows of the balls of shadow-hidden ordnance. But the scene, the uproar, the voices of the wind were real—a better cordial to my spirits than a gallon of the mellowest vintage below; and presently, when the cold was beginning to pierce me, my courage was so much the better for this excursion into the hoarse and black and gleaming realities of the night, that my heart beat at its usual measure as I passed through the hatch and went again to the cook-room.

I was, however, sure that if I sat here long, listening and thinking, fear would return. A small fire still burned; I put a saucepan on it, and popped in a piece of the fresh-water ice, but on handling the brandy I found it hard set. The heat of the oven was not sufficiently great to thaw me a dram; so to save further trouble in this way I took the chopper and at one blow split open the jar, and then there lay before me the solid body of the brandy, from which I chipped off as much as I needed, and thus procured a hot and animating draught.

Raking out the fire, I picked up the lanthorn and was about to go, then halted, considering whether I should not stow the frozen provisions away. It was a natural thought, seeing how precious food was to me. But, alas! it mattered not where they lay; they were as secure here as if they were snugly hidden in the bottom of the hold. It was the white realm of death; if ever a rat had crawled in this ship, it was, in its hiding-place, as stiff and idle as the frozen vessel. So I let the lump of brandy, the ice, ham, and so forth, rest where they were, and went to the cabin I had chosen, involuntarily peeping at the figures as I passed, and hurrying the faster because of the grim and terrifying liveliness put into the man who sat starting from the table by the swing of the lanthorn in my hand.

I shut the door and hung the lanthorn near the cot, having the flint and box in my pocket. There was indeed an abundance of candles in the vessel; nevertheless, it was my business to husband them with the utmost niggardliness. How long I was to be imprisoned here, if indeed I was ever to be delivered, Providence alone knew; and to run short of candles would add to the terrors of my existence, by forcing me either to open the hatches and ports for light, and so filling the ship with the deadly air outside, or living in darkness. There were a cloak and a coat in the cot, but they would not suffice. The fine cloak I had taken from the man on the rocks was on deck, and till now I had forgotten it; there was, however, plenty of apparel in the corner to serve as wraps, and having chosen enough to smother me I vaulted into the cot, and so covered myself that the clothes were above the level of the sides of the cot.

I left the lanthorn burning whilst I made sure my bed was all right, and lay musing, feeling extremely melancholy; the hardest part was the thought of those two men watching in the cabin. The most fantastic alarms possessed me. Suppose their ghosts came to the ship at midnight, and, entering their bodies, quickened them into walking? Suppose they were in the condition of cataleptics, sensible of what passed around them, but paralysed to the motionlessness and seeming insensibility of death? Then the very garments under which I lay were of a proper kind to keep a man in my situation quaking. My imagination went to work to tell me to whom they had belonged, the bloody ends their owners had met at the hands of the miscreants who despoiled them. I caught myself listening—and there was enough to hear, too, what with the subdued roaring of the wind, the splintering of ice, the occasional creaking—not unlike a heavy booted tread—of the fabric of the schooner—to the blasts of the gale against her masts, or to a movement in the bed on which she reposed.

But plain sense came to my rescue at last. I resolved to have no more of these night fears, so, blowing out the candle, I put my head on the coat that formed my pillow, resolutely kept my eyes shut, and after awhile fell asleep.

Chapter XIII.
I Explore the Hold and Forecastle

It was pitch dark when I awoke, and I conceived it must be the middle of the night, but to my astonishment, on lighting the lanthorn and looking at the watch, which I had taken the precaution to wind up overnight, I saw it wanted but twenty minutes of nine o'clock, so that I had passed through twelve hours of solid sleep. However, it was only needful to recollect where I was, and to cast a glance at the closed door and port, to understand why it was dark. I had slept fairly warm, and awoke with no sensation of cramp; but the keen air had caused the steam of my breath to freeze upon my mouth in such a manner that, when feeling the sticky inconvenience I put my finger to it, it fell like a little mask; and I likewise felt the pain of cold in my face to such an extent that had I been blistered there my cheeks, nose, and brow could not have smarted more. This resolved me henceforward to wrap up my head and face before going to rest.

I opened the door and passed out, and observed an amazing difference between the temperature of the air in which I had been sleeping and that of the atmosphere in the passage—a happy discovery, for it served to assure me that, if I was careful to lie under plenty of coverings and to keep the outer air excluded, the heat of my body would raise the temperature of the little cabin; nor, providing the compartment was ventilated throughout the day, was there anything to be feared from the vitiation of the air by my own breathing.

My first business was to light the fire and set my breakfast to thaw, and boil me a kettle of water; and some time after I went on deck to view the weather and to revolve in my mind the routine of the day. On opening the door of the companion-hatch I was nearly blinded by the glorious brilliance of the sunshine on the snow; after the blackness of the cabin it was like looking at the sun himself, and I had to stand a full three minutes with my hand upon my eyes before I could accustom my sight to the dazzling glare. It was fine weather again; the sky over the glass-like masts of the schooner was a clear dark blue, with a few light clouds blowing over it from the southward. The wind had shifted at last; but, pure as the heavens were, the breeze was piping briskly with the weight and song of a small gale, and its fangs of frost, even in the comparative quiet of the sheltered deck, bit with a fierceness that had not been observable yesterday.

The moment I had the body of the vessel in my sight I perceived that she had changed her position since my last view of her. Her bows were more raised, and she lay over further by the depth of a plank. I stared earnestly at the rocky slopes on either hand, but could not have sworn their figuration was changed. An eager hope shot into my mind, but it quickly faded into an emotion of apprehension. It was conceivable indeed that on a sudden some early day I might find the schooner liberated and afloat, and this was the first inspiriting flush; but then came the fear that the disruption and volcanic throes of the ice might crush her, a fear rational enough when I saw the height she lay above the sea, and how by pressure those slopes which formed her cradle might be jammed and welded together. The change of her posture then fell upon me with a kind of shock, and determined me, when I had broken my fast, to search her hold for a boat or for materials for constructing some ark by which I might float out to sea, should the ice grow menacing and force me from the schooner.

I made a plentiful meal, feeling the need of abundance of food in such a temperature as this, and heartily grateful that there was no need why I should stint myself. The having to pass the two figures every time I went on deck and returned was extremely disagreeable and unnerving, and I considered that, after searching the hold, the next duty I owed myself was to remove them on deck, and even over the side, if possible, for one place below was as sure to keep them haunting me as another, and they would be as much with me in the forecastle as if I stowed them away in the cabin adjoining mine.

Whilst I ate, my mind was so busy with considerations of the change in the ship's posture during the night that it ended in determining me to take a survey of her from the outside, and then climb the cliffs and look around before I fell to any other work. I fetched the cloak I had stripped the body on the rocks of and thawed and warmed it, and put it on, and a noble covering it was, thick, soft, and clinging. Then, arming myself with a boarding-pike to serve as a pole, I dropped into the fore-chains and thence stepped on to the ice, and very slowly and carefully walked round the schooner, examining her closely, and boring into the snow upon her side with my pike wherever I suspected a hole or indent. I could find nothing wrong with her in this way, though what a thaw might reveal I could not know. Her rudder hung frozen upon its pintles, and looked as it should. Some little distance abaft her rudder, where the hollow or chasm sloped to the sea, was a great split three or four feet wide; this had certainly happened in the night, and I must have slept as sound as the dead not to hear the noise of it. Such a rent as this sufficed to account for the subsidence of the after-part of the schooner and her further inclination to larboard. Indeed, the hollow was now coming to resemble the "ways" on which ships are launched; and you would have conceived by the appearance of it that if it should slope a little more yet, off would slide the schooner for the sea, and in the right posture too—that is, stern on. But I prayed with all my might and main for anything but this. It would have been very well had the hollow gone in a gentle declivity to the wash of the sea, to the water itself, in short; but it terminated at the edge of a cliff, not very high indeed, but high enough to warrant the prompt foundering of any vessel that should launch herself off it. Happily the keel was too solidly frozen into the ice to render a passage of this description possible; and the conclusion I arrived at after careful inspection was that the sole chance that could offer for the delivery of the vessel to her proper element was in the cracking up and disruption of the bed on which she lay.

Having ended my survey of the schooner, I addressed myself to the ascent of the starboard slope, and scaled it much more easily than I had yesterday managed to make my way over the rocks. I climbed to the highest block that was nearest me on the summit, and here I had a very large view of the scene. Much to my astonishment, the first objects which encountered my eye were four icebergs, floating detached but close together at a distance of about three miles on my side of the north-east trend of the island. I counted them and made them four. They swam low, and it was very easily seen they had formed part of the coast there, though, as the form of the ice that way was not familiar to me, and as, moreover, the glare rendered the prospect very deceptive, I could not distinguish where the ruptures were. But one change in the face of this white country I did note, and that was the entire disappearance of two of the most beautiful of the little crystal cities that adorned the northward range. The gale of the night had wrought havoc, and the unsubstantiality of this dazzling kingdom of ice was made startlingly apparent by the evanishment of the delicate glassy architecture, and by those four white hills floating like ships under their courses and topsails out upon the flashing hurry and leaping blue and yeast of the water.

It was blowing harder than I had imagined. The wind was extraordinarily sharp, and the full current of it not long to be endured on my unsheltered eminence. The sea, swelling up from the south, ran high, and was full of seething and tumbling noises, and of the roaring of the breakers, dashing themselves against the ice in prodigious bodies of foam, which so boiled along the foot of the cliffs that their fronts, rising out of it, might have passed for the spume itself freezing as it leapt into a solid mass of glorious brilliance. The eye never explored a scene more full of the splendour of light and of vivid colour. Here and there the rocks shone prismatically as though some flying rainbow had shivered itself upon them and lay broken. The blue of the sea and sky was deepened into an exquisite perfection of liquid tint by the blinding whiteness of the ice, which in exchange was sharpened into a wonderful effulgence by the hues above and around it. Again and again, along the whole range, far as the sight could explore, the spray rose in stately clouds of silver, which were scattered by the wind in meteoric scintillations of surpassing beauty, flashing through the fires of the sun like millions of little blazing stars. There were twenty different dyes of light in the collection of spires, fanes, and pillars near the schooner, whose masts, yards, and gear mingled their own particular radiance with that of these dainty figures; and wherever I bent my gaze I found so much of sun-tinctured loveliness, and the wild white graces of ice-forms and the dazzle of snow-surfaces softening into an azure gleaming in the far blue distances, that but for the piercing wind I could have spent the whole morning in taking into my mind the marvellous spirit of this ocean picture, forgetful of my melancholy condition in the intoxication of this draught of free and spacious beauty.

Satisfied as to the state of the ice and the posture of the schooner, viewed from without, I sent a slow and piercing gaze along the ocean line, and then returned to the ship. The strong wind, the dance of the sea, the grandeur of the great tract of whiteness, vitalized by the flying of violet cloud-shadows along it, had fortified my spirits, and being free (for a while) of all superstitious dread, I determined to begin by exploring the forecastle and ascertaining if more bodies were in the schooner than those two in the cabin and the giant form on deck. I threw some coal on the fire, and placed an ox-tongue along with the cheese and a lump of the frozen wine in a pannikin in the oven (for I had a mind to taste the vessel's stores, and thought the tongue would make an agreeable change), and then putting a candle into the lanthorn walked very bravely to the forecastle and entered it.

I was prepared for the scene of confusion, but I must say it staggered me afresh with something of the force of the first impression. Sailors' chests lay open in all directions, and their contents covered the decks. There was the clearest evidence here that the majority of the crew had quitted the vessel in a violent hurry, turning out their boxes to cram their money and jewellery into their pockets, and heedlessly flinging down their own and the clothes which had fallen to their share. This I had every right to suppose from the character of the muddle on the floor; for, passing the light over a part of it, I witnessed a great variety of attire of a kind which certainly no sailor in any age ever went to sea with; not so fine perhaps as that which lay in the cabins, but very good nevertheless, particularly the linen. I saw several wigs, beavers of the kind that was formerly carried under the arm, women's silk shoes, petticoats, pieces of lace, silk, and so forth; all directly assuring me that what I viewed was the contents of passengers' luggage, together with consignments and such freight as the pirates would seize and divide, every man filling his chest. Perhaps there was less on the whole than I supposed, the litter looking great by reason of everything having been torn open and flung down loose.

I trod upon these heaps with little concern; they appealed to me only as a provision for my fire should I be disappointed in my search for coal. The hammocks obliged me to move with a stooped head; it was only necessary to feel them with my hand—that is, to test their weight by pushing them in the middle—to know if they were tenanted. Some were heavier than the others, but all of them much lighter than they would have been had they contained human bodies; and by this rapid method I satisfied my mind that there were no dead men here as fully as if I had looked into each separate hammock.

This discovery was exceedingly comforting, for, though I do not know that I should have meddled with any frozen man had I found him in this place, his being in the forecastle would have rendered me constantly uneasy, and it must have come to my either closing this part of the ship and shrinking from it as from a spectre-ridden gloom, or to my disposing of the bodies by dragging them on deck—a dismal and hateful job. There were no ports, but a hatch overhead. Wanting light—the candle making the darkness but little more than visible—I fetched from the arms-room a handspike that lay in a corner, and, mounting a chest, struck at the hatch so heartily that the ice cracked all around it and the cover rose. I pushed it off, and down rolled the sunshine in splendour.

Everything was plain now. In many places, glittering among the clothes, were gold and silver coins, a few silver ornaments such as buckles, and watches—things not missed by the pirates in the transport of their flight. In kicking a coat aside I discovered a couple of silver crucifixes bound together, and close by were a silver goblet and the hilt of a sword broken short off for the sake of the metal it was of. Nothing ruder than this interior is imaginable. The men must have been mighty put to it for room. There was a window in the head, but the snow veiled it. Maybe the rogues messed together aft, and only used this forecastle to lie in. Right under the hatch, where the light was strongest, was a dead rat. I stooped to pick it up, meaning to fling it on to the deck, but its tail broke off at the rump, like a pipe-stem.

Close against the after bulkhead that separated the forecastle from the cook-room was a little hatch. There was a quantity of wearing-apparel upon it, and I should have missed it but for catching sight of some three inches of the dark line the cover made in the deck. On clearing away the clothes I perceived a ring similar to that in the lazarette hatch, and it rose to my first drag and left me the hold yawning black below. I peered down and observed a stout stanchion traversed by iron pins for the hands and feet. The atmosphere was nasty, and to give it time to clear I went to the cook-house and warmed myself before the fire.

The fresh air blowing down the forecastle hatch speedily sweetened the hold. I lowered the lanthorn and followed, and found myself on top of some rum or spirit casks, which on my hitting them returned to me a solid note. There was a forepeak forward in the bows, and the casks went stowed to the bulkhead of it; the top of this bulkhead was open four feet from the upper deck, and on holding the lanthorn over and putting my head through I saw a quantity of coals. If the forepeak went as low as the vessel's floor, then I calculated there would not be less than fifteen tons of coal in it. This was a noble discovery to fall upon, and it made me feel so happy that I do not know that the assurance of my being immediately rescued from this island could have given a lighter pulse to my heart.

The candle yielded a very small light, and it was difficult to see above a yard or so ahead or around. I turned my face aft, and crawled over the casks and came to under the main-hatch, where lay coils of hawser, buckets, blocks, and the like, but there was no pinnace, though here she had been stowed, as a sailor would have promptly seen. A little way beyond, under the great cabin, was the powder-magazine, a small bulkheaded compartment with a little door, atop of which was a small bull's-eye lamp. I peered warily enough, you will suppose, into this place, and made out twelve barrels of powder. I heartily wished them overboard; and yet, after all, they were not very much more dangerous than the wine and spirits in the lazarette and fore-hold.

The run remained to be explored—the after part, I mean, under the lazarette deck to the rudder-post—but I had seen enough; crawling about that black interior was cold, lonesome, melancholy work, and it was rendered peculiarly arduous by the obligation of caution imposed by my having to bear a light amid a freight mainly formed of explosives and combustible matter. I had found plenty of coal, and that sufficed. So I returned by the same road I had entered, and sliding to the bulkhead door to keep the cold of the forecastle out of the cook-room, I stirred the fire into a blaze and sat down before it to rest and think.

Chapter XIV.
An Extraordinary Occurrence

After the many great mercies which had been vouchsafed me, such as my being the only one saved of all the crew of the *Laughing Mary*, my deliverance from the dangers of an open boat, my meeting with this schooner and discovering within her everything needful for the support of life, I should have been guilty of the basest ingratitude had I repined because there was no boat in the ship. Yet for all that I could not but see it was a matter that concerned me very closely. Should the vessel be crushed, what was to become of me? It was easy to propose to myself the making of a raft or the like of such a fabric; but everything was so hard frozen that, being single-handed, it was next to impossible I should be able to put together such a contrivance as would be fit to live in the smallest sea-way.

However, I was resolved not to make myself melancholy with these considerations. The good fortune that had attended me so far might accompany me to the end, and maybe I was the fitter just then to take a hopeful view of my condition because of the cheerfulness awakened in me by the noble show of coal in the forepeak. At twelve o'clock by the watch in my pocket I got my dinner. I had a mind for a lighter drink than brandy, and went to the lazarette and cut out a block of the wine in the cask I had opened; I also knocked out the head of a tierce of beef, designing a hearty regale for supper. You smile, perhaps, that I should talk so much of my eating; but if on shore, amid the security of existence there, it is the one great business of life, that is to say, the one great business of life after love, what must it be to a poor shipwrecked wretch like me, who had nothing else to think of but his food?

Yet I could not help smiling when I considered how I was carrying my drink about in my fingers. What the wine was I do not know; it looked like claret but was somewhat sweet, and was the most generous wine I ever tasted, spite of my having to drink it warm, for if I let the cup out of my hand to cool, lo! when I looked it was ice!

Whilst I sat smoking my pipe it entered my head to presently turn those two silent gentlemen in the cabin out of it. It was a task from which I shrank, but it must be done. To be candid, I dreaded the effects of their dismal companionship on my spirits. I had been in the schooner two days only; I had been heartened by the plenty I had met with, a sound night's rest, the fire, and my escape from the fate that had certainly overtaken me had I gone away in the boat. But being of a superstitious nature and never a lover of solitude, I easily guessed that in a few days the weight of my loneliness would come to press very heavily upon me, and that if I suffered those figures to keep the cabin I should find myself lying under a kind of horror which might end in breaking down my manhood and perhaps in unsettling my reason.

But how was I to dispose of them? I meditated this matter whilst I smoked. First I thought I would drag them to the fissure or rent in the ice just beyond the stern of the schooner and tumble them into it. But even then they would still be with me, so to speak—I mean, they would be neighbours though out of sight; and my eagerness was to get them away from this island altogether, which was only to be done by casting them into the sea. Why, though I did not mention the matter in its place, I was as much haunted last night by the man on deck and the meditating figure on the rocks as by the fellows in the cabin; and, laugh as you may at my weakness, I do candidly own my feeling was, if I did not contrive that the sea should carry those bodies away, I should come before long to think of them as alive, no matter in what part of the island I might bear them to, and at night-time start at every sound, hear their voices in the wind, see their shapes in the darkness, and even by day dread to step upon the cliffs.

That such fancies should possess me already shows how necessary it was I should lose no time to provide against their growth; so I settled my scheme thus: first I was to haul the figures as best I could on to the deck; then, there being three, to get them over the side, and afterwards by degrees to transport the four of them to some steep whence they would slide of themselves into the ocean. Yet so much did I dread the undertaking, and abhor the thought of the tedious time I foresaw it would occupy me, that I cannot imagine any other sort of painful and distressing work that would not have seemed actually agreeable as compared with this.

My pipe being smoked out, I stepped into the cabin, and ascending the ladder threw off the companion-cover and opened the doors, and then went to the man that had his back to the steps, but my courage failed me; he was so lifelike, there was so wild and fierce an earnestness in the expression of his face, so inimitable a picture of horror in his starting posture, that my hands fell to my side and I could not lay hold of him. I will not stop to analyse my fear or ask why, since I knew that this man was dead, he should have terrified me as surely no living man could; I can only repeat that the prospect of touching him, and laying him upon the deck and then dragging him up the ladder, was indescribably fearful to me, and I turned away, shaking as if I had the ague.

But it had to be done, nevertheless; and after a great deal of reasoning and self-reproach I seized him on a sudden, and, kicking away the bench, let him fall to the deck. He was frozen as hard as stone and fell like stone, and I looked to see him break, as a statue might that falls lumpishly. His arms remaining raised put him into an attitude of entreaty to me to leave him in peace; but I had somewhat mastered myself, and the hurry and tumult of my spirits were a kind of hot temper; so catching him by the collar, I dragged him to the foot of the companion-steps, and then with infinite labour and a number of sickening pauses hauled him up the ladder to the deck.

I let him lie and returned, weary and out of breath. He had been a very fine man in life, of beauty too, as was to be seen in the shape of his features and the particular elegance of his chin, despite the distortion of his last unspeakable dismay; and with his clothes I guessed his weight came hard upon two hundred pounds, no mean burden to haul up a ladder.

I went to the cook-house for a dram and to rest myself, and then came back to the cabin and looked at the other man. His posture has been already described. He made a very burly figure in his coat, and if his weight did not exceed the other's it was not likely to be less. Nothing of his head was visible but the baldness on the top and the growth of hair that ringed it, and the fluffing up of his beard about his arms in which his face was sunk. I touched his beard with a shuddering finger, and noted that the frost had made every hair of it as stiff as wire. It would not do to stand idly contemplating him, for already there was slowly creeping into me a dread of seeing his face; so I took hold of him and swayed him from the table, and he fell upon the deck sideways, preserving his posture, so that his face remained hidden. I dragged him a little way, but he was so heavy and his attitude rendered him as a burthen so surprisingly cumbrous that I was sure I could never of my own strength haul him up the ladder. Yet neither was it tolerable that he should be there. I thought of contriving a tackle called a whip, and making one end fast to him and taking the other end to the little capstan on the main deck; but on inspecting the capstan I found that the frost had rendered it immovable, added to which there was nothing whatever to be done with the iron-hard gear, and therefore I had to give that plan up.

Then, thought I, if I was to put him before the fire, he might presently thaw into some sort of suppleness, and so prove not harder than the other to get on deck. I liked the idea, and without more ado dragged him laboriously into the cook-room and laid him close to the furnace, throwing in a little pile of coal to make the fire roar.

I then went on deck, and easily enough, the deck being slippery, got my first man to where the huge fellow was that had sentinelled the vessel when I first looked down upon her; but when I viewed the slopes, broken into rocks, which I, though unburdened, had found hard enough to ascend, I was perfectly certain I should never be able to transport the bodies to the top of the cliffs, I must either let them fall into the great split astern of the ship, or lower them over the side and leave the hollow in which the schooner lay to be their tomb.

I paced about, not greatly noticing the cold in the little valley, and relishing the brisk exercise, scheming to convey the bodies to the sea, for I was passionately in earnest in wishing the four of them away; but to no purpose. I had but my arms, and scheme as I would, I could not make them stronger than they were. It was still blowing a fresh bright gale from the south; the sea, as might be known by the noise of it, beat very heavily against the cliffs of ice; and the extremity of the hollow, where it opened to the ocean but without showing it, was again and again veiled by a vast cloud of spray, the rain of which I could hear ringing like volleys of shot as the wind smote it and drove it with incredible force against the rocks past the brow of the north slope. I thought to myself there should be power in this wind to quicken the sliding of even so mighty a berg as this island northwards. Every day should steal it by something, however inconsiderable, nearer to warmer regions, and no gale, nay, no gentle swell even, but must help to crack and loosen it into pieces. "Oh," cried I, "for the power to rupture this bed, that the schooner might slip into the sea! Think of her running north before such a gale as this, steadily bearing me towards a more temperate clime, and into the road of ships!" I clenched my hands with a wild yearning in my heart. Should I ever behold my country again? should I ever meet a living man? The white and frozen steeps glared a bald reply; and I heard nothing but menace in the shrill noises of the wind and the deep and thunderous roaring of the ocean.

It was mighty comforting, however, on returning to the cabin to find it vacant, to be freed from the scare of the sight of the two silent figures. I drew my breath more easily and stopped to glance around. It was the barest cabin I was ever in—uncarpeted, with no other seats than the little benches. I looked at the crucifix, and guessed from the sight of it that, whatever might be the vessel's nation, she had not been sailed by Englishmen. I peeped into poor Polly's cage—if a parrot it was—and the sight of the rich plumage carried my imagination to skies of brass, to the mysterious green solitude of tropic forests, to islands fringed with silver surf, in whose sunny flashing sported nude girls of faultless forms, showing their teeth of pearl in merry laughter, winding amorously with the blue billow, and filling the aromatic breeze with the melody of their language of the sun. Ha! thought I, sailors see some changes in their time; and with a hearty sigh I stepped into the cook-room.

I started, stopped, and fell back a pace with a cry. When I had put the figure before the fire he was in the same posture in which he had sat at the table, that is, leaning forward with his face hid in his arms; I had laid him on his side, with his face to the furnace, and in that attitude you would have supposed him a man sound asleep with his arms over his face to shield it from the heat. But now, to my unspeakable astonishment, he lay on his back, with his arms sunk to his side and resting on the deck, and his face upturned.

I stared at him from the door as if he was the Fiend himself. I could scarce credit my senses, and my consternation was so great that I cannot conceive of any man ever having laboured under a greater fright. I faintly ejaculated 'Good God!' several times, and could hardly prevent my legs from running away with me. You see, it was certain he must have moved of his own accord to get upon his back. I was prepared for the fire to thaw him into limberness, and had I found him straightened somewhat I should not have been surprised. But there was no power in fire to stretch him to his full length and turn him over on his back. What living or ghostly hand had done this thing? Did spirits walk this schooner after all? Had I missed of something more terrible than any number of dead men in searching the vessel?

I had made a great fire and its light was strong, and there was also the light of the lanthorn; but the furnace flames played very lively, completely overmastering the steady illumination of the candle, and the man's figure was all a-twitch with moving shadows, and a hundred fantastic shades seemed to steal out of the side and bulkheads and disappear upon my terrified gaze. Then, thought I, suppose after all that the man should be alive, the vitality in him set flowing by the heat? I minded myself of my own simile of the current checked by frost, yet retaining unimpaired the principle of motion; and getting my agitation under some small control, I approached the body on tiptoe and held the lanthorn to its face.

He looked a man of sixty years of age; his beard was grey and very long, and lay upon his breast like a cloud of smoke. His eyes were closed; the brows shaggy, and the dark scar of a sword-wound ran across his forehead from the corner of the left eye to the top of the right brow. His nose was long and hooked, but the repose in his countenance, backed by the vague character of the light in which I inspected him, left his face almost expressionless. I was too much alarmed to put my ear to his mouth to mark if he breathed, if indeed the noise of the burning fire would have permitted me to distinguish his respiration. I drew back from him, and put down the lanthorn and watched him. Thought I, it will not do to believe there is anything supernatural here. I can swear there is naught living in this ship, and am I to suppose, assuming she is haunted, that a ghost, which I have always read and heard of as an essence, has in its shadowy being such quality of *muscle* as would enable it to turn that heavy man over from his side on to his back? No, no, thought I! depend upon it, either he is alive and may presently come to himself, or else in some wonderful way the fire in thawing him has so wrought in his frozen fibres as to cause him to turn.

Presently his left leg, that was slightly bent towards the furnace, stretched itself out to its full length, and my ear caught a faint sound, as of a weak and melancholy sigh. Gracious heaven, thought I, he *is* alive! and with less of terror than of profound awe, now that I saw there was nothing of a ghostly or preternatural character in this business, I approached and bent over him. His eyes were still shut, and I could not hear that he breathed; there was not the faintest motion of respiration in his breast nor stir in the hair, that was now soft, about his mouth. Yet, so far as the light would suffer me to judge, there was a complexion in his face such as could only come with flowing blood, however languid its circulation, and putting this and the sigh and the movement of the leg together, I felt convinced that the man was alive, and forthwith fell to work, very full of awe and amazement to be sure, to help nature that was struggling in him.

My first step was to heat some brandy, and whilst this was doing I pulled open his coat and freed his neck, fetching a coat from the cabin to serve as a pillow for his head. I next removed his boots and laid bare his feet (which were encased in no less than four pairs of thick woollen stockings, so that I thought when I came to the third pair I should find his legs made of stockings), and after bathing his feet in hot water, of which there was a kettleful, I rubbed them with hot brandy as hard as I could chafe. I then dealt with his hands in the like manner, having once been shipmate with a seaman who told me he had seen a sailor brought to by severe rubbing of his extremities after he had been carried below supposed to be frozen to death, and continued this exercise till I could rub no longer. Next I opened his lips and, finding he wanted some of his front teeth, I very easily poured a dram of brandy into his mouth. Though I preserved my astonishment all this while, I soon discovered myself working with enthusiasm, with a most passionate longing indeed to recover the man, not only because it pleased me to think of my being an instrument under God of calling a human being, so to speak, out of his grave, but because I yearned for a companion, some one to address, to lighten the hideous solitude of my condition and to assist me in planning our deliverance.

I built up a great fire, and with much trouble, for he was very heavy, disposed him in such a manner before it that the heat was reflected all over the front of him from his head to his feet. I likewise continued to chafe his extremities, remitting this work only to rest, and finding that the brandy had stolen down his throat, I poured another dram in and then another, till I think he had swallowed a pint. This went on for an hour, during which time he never exhibited the least signs of life; but on a sudden he sighed deep, a tremor ran through him, he sighed again and partly raised his right hand, which fell to the deck with a blow; his lips twitched, and a small convulsion of his face compelled the features into the similitude of a grin that instantly faded; then he fetched a succession of sighs and opened his eyes full upon me.

I was warm enough with my work, but when I observed him looking at me I turned of a death-like cold, and felt the dew of an intolerable emotion wet in the palms of my hands. There was no speculation in his stare at first; his eyes lay as coldly upon me as those of a fish; but as life quickened in him so his understanding awoke; he slightly knitted his brows, and very slowly rolled his gaze off me to the furnace and so over as much of the cook-room as was before him. He then started as if to sit up, but fell back with a slight groan and looked at me again.

"What is this?" said he in French, in a very hollow feeble voice.

I knew enough of his language to enable me to know he spoke in French, but that was all. I could not speak a syllable of that tongue.

"You'll be feeling better presently; you must not expect your strength to come in a minute," said I, taking my chance of his understanding me, and speaking that he might not think me a ghost, for I doubt not I was as white as one; since, to be plain, the mere talking to a figure that I had got to consider as sheerly dead as anybody in a graveyard was alarming enough, and then again there was the sound of my own voice, which I had not exerted in speech for ages, as it seemed to me.

He faintly nodded his head, by which I perceived he understood me, and said very faintly in English, but with a true French accent, "This is a hard bed, sir."

"I'll speedily mend that," said I, and at once fetched a mattress from the cabin next mine; this I placed beside him, and dragged him on to it, he very weakly assisting. I then brought clothes and rugs to cover him with, and made him a high pillow, and as he lay close to the furnace he could not have been snugger had he had a wife to tuck him up in his own bed.

I was very much excited; my former terrors had vanished, but my awe continued great, for I felt as if I had wrought a miracle, and I trembled as a man would who surveys some prodigy of his own creation. It was yet to be learnt how long he had been in this condition; but I was perfectly sure he had formed one of the schooner's people, and as I had guessed her to have been here for upwards of fifty years, the notion of that man having lain torpid for half a century held me under a perpetual spell of astonishment; but there was no more horror in me nor fright. He followed me about with his eyes but did not offer to speak; perhaps he could not. I put a lump of ice into the kettle, and when the water boiled made him a pint of steaming brandy punch, which I held to his lips in a pannikin whilst I supported his back with my knee; he supped it slowly and painfully but with unmistakable relish, and fetched a sigh of contentment as he lay back. But he would need something more sustaining than brandy and water; and as I guessed his stomach, after so prodigious a fast, would be too weak to support such solids as beef or pork or bacon, I mused a little, turning over in my mind the contents of the larder (as I call it), all which time he eyed me with bewilderment growing in his face; and I then thought I could not do better than manufacture him a broth of oatmeal, wine, bruised biscuit, and a piece of tongue minced very small.

This did not take me long in doing, the tongue being near the furnace and soft enough for the knife, and there was nothing to melt but the wine. When the broth was ready I kneeled as before and fed him. He ate greedily, and when the broth was gone looked as if he would have been glad for more.

"Now, sir," says I, "sleep if you can;" with which he turned his head and in a few minutes was sound asleep, breathing regularly and deeply.

Chapter XV.
The Pirate's Story

I<small>T</small> was now time to think of myself. The watch showed the hour to be after six. Whilst my supper was preparing I went on deck to close the hatches to keep the cold out of the ship, and found the weather changed, the wind having shifted directly into the west, whence it was blowing with a good deal of violence upon the ice, ringing over the peaks and among the rocks with a singular clanking noise in its crying, as though it brought with it the echo of thousands of bells pealing in some great city behind the sea. It also swept up the gorge that went from our hollow to the edge of the cliff in a noisy fierce hooting, and this blast was very freely charged with the spray of the breakers which boiled along the island. The sky was overcast with flying clouds of the true Cape Horn colour and appearance.

I closed the fore-scuttle, but on stepping aft came to the two bodies, the sight of which brought me to a stand. Since there was life in one, thought I, life may be in these, and I felt as if it would be like murdering them to leave them here for the night. But, said I to myself, after all, these men are certainly insensible if they be not dead; the cold that freezes on deck cannot be different from the cold that froze them below; they'll not be better off in the cabin than here. It will be all the same to them, and to-morrow I shall perhaps have the Frenchman's help to carry them to the furnace and discover if the vital spark is still in them.

To be candid, I was the more easily persuaded to leave them to their deck lodging by the very grim, malignant, and savage appearance of the great figure that had leaned against the rail. Indeed, I did not at all like the notion of such company in the cabin through the long night. Added to this, his bulk was such that, without assistance, I could only have moved him as you move a cask, by rolling it; and though this might have answered to convey him to the hatch, I stood to break his arms and legs off, and perhaps his head, so brittle was he with frost, by letting his own weight trundle him down the ladder.

So I left them to lie and came away, flinging a last look round, and then closing the companion-door upon me. The Frenchman, as I may call him, was sleeping very heavily and snoring loudly.

I got my supper, and whilst I ate surveyed the mound of clothes he made on the deck—a motley heap indeed, with the colours and the finery of the lace and buttons of the coats I had piled upon him—and fell into some startling considerations of him. Was it possible, I asked myself, that he could have lain in his frozen stupor for fifty years? But why not? for suppose he had been on this ice but a year only, nay, six months—an absurdity in the face of the manifest age of the ship and her furniture— would not six months of lifelessness followed by a resurrection be as marvellous as fifty years? Had he the same aspect when the swoon of the ice seized him as he has now? I answered yes, for the current of life having been frozen, his appearance would remain as it was.

I lighted my pipe and sat smoking, thinking he would presently awake; but his slumber was as deep as the stillness I had thawed him out of had been, and he lay so motionless that, but for his snoring and harsh breathing, I should have believed him lapsed into his former state.

At eight o'clock the fire was very low. Nature was working out her own way with this Frenchman, and I determined to let him sleep where he was, and take my chance of the night. At all events he could not alarm me by stirring, for if I heard a movement I should know what it was. So, loitering to see the last gleam of the fire extinguished, I took my lanthorn and went to bed, but not to sleep.

The full meaning of the man awakening into life out of a condition into which he had been plunged, for all I knew, before I was born, came upon me very violently in the darkness. There being nothing to divert my thoughts, I gave my mind wholly to it, and I tell you I found it an amazing terrifying thing to happen. Indeed, I do not know that the like of such an adventure was ever before heard of, and I well recollect thinking to myself, "I would give my left hand to know of other cases of the kind—to be assured that this recovery was strictly within the bounds of nature," that I might feel I was not alone, so strongly did the thoughts of a satanic influence operating in this business crowd upon me—that is to say, as if I was involuntarily working out some plan of the devil.

The gale made a great roaring. The ship's stern lay open to the gorge, and but for her steadiness I might have supposed myself at sea. There was indeed an incessant thunder about my ears often accompanied by the shock of a mass of spray flung thirty feet high, and falling like sacks of stones upon the deck. Once I felt the vessel rock; I cannot tell the hour, but it was long past midnight, and by the noise of the wind I guessed it was blowing a whole gale. The movement was extraordinary—whether sideways or downwards I could not distinguish; but, seasoned as my stomach was to the motion of ships, this movement set up a nausea that lasted some while, acting upon me as I have since learned the convulsion of an earthquake does upon people. It took off my mind from the Frenchman, and filled me with a different sort of alarm altogether, for it was very evident the gale was making the ice break; and, thought I to myself, if we do not mind our eye we shall be crushed and buried. But what was to be done? To quit the ship for that piercing flying gale, charged with sleet and hail and foam, was merely to languish for a little and then miserably expire of frost. No, thought I, if the end is to come let it find me here; and with that I snugged me down amid the coats and cloaks in my cot, and, obstinately holding my eyes closed, ultimately fell asleep.

It was late when I awoke. I lighted the lanthorn, but upon entering the passage that led to the cabin I observed by my own posture that the schooner had not only heeled more to larboard, but was further "down by the stern" to the extent of several feet. Indeed, the angle of inclination was now considerable enough to bring my shoulder (in the passage) close against the starboard side when I stood erect. The noise of the gale was still in the air, and the booming and boiling of the sea was uncommonly loud. I walked straight to the cook-room, and, putting the lanthorn to the Frenchman, perceived that he was still in a heavy sleep, and that he had lain through the night precisely in the attitude in which I had left him. His face was so muffled that little more than his long hawk's-bill nose was discernible. It was freezingly cold, and I made haste to light the fire. There was still coal enough in the corner to last for the day, and before long the furnace was blazing cheerfully. I went to work to make some broth and fry some ham, and melt a little block of the ruby-coloured wine; and whilst thus occupied, turning my head a moment to look at the Frenchman, I found him half started up, staring intently at me.

This sudden confrontment threw me into such confusion that I could not speak. He moved his head from side to side, taking a view of the scene, with an expression of the most inimitable astonishment painted upon his countenance. He then brought the flat of his hand with a dramatic blow to his forehead, the scar on which showed black as ink to the fire-glow, and sat erect.

"Where have I been?" he exclaimed in French.

"Sir," said I, speaking with the utmost difficulty, "I do not understand your language. I am English. You speak my tongue. Will you address me in it?"

"English!" he exclaimed in English, dropping his head on one side, and peering at me with an incredible air of amazement. "How came you here? You are not of our company? Let me see..." Here he struggled with recollection, continuing to stare at me from under his shaggy eyebrows as if I was some frightful vision.

"I am a shipwrecked British mariner," said I, "and have been cast away upon this ice, where I found your schooner."

"Ha!" he interrupted with prodigious vehemence, "certainly; we are frozen up—I remember. That sleep should serve my memory so!" He made as if to rise, but sat again. "The cold is numbing; it would weaken a lion. Give me a hot drink, sir."

I filled a pannikin with the melted wine, which he swallowed thirstily. "More!" cried he. "I seem to want life."

Again I filled the pannikin.

"Good!" said he, fetching a sigh as he returned the vessel; "you are very obliging, sir. If you have food there, we will eat together."

I give the substance of his speech, but not his delivery of it, nor is it necessary that I should interpolate my rendering with the French words he used.

The broth being boiled, I gave him a good bowl of it along with a plate of bacon and tongue, some biscuit and a pannikin of hot brandy and water, all which things I put upon his knees as he sat up on the mattress, and to it he fell, making a rare meal. Yet all the while he ate he acted like a man bewitched, as well he might, staring at me and looking round and round him, and then dropping his knife to strike his brow, as if by that kind of blow he would quicken the activity of memory there.

"There is something wrong," said he presently. "What is it, sir? This is the cook-room. How does it happen that I am lying here?"

I told him exactly how it was, adding that if it had not been for his posture, which obliged me to thaw in order to carry him, he would now be on deck with the others, awaiting the best funeral I could give him.

"Who are the others?" asked he.

"I know not," said I. "There were four in all, counting yourself; one sits frozen to death on the rocks. I met him first, and took this watch from his pocket that I might tell the time."

He took the watch in his hands, and asked me to bring the lanthorn close.

"Ha!" cried he, "this was Mendoza's—the captain's. I remember; he took it for the sake of this letter upon it. He lies dead on the rocks? We missed him, but did not know where he had gone."

Then, raising his hand and impulsively starting upon the mattress, he cried, whilst he tapped his forehead, "It has come back! I have it! Guiseppe Trentanove and I were in the cabin; he had fallen blind with the glare of the ice—if that was it. We confronted each other. On a sudden he screamed out. I had put my face into my arms, and felt myself dying. His cry aroused me. I looked up, and saw him leaning back from the table with his eyes fixed and horror in his countenance. I was too feeble to speak— too languid to rise. I watched him awhile, and then the drowsiness stole over me again, and my head sank, and I remember no more."

He shuddered, and extended the pannikin for more liquor. I filled it with two-thirds of brandy and the rest water, and he supped it down as if it had been a thimbleful of wine.

"By the holy cross," cried he, "but this is very wonderful, though. How long have you been here, sir?"

"Three days."

"Three days! and I have been in a stupor all that time—never moving, never breathing?"

"You will have been in a stupor longer than that, I expect," said I.

"What is this month?" he cried.

"July," I replied.

"July—July!" he muttered. "Impossible! Let me see"—he began to count on his fingers—"we fell in with the ice and got locked in November. We had six months of it, I recollect no more. Six months of it, sir; and suppose the stupor came upon me then, the month at which my memory stops would be April. Yet you call this July; that is to say, *four months of oblivion*; impossible!"

"What was the year in which you fell in with the ice?" said I.

"The year?" he exclaimed in a voice deep with the wonder this question raised in him; "the year? Why, man, what year but *seventeen hundred and fifty-three*!"

"Good God!" cried I, jumping to my feet with terror at a statement I had anticipated, though it shocked me as a new and frightful revelation.

"Do you know what year this is?"

He looked at me without answering.

"It is eighteen hundred and one," I cried, and as I said this I recoiled a step, fully expecting him to leap up and exhibit a hundred demonstrations of horror and consternation; for this I am persuaded would have been my posture had any man roused me from a slumber and told me I had been in that condition for eight-and-forty years.

He continued to view me with a very strange and cunning expression in his eyes, the coolness of which was inexpressibly surprising and bewildering and even mortifying; then presently grasping his beard, looked at it; then put his hands to his face and looked at them; then drew out his feet and looked at *them*; then very slowly, but without visible effort, stood up, swaying a little with an air of weakness, and proceeded to feel and strike himself all over, swinging his arms and using his legs; after which he sat down and pulled the clothes over his naked feet, and fixing his eyes on me afresh, said, "What do you say this year is, sir?"

"Eighteen hundred and one," I replied.

"Bah!" said he, and shook his head very knowingly. "No matter; you have been shipwrecked too! Sir, shipwreck shuffles dates as a player does cards, and the best of us will go wrong in famine, loneliness, cold, and peril. Be of good cheer, my friend; all will return to you. Sit, sir, that I may hear your adventures, and I will relate mine."

I saw how it was—he supposed me deranged, a mortifying construction to place upon the language of a man who had restored him to life; yet a few moments' reflection taught me to see the reasonableness of it, for unless he thought me crazy he must conclude I spoke the truth, and it was inconceivable he should believe that he had lain in a frozen condition for eight-and-forty years.

I stirred the fire to make more light and sat down near the furnace. His appearance was very striking. The scar upon his forehead gave a very dark sullen look to his brows; his eyes were small and were half lost in the dusky hollows in which they were set, and I observed an indescribably leering, cunning expression in them, something of which I attributed to the large quantity of liquor he had swallowed. This contrasted oddly with the respectable aspect he took from his baldness—that is, from the nakedness of his poll, for, as I have before said, his hair fell long and plentifully, in a ring a little above the ears, so that you would have supposed at some late period of his life he had been scalped.

I know not how it was, but I felt no joy in this man's company. For some companion, for some one to speak with, I had yearned again and again with heart-breaking passion; and now a living man sat before me, yet I was sensible of no gladness. In truth, I was overawed by him; he frightened me as one risen from the dead. Here was a creature that had entered, as it seemed to me, those black portals from which no man ever returns, and had come back, through my instrumentality, after hard upon fifty years of the grave. Reason as I might that it was all perfectly in nature, that there was nothing necromantic or diabolic in it, that it could not have happened had it not been natural, my spirits were as much oppressed and confounded by his sitting there alive, talking, and watching me, as if, being truly dead, life had entered him on a sudden, and he had risen and walked.

I have no doubt the disorder my mind was in helped to persuade him that I had not the full possession of my senses. He ran his eye over my figure and then round the cook-room, and said, "I am impatient to learn your story, sir."

"Why, sir," said I, "my story is summed up in what I have already told you." But that he might not be at a loss—for to be sure he had only very newly collected his intellects—I related my adventures at large. He drew nearer to the furnace whilst I talked, bringing his covering of clothes along with him, and held out his great hands to toast at the fire, all the time observing me with scarce a wink of the eye. Arrived at the end of my tale, I told him how only last night I had dragged his companion on deck, and how he was to have followed but for his posture.

"Ha!" cried he, "you might have caused my flesh to mortify by laying me close to the fire. It would have been better to rub me with snow."

He poked up one foot after the other to count his toes, fearing some had come away with his stockings, and then said, "Well, and how long should I have slept had you not come? Another week! By St. Paul, I might have died. Have you my stockings, sir?"

I gave them to him, and he pulled them over his legs and then drew on his boots and stood up, the coats and wraps tumbling off him as he rose.

"I can stand," says he. "That is good."

But in attempting to take a step he reeled and would have fallen had I not grasped his arm.

"Patience, my friend, patience!" he muttered as if to himself. "I must lie a little longer," and with that he kneeled and then lay along the mattress. He breathed heavily and pointed to the pannikin. I asked him whether he would have wine or brandy; he answered, "Wine," so I melted a draught, which dose, I thought, on top of what he had already taken, would send him to sleep; but instead it quickened his spirits, and with no lack of life in his voice he said, "What is the condition of the vessel?"

I told him that she was still high and dry, adding that during the night some sort of change had happened which I should presently go on deck to remark.

"Think you," says he, "that there is any chance of her ever being liberated?"

I answered, "Yes, but not yet; that is, if the ice in breaking doesn't destroy her. The summer season has yet to come, and we are progressing north; but now that you are with me it will be a question for us to settle, whether we are to wait for the ice to release the schooner or endeavour to effect our escape by other means."

A curious gleam of cunning satisfaction shone in his eyes as he looked at me; he then kept silence for some moments, lost in thought.

"Pray," said I, breaking in upon him, "what ship is this?"

He started, deliberated an instant, and answered, "The *Boca del Dragon*."[2]

"A Spaniard?"

He nodded.

"She was a pirate?" said I.

"How do you know that?" he cried with a sudden fierceness.

"Sir," said I, "I am a British sailor who has used the sea for some years, and know the difference between a handspike and a poop-lanthorn. But what matters? She is a pirate no longer."

He let his eyes fall from my face and gazed round him with the air of one who cannot yet persuade his understanding of the realities of the scene he moves in.

[2] So in Mr. Rodney's manuscript.

"Tut!" cried he presently, addressing himself, "what matters the truth, as you say? Yes, the *Boca del Dragon* is a pirate. You have of course rummaged her, and guessed her character by what you found?"

"I met with enough to excite my suspicion," said I. "The ship's company of such a craft as this do not usually go clothed in lace and rich cloaks, and carry watches of this kind," tapping my breast, "in their fobs and handfuls of gold in their pockets."

"Unless——" said he.

"Unless," I answered, "their flag is as black as our prospects."

"You think them black?" cried he, the look of resentment that was darkening his face dying out of it. "The vessel is sound, is not she?"

I replied that she appeared so, but it would be impossible to be sure until she floated.

"The stores?"

"They are plentiful."

"They should be!" he cried; "we have the liquor and stores of a galleon and two carracks in our hold, apart from what we originally laid in for the cruise. Everything will have been kept sweet by the cold."

"All the stores seem sound," said I; "we shall not starve—no, not if we were to be imprisoned here for three years. But all the same our prospects are black, for here is the ship high and fixed; the ice in parting may crush her, and we have no boat."

"May, may!" he cried with a Frenchman's vehemence. "You have *may* and you also have *may not* in your language. Let me feel my strength improving; we shall then find means of throwing a light upon these black prospects of yours."

He smiled, or rather grinned, his fangs making the latter term fitter for the mirthless grimace he made.

"May I ask your name?" said I.

"Jules Tassard, at your service," said he, "third in command of the *Boca del Dragon*, but good as Mate Trentanove, and good as Captain Mendoza, and good as the cabin boy Fernando Prado; for we pirates are republicans, sir, we know no social distinctions save those we order for the convenience of working ship. Now let me tell you the story of our disaster. We had come out of the Spanish Main into the South Seas, partly to escape some British and French cruisers which were after us and others of our kind, and partly because ill-luck was against us, and we could not find our account in those waters. We sailed in December two years ago——"

"Making the year——?" I interrupted.

He started, and then grinned again.

"Ah, to be sure!" cried he, "this is eighteen hundred and one; but to keep my tale in countenance," he went on in a satirical apologetic way, "let me call the year in which we sailed for the South Sea seventeen hundred and fifty-one. What matters forty or fifty years to the shipwrecked? Is not one day of an open boat, with no society but the devils of memory and no hope but the silence at the bottom of the sea, an eternity? Fill me that pannikin, my friend. I thank you. To proceed: we cruised some months in the South Sea and took a number of ships. One was a privateer that had plundered a British Indiaman in the Southern Ocean, and had entered the South Sea by New Holland. This fellow was full of fine clothes and had some silver in her. We took what we wanted, and let her go with her people under hatches, her yards square, her helm amidships, and her cabin on fire. Our maxim is, 'No witnesses!' That is the pirate's philosophy. Who gives us quarter unless it be to hang us? But to continue: we did handsomely, but were a long time about it, and after careening and filling up with water 'twixt San Carlos and Chiloe we set sail for the Antilles. Like your brig, we were blown south. The weather was ferocious. Gale after gale thundered down upon us, forcing us to fly before it. We lost all reckoning of our position; for days, for weeks, sea and sky were enveloped in clouds of snow, in the heart of which drove our frozen schooner. We were none of us of a nationality fit to encounter these regions; we carried most of us the curly hair of the sun, the chocolate cheek of the burning zone, and the ice chained the crew, crouching like Lascars, below. We swept past many vast icebergs, which would leap on a sudden out of the white whirl of thickness, often so close aboard that the recoil of the surge striking against the mass would flood our decks. At all moments of the day and night we were prepared to feel the shock of the vessel crushing her bows against one of these stupendous hills. The cabin resounded with Salves and Aves, with invocations to the saints, promises, curses, and litanies. The cold does not make men of the Spaniards, who are but indifferent seamen in temperate climes, and we were chiefly Spanish with consciences as red as your English flag."

He grinned, emptied the pannikin, and stretched his hands to the fire to warm them.

"One morning, the weather having cleared somewhat, we found ourselves surrounded by ice. A great chain floated ahead of us, extending far into the south. The gale blew dead on to this coast; we durst not haul the schooner to the wind, and our only chance lay in discovering some bay where we might find shelter. Such a bay it was my good luck to spy, lying directly in a line with the ship's head. It was formed of a great steep of ice jutting a long way slantingly into the sea, the width between the point and the main being about a third of a mile. I seized the helm, and shouted to the men to hoist the head of the mainsail that she might round to when I put the helm down. But the fellows were in a panic terror and stood gaping at what they regarded as their doom, calling upon the

Virgin and all the saints for help and mercy. Into this bay did we rush on top of a huge sea, Trentanove and the captain and I swinging with set teeth at the tiller, that was hard a-lee; she came round, but with such way upon her that she took a long shelving beach of ice and ran up it to the distance of half her own length, and there she lay, with her rudder within touch of the wash of the water. The men, regarding the schooner as lost, and concluding that if she went to pieces her boats would be destroyed, and with them their only chance to escape from the ice, fell frantic and lost their wits altogether. They roared, 'To the boats! to the boats!' The captain endeavoured to bring them to their senses; he and I and the mate, and Joam Barros, the boatswain—a Portuguese—went among them pistols in hand, entreating, cursing, threatening. 'Think of the plunder in this hold! Will you abandon it without an effort to save it? What think you are your chances for life in open boats in this sea? The schooner lies protected here; the weather will moderate presently, and we may then be able to slide her off.' But reason as we would the cowardly dogs refused to listen. They had broached a spirit-cask aft, and passed the liquor along the decks whilst they hoisted the pinnace out of the hold and got the other boats over. The drink maddened, yet left them wild with fear too. They would not wait to come at the treasure in the run—the fools believed the ship would tumble to pieces as she stood—but entered the forecastle and the officers' cabins, and routed about for whatever money and trinkets they might stuff into their pockets without loss of time; and then provisioning the boats, they called to us to join them, but we said, No, on which they ran the boats down to the water, tumbled into them, and pulled away round the point of ice. We lost sight of them then, and I have little doubt that they all perished shortly afterwards."

He ceased. I was anxious to hear more.

"You had been six months on the ice when the stupor fell upon you?"

"Ay, about six months. The ice gathered about us and built us in. I recollect it was three days after we stranded that, going on deck, I saw the bay (as I term it) filled with ice. We drew up several plans to escape, but none satisfied us. Besides, sir, we had a treasure on board which we had risked our necks to get, and we were prepared to go on imperilling our lives to save it. 'Twas natural. We had a great store of coal forwards and amidships, for we had faced the Horn in coming and knew what we had to expect in returning. We were also richly stocked with provisions and drink of all sorts. There were but four of us, and we dealt with what we had as if we designed it should last us fifty years. But the cold was frightful; it was not in flesh and blood to stand it. One day—we had been locked up about five months—Mendoza said he would get upon the rocks and take a view of the sea. He did not return. The others were too weak to seek him, and they were half blind besides; I went, but the ice was full of caves and hollows, and the like, and I could not find him, nor could I look for him long, the cold being the hand of death itself up there. The time went by; Trentanove went stone-blind, and I had to put food and drink into his hands that he might live. A week before the stupor came upon me I went on deck and saw Joam Barros leaning at the rail. I called to him, but he made no reply. I approached and looked at him, and found him frozen. Then happened what I have told you. We were in the cabin, the mate seated at the table, waiting for me to lead and support him to the cook-room, for he was so weak he could scarce carry his weight. A sudden faintness seized me, and I sank down upon the bench opposite him, letting my head fall upon my arms. His cry startled me—I looked up—saw him as I have said; but the cabin then turned black, my head sank again, and I remember no more."

He paused and then cried in French, "That is all! They are dead—Jules Tassard lives! The devil is loyal to his own!" and with that he lay back and burst into laughter.

"And this," said I, "was in seventeen hundred and fifty-three?"

"Yes," he answered; "and this is eighteen hundred and one—eight-and-forty years afterwards, hey?" and he laughed out again. "I've talked so much," said he, "that, d'ye know, I think another nap will do me good. What coals have you found in the ship?"

I told him.

"Good," he cried; "we can keep ourselves warm for some time to come, anyhow."

And so saying, he pulled a rug up to his nose and shut his eyes.

Chapter XVI.
I Hear of a Great Treasure

I LIGHTED a pipe and sat pondering his story a little while. There was no doubt he had given me the exact truth so far as his relation of it went. As it was certain then that the *Boca del Dragon* (as she was called) had been fixed in the ice for hard upon fifty years, the conclusion I formed was that she had been blown by some hundreds of leagues further south than the point to which the *Laughing Mary* had been driven; that this ice in which she was entangled was not then drifting northwards, but was in the grasp of some polar current that trended it south-easterly; that in due course it was carried to the Antarctic main of ice, where it lay compacted; after which, through stress of weather or by the agency of a particular temperature, a great mass of it broke away and started on that northward course which bergs of all magnitude take when they are ruptured from the frozen continent.

This theory may be disputed, but it matters not. My business is to relate what befell me; if I do my share honestly the candid reader will not, I believe, quarrel with me for not being able to explain everything as I go along.

The Frenchman snored, and I sat considering him. The impression he had made upon me was not agreeable. To be sure he had suffered heavily, and there was something not displeasing in the spirit he discovered in telling the story—a spirit I am unable to communicate, as it owed everything to French vivacity largely spiced with devilment, and to sudden turns and ejaculations beyond the capacity of my pen to imitate. But a professional fierceness ran through it too; it was as if he had licked his chops when he talked of dismissing the captured ship with her people confined below and her cabin on fire. He had been as good as dead for nearly fifty years, yet he brought with him into life exactly the same qualities he had carried with him in his exit. Hence I never now hear that expression taken from the Latin, "*Of the dead speak nothing unless good*," without despising it as an unworthy concession to sentiment; for I have not the least doubt in my mind that, spite of deathbed repentances and all the horrors which crowd upon the imagination of a bad man in his last moments—I say I have not the least doubt that of every hundred persons who die, ninety-nine of them, could they be raised from the dead, no matter how many years or even centuries they might have lain in their graves, would exhibit their original natures, and pursue exactly the same courses which made them loved or scorned or feared or neglected before, which brought them to the gallows or which qualified them to die in peace with faces brightening to the opening heavens. If Nero did not again fire Rome he would be equal to crimes as great, and desire nothing better than the opportunity for them. Caesar would again be the tyrant, and the sword of Brutus would once more fulfil its mission. Richard III. would emerge in his winding-sheet with the same humpbacked character in which he had expired, the Queen of Scots return warm to her gallantries, and the Stuarts repeat those blunders and crimes which terminated in the headsman or in banishment.

But these are my thoughts of to-day; I was of another temper whilst I sat smoking and listening to the snoring of Monsieur Jules Tassard. Now that I had a companion should I be able to escape from this horrid situation? He had spoken of chests of silver—where was the treasure? in the run? There might be booty enough in the hold to make a great man, a fine gentleman of me ashore. It would be a noble ending to an amazing adventure to come off with as much money as would render me independent for life, and enable me to turn my back for ever upon the hardest calling to which the destiny of man can wed him.

Of such were the fancies which hurried through my mind, coupled with visitations of awe and wonder when I cast my eyes upon the sleeping Frenchman. After all it was ridiculous that I should feel mortified because he supposed me crazy in the matter of dates. How was it conceivable he should believe he had lain lifeless for eight-and-forty years? I knew a man who after a terrible adventure had slept three days and nights without stirring; the assurances of the people about him failed to persuade him that he had slumbered so long, and it was not until he walked abroad and met a hundred evidences as to the passage of the time during which he had slept that he allowed himself to become convinced.

I wished to see how the schooner lay and what change had befallen the ice in the night, and went on deck. It was blowing a whole gale of wind from the north-west. Inside the ship, with the hatches on, and protected moreover by the sides of the hollow in which she lay, it would have been impossible to guess at the weight of the gale, though all along I had supposed it to be storming pretty fiercely by the thunderous humming noise which resounded in the cabin. But I had no notion that so great a wind raged till I gained the deck and heard the prodigious bellowing of it above the rocks. The sky was one great cloud of slate, and there was no flying darkness or yellow scud to give the least movement of life to it. The sea was swelling very furiously, and I could divine its tempestuous character by clouds of spray which sped like volumes of steam under the sullen dusky heavens high over the mastheads. The schooner lay with a list of about fifteen degrees and her bows high cocked. I looked over the stern and saw that the ice had sunk there, and that there were twenty great rents and yawning seams where I had before noticed but one. A vast block of ice had fallen on the starboard side, and lay so close on the quarter that I could have sprung on to it. No other marked changes were observable, but there were a hundred sounds to assure me that neither the sea nor the gale was wholly wasting its strength upon this crystal territory, and that if I thought proper to climb the slope and expose myself to the wind, I should behold a face of ice somewhat different from what I had before gazed upon.

But the bitter cold held me in dread, and there was no need besides for me to take a survey. All that concerned me lay in the hollow in which the schooner was frozen; but so far as the slopes were concerned I could see nothing to render me uneasy. The declivities were gradual, and there was little fear of even a violent convulsion throwing the ice upon us. The danger lay below, under the keel; if the ice split, then down would drop the ship and stave herself, or if she escaped that peril she must be so wedged as to render the least further pressure of the ice against her sides destructive.

I was about to go below again, when my eye was taken by the two figures lying upon the deck. No dead bodies ever looked more dead, but after the wondrous restoration of the Frenchman I could not view their forms without fancying that they were but as he had been, and that if they were carried to the furnace and treated with brandy and rubbing and the like they might be brought to. Full of thoughts concerning them I stepped into the cabin, and, going to the cook-room, found Tassard still heavily sleeping. The coal in the corner was low, and as it wanted an hour of dinner-time I took the lanthorn and a bucket and went into the forepeak, and after several journeys stocked up a good provision of coal in the corner. I made noise enough, but Tassard slept on. When this was ended I boiled some water to cleanse myself, and then set about getting the dinner ready.

The going into the forepeak had put my mind upon the treasure, which, as I had gathered from the Frenchman's narrative, was somewhere hidden in the schooner—in the run, as I doubted not; I mean in the hold, under the lazarette, for you will recollect that, being weary and half-perished with the cold, I had turned my back on that dark part after having looked into the powder-room. All the time I was fetching the coal and dressing the dinner my imagination was on fire with fancies of the treasure in this ship. The Frenchman had told me that they had been well enough pleased with their hauls in the South Sea to resolve them upon heading round the Horn for their haunt, wherever it might be, in the Spanish main; and I had too good an understanding of the character of pirates to believe that they would have quitted a rich hunting-field before they had handsomely lined their pockets. What, then, was the treasure in the run, if indeed it were there? I recalled a dozen stories of the doings of the buccaneers, not to speak of the famous Acapulco ship taken by Anson a little before the year in which the *Boca del Dragon* was fishing in those waters; and I feasted my fancy with all sorts of sparkling dreams of gold and silver and precious stones, of the costly ecclesiastical furniture of New Spain, of which methought I found a hint in that silver crucifix in the cabin, of rings, sword-hilts, watches, buckles, snuff-boxes, and the like. Lord! thought I, that this island were of good honest mother earth instead of ice, that we might bury the pirate's booty if we could not save the ship, and make a princely mine of its grave, ready for the mattock should we survive to fetch it!

I was mechanically stirring the saucepan full of broth I had prepared, lost in these golden thoughts, when the Frenchman suddenly sat up on his mattress.

"Ha!" cried he, sniffing vigorously, "I smell something good—something I am ready for. There is no physic like sleep," and with that he stretched out his arms with a great yawn, then rose very agilely, kicking the clothes and mattress on one side and bringing a bench close to the furnace. "What time is it, sir?"

"Something after twelve by the captain's watch," said I, pulling it out and looking at it. "But 'tis guesswork time."

"The *captain's watch*?" cried he, with a short loud laugh. "You are modest, Mr. —— "

"Paul Rodney," said I, seeing he stopped for my name.

"Yes, modest, Mr. Paul Rodney. That watch is yours, sir; and you mean it shall be yours."

"Well, Mr. Tassard," said I, colouring in spite of myself, though he could not witness the change in such a light as that, "I felt this, that if I left the watch in the captain's pocket it was bound to go to the bottom ultimately, and—— "

"Bah!" he interrupted, with a violent flourish of the hand. "Let us save the schooner, if possible; there will be more than one watch for your pocket, more than one doubloon for your purse. Meanwhile, to dinner! My stupor has converted me into an empty hogshead, and it will take me a fortnight of hard eating to feel that I have broken my fast."

With a blow of the chopper he struck off a lump of the frozen wine, and then fell to, eating perhaps as a man might be expected to eat who had not had a meal for eight-and-forty years.

"There are two of your companions on deck," said I.

He started.

"Frozen," I continued; "they'll be the bodies of Trentanove and Joam Barros?"

He nodded.

"There is no reason why they should be deader than you were. It is true that Barros has been on deck whilst you have been below; but after you pass a certain degree of cold fiercer rigours cannot signify."

"What do you propose?" said he, looking at me oddly.

"Why, that we should carry them to the fire and rub them, and bring them to if we can."

"Why?"

I was staggered by his indifference, for I had believed he would have shown himself very eager to restore his old companions and shipmates to life. I was searching for an answer to his strange inquiry, "Why?" when he proceeded,—

"First of all, my friend Trentanove was stone-blind, and Barros nearly blind. Unless you could return them their sight with their life they would curse you for disturbing them. Better the blackness of death than the blackness of life."

"There is the body of the captain," said I.

He grinned.

"Let them sleep," said he. "Do you know that they are cutthroats, who would reward your kindness with the poniard that you might not tell tales against them or claim a share of the treasure in this vessel? Of all desperate villains I never met the like of Barros. He loved blood even better than money. He'd quench his thirst before an engagement with gunpowder mixed in brandy. I once saw him choke a man—tut! he is very well—leave him to his repose."

In the glow of the fire he looked uncommonly sardonic and wild, with his long beard, bald head, flowing hair, shaggy brows, and little cunning eyes, which seemed in their smallness to share in his grin, and yet did not; and though to be sure he was some one to talk to and to make plans with for our escape, yet I felt that if he were to fall into a stupor again it would not be my hands that should chafe him into being.

"You knew those men in life," said I. "If the others are of the same pattern as the Portuguese, by all means let them lie frozen."

"But, my friend," said he, calling me *mon ami*, which I translate, "that's not it, either. Do you know the value of the booty in this schooner?"

I answered, No; how was I to know it? I had met with nothing but wearing apparel, and some pieces of money, and a few watches in the forecastle. He knit his brows with a fierce suspicious gleam in his eyes.

"But you have searched the vessel?" he cried.

"I have searched, as you call it—that is, I have crawled through the hold as far as the powder-room."

"And further aft?"

"No, not further aft."

His countenance cleared.

"You scared me!" said he, fetching a deep breath. "I was afraid that some one had been beforehand with us. But it is not conceivable. No! we shall look for it presently, and we shall find it."

"Find what, Mr. Tassard?" said I.

He held up the fingers of his right hand: "One, two, three, four, five—five chests of plate and money; one, two, three—three cases of virgin silver in ingots; one chest of gold ingots; one case of jewellery. In all——" he paused to enter into a calculation, moving his lips briskly as he whispered to himself—"between ninety and one hundred thousand pounds of your English money."

I stifled the amazement his words excited, and said coldly, "You must have met with some rich ships."

"We did well," he answered. "My memory is good"—he counted afresh on his fingers—"ten cases in all. Fortune is a strange wench, Mr. Rodney. Who would think of finding her lodged on an iceberg? Now bring those others up there to life, and you make us five. What would follow, think you? what but this?"

He raised his beard and stroked his throat with the sharp of his hand. Then, swallowing a great draught of brandy, he rose and stopped to listen.

"It is blowing hard," said he; "the harder the better. I want to see this island knocked into bergs. Every sea is as good as a pickaxe. Hark! there are those crackling noises I used to hear before I fell into a stupor. Where do you sleep?"

I told him.

"My berth is the third," said he. "I wish to smoke, and will fetch my pipe."

He took the lanthorn and went aft, acting as if he had left that berth an hour ago, and I understood in the face of this ready recurrence of his memory how impossible it would be ever to make him believe he had been practically lifeless since the year 1753. When he returned he had on a hairy cap, with large covers for the ears, and a big flap behind that fell to below his collar, and was almost as long as his hair. He wanted but a couple of muskets and an umbrella to closely resemble Robinson Crusoe, as he is made to figure in most of the cuts I have seen. He produced a pipe of the Dutch pattern, with a bowl carved into a death's head, and great enough to hold a cake of tobacco. The skull might have been a child's for size, and though it was dyed with tobacco juice and the top blackened, with the live coals which had been held to it, it was so finely carved that it looked very ghastly and terribly real in his hand as he sat puffing at it.

He eyed me steadfastly whilst he smoked, as if critically taking stock of me, and presently said, "The devil hath an odd way of ordering matters. What particular merit have I that I should have been the one hit upon by you to thaw? Had you brought any one of the others to, he would have advised you against reviving us, and so I should have passed out of my frosty sleep into death as quietly, ay, and as painlessly, as that puff of smoke melts into clear air."

"Then perhaps you do not think you are obliged by my awakening you to life?" said I.

"Yes, my friend, I am much obliged," said he with vivacity. "Any fool can die. To live is the true business of life. Mark what you do: you make me know tobacco again, you enable me to eat and drink, and these things are pleasures which were denied me in that cabin there. You recall me to the enjoyment of my gains, nay, of more—of my own and the gains of our company. You make me, as you make yourself, a rich man; the world opens before me anew, and very brilliantly—to be sure, I am obliged."

"The world is certainly before you, as it is before me," said I, "but that's all; we have got to get there."

He flourished his pipe, and 'twas like the flight of Death through the gloomy fire-tinctured air.

"That must come. We are two. Yesterday you were one, and I can understand your despair. But these arms—stupor has not wasted so much as the dark line of a finger-nail of muscle. You too are no girl. Courage! between us we shall manage. How long is it since you sailed from England?"

"We sailed last month a year from the Thames for Callao."

"And what is the news?" said he, taking a pannikin of wine from the oven and sipping it. "Last year! 'Tis twelve years since I was in Paris and three years since we had news from Europe."

News! thought I; to tell this man the news, as he calls it, would oblige me to travel over fifty years of history.

"Why, Mr. Tassard," said I, "there's plenty of things happening, you know, for Europe's full of kings and queens, and two or more of them are nearly always at loggerheads; but sailors—merchantmen like myself— hear little of what goes on. We know the name of our own sovereign and what wages sailors are getting; that's about it, sir. In fact, at this moment I could tell you more about Chili and Peru than England and France."

"Is there war between our nations?" he asked.

"Yes," said I.

"Ha!" he cried, "I doubt if this time you will come off so easily. You have good men in Hawke and Anson; but Jonquière and St. George, hey? and Maçon, Cellie, Letenduer!"

He shook his head knowingly, and an air of complacency, that would be indescribable but for the word French, overspread his face. I knew the name of Jonquière as an admiral who had fought us in 1748 or thereabouts; of the others I had never heard. But I held my peace, which

I suppose he put down to good manners, for he changed the subject by asking if I was married. I answered, No, and inquired if *he* had a wife.

"A wife!" cried he; "what should a man of my calling do with a wife? No, no! we gather such flowers as we want off the high seas, and wear them till the perfume palls. They prove stubborn though; our graces are not always relished. Trentanove reckoned himself the most killing among us, and by St. Barnabas he proved so, for three ladies—passengers of beauty and distinction—slew themselves for his sake. Do you understand me? They preferred the knife to his addresses. *I*," said he, tapping his breast and grinning, "was always fortunate."

He looked a complete satyr as he thus spoke, with his hairy cap, grey beard, long nose, little cunning shining eyes, and broken fangs; and a chill of disgust came upon me. But I had already seen enough of him to understand that he was a man of a very formidable character, and that he had awakened after eight-and-forty years of insensibility as real a pirate at heart as ever he had been, and that it therefore behoved me to deal very warily with him, and above all not to let him suspect my thoughts. Yet he seemed a person superior to the calling he had adopted. His English was good, and his articulation indicated a quality of breeding. Whilst he smoked his pipe out he told me a story of an action between this schooner and a French Indiaman. I will not repeat it; it was mere butchery, with features of diabolic cruelty; but what affected me more violently than the horrors of the narrative was his cool and easy recital of his own and the deeds of his companions. You saw that he had no more conscience in him than the death's head he puffed at, and that his idea was there was no true greatness to be met with out of enormity. Well, thought I, as I stepped to the corner for some coal, if I was afraid of this creature when he was dead, to what condition of mind shall I be reduced by his being alive?

Chapter XVII.
The Treasure

WHEN his pipe was out he rose and made several strides about the cook-room, then took the lanthorn, and entering the cabin stood awhile surveying the place.

"So this would have been my coffin but for you, Mr. Rodney?" said he. "I was in good company, though," pointing over his shoulder at the crucifix with his thumb. "Lord, how the rogues prayed and cursed in this same cabin! In fine weather, and when all was well, the sharks in our wake had more religion than they; but the instant they were in danger, down they tumbled upon their quivering knees, and if heaven was twice as big as it is, it could not have held saints enough for those varlets to petition."

"You were nearly all Spaniards?"

"Ay; the worst class of men a ship could enter these seas with. But for our calling they are the fittest of all the nations in the world; better even than the Portuguese, and with truer trade instincts than the trained mulatto—nimbler artists in roguery than ever a one of them. I despise their superstition, but they are the better pirates for it. They carry it as a man might a feather bed; it enables them to fall soft. D'ye take me?" He gave one of his short loud laughs, and said, "I hope this slope won't increase. The angle's stiff enough as it is. 'Twill be like living on the roof of a house. I have a mind to see how she lies. What d'ye say, Mr. Rodney? shall I venture into the open?"

"Why not?" said I. "You can move briskly. You have as much life as ever you had."

"Let's go, then," he exclaimed, and climbing the ladder he pushed open the companion-door and stepped on to the deck. I followed with but little solicitude, as you may suppose, as to what might attend his exposure. The blast of the gale though it was broken into downwards eddying dartings by the rocks, made him bawl out with the sting of it, and for some moments he could think of nothing but the cold, stamping the deck, and beating his hands.

"Ha!" cried he, grinning to the smart of his cheeks, "this is not the cook-room, eh? Great thunder, you will not have it that this ice has been drifting north? Why, man, 'tis icier by twenty degrees than when we were first locked up."

"I hope not," said I; "and I think not. Your blood doesn't course strong yet, and you are fresh from the furnace. Besides, it is blowing a bitter cold gale. Look at that sky and listen to the thunder of the sea!"

The commotion was indeed terribly uproarious. The spume as before was blowing in clouds of snow over the ice, and fled in very startling flashes of whiteness under the livid drapery of the sky. The wind itself sounded like the prolonged echo of a discharge of monster ordnance, and it screeched and whistled hideously where it struck the peaks and edges of the cliffs and swept through the schooner's masts. The rending noises of the ice in all directions were distinct and fearful. The Frenchman looked about him with consternation, and to my surprise crossed himself.

"May the blessed Virgin preserve us!" he said. "Do you say we have drifted north? If this is not the very heart of the south pole you shall persuade me we are on the equator."

"It cannot storm too terribly for us, as you just now said," I replied. "I want this island to go to pieces."

As I said this a solid pillar of ice just beyond the brow of the hill on the starboard side was dislodged or blown down; it fell with a mighty crash, and filled the air with crystal splinters. Tassard started back with a faint cry of "Bon Dieu!"

"Judge for yourself how the ship lies," said I; "this is freezing work."

He went aft and looked over the stern, then walked to the larboard rail and peered over the side.

"Is there ice beyond that opening?" he asked, pointing over the taffrail.

"No," I answered; "that goes to the sea. There is a low cliff beyond. Mark that cloud of white; it is the spray hurled athwart the mouth of this hollow."

"Good," he mumbled with his teeth chattering. "The change is marvellous. There was ice for a quarter of a mile where that slope ends. 'Tis too cold to converse here."

"*There* are your companions," said I, pointing to the two bodies lying a little distance before the mainmast.

He marched up to them, and exclaimed, "Yes, this is Trentanove and that is Barros. Both were blind, but they are blinder now. Would they thank you to arouse them out of their comfortable sleep and force them to feel as I do, this cold to which they are now as insensible as I was? By heaven, for my part, I can stand it no longer;" and with that he ran briskly to the hatch.

I followed him to the cook-room and he crept so close to the furnace that I thought he had a mind to roast himself. No doubt, newly come to life as he was, the cold hurt him more than me, and maybe the tide of those animal spirits which had in his former existence furnished him with a brute courage had not yet flowed full to his mind; still I questioned even in his heydey if there had ever been much more than the swashbuckler in him, which opinion, however, could only increase the anxiety his companionship was like to cause me by obliging me to understand that I must prepare myself for treachery, and on no account whatever to suppose for a moment that he was capable of the least degree of gratitude or was to be swerved from any design he might form by considerations of my claim upon him as his preserver.

It is among the wonders of human nature that antagonisms should be found to flourish under such conditions of hopelessness, misery, and anguish as make those who languish under them the most pitiful wretches under God's eye. But so it has been, so it is, so it will ever be. Two men in an open boat at sea, their lips frothing with thirst, their eyes burning with famine, shall fall upon each other and fight to the death. Two men on an island, two miserable castaways whose dismal end can only be a matter of a week or two, eye each other morosely, give each other injurious words, break away and sullenly live, each man by himself, on opposite sides of their desert prison. Beasts do not act thus, nor birds, nor reptiles—only man. What was in the Frenchman Tassard's mind I do not know; in mine was fear, dislike, profound distrust, a great uneasiness, albeit we were alone, we were brothers in affliction and distress, as completely sundered from the world to which we belonged as if we lay stranded in the icy moon, speaking in the same tongue and believing in the same God!

The heat comforted him presently, and he put a lump of wine into the oven to melt, and this comforted him also.

"I can converse now," said he. "Perhaps after all the danger lies more in the imagination than in the fact. But it is a hideous naked scene, and needs no such colouring as the roaring of wind, the rushing of seas, and the crashing falls of masses of ice to render it frightful."

"You tell me," said I, "that when you fell asleep"—I would sometimes express his frozen state thus—"there was a quarter of a mile of ice beyond the schooner's stern."

"At least a quarter of a mile," he answered. "Day after day it would be built up till it came to a face of that extent."

I thought to myself if it has taken forty-eight years of the wear and tear of storm and surge to extinguish a quarter of a mile, how long a time must elapse before this island splits up? But then I reflected that during the greater part of those years this seat of ice had been stuck very low south where the cold was so extreme as to make it defy dissolution; that since then, it was come away from the main and stealing north, so that what might have taken thirty years to accomplish in seventy degrees of south latitude, might be performed in a day on the parallel of sixty degrees in the summer season in these seas.

Tassard continued speaking with the pannikin in his hand, and his eyes shut as if to get the picture of the schooner's position fair before his mind's vision: "There was a quarter of a mile of ice beyond the ship: I have it very plain in my sight: it was a great muddle of hillocks, for the ice pressed thick and hard, and raised us and vomited up peaks and rocks to the squeeze. Suppose I have been asleep a week?" Here he opened his eyes and gazed at me.

"Well?" said I.

"I say," he continued in the tone of one easily excited into passion, "a week. It will not have been more. It is impossible. Never mind about your eighteen hundred and one," showing his fangs in a sarcastic grin; "a week is long enough, friend. Then this is what I mean to say: that the breaking away of a quarter of a mile of ice in a week is fine work, full of grand promise: the next wrench—which might come now as I speak, or to-morrow, or in a week—the next wrench may bring away the rock on which we are lodged, and the rest is a matter of patience—which we can afford, hey? for we are but two—there is plenty of meat and liquor and the reward afterwards is a princely independence, Mr. Paul Rodney."

I was struck with the notion of the bed of ice on which the schooner lay going afloat, and said, "Are sea and wind to be helped, think you? If the block on which we lie could be detached, it might beat a bit against its parent stock, but would not unite again. The schooner's canvas might be made to help it along—though suppose it capsized!"

"We must consider," said he; "there is no need to hurry. When the wind falls we will survey the ice."

He warmed himself afresh, and after remaining silent with the air of one turning many thoughts over in his mind, he suddenly cried, "D'ye know I have a mind to view the plate and money below. What say you?"

His little eyes seemed to sparkle with suspicion as he directed them at me. I was confident he suspected I had lied in saying I knew nothing of this treasure and that he wanted to see if I had meddled with those chests. One of the penalties attached to a man being forced to keep the company of liars is, he himself is never believed by them. I answered instantly, "Certainly; I should like to see this wonderful booty. It is right that we should find out at once if it is there; for supposing it vanished we should be no better than madmen to sit talking here of the fine lives we shall live if ever we get home."

He picked up the lanthorn and said, "I must go to your cabin: it was the captain's. The keys of the chests should be in one of his boxes."

He marched off, and was so long gone that I was almost of belief he had tumbled down in a fit. However, I had made up my mind to act a very wary part; and particularly never to let him think I distrusted him, and so I would not go to see what he was about. But what I did was this: the arms-room was next door: I lighted a candle, entered it, and swiftly armed myself with a sort of dagger, a kind of boarding-knife, a very murderous little two-edged sword, the blade about seven inches long, and the haft of brass. There were some fifty of these weapons, and I took the first that came to my hand and dropped it into the deep side pocket of my coat and returned to the cook-room. It was not that I was afraid of going unarmed with this man into the hold: there was no more danger to me there than here: should he ever design to despatch me, one place was the same as another, for the dead above could not testify: there were no witnesses in this white and desolate kingdom. What resolved me to go armed was the fear that should the treasure be missing—and who was to swear that the schooner had never been visited once in eight-and-forty years?—the Frenchman, who was persuaded his stupor had not lasted above a week, and who was doubtless satisfied the chests were in the hold down to the period when he lost recollection, would suspect me of foul play, and in the barbarous rage of a pirate fall upon and endeavour to kill me. Thus you will see that I had no very high opinion of the morals and character of the man I had given life to; and indeed, after I had armed myself and was seated again before the furnace, I felt extremely melancholy, and underwent the severest dejection of spirits that had yet visited me, fearing that my humanity had achieved nothing more than to bring me into the society of a devil, who would prove a fixed source of anxiety and misery to me. Was it conceivable that the others should be worse than, or even as bad as, this creature? His hair showed him hoary in vice. The Italian was a handsome man, and let him have been as profligate as he would, as cruel and fierce a pirate as Tassard had painted him, he would at all events have proved a sightly companion, and harmless as being blind, though to be sure for that reason of no use to me. Yet though his blindness would have made him a burden, I had rather have thawed him into life than the Frenchman.

The mere thought of feeling under an obligation to arm myself filled me with such vindictive passions that I protest as I sat alone waiting for him. I felt as if it were a duty I owed myself to return him to the condition in which I found him, which was to be easily contrived by my binding him in his sleep and dragging him to the deck and leaving him to stupefy alongside the body of the giant Joam Barros. "Peace!" cried I to myself with a shiver; "villain that thou art to harbour such thoughts! Thou art a hundred-fold worse than the wretch against whom Satan is setting thee plotting to think thus vilely." I gulped down this bolus of conscience with the help of a draught of wine, and it did me good. Lord, how dangerous is loneliness to a man! Depend upon it, your seeker after solitude is only hunting for the road that leads to Bedlam.

It might be that he was long because of having to seek for the keys; but my own conviction was that he found the keys easily and stayed to rummage the boxes for such jewels and articles of value as he might there find. I think he was gone near half an hour; he then returned to the cook-house, saying briefly, "I have the keys," and jingling them, and after warming himself, said, "Let us go."

I was moving towards the forecastle.

"Not that way for the run," cried he.

"Is there a hatch aft?" I asked.

"Certainly; in the lazarette."

"I wish I had known that," said I; "I should have been spared a stifling scramble over the casks and raffle forwards."

He led the way, and coming to the trap hatch that conducted to the lazarette, he pulled it open and we descended. He held the lanthorn and threw the light around him and said, "Ay, there are plenty of stores here. We reckoned upon provisions for twelve months, and we were seventy of a crew."

A strange figure he looked, just touched by the yellow candle-light, and standing out upon the blackness like some vision of a distempered fancy, in his hair-cap and flaps, and with his long nose and beard and little eyes shining as he rolled them here and there. We made our way over the casks, bales, and the like, till we were right aft, and here there was a small clear space of deck in which lay a hatch. This he lifted by its ring, and down through the aperture did he drop, I following. The lazarette deck came so low that we had to squat when still or move upon our knees. At the foremost end of this division of the ship, so far as it was possible for my eyes to pierce the darkness—for it seems that this run went clear to the fore-hold bulkhead, that is to say, under the powder-room, to where the fore-hold began—were stowed the spare sails, ropes for gear, and a great variety of furniture for the equipment of a ship's yards and masts. But immediately under the hatch stood several small chests and cases, painted black, stowed side by side so that they could not shift.

Tassard ran his eye over them, counting. "Right!" cried he; "hold the lanthorn, Mr. Rodney."

I took the light from him, and, pulling the keys from his pocket, he fell to trying them at the lock of the first chest. One fitted; the bolt shot with a hard click, like cocking a trigger, and he raised the lid. The chest was full of silver money. I picked up a couple of the coins, and, bringing them to the candle, perceived them to be Spanish pieces of eight. The money was tarnished, yet it reflected a sort of dull metallic light. The Frenchman grasped a handful and dropped them, as though, like a child, he loved to hear the chink the pieces made as they fell.

"There's a brave pocketful there," said I.

"Tut!" cried he, scornfully. " 'Tis a mere show of money; resolve it into gold and it becomes a lean bit of plunder. This we got from the *Conquistador*; it was all she had in this way; destined for some monastery, I recollect; but disappointment is good for holy fathers; it makes them more earnest in their devotions and keeps their paunches from swelling."

He let fall the lid of the chest, which locked itself, and then, after a short trial of the keys, opened the one beside it. This was stored to the top with what I took to be pigs of lead, and when he pulled out one and bade me feel the weight of it I still thought it was lead, until he told me it was virgin silver.

"This was good booty!" cried he, taking the lanthorn and swinging it over the blocks of metal. "It would have been missed but for me. Our men had found it in the hold of the buccaneer in a chest half as deep again as this, and thought it to be a case of marmalade, for there were two layers of boxes of marmalade stowed on top. I routed them out and found those pretty bricks of ore snug beneath. I believe Mendoza made the value of the two chests—silver though it be—to be equal to six thousand pounds of your money."

The next chest he opened was filled with jewellery of various kinds, the fruits, I daresay, of a dozen pillages, for not only had this pirate robbed honest traders but a picaroon as well that had also plundered in her turn another of her own kidney; so that, as I say, this chest of jewellery might represent the property of the passengers of as many as a dozen vessels. It was as if the contents of the shop of a jeweller who was at once a goldsmith and a silversmith had been emptied into this chest; you could scarce name an ornament that was not here—watches, snuff-boxes, buckles, bracelets, pounce-boxes, vinaigrettes, earrings, crucifixes, stars for the hair, necklaces—but the list grows tiresome; in silver and gold, but chiefly in gold; all shot together and lying scramble fashion, as if they had been potatoes.

"This is a fine sight," said Tassard, poring upon the sparkling mass with falcon nose and ravenous eyes. "Here is a dainty little watch. Fifty guineas would not purchase it in London or Paris. Where is the white breast upon which that cross there once glittered? Ha! the perfume has faded," bringing a vinaigrette to his hawk's bill; "the soul is gone; the body is the immortal part in this case. Now, my friend, talk to me of the patient drudgery of honourable life after this," collecting the chests, so to say, to my view with a sweep of the hand; "men will break their hearts for a hundred livres ashore and be hanged for the price of a pinchbeck dial. When I was in London I saw five men carted to the gallows; one had forged, one was a highwayman—I forget the others' businesses; but I recollect on inquiring the value of their baggings—that for which they were hanged—it did not amount to four guineas a man. Look at this!" He swept his great hand again over the chests. "Is not here something worth going to the scaffold for?"

His bosom swelled, his eyes sparkled, and he made as if to strike a heroic posture, but this he could not contrive on his hams.

I was thunder-struck, as you will suppose, by the sight of all this treasure, and looked and stared like a fool, as if I was in a dream. I had never seen so many fine things before, and indulged in the most extravagant fancies of their worth. Here and there in the glittering huddle my eye lighted on an object that was a hundred, perhaps two hundred, years old: a cup very choicely wrought, that may have been in a family for several generations; a watch of a curious figure, and the like. There might have been the pickings of the cabins, trunks, and portmanteaux of a hundred opulent men and women in this chest, and, so far as I could judge from what lay atop, the people plundered represented several nationalities.

But there were other chests and cases to explore—ten in all: two of these were filled with silver money, a third with plate, a fourth with English, French, Spanish, and Portugal coins in gold; but the one over which Tassard hung longest in a transport that held him dumb, was the smallest of all, and this was packed with gold in bars. The stuff had the appearance of mouldy yellow soap, and having no sparkle nor variety did not affect me as the jewellery had, though in value this chest came near to being worth as much as all the others put together. The fixed transported posture of the pirate, his little shining eyes intent upon the bars, his form in the candle-light looking like a sketch of a strange, wildly-apparelled man done in phosphorus, coupled with the loom of the black chests, the sense of our desolation, the folly of our enjoyment of the sight of the treasure in the face of our pitiable and dismal plight, the melancholy storming of the wind, moaning like the rumble of thunder heard in a vault, and above all the feeling of unreality inspired by the thought of my companion having lain for eight-and-forty years as good as dead, combined to render the scene so startlingly impressive that it remains at this hour painted as vividly upon the eye of memory as if I had come from it five minutes ago.

"So!" cried the Frenchman suddenly, slamming the lid of the chest. "'Tis all here! Now then to the business of considering how to come off with it."

He thrust the keys in his pocket, and we returned to the cook-room.

Chapter XVIII.
We Talk over our Situation

THAT night, as afterwards, Tassard occupied the berth that he was used to sleep in before he was frozen. Although I had not then the least fear that he would attempt any malignant tricks with me whilst we remained in this posture, the feeling that he lay in the berth next but one to mine made me uneasy in spite of my reasoning; and I was so nervous as to silently shoot a great iron bolt, so that it would have been impossible to enter without beating the door in.

In sober truth, the sight of the treasure had put a sort of fever into my imagination, of the heat and effects of which I was not completely sensible until I was alone in my cabin and swinging in the darkness. That the value of what I had seen came to ninety or a hundred thousand pounds of our money I could not doubt; and I will not deny that my fancy was greatly excited by thinking of it. But there was something else. Suppose we should have the happiness to escape with this treasure, then I was perfectly certain the Frenchman would come between me and my share of it. This apprehension threading my heated thoughts of the gold and silver kept me restless during the greater part of the night, and I also held my brains on the stretch with devices for saving ourselves and the treasure; yet I could not satisfy my mind that anything was to be done unless Nature herself assisted us in freeing the schooner.

However, as it happened, the gale roared for a whole week, and the cold was so frightful and the air so charged with spray and hail that we were forced to lie close below with the hatches on for our lives. It was true Cape Horn weather, with seas as high as cliffs, and a westering tendency in the wind that flung sheets of water through the ravine, which must have quickly filled the hollow and built us up in ice to the height of the rails but for the strong slope down which the water rushed as fast as it was hurled.

I never needed to peep an inch beyond the companion-way to view the sky; nor for the matter of that was there ever any occasion to leave the cabin to guess at the weather, for the perpetual thunder of it echoed strong in every part of the vessel below, and the whole fabric was constantly shivering to the blows of the falls of water on her decks.

At first the Frenchman and I would sit in the greatest fear imaginable, constantly expecting some mighty disaster, such as the rending of the ice under our keel and our being swallowed up, or the coming together of the slopes in such a manner as to crush the ship, or the fall upon her of ice weighty enough to beat her flat; though perhaps this we least feared, for unless the storm changed the whole face of the cliffs, there was no ice in our neighbourhood to serve us in that way. But as the time slipped by and nothing worse happened than one sharp movement only in the vessel, following the heels of a great noise like a cannon discharged just outside; though this movement scared us nearly out of our senses, and held us in a manner dumbfounded for the rest of the day; I say, the time passing and nothing more terrifying than what I have related happening, we took heart and waited with some courage and patience for the gale to break, never doubting that we should find a wonderful change when we surveyed the scene from the heights.

We lived well, sparing ourselves in nothing that the vessel contained, the abundance rendering stint idle; the Frenchman cooked, for he was a better hand than I at that work, and provided several relishable sea-pies, cakes, and broths. As for liquor, there was enough on board to drown the pair of us twenty times over: wines of France, Spain, Portugal, very choice fine brandy, rum in plenty, such variety indeed as enabled us to brew a different kind of punch every day in the seven. But we were much more careful with the coal, and spared it to the utmost by burning the hammocks, bedding, and chests that lay in the forecastle; that is to say, we burnt these things by degrees, the stock being excessive, and by judiciously mixing them with coal and wood, they made good warming fires, and as tinder lasted long too.

We occupied one morning in thoroughly overhauling the forecastle for such articles of value as the sailors had dropped or forgotten in their flight; but found much less than I had expected from the sight of the money and other things on the deck. There was little in this way to be found in the cabins: I mean in the captain's cabin which I used, and the one next it that had been the mate's, for of course I did not search Mr. Tassard's berth. But though it was quite likely that the seamen had plundered these cabins before they left the ship, I was also sure that the Frenchman had made a clean sweep of what they had overlooked when he pretended to search for the keys of the treasure-chests; and this suspicion I seemed to find confirmed by the appearance of the captain's boxes. One of these boxes contained books, papers, a telescope, some nautical instruments, and the like. I looked at the books and the papers, in the hope of finding something to read; but they were written and printed in the Spanish tongue, and might have been Hebrew for all the good they were to me.

Our life was extraordinarily dismal and melancholy, how much so I am unable to express. It was just the same as living in a dungeon. There was no crevice for the daylight to shine through, and had there been we must have closed it to keep the cold out. Nothing could be imagined more gloomy to the spirits than the perpetual night of the schooner's interior. The furnace, it is true, would, when it flamed heartily, throw a brightness about it; but often it sank into redness that did but empurple the gloom. We burned but one candle at a time, and its light was very small, so that our time was spent chiefly in a sullen twilight. Added to all this was my dislike of my companion. He would half fuddle himself with liquor, and in that condition hiccup out twenty kinds of villainous yarns of piracy, murder, and bloodshed, boasting of the number of persons he had despatched, of his system of torturing prisoners to make them confess what they had concealed and where. He would drivel about his amours, of the style in which he lived when ashore, and the like; but whether reticence had grown into a habit too strong even for drink to break down, he never once gave me so much as a hint touching his youth and early life. He was completely a Frenchman in his vanity, and you would have thought him entirely odious and detestable for this excessive quality in him alone. Methinks I see him now, sitting before me, with one half of him reflecting the light of the furnace, his little eyes twinkling with a cruel merriment of wine, telling me a lying story of the adoration of a noble, queenly-looking captive for his person—some lovely Spanish court lady whom, with others, they had taken out of a small frigate bound to old Spain. To test her sincerity he offered to procure her liberty at the first opportunity that offered; but she wept, raved, tore her hair. No; without her Jules life would be unendurable; her husband, her country, her king, nay, even the allurements and sparkle of the court, had grown disgusting; and so on, and so on. And I think a monkey would have burst into laughter to see the bald-headed old satyr beat his bosom, flourish his arms, ogle, languish, and simper, all with a cut-throat expression, too, soften his voice, and act in short as if he was not telling me as big a lie as was ever related on shipboard.

It naturally rendered me very melancholy to reflect that I had restored this old villain to life, and I protest it was a continuous shock to such religious feelings as I had managed to preserve to reflect that what had been as good as nearly half a century of death had done nothing for this elderly rogue's morals. It entered my head once to believe that if I could succeed in getting him to believe he had lain frozen for eight-and-forty years, he might be seized with a fright (for he was a white-livered creature), and in some directions mend, and so come to a sense of the service I had done him, of which he appeared wholly insensible, and qualify me to rid my mind of the fears which I entertained concerning our association, should we manage to escape with the treasure. I said to him bluntly—not *apropos* (to use his own lingo) of anything we were talking about,—

" 'Tis odd, Mr. Tassard, you should doubt my assurance that this is the year eighteen hundred and one."

He stared, grinned, and said, "Do you think so?"

"Well," said I, "perhaps it is not so odd after all; but you should suffer me to have as good an idea of the passage of time as yourself. You cannot tell me how long your stupor lasted."

"Two days if you like!" he interrupted vehemently. "Why more? Why longer than a day? How do you know that I had sunk into the condition in which you found me longer than an hour or two when you landed? How do you know, hey? How do you know?" and he snapped his fingers.

"I know by the date you name and by the year that this is," said I defiantly.

He uttered a coarse French expression and added, "You want to prove that I have been insensible for forty-eight years."

"It is the fact," said I.

He looked so wild and fierce that I drew myself erect ready for him if he should fall upon me. Then, slowly wagging his head whilst the anger in his face softened out, he said, "Who reigns in France now?"

I said, "There is no king; he was beheaded."

"What was his name?" said he.

"Louis the Sixteenth," I answered.

"Ha!" cried he, with an arch sneer; "Louis the Sixteenth, hey? Are you sure it wasn't Louis the Seventeenth?"

"He is dead too."

"This is news, Mr. Rodney," said he scornfully.

"Whilst you have been here," said I, "many mighty changes have happened. France has produced as great a general and as dangerous a villain as the world ever beheld; his name is Buonaparte."

He shrugged his shoulders with an air of mocking pity.

"Who is your king?" he asked.

"George the Third," said I; "God bless him!"

"So—George and Louis—Louis and George. I see how it is. Stick to your dates, sir. But, my friend, never set up as a schoolmaster."

This sally seemed to delight him, and he burst into a loud laugh.

"Eighteen hundred and one!" he cried. "A man I knew once lost ten thousand livres at a *coup*. What do you think happened? They settled in him here;" he patted his belly: "he went about bragging to everybody that he was made of money, and was nicknamed the walking bourse. One day he asked a friend to dine with him; when the bill was presented he felt in his pockets, and exclaimed, 'I left my purse at home. No matter; there is plenty here;' with which he seized a table-knife and ripped himself open. Eighteen hundred and one, d'ye call it? *Soit.* But let it be *your* secret, my friend. The world will not love you for making it fifty years older than it is."

It was ridiculous to attempt to combat such obstinacy as this, and as the subject produced nothing but excitement and irritation, I dropped it and meddled with it no more, leaving him to his conviction that I was cracked in this one particular. In fact, it was a matter of no consequence at all; what came very much closer home was the business of our deliverance, and over this we talked long and very earnestly, for he forgot to be mean and fierce and boastful, and I to dislike and fear him, when we spoke of getting away with our treasure, and returning to our native home.

For hour after hour would we go on plotting and planning and scheming, stepping about the cook-house in our earnestness, and entirely engrossed with the topic. His contention was that if we were to save the money and plate, we must save the schooner.

"Unless we build a vessel," said I.

"Out of what?"

"Out of this schooner."

"Are you a carpenter?" said he.

"No," I replied.

"Neither am I," said he. "It's possible we might contrive such a structure as would enable us to save our lives; but we have not the skill to produce a vessel big enough to contain those chests as well as ourselves, and the stores we should require to take. Besides, do you know there is no labour more fatiguing than knocking such a craft as this to pieces?"

This I very well believed, and it was truer of such a vessel as the *Boca del Dragon* that was a perfect bed of timber, and, like the *Laughing Mary*, built as if she was to keep the seas for three hundred years.

"And supposing," said he, "after infinite toil we succeeded in breaking up as much of her as we wanted, what appliances have we for reshaping the curved timbers? and where are we to lay the keel? Labour as we might, the cold would prove too much for us. No, Mr. Rodney, to save the treasure, ay, and to save ourselves, we must save the ship. Let us put our minds to that."

In this way we would reason, and I confess he talked very sensibly, taking very practical views, and indicating difficulties which my more ardent and imaginative nature might have been blind to till they immovably confronted me, and rendered days of labour useless. But how was the ship to be saved? Was it possible to force Nature's hand; in other words, to anticipate our release by the dissolution of the ice? We were both agreed that this was the winter season in these seas, though he instantly grew sulky if I mentioned the month, for he was as certain I was as mad in this, as in the year, and he would eye me very malignantly if I persisted in calling it July. But, as I have said, we were both agreed that the summer was to come, and though we could not swear that the ice was floating northwards, we had a right to believe so, in spite of the fierceness of the cold, this being the trick of all these frozen estates when they fetch to the heights under which we lay; and we would ask each other whether we should let our hands and minds rest idle and wait to see what the summer would do for us, or essay to launch the schooner.

"If," said he, "we wait for the ice to break up it may break us up too."

"Yes," said I, "but how are we to cut the vessel out of the ice in which she is seated to above the garboard streak? Waiting is odious and intolerable work; but my own conviction is, nothing is to be done till the sun comes this way, and the ice crumbles into bergs. The island is leagues long, and vanishes in the south; but it is wasting fast in the north, and when this gale is done I shall expect to see twenty bergs where it was before all compact."

As you may guess, our long conversations left us without plans, bitter as was our need, and vigorous as were our efforts to strike upon some likely scheme. However, if they achieved no more, they served to beguile the time, and what was better yet, they took my companion's mind off his nauseous and revolting recollections, so that it was only now and again when he had drained a full bowl, and his little eyes danced in their thick-shagged caves, that he regaled me with his memories of murder, rapine, plank-walking, hanging, treacheries of all kinds, and cruelties too barbarous for belief.

Chapter XIX.
We Take a View of the Ice

For seven days the gale raged with uncommon violence: it then broke, and this brought us into the first week of August. The wind fell in the night, and I was awakened by the silence, which you will not think strange if you consider how used were my ears to the fierce seething and strong bellowing of the blast. I lay listening, believing that it had only veered, and that it would come on again in gusts and guns; but the stillness continued, and there was no sound whatever, saving the noises of the ice, which broke upon the air like slow answers from batteries near and distant, half whose cannons have been silenced.

I slept again, and when I awoke it was half-past nine o'clock in the morning. The Frenchman was snoring lustily. I went on deck before entering the cook-house, and had like to have been blinded by the astonishing brilliance of the sunshine upon the ice and snow. All the wind was gone. The air was exquisitely frosty and sharp. But there was a heavy sound coming from the sea which gave me to expect the sight of a strong swell. The sky was a clear blue, and there was no cloud on as much of its face as showed betwixt the brows of the slopes.

The schooner was a most wonderful picture of drooping icicles. A more beautiful and radiant sight you could not figure. From every rope, from the yards forward, from the rails, from whatever water could run in a stream, hung glorious ice-pendants of prismatic splendour. No snow had fallen to frost the surfaces, and every pendant was as pure and polished as cut-glass and reflected a hundred brilliant colours. The water hurled over and on the schooner had frozen upon the masts, rigging, and decks, and as this ice, like the pendants, was very sparklingly bright, it gave back all the hues of the sunbeam, so that, stepping from the darkness of the cabin into this effulgent scene, you might easily have persuaded yourself that before you stood the fabric of a ship fashioned out of a rainbow.

My attention, however, was quickly withdrawn from this shining spectacle by the appearance of the starboard cliff over against our quarter. The whole shoulder of it had broken away and I could just catch a view of the horizon of the sea from the deck by stretching my figure. The sight of the ocean showed me that the breakage had been prodigious, for to have come to that prospect before, I should have had to climb to the height of the main lower masthead. No other marked or noteworthy change did I detect from the deck; but on stepping to the larboard side to peer over I spied a split in the ice that reached from the very margin of the ravine, I mean to that end of it where it terminated in a cliff, to past the bows of the schooner by at least four times her own length.

I returned to the cook-room and went about the old business of lighting the fire and preparing the breakfast—this job by an understanding between the Frenchman and me, falling to him who was first out of bed—and in about twenty minutes Tassard arrived.

"The wind is gone," said he.

"Yes," I replied, "it is a bright still morning. I have been on deck. There has been a great fall of ice close to."

"Does it block us?"

"No, on the contrary, it clears the way to the sea; the ocean is now visible from the deck. Not that it mends our case," I added. "But there is a great rent in the ice that puts a fancy into my head; I'll speak of it later after a closer look."

The breakfast was ready, and we fell to in a hurry, the Frenchman gobbling like a hog in his eagerness to make an end. When we were finished he wrapped himself up in three or four coats and cloaks, warming the under ones before folding them about him, and completing his preparations for the excursion by swallowing half a pint of raw brandy. I bade him arm himself with a short-headed spear to save his neck; and thus equipped we went on deck.

He stood stock-still with his eyes shut on emerging through the hatch, crying out with a number of French oaths that he had been struck blind. This I did not believe, though I readily supposed that the glare made his eyeballs smart so as to cause him a good deal of agony. Indeed, all along I had been surprised that he should have found his sight so easily after having sat in blindness for forty-eight years, and it was not wonderful that the amazing brilliance on deck, smiting his sight on a sudden, should have caused him to cry out as if he had lost the use of his eyes for ever.

I waited patiently, and in about ten minutes he was able to look about him, and then it was not long before he could see without pain. He stood a minute gazing at the glories upon the rigging, and in that piercing light I noticed the unwholesome colour of his face. His cap hid the scar, and nothing of his countenance was to be seen but the cheeks, eyes, and nose; he was much more wrinkled than I had supposed, and methought the spirit of cruelty lay visible in every line. I had never seen eyes so full of cunning and treachery—so expressive, I should say, of these qualities; yet they were no bigger than mere punctures. I was sensible of a momentary fear of the man—not, let me say, an emotion of cowardice—but a sort of mixture of alarm and awe, such as a ghost might inspire. This I put down to the searching light in which I watched him for a moment or two, an irradiation subtle enough to give the sharpest form to expression, to exquisitely define every meaning that was distinguishable in his graveyard physiognomy. I left him to stare and judge for himself of the posture in which the long hard gale had put the schooner and stepped over to the two bodies. They were shrouded in ice from head to foot, as though they had each man been packed in a glass case cunningly wrought to their shapes. Their faces were hid by the crystal masks. Tassard joined me.

"Small chance for your friends now," said I, "even if you were agreeable to my proposal to attempt to revive them."

"So!" cried he, touching the body of the mate with his foot; "and this is the end of the irresistible Trentanove! for what conquests has Death robed him so bravely? See, the colours shine in him like fifty different kinds of ribbands. Poor fellow! he could not curl his moustachios now, though the loveliest eyes in Europe were fixed in passionate admiration on him. He'll never slit another throat, nor hiccup Petrarch over a goblet nor remonstrate with me on my humanity. Shall we toss the bodies over the side?"

"They are your friends," said I; "do as you please."

"But we must empty their pockets first. Business before sentiment, Mr. Rodney."

He stirred the figure again with his foot.

"Well, presently," said he, "this armour will want the hatchet. Now, my friend, to view the work of the gale."

The increased heel of the ship brought the larboard fore-channel low, and we stepped without difficulty from it on to the ice. The rent or fissure that I have before spoken of went very deep; it was nearly two feet wide in places, but, though the light poured brilliantly upon it, I could see no bottom.

"If only such another split as this would happen t'other side," said the Frenchman, "I believe this block would go adrift."

"Well," said I, after musing a little whilst I ran my eye over the hollows, "I'll tell you what was in my mind just now. There is a great quantity of gunpowder in the hold; ten or a dozen barrels. By dropping large parcels of it into the crevices on the right there, and firing it with slow-matches—"

He interrupted me with a cry: "By St. Paul, you have it! What crevices have you?"

We walked briskly round the vessel, and all about her beam and starboard quarter I found, in addition to the seams I had before noticed, many great cracks and fissures, caused no doubt by the fall of the shoulder of the slope. I pushed on further yet, going down the ravine, as I have called it, until I came to the edge; and here I looked down from a height of some twelve or fourteen feet—so greatly had the ice sunk or been changed by the weather—upon the ocean. I called to Tassard. He approached warily. I believe he feared I might be tempted to give him a friendly shove over the edge.

"Observe this hollow," said I; "the split there goes down to the water, and you may take it that the block is wholly disconnected on that side. Now look at the face of the ice," said I, pointing to the starboard or right-hand side; "that crack goes as far as the vessel's quarter, and the weakness is carried on to past the bows by the other rents. Mr. Tassard, if we could burst this body of ice by an explosion from its moorings ahead of the bowsprit, where it is all too compact, this cradle with the schooner in it will go free of the parent body."

He answered promptly, "Yes; it is the one and only plan. That crack to starboard is like telling us what to do. It is well you came here. We should not have seen it from the top. This valley runs steep. You must expect no more than the surface to be liberated, for the foot of the cliff will go deep."

"I desire no more."

"Will the ship stand such a launch, supposing we bring it about?" said he.

I responded with one of his own shrugs, and said, "Nothing is certain. We have one of two courses to choose: to venture this launch, or stay till the ice breaks up, and take our chance of floating or of being smashed."

"You are right," he exclaimed. "Here is an opportunity. If we wait, bergs may gather about this point and build us in. As to this island dissolving, we are yet to know which way 'tis heading. Suppose it should be travelling south, hey!"

He struck the ice with his spear, and we toiled up the slippery rocks with difficulty to the ship. We walked past the bows to the distance of the vessel's length. Here were many deep holes and cracks, and as if we were to be taught how these came about, even whilst we were viewing them an ear-splitting crash of noise happened within twenty fathoms of us, a rock many tons in weight rolled over, and left a black gulf behind it.

The Frenchman started, muttered, and crossed himself. "Holy Virgin!" he cried, rolling his eyes. "Let us return to the schooner. We shall be swallowed up here."

I own I was not a little terrified myself by the sudden loud blast and the thunder of the uprooted rock, and the sight of the huge black rent; but I meant to view the scene from the top, and to consider how best to dispose of the powder in the cracks, and said, "There is nothing to be done on board; skulking below will not deliver us or preserve the treasure. Here are several fissures big enough to receive barrels of gunpowder. See, Mr. Tassard, as they stand they cover the whole width of the hollow."

And I proceeded to give him my ideas as to lowering, fixing the barrels, and the like. He nodded his head, and said, "Yes, very good;

yes, it will do," and so on; but was too scared in his heart, I believe, to see my full meaning. He was perpetually moving, as if he feared the ice would split under his feet, and his eyes travelled over the face of the rocks with every manifestation of alarm in their expression. I wondered how so poor a creature should ever have had stomach enough to serve as a pirate; no doubt his spirit had been enfeebled by his long sleep; but then it is also true that the greatest bullies and most bloodthirsty rogues prove themselves despicable curs under conditions which make no demand upon their temper or their lust for plunder.

He would have returned to the ship, had I encouraged him, but on seeing me start to climb to the brow he followed. The prospect disappointed me. I had expected to witness a variety of surprising changes; but southward the scene was scarce altered. It was a wonderfully fair morning, the sky clear from sea-line to sea-line, and of a very soft blue, the ocean of a like hue, with a high swell running, that was a majestic undulation even from the height at which I surveyed it. The sun stood over the ice in the north-east, and the dazzle kept me weeping, so intolerable was the effulgence. Half of the delicate architecture that had enriched the slopes and surfaces that way was swept down, and ice lay piled in places to an elevation of many feet, where before it had been flat or hollow. However, there was no question but that the gale had played havoc with the north extremity of the island: I counted no less than twenty bergs floating off the main, and it was quite likely the sea was crowded beyond, though my sight could not travel so far.

However, when I came to look close, and to recollect the features of the shore as they showed when I first landed, I found some vital changes near at hand. Where my haven had been the ice had given way and left a gap half a mile broad and a hundred feet deep. The fall on the schooner's starboard quarter was very heavy, and the ice was split in all directions; and in parts was so loose that a point of cliff hard upon the sea rocked with the swell. When Tassard came to a stand he looked about him north and south, shading his eyes with his hand, and then swearing very savagely in French, he cried out in English, freely employing oaths as he spoke,—

"Why, here's as much ice as there was before I fell asleep! See yonder!" pointing to the south. "It dies out in the distance. If it does not join the pole there, may the devil rise before me as I speak. Thunder and fury! I had hoped to see it shrivelled to an ordinary berg!"

"What! in a week?" cried I, as if I believed his stupor had not lasted longer.

He returned no answer and gaped about him full of consternation and passion.

"And are we to wait for our deliverance till this continent breaks up?" he bawled. "The day of judgment will be a thing of the past by that time. Travelling north! 'sdeath!" he roared, his mouth full of the expletives of his day, French and English. "Who but a madman could suppose that this ice is not as fixed as the antarctic circle to which it is moored? Why, six months ago it was no bigger than it is now!" And he sent a furious terrified gate into the white solitudes vanishing in azure faintness in the south-west.

It was not a thing to reason upon. I was as much disappointed as he by the trifling changes the gale had made, and my heart felt very heavy at the sight of the great field disappearing in the south. The bergs in the north signified little. It is true they indicated demolition, but demolition so slow as to be worthless to us. It was not to be questioned that the island was proceeding north, but at what rate? Here, perhaps, might be a frozen crescent of forty or fifty leagues: and at what speed, appreciable enough to be of the least consequence to our calculations, should such a body travel?

I looked at the Frenchman.

"This must decide us!" said I. "We must fix on one of two courses: endeavour to launch the ship by blowing up the ice, or turn to and rig up the best arrangement we can contrive and put to sea."

"Yes," he answered, scowling as he darted his enraged eyes over the ice. "Better set a slow match in the magazine and drink ourselves senseless, and so blow ourselves to hell, than linger here in the hope that this continent will dissolve and release us. Where's Mendoza's body?"

I stared about me, and then pointing to the huge gap the ice had made, answered, "It was there. Where it is now I know not."

He shrugged his shoulders, took another view of the ice and the ocean, and then cried impatiently, "Let us return! the powder-barrels must have the first chance." And he made for the schooner, savagely striking the ice with his spear and growling curses to himself as he ploughed and climbed and jumped his way along.

Chapter XX.
A Merry Evening

BY the time we had reached the bottom of the hollow Tassard was blowing like a bellows with the uncommon exertion; and swearing that he felt the cold penetrating his bones, and that he should be stupefied again if he did not mind, he climbed into the ship and disappeared. I loved him so little that secretly I very heartily wished that nature would make away with him: I mean that something it would be impossible in me to lay to my conscience should befall him, as becoming comatose again, and so lying like one dead. Assuredly in such a case it was not this hand that would have wasted a drop of brandy in returning an evil, white-livered, hectoring old rascal to a life that smelled foully with him and the like of him.

It was so still a day that the cold did not try me sorely: there was vitality if not warmth in the light of the sun, and I was heated with clambering. So I stayed a full half-hour after my companion had vanished examining the ice about the schooner; which careful inspection repaid me to the extent of giving me to see that if by blasts of gunpowder I could succeed in rupturing the ice ahead of the schooner's bows there was a very good chance of the mass on which she lay going adrift. Yet I will not deny that though I recognized this business of dislocation as our only chance—for I could see little or nothing to be done in the way of building a boat proper to swim and ply—I foreboded a dismal issue to our adventure, even should we succeed in separating this block from the main. In fine, what I feared was that the weight of the schooner would overset the ice and drown her and us.

I entered the ship and found Tassard roasting himself in the cook-house.

"How melancholy is this gloom," said I, "after the glorious white sunshine!"

"Yes," said he, "but it is warm. That is enough for me. Curse the cold, say I. It robs a man of all spirit. To grapple with this rigour one should have fed all one's life on blubber. I defy a man to be brave when he is half-frozen. I feel a match for any three men now; but on the heights a flea would have made me run."

He pulled a pot from the bricks and filled his pannikin.

"I have been surveying the ice," said I, drawing to the furnace, "and have very little doubt that if we wisely bestow the powder in great quantities we shall succeed in dislocating the bed on which we are lying."

"Good!" he cried.

"But after?" said I.

"What?"

"As much of this bed as may be dislodged will not be deep: icebergs, as of course you know, capsize in consequence of their becoming top-heavy by the wasting of the bulk that is submerged. This block will make but a small berg should we liberate it, and I very much fear that the weight of the schooner will overset it the instant we are launched."

"Body of Moses!" he cried angrily, knitting his brows, whereby he stretched the scar to half its usual width, "what's to be done, then?"

"She is a full ship," said I, "and weighty. If the liberated ice be thin she may sit up on it and keep it under. We have a right to hope in that direction, perhaps. Yet there is another consideration. She may leak like a sieve!"

"Why?" he exclaimed. "She took the ice smoothly; she has not been strained; she was as tight as a bottle before she stranded; the coating of ice will have cherished her; and a stout ship like this does not suffer from six months of lying up!"

Six months, thought I!

"Well, it may be as you say; but if she leaks it will not be in our four arms to keep her free."

He exclaimed hotly, "Mr. Rodney, if we are to escape, we must venture something. To stay here means death in the end. I am persuaded that this ice is joined with some vast main body far south and that it does not move. What is there, then, to wait for? There is promise in your gunpowder proposal. If she capsizes then the devil will get his own." And with a savage flourish of the pannikin he put it to his lips and drained it.

His sullen determination that we should stand or fall by my scheme was not very useful to me. I had looked for some shrewdness in him, some capacity of originating and weighing ideas; but I found he could do little more than curse and swagger and ply his can, in which he found most of his anecdotes and recollections and not a little of his courage. I pulled out my watch, as I must call it, and observed that it was hard upon one o'clock.

" 'Tis lucky," said he, eying the watch greedily and coming to it away from the great subject of our deliverance as though the sight of the fine gold thing with its jewelled letter extinguished every other thought in him, "that you removed that watch from Mendoza. But he will have carried other good things to the bottom with him, I fear."

"His flask and tobacco-box I took away," said I. "He had nothing of consequence besides."

"They must go into the common-chest," cried he; " 'tis share and share, you know."

"Ay," said I, "but what I found on Mendoza is mine by the highest right under heaven. If I had not taken the things, they would now be at the bottom of the sea."

"What of that?" cried he savagely. "If we had not plundered the galleon, she might have been wrecked and taken all she had down with her. Yet should such a consideration hinder a fair division as between us—between you who had nothing to do with the pillage and me who risked my life in it?"

I said, "Very well; be it as you say," appearing to consent, for there was something truly absurd in an altercation about a few guineas' worth of booty in the face of our melancholy and most perilous situation; though it not only enabled me to send a deeper glance into the mind of this man than I had yet been able to manage, but made me understand a reason for the bloody and furious quarrels which have again and again arisen among persons standing on the brink of eternity, to whom a cup of drink or the sight of a ship had been more precious than the contents of the Bank of England.

I set about getting the dinner.

"Whilst you are at that work," cried he, starting up, "I'll overhaul the pockets of the bodies on deck;" and, picking up a chopper, away he went, and I heard him cursing in his native tongue as he stumbled to the companion-ladder through the darkness in the cabin.

His rapacity was beyond credence. There was an immense treasure in the hold, yet he could not leave the pockets of the two poor wretches on deck alone. I did not envy him his task. The frozen figures would bear a deal of hammering; and besides he had to work in the cold. Ah, thought I with a groan, I should have left him to make one of them!

I had finished my dinner by the time he arrived. He produced the watch I had taken from and returned to the mate's pocket when I had searched him for a tinder-box; also a gold snuff-box set with diamonds, and a few Spanish pieces in gold. On seeing these things I remembered that I had found some rings and money in his pockets whilst overhauling him for means to obtain fire; but I held my peace.

"Should not we have been imbeciles to sacrifice these beauties?" he cried, viewing the watch and snuff-box with a rapturous grin.

"They were hard to come at, I expect?"

"No," he answered, pocketing them and turning to a piece of beef in the oven. "I knocked away the ice and after a little wrenching got at the pockets. But poor Trentanove! d'ye know, his nose came away with the mask of ice! He is no longer lovely to the sight!" He broke into a guffaw, then stuffed his mouth full and talked in the intervals of chewing. "There was nothing worth taking on Barros. They are both overboard."

"Overboard!" I cried.

"Why, yes," said he. "They are no good on deck. I stood them against the rail, then tipped them over."

This was an illustration of his strength I did not much relish.

"I doubt if I could have lifted Barros," said I.

"Not you!" he exclaimed, running his eye over me. "A dead Dutchman would have the weight of a fairy alongside Barros."

"Well, Mr. Tassard," said I, "since you are so strong, you will be very useful to our scheme. There is much to be done."

"Give me a sketch of your plans, that I may understand you," he exclaimed, continuing to eat very heartily.

"First of all," said I, "we shall have to break the powder-barrels out of the magazine and hoist them on deck. There are tackles, I suppose?"

"You should be able to find what you want among the boatswain's stores in the run," he replied.

"There are some splits wide enough to receive a whole barrel of powder," said I. "I counted four such yawns all happily lying in a line athwart the ice past the bows. I propose to sink these barrels twenty feet deep, where they must hang from a piece of spar across the aperture."

He nodded.

"Have you any slow-matches aboard?"

"Plenty among the gunner's stores," he replied.

"There are but you and me," said I; "these operations will take time. We must mind not to be blown up by one barrel whilst we are suspending another. We shall have to lower the barrels with their matches on fire and they must be timed to burn an hour."

"Ay, certainly, at least an hour," he exclaimed. "Two hours would be better."

"Well, that must depend upon the number of parcels of matches we meet with. There will be a good many mines to spring, and one must not explode before another. 'Tis the united force of the several blasts which we must reckon on. The contents of at least four more barrels of powder we must distribute amongst the other chinks and splits in such parcels as they will be able to receive."

"And then?"

"And then," said I, "we must await the explosion and trust to the mercy of Heaven to help us."

He made a hideous face, as if this was a sort of talk to nauseate him, and said, "Do you propose that we should remain on board or watch the effects from a distance?"

"Why, remain on board of course," I answered. "Suppose the mines liberated the ice on which the schooner lies and it floated away, what should we, watching at a distance, do?"

"True," cried he, "but it is cursed perilous. The explosion might blow the ship up."

"No, it will not do that. We shall be bad engineers if we bring such a thing about. The danger will be—providing the schooner is released—in her capsizing, as I have before pointed out."

"Enough!" cried he, charging his pannikin for the third time. "We must chance her capsizing."

"If I had a crew at my back," said I, "I would carry an anchor and cable to the shoulder of the cliff at the end of the slope to hold the ship if she swam. I would also put a quantity of provisions on the ice along with materials for making us shelter and the whole of the stock of coal, so that we could go on supporting life here if the schooner capsized."

"Then," said he, "you would remain ashore during the explosion?"

"Most certainly. But as all these preparations would mean a degree of labour impracticable by us two men, I am for the bold venture—prepare and fire the mines, return to the ship, and leave the rest to Providence."

He made another ugly face and indulged himself in a piece of profanity that was inexpressibly disgusting and mean in the mouth of a man who was used to cross himself when alarmed and swear by the saints. But perhaps he knew, even better than I, how little he had to expect from Providence. He filled his pipe, exclaiming that when he had smoked it out we should fall to work.

Now that I had settled a plan I was eager to put it into practice—hot and wild indeed with the impatience and hope of the castaway animated with the dream of recovering his liberty and preserving his life; and I was the more anxious to set about the business at once, on account of the weather being fair and still, for if it came on to blow a stormy wind again we should be forced as before under hatches. But I had to wait for the Frenchman to empty his pipe. He was so complete a sensualist that I believe nothing short of terror could have forced him to shorten the period of a pleasure by a second of time. He went on puffing so deliberately, with such leisurely enjoyment of the flavour of the smoke, that I expected to see him fall asleep; and my patience becoming exhausted I jumped up; but by this time his bowl held nothing but black ashes.

"Now," cried he, "to work."

And he rose with a prodigious yawn and seized the lanthorn. Our first business was to hunt among the boatswain's stores in the run for tackles to hoist the powder-barrels up with. There was a good collection, as might have been expected in a pirate whose commerce lay in slinging goods from other ships' holds into her own; but the ropes were frozen as hard as iron, to remedy which we carried an armful to the cook-house, and left the tackles to lie and soften. We also conveyed to the cook-house a quantity of ratline stuff—a thin rope used for making of the steps in the shroud ladders; this being a line that would exactly serve to suspend the smaller parcels of powder in the splits. Before touching the powder-barrels we put a lighted candle into the bull's eye lamp over the door and removed the lanthorn to a safe distance. Tassard was perfectly well acquainted with the contents of this storeroom, and on my asking for the matches put his hand on one of several bags of them. They varied in length, some being six inches and some making a big coil. There was nothing for it but to sample and test them, and this I told Tassard could be done that evening. The main hatch was just forward of the gun-room bulkhead; we seized a handspike apiece and went to work to prize the cover open. It was desperate tough labour; as bad as trying to open an oyster with a soft blade. The Frenchman broke out into many strange old-fashioned oaths in his own tongue, imagining the hatch to be frozen; but though I don't doubt the frost had something to do with it, its obstinacy was mainly owing to time, that had soldered it, so to speak, with the stubbornness that eight-and-forty years will communicate to a fixture which ice has cherished and kept sound.

We got the hatch open at last—be pleased to know that I am speaking of the hatch in the lower deck, for there was another immediately over it on the upper or main deck—and returning to the powder-room rolled the barrels forward ready for slinging and hoisting away when we should have rigged a tackle aloft. We had not done much, but what we had done had eaten far into the afternoon.

"I am tired and hungry and thirsty," said the Frenchman. "Let us knock off. We have made good progress. No use opening the main-deck hatch to-night: the vessel is cold enough even when hermetically corked."

"Very well," said I, bringing my watch to the lanthorn and observing the time to be sundown: so, carefully extinguishing the candle in the bull's-eye lamp, we took each of us a bag of matches and went to the cook-room.

There was neither tea nor coffee in the ship. I so pined for these soothing drinks that I would have given all the wine in the vessel for a few pounds of either one of them. A senseless, ungracious yearning, indeed, in the face of the plenty that was aboard! but it was the plenty, perhaps, that provoked it. There was chocolate, which the Frenchman frothed and drank with hearty enjoyment; he also devoured handfuls of *succades*, which he would wash down with wine. These things made me sick, and for drink I was forced upon the spirits and wine, the latter of which was so generous that it promised to combine with the enforced laziness of my life under hatches to make me fat; so that I am of opinion had we waited for the ice to release us, I should have become so corpulent as to prove a burden to myself.

I mention this here that you may find an excuse in it for the only act of folly in the way of drinking that I can lay to my account whilst I was in this pirate; for I must tell you that, on returning to the furnace, we, to refresh us after our labour, made a bowl of punch, of which I drank so plentifully that I began to feel myself very merry. I forgot all about the matches and my resolution to test them that night. The Frenchman, enjoying my condition, continued to pledge me till his little eyes danced in his head. Luckily for me, being at bottom of a very jolly disposition, drink never served me worse than to develop that quality in me. No man could ever say that I was quarrelsome in my cups. My progress was marked by stupid smiles, terminating in unmeaning laughter. The Frenchman sang a ballad about love and Picardy, and the like, and I gave him "Hearts of Oak," the sentiments of which song kept him shrugging his shoulders and drunkenly looking contempt.

We continued singing alternately for some time, until he fell to setting up his throat when I was at work, and this confused and stopped me. He then favoured me with what he called the Pirate's Dance, a very wild, grotesque movement, with no elegance whatever to be hurt by his being in liquor; and I think I see him now, whipping off his coat, and sprawling and flapping about in high boots and a red waistcoat, flourishing his arms, snapping his fingers, and now and again bursting into a stave to keep step to. When he was done, I took the floor with the hornpipe, whistling the air, and double-shuffling, toe-and-heeling, and quivering from one leg to another very briskly. He lay back against the bulkhead grasping a can half full of punch, roaring loudly at my antics; and when I sank down, breathless, would have had me go on, hiccuping that though he had known scores of English sailors, he had never seen that dance better performed.

By this time I was extremely excited and extraordinarily merry, and losing hold of my judgment, began to indulge in sundry pleasantries concerning his nation and countrymen, asking with many explosions of laughter, how it was that they continued at the trouble of building ships for us to use against them, and if he did not think the "flower de louse" a neater symbol for people who put snuff into their soup and restricted their ablutions to their faces than the tricolour, being too muddled to consider that he was ignorant of that flag; and in short I was so offensive, in spite of my ridiculous merriment, that his savage nature broke out. He assailed the English with every injurious term his drunken condition suffered him to recollect; and starting up with his little eyes wildly rolling, he clapped his hand to his side, as if feeling for a sword, and calling me by a very ugly French word, bade me come on, and he would show me the difference between a Frenchman and a beast of an Englishman.

I laughed at him with all my might, which so enraged him that, swaying to right and left, he advanced as if to fall upon me. I started to my feet and tumbled over the bench I had jumped from, and lay sprawling; and the bench oversetting close to him, he kicked against it and fell too, fetching the deck a very hard blow. He groaned heavily and muttered that he was killed. I tried to rise, but my legs gave way, and then the fumes of the punch overpowered me, for I recollect no more.

When I awoke it was pitch dark. My hands, legs, and feet seemed formed of ice, my head of burning brass. I thought I was in my cot, and felt with my hands till I touched Tassard's cold bald head, which so terrified me that I uttered a loud cry and sprang erect. Then recollection returned, and I heartily cursed myself for my folly and wickedness. Good God! thought I, that I should be so mad as to drown my senses when never was any wretch in such need of all his reason as I!

The boatswain's tinder-box was in my pocket; I groped, found a candle, and lighted it. It was twenty minutes after three in the morning. Tassard lay on his back, snoring hideously, his legs overhanging the capsized bench. I pulled and hauled at him, but he was too drunk to awake, and that he might not freeze to death I fetched a pile of clothes out of his cabin and covered him up, and put his head on a coat.

My head ached horribly, but not worse than my heart. When I considered how our orgy might have ended in bloodshed and murder, how I had insulted God's providence by drinking and laughing and roaring out songs and dancing at a time when I most needed His protection, with Death standing close beside me, as I may say, I could have beaten my head against the deck in the anguish of my contrition and shame. My passion of sorrow was so extravagant, indeed, that I remember looking at the Frenchman as if he was the devil incarnate, who had put himself in my way to thaw and recover, that he might tempt me on to the loss of my soul. Fortunately these fancies did not last. I was parched with thirst, but the water was ice, and there was no fire to melt it with; so I broke off some chips and sucked them, and held a lump to my forehead. I went to my cabin and got into my hammock, but my head was so hot, and ached so furiously, and I was so vexed with myself besides, that I could not sleep. The schooner was deathly still; there was not apparently the faintest murmur of air to awaken an echo in her; nothing spoke but the near and distant cracking of the ice. It was miserable work lying in the cabin sleepless and reproaching myself, and as my burning head robbed the cold of its formidableness, I resolved to go on deck and take a brisk turn or two.

The night was wonderfully fine; the velvet dusk so crowded with stars that in parts it resembled great spaces of cloth of silver hovering. I turned my eyes northwards to the stars low down there and thought of

England and the home where I was brought up until the tears gathered, and with them went something of the dreadful burning aching out of my head. Those distant, silent, shining bodies amazingly intensified the sense of my loneliness and remoteness, and yonder Southern Cross and the luminous dust of the Magellanic clouds seemed not farther off than my native country. It is not in language to express the savage naked beauty, the wild mystery of the white still scene of ice, shining back to the stars with a light that owed nothing to their glory; nor convey how the whole was heightened to every sense by the element of fear, put into the picture by the sounds of the splitting ice, and the softened regular roaring of the breakers along the coast.

I started with fresh shame and horror when I contrasted this ghastly calmness of pale ice and the brightness of the holy stars looking down upon it, with our swinish revelry in the cabin, and I thought with loathing of the drunken ribaldry of the pirate and my own tipsy songs piercing the ear of the mighty spirit of this solitude. The exercise improved my spirits; I stepped the length of the little raised deck briskly, my thoughts very busy. On a sudden the ice split on the starboard hand with a noise louder than the explosion of a twenty-four pounder. The schooner swayed to a level keel with so sharp a rise that I lost my balance and staggered. I recovered myself, trembling and greatly agitated by the noise and the movement coming together, without the least hint having been given me, and grasping a backstay, waited, not knowing what was to happen next. Unless it be the heave of an earthquake, I can imagine no motion capable of giving one such a swooning, nauseating, terrifying sensation as the rending of ice under a fixed ship. In a few moments there were several sharp cracks, all on the starboard side, like a snapping of musketry, and I felt the schooner very faintly heave, but this might have been a deception of the senses, for though I set a star against the masthead and watched it, there was no movement. I looked over the side and observed that the split I had noticed on the face of the cliff had by this new rupture been extended transversely right across the schooner's starboard bow, the thither side being several feet higher than on this. It was plain that the bed on which the vessel rested had dropped so as to bring her upright, and I was convinced by this circumstance alone, that if I used good judgment in disposing of the powder the weight of the mass would complete its own dislocation.

I stepped a little way forward to obtain a clearer sight of the splits about the schooner, and on putting my head over, I was inexpressibly dismayed and confounded by the apparition of a man with his arms stretched out before him, his face upturned, and his posture that of starting back as though terrified at beholding me. I had met with several frights whilst I had been on this island, but none worse than this, none that so completely paralysed me as to very nearly deprive me of the power of breathing. I stared at him, and he seemed to stare at me, and I know not which of the two was the more motionless. The whiteness made a light of its own, and he was perfectly plain. I blinked and puffed, conceiving it might be some illusion of the wine I had drunk, and finding him still there, and acting as though he warded me off in terror, as if my showing myself unawares had led him to think me the devil—I say finding him perfectly real, I was seized with an agony of fear, and should have rushed to my cabin had my legs been equal to the task of transporting me there. *Then*, thought I, idiot that you are, what think you, you fool, is it but the body of Trentanove? Sure enough it was, and putting my head a little farther over the rail, I saw the figure of the Portuguese Barros lying close under the bends. No doubt it was the movement of the ice that had shot the Italian into the lifelike posture, it being incredible he should have fallen so on being tumbled overboard by the Frenchman. But there he was, resting against a lump of ice, looking as living in his frozen posture as ever he had showed in the cabin.

The shock did my head good; I went below and got into my cot, and after tossing for half an hour or so fell asleep. I awoke and went to the cook-house, where I found Tassard preparing the breakfast, and a great fire burning. I hardly knew what reception he would give me, and was therefore not a little agreeably surprised by his thanking me for covering him up.

"You have a stronger head than mine," said he. "The punch used you well. You made me laugh, though. You was very diverting."

"Ay, much too diverting to please myself," said I; and I sounded him cautiously to remark what his memory carried of my insults, but found that he recollected nothing more than that I danced with vigour, and sang well.

I said nothing about my contrition, my going on deck, and the like, contenting myself with asking if he had heard the explosion in the night.

"No," cried he, staring and looking eagerly.

"Well, then," said I, "there has happened a mighty crack in the ice, and I do soberly believe that with the blessing of God we shall be able by blasts of powder to free the block on which the schooner rests."

"Good!" cried he; "come, let us hurry with this meal. How is the weather?"

"Quiet, I believe. I have not been on deck since the explosion aroused me early this morning."

Whilst we ate he said, "Suppose we get the schooner afloat, what do you propose?"

"Why," I answered, "if she prove tight and seaworthy, what but carry her home?"

"What, you and I alone?"

"No," said I, "certainly not; we must make shift to sail her to the nearest port, and ship a crew."

He looked at me attentively, and said, "What do you mean by home?"

"England," said I.

He shrugged his shoulders and exclaimed in French, "'Tis natural." Then proceeding in English, "Pray," said he, showing his fangs, "do not you know that the *Boca del Dragon* is a pirate? Do you want to be hanged that you propose to carry her to a port to ship men?"

"I have no fear of that," said I; "after all these years she'll be as clean forgotten as if she had never had existence."

"Look ye here, Mr. Rodney," cried he in a passion, "let's have no more of this snivelling nonsense about *years*. You may be as mad as you please on that point, but it shan't hang *me*. It needs more than a few months to make men forget a craft that has carried on such traffic as our hold represents. You'll not find me venturing myself nor the schooner into any of your ports for men. No, no, my friend. I am in no stupor now, you know; and I've slept the punch off also, d'ye see. What, betray our treasure and be hanged for our generosity?"

He made me an ironical bow, grinning with wrath.

"Let's get the schooner afloat first," said I.

"Ay, that's all very well," he cried; "but better stop here than dangle in chains. No, my friend; our plan must be a very different one from your proposal. I suppose you want your share of the booty?" said he, snapping his fingers.

"I deserve it," said I, smiling, that I might soften his passion.

"And yet you would convey the most noted pirate of the age, with plunder in her to the value of thousands of doubloons, to a port in which we should doubtless find ships of war, a garrison, magistrates, governors, prisons, and the whole of the machinery it is our business to give our stern to! *Ma foi*, Mr. Rodney! sure you are out in something more than your reckoning of time?"

"What do you propose?" said I.

"Ha!" he exclaimed, whilst his little eyes twinkled with cunning, "now you speak sensibly. What do I propose? This, my friend. We must navigate the schooner to an island and bury the treasure; then head for the shipping highways, and obtain help from any friendly merchantmen we may fall in with. *Home* with us means the Tortugas. There we shall find the company we need to recover for us what we shall have hidden. We shall come by our own then. But to sail with this treasure on board— without a crew to defend the vessel—by this hand! the first cruiser that sighted us would make a clean sweep, and then, ho, for the hangman, Mr. Rodney!"

How much I relished this scheme you will imagine; but to reason with him would have been mere madness. I knitted my brows and seemed to reflect, and then said, "Well, there is a great deal of plain, good sense in what you say. I certainly see the wisdom of your advice in recommending that we should bury the treasure. Nor must we leave anything on board to convict the ship of her true character."

His greedy eyes sparkled with self-complacency. He tapped his forehead and cried, "Trust to this. There is mind behind this surface. Your plan for releasing the schooner is great; mine for preserving the treasure is great too. You are the sailor, I the strategist; by combining our genius, we shall oppose an invulnerable front to adversity, and must end our days as Princes. Your hand, Paul!"

I laughed and gave him my hand, which he squeezed with many contortions of face and figure; but though I laughed I don't know that I ever so much disliked and distrusted and feared the old leering rogue as at that moment.

"Come!" cried I, jumping up, "let's get about our work." And with that I pulled open a bag of matches, and fell to testing them. They burnt well. The fire ate into them as smoothly as if they had been prepared the day before. They were all of one thickness. I cut them to equal lengths, and fired them and waited watch in hand; one was burnt out two minutes before the other, and each length took about ten minutes to consume. This was good enough to base my calculations upon.

Chapter XXI.
We Explore the Mines

I DON'T design to weary you with a close account of our proceedings. How we opened the main-deck hatch, rigged up tackles, clapping purchases on to the falls, as the capstan was hard frozen and immovable; how we hoisted the powder-barrels on deck and then, by tackles on the foreyard, lowered them over the side; how we filled a number of bags which we found in the forecastle with powder; how we measured the cracks in the ice and sawed a couple of spare studding-sail booms into lengths to serve as beams whereby to poise the barrels and bags; would make but sailor's talk, half of which would be unintelligible and the rest wearisome.

The Frenchman worked hard, and we snatched only half an hour for our dinner. The split that had happened in the ice during the night showed by daylight as a gulf betwixt eight and ten feet wide at the seawards end, thinning to a width of three feet, never less, to where it ended, ahead of the ship, in a hundred cracks in the ice that showed as if a thunderbolt had fallen just there. I looked into this rent, but it was as black as a well past a certain depth, and there was no gleam of water. When we went over the side to roll our first barrel of powder to the spot where we meant to lower it, the Frenchman marched up to the figure of Trentanove, and with no more reverence than a boy would show in throwing a stone at a jackass, tumbled him into the chasm. He then stepped up to the body of the Portuguese boatswain, dragged him to the same fissure, and rolled him into it.

"There!" cried he; "now they are properly buried."

And with this he went coolly on with his work.

I said nothing, but was secretly heartily disgusted with this brutal disposal of his miserable shipmates' remains. However, it was his doing, not mine; and I confess the removal of those silent witnesses was a very great relief to me, albeit when I considered how Tassard had been awakened, and how both the mate and the boatswain might have been brought to by treatment, I felt as though, after a manner, the Frenchman had committed a murder by burying them so.

It blew a small breeze all day from the south-west, the weather keeping fine. It was ten o'clock in the morning when we started on our labour, and the sun had been sunk a few minutes by the time we had rigged the last whip for the lowering and poising of the powder. This left us nothing to do in the morning but light the matches, lower the powder into position, and then withdraw to the schooner and await the issue. Our arrangements comprised, first, four barrels of powder in deep yawns ahead of the vessel, directly athwart the line of her head; second, two barrels, a wide space between them, in the great chasm on the starboard side; third, about fifty very heavy charges in bags and the like for the further rupturing of many splits and crevices on the larboard bow of the ship, where the ice was most compact. What should follow the mighty blast no mortal being could have foretold. I had no fear of the charges injuring the vessel—that is to say, I did not fear that the actual explosion would damage her: but as the effect of the bursting of such a mass of powder as we designed to explode upon so brittle a substance as ice was not calculable, it was quite likely that the vast discharge, instead of loosening and freeing the bed of ice, might rend it into blocks, and leave the schooner still stranded and lying in some wild posture amid the ruins.

But the powder was our only trumps; we had but to play it and leave the rest to fortune.

We got our supper and sat smoking and discussing our situation and chances. Tassard was tired, and this and our contemplation of the probabilities of the morrow sobered his mind, and he talked with a certain gravity. He drank sparely and forbore the hideous recollections or inventions he was used to bestow on me, and indeed could find nothing to talk about but the explosion and what it was to do for us. I was very glad he did not again refer to his project to bury the treasure and carry the schooner to the Tortugas. The subject fired his blood, and it was such nonsense that the mere naming of it was nauseous to me. Eight-and-forty years had passed since his ship fell in with this ice, and not tenfold the treasure in the hold might have purchased for him the sight of so much as a single bone of the youngest of those associates whom he idly dreamt of seeking and shipping and sailing in command of. Yet, imbecile as was his scheme, having regard to the half-century that had elapsed, I clearly witnessed the menace to me that it implied. His views were to be read as plainly as if he had delivered them. First and foremost he meant that I should help him to sail the schooner to an island and bury the plate and money; which done he would take the first opportunity to murder me. His chance of meeting with a ship that would lend him assistance to navigate the schooner would be as good if he were alone in her as if I were on board too. There would be nothing, then, in this consideration to hinder him from cutting my throat after we had buried the treasure and were got north. Two motives would imperatively urge him to make away with me; first, that I should not be able to serve as a witness to his being a pirate, and next that he alone should possess the secret of the treasure.

He little knew what was passing in my mind as he surveyed me through the curls of smoke spouting up from his death's-head pipe. I talked easily and confidentially, but I saw in his gaze the eyes of my murderer, and was so sure of his intentions that had I shot him in self-defence, as he sat there, I am certain my conscience would have acquitted me of his blood.

I passed two most uneasy hours in my cot before closing my eyes. I could think of nothing but how to secure myself against the Frenchman's treachery. You would suppose that my mind must have been engrossed with considerations of the several possibilities of the morrow; but that was not so. My reflections ran wholly to the bald-headed evil-eyed pirate whom in an evil hour I had thawed into being, and who was like to discharge the debt of his own life by taking mine. The truth is, I had been too hard at work all day, too full of the business of planning, cutting, testing, and contriving, to find leisure to dwell upon what he had said at breakfast, and now that I lay alone in darkness it was the only subject I could settle my thoughts to.

However, next morning I found myself less gloomy, thanks to several hours of solid sleep. I thought, what is the good of anticipating? Suppose the schooner is crushed by the ice or jammed by the explosion? Until we are under way, nay, until the treasure is buried, I have nothing to fear, for the rogue cannot do without me. And, reassuring myself in this fashion, I went to the cook-room and lighted the fire; my companion presently arrived, and we sat down to our morning meal.

"I dreamt last night," said he, "that the devil sat on my breast and told me that we should break clear of the ice and come off safe with the treasure—there is loyalty in the Fiend. He seldom betrays his friends."

"You have a better opinion of him than I," said I; "and I do not know that you have much claim upon his loyalty either, seeing that you will cross yourself and call upon the Madonna and saints when the occasion arises."

"Pooh, mere habit," cried he, sarcastically. "I have seen Barros praying to a little wooden saint in a gale of wind and then knock its head off and throw it overboard because the storm increased." And here he fell to talking very impiously, professing such an outrageous contempt for every form of religion, and affirming so ardent a belief in the goodwill of Satan and the like, that I quitted my bench at last in a passion, and told him that he must be the devil himself to talk so, and that for my part his sentiments awoke in me nothing but the utmost scorn, loathing, and horror of him.

His face fell, and he looked at me with the eye of one who takes measure of another and does not feel sure.

"Tut!" cried he, with a feigned peevishness; "what are my sentiments to you, or yours to me? you may be a Quaker for all I care. Come, fill your pannikin and let us drink a health to our own souls!"

But though he said this grinning, he shot a savage look of malice at me, and when he put his pannikin down his face was very clouded and sulky.

We finished our meal in silence, and then I rose, saying, "Let us now see what the gunpowder is going to do for us."

My rising and saying this worked a change in him. He exclaimed briskly, "Ay, now for the great experiment," and made for the companion-steps with an air of bustle.

The wind as before was in the south-west, blowing without much weight; but the sky was overcast with great masses of white clouds with a tint of rainbows in their shoulders and skirts, amid which the sky showed in a clear liquid blue. Those clouds seemed to promise wind and perhaps snow anon; but there was nothing to hinder our operations. We got upon the ice, and went to work to fix matches to the barrels and bags, and to sling them by the beams we had contrived ready for lowering when the matches were fired, and this occupied us the best part of two hours. When all was ready I fired the first match, and we lowered the barrel smartly to the scope of line we had settled upon; so with the others. You may reckon we worked with all imaginable wariness, for the stuff we handled was mighty deadly, and if a barrel should fall and burst with the match alight, we might be blown in an instant into rags, it being impossible to tell how deep the rents went.

The bags being lighter there was less to fear, and presently all the barrels and bags with the matches burning were poised in the places and hanging at the depth we had fixed upon, and we then returned to the schooner, the Frenchman breaking into a run and tumbling over the rail in his alarm with the dexterity of a monkey.

Each match was supposed to burn an hour, so that when the several explosions happened they might all occur as nearly as possible at once, and we had therefore a long time to wait. The margin may look unreasonable in the face of our despatch, but you will not think it unnecessary if you consider that our machinery might not have worked very smooth, and that meanwhile all that was lowered was in the way of exploding. So interminable a period as now followed I do believe never before entered into the experiences of a man. The cold was intense, and we had to move about; but also were we repeatedly coming to a halt to look at our watches and cast our eyes over the ice. It was like standing under a gallows with the noose around the neck waiting for the cart to move off. My own suspense became torture; but I commanded my face. The Frenchman, on the other hand, could not control the torments of his expectation and fear.

"Holy Virgin!" he would cry, "suppose we are blown up too? suppose we are engulfed in the ice? suppose it should be vomited up in vast blocks which in falling upon us must crush us to pulp and smash the decks in?"

At one moment he would call himself an idiot for not remaining on the rocks at a distance and watching the explosion, and even make as if to jump off the vessel, then immediately recoil from the idea of setting his foot upon a floor that before he could take ten strides might split into chasms, with hideous uproar under him. At another moment he would run to the companion and descend out of my sight, but reappear after a minute or two wildly shaking his head and swearing that if waiting was insupportable in the daylight, it was ten thousand times worse in the gloom and solitude of the interior.

I was too nervous and expectant myself to be affected by his behaviour; but his dread of the explosion upheaving lumps of ice was sensible enough to determine me to post myself under the cover of the hatch and there await the blast, for it was a stout cover and would certainly screen me from the lighter flying pieces.

It was three or four minutes past the hour and I was looking breathlessly at my watch when the first of the explosions took place. Before the ear could well receive the shock of the blast the whole of the barrels exploded along with some twelve or fourteen parcels. Tassard, who stood beside me, fell on his face, and I believed he had been killed. It was so hellish a thunder that I suppose the blowing up of a first-rate could not make a more frightful roar of noise. A kind of twilight was caused by the rise of the volumes of white smoke out of the ice. The schooner shook with such a convulsion that I was persuaded she had been split. Vast showers of splinters of ice fell as if from the sky, and rained like arrows through the smoke, but if there were any great blocks uphove they did not touch the ship. Meanwhile, the other parcels were exploding in their places sometimes two and three at a time, sending a sort of sickening spasms and throes through the fabric of the vessel, and you heard the most extraordinary grinding noises rising out of the ice all about, as though the mighty rupture of the powder crackled through leagues of the island. I durst not look forth till all the powder had burst, lest I should be struck by some flying piece of ice, but unless the schooner was injured below she was as sound as before, and in the exact same posture, as if afloat in harbour, only that of course her stern lay low with the slope of her bed.

I called to Tassard and he lifted his head.

"Are you hurt?" said I.

"No, no," he answered. "'Tis a Spaniard's trick to fling down to a broadside. Body of St. Joseph, what a furious explosion!" and so saying he crawled into the companion and squatted beside me. "What has it done for us?"

"I don't know yet," said I; "but I believe the schooner is uninjured. *That* was a powerful shock!" I cried, as a half-dozen of bags blew up together in the crevices deep down.

The thunder and tumult of the rending ice accompanied by the heavy explosions of the gunpowder so dulled the hearing that it was difficult to speak. That the mines had accomplished our end was not yet to be known; but there could not be the least doubt that they had not only occasioned tremendous ruptures low down in the ice, but that the volcanic influence was extending far beyond its first effects by making one split produce another, one weak part give way and create other weaknesses, and so on, all round about us and under our keel, as was clearly to be gathered by the shivering and spasms of the schooner, and by the growls, roars, blasts, and huddle of terrifying sounds which arose from the frozen floor.

It was twenty minutes after the hour at which the mines had been framed to explode when the last parcel burst; but we waited another quarter of an hour to make sure that it *was* the last, during all which time the growling and roaring noises deep down continued, as if there was a battle of a thousand lions raging in the vaults and hollows underneath. The smoke had been settled away by the wind, and the prospect was clear. We ran below to see to the fire and receive five minutes of heat into our chilled bodies, and then returned to view the scene.

I looked first over the starboard side and saw the great split that had happened in the night torn in places into immense yawns and gulfs by the fall of vast masses of rock out of its sides; but what most delighted me was the hollow sound of washing water. I lifted my hand and listened.

" 'Tis the swell of the sea flowing into the opening!" I exclaimed.

"That means," said Tassard, "that this side of the block is dislocated from the main."

"Yes," cried I. "And if the powder ahead of the bows has done its work, the heave of the ocean will do the rest."

We made our way on to the forecastle over a deep bed of splinters of ice, lying like wood-shavings upon the deck, and I took notice as I walked that every glorious crystal pendant that had before adorned the yards, rigging, and spars had been shaken off. I had expected to see a wonderful spectacle of havoc in the ice where the barrels of gunpowder had been poised, but saving many scores of cracks where none was before, and vast ragged gashes in the mouths of the crevices down which the barrels had been lowered, the scene was much as heretofore.

The Frenchman stared and exclaimed, "What has the powder done? I see only a few cracks."

145

"What it may have done, I don't know," I answered; "but depend on't such heavy charges of powder must have burst to some purpose. The dislocation will be below; and so much the better, for 'tis *there* the ice must come asunder if this block is to go free."

He gazed about him, and then rapping out a string of oaths, English, Italian, and French, for he swore in all the languages he spoke, which, he once told me, were five, he declared that for his part he considered the powder wasted, that we'd have done as well to fling a hand-grenade into a fissure, that a thousand barrels of powder would be but as a popgun for rending the schooner's bed from the main, and in short, with several insulting looks and a face black with rage and disappointment, gave me very plainly to know that I had not only played the fool myself, but had made a fool of him, and that he was heartily sorry he had ever given himself any trouble to contrive the cursed mines or to assist me in a ridiculous project that might have resulted in blowing the schooner to pieces and ourselves with it.

I glanced at him with a sneer, but took no further notice of his insolence. It was not only that he was so contemptible in all respects, a liar, a rogue, a thief, a poltroon, hoary in twenty walks of vice, there was something so unearthly about a creature that had been as good as dead for eight-and-forty years, that it was impossible anything he said could affect me as the rancorous tongue of another man would. I feared and hated him because I knew that in intent he was already my assassin; but the mere insolences of so incredible a creature could not but find me imperturbable.

And perhaps in the present instance my own disappointment put me into some small posture of sympathy with his passion. Had I been asked before the explosions happened what I expected, I don't know that I should have found any answer to make; and yet, though I could not have expressed my expectations, which after all were but hopes, I was bitterly vexed when I looked over the bows and found in the scene nothing that appeared answerable to the uncommon forces we had employed. Nevertheless, I felt sure that my remark to the Frenchman was sound. A great show of uphove rocks and fragments of ice might have satisfied the eye; but the real work of the mines was wanted below; and since the force of the mighty explosion must needs expend itself somewhere, it was absurd to wish to see its effects in a part where its volcanic agency would be of little or no use.

"There is nothing to be seen by staring!" exclaimed the Frenchman presently, speaking very sullenly. "I am hungry and freezing, and shall go below!" And with that he turned his back and made off, growling in his throat as he went.

I got upon the ice and stepped very carefully to the starboard side and looked down the vast split there. The sea in consequence of the slope did not come so far, but I could hear the wash of the water very plain. It was certain that the valley in which we lay was wholly disconnected from the main ice on this side. I passed to the larboard quarter, and here too were cracks wide and deep enough to satisfy me that its hold was weak. It was forward of the bows where the barrels had been exploded that the ice was thickest and had the firmest grasp; but its surface was violently and heavily cracked by the explosions, and I thought to myself if the fissures below are as numerous, then certainly the swell of the sea ought to fetch the whole mass away. But I was now half frozen myself and pining for warmth. It was after one o'clock. The wind was piping freshly, and the great heavy clouds in swarms drove stately across the sky.

"It may blow to-night," thought I; "and if the wind hangs as it is, just such a sea as may do our business will be set running." And thus musing I entered the ship and went below.

Chapter XXII.
A Change Comes Over the Frenchman

TASSARD was dogged and scowling. Such was his temper that had I been a small or weak man, or a person likely to prove submissive, he would have given a loose to his foul tongue and maybe handled me very roughly. But my demeanour was cold and resolved, and not of a kind to improve his courage. I levelled a deliberate semi-contemptuous gaze at his own fiery stare, and puzzled him, too, I believe, a good deal by my cool reserve. He muttered whilst we ate, drinking plentifully of wine, and garnishing his draughts with oaths and to spare; and then, after falling silent and remaining so for the space of twenty minutes, during which I lighted my pipe and sat with my feet close to the furnace, listening with eager ears to the sounds of the ice and the dull crying of the wind, he exclaimed sulkily, "Your scheme is a failure. The schooner is fixed. What's to be done now?"

"I don't know that my scheme is a failure," said I. "What did you suppose? that the blast would blow the ice with the schooner on it into the ocean clear of the island? If the ice is so shaken as to enable the swell to detach it, my scheme will have accomplished all I proposed."

"*If!*" he cried scornfully and passionately. "*If* will not deliver us nor save the treasure. I tell you the schooner is fixed—as fixed as the damned in everlasting fire. Be it so!" he cried, clenching his fist. "But you must meddle no more! The *Boca del Dragon* is mine—*mine*, d'ye see, now that they're all dead and gone but me"—smiting his bosom—"and if ever she is to float, let nature or the devil launch her: no more explosions with the risks your failure has made her and me run!"

His voice sank; he looked at me in silence, and then with a wild grin of anger he exclaimed, "What made you awake me? I was at peace—neither cold, hungry, nor hopeless! What demon forced you to bring me to this—to bring me back to *this*?"

"Mr. Tassard," said I coldly, "I don't ask your pardon for my experiment; I meant well, and to my mind it is no failure yet. But for disturbing your repose I do sincerely beg your forgiveness, and solemnly promise you, if you will return to the state in which I found you, that I will not repeat the offence."

He eyed me from top to toe in silence, filled and lighted his hideous pipe, and smoked with his back turned upon me.

Had there been another warm place in the schooner I should have retired to it, and left this surly and scandalous savage to the enjoyment of his own company. His temper rendered me extremely uneasy. The arms-room was full of weapons; he might draw a pistol upon me and shoot me dead before I should have time to clench my hand. Nor did I conceive him to have his right mind. His panic terrors and outbursts of rage were such extremes of behaviour as suggested some sort of organic decay within. He had been for eight-and-forty years insensible; in all that time the current of life had been frozen in him, not dried up and extinguished; therefore, taking his age to be fifty-five when the frost seized him, he would now be one hundred and three years old, having subsisted into this great span of time in fact, though confronting me with the aspect of an elderly man merely. Death ends time, but this man never had been dead, or surely it would not have been in the power of brandy and chafing and fire to arouse him; and though all the processes of nature had been checked in him for near half a century, yet he must have been throughout as much alive as a sleeping man, and consequently when he awoke he arose with the weight of a hundred and three years upon his brain, which may suffice to account for the preternatural peculiarities of his character.

After sitting a long while sullenly smoking in silence, he fetched his mattress and some covers, lay down upon it, and fell fast asleep. I admired and envied this display of confidence, and heartily wished myself as safe in his hands as he was in mine. The afternoon passed. I was on deck a half-dozen times, but never witnessed the least alteration in the ice. My spirits sank very low. There was bitter remorseless defiance in the white, fierce rigid stare of the ice, and I could not but believe with the Frenchman that all our labour and expenditure of powder was in vain. There was no more noticeable weight in the wind, but the sea was beginning to beat with some strength upon the coast, and the schooner sometimes trembled to the vibrations of the blows. There was also a continuous crackling noise coming up out of the ice, and just as I came on deck on my third visit, a block of ice, weighing I dare say a couple of hundred tons, fell from the broken shoulder on the starboard quarter, and plunged with a roar like a thunder-clap into the chasm that had opened in the night.

I sat before the furnace extremely dejected, whilst the Frenchman snored on his mattress. I could no longer flatter myself that the explosions had made the impression I had expected on the ice, and my mind was utterly at a loss. How to deliver myself from this horrible situation I could not imagine. As to the treasure, why, if the chests had all been filled with gold, they might have gone to the bottom there and then for me, so utterly insignificant did their value seem as against the pricelessness of liberty and the joy of deliverance. Had I been alone I should have had a stouter heart, I dare say, for then I should have been able to do as I pleased; but now I was associated with a bloody-minded rogue whose soul was in the treasure, and who was certain to oppose any plan I might propose for the construction of a boat or raft out of the material that formed the schooner. The sole ray of hope that gleamed upon me broke out of the belief that this island was going north, and that when we had come to the height of the summer in these seas, the wasting of the coast or the dislocation of the northern mass would release us.

Yet this was but poor comfort too; it threatened a terrible long spell of waiting, with perhaps disappointment in the end, and months of enforced association with a wretch with whom I should have to live in fear of my life.

When I was getting supper Tassard awoke, quitted his mattress, and came to his bench.

"Has anything happened whilst I slept?" said he.

"Nothing," I answered.

"The ice shows no signs of giving?"

"I see none," said I.

"Well," cried he, with a sarcastic sneer, "have you any more fine schemes?"

" 'Tis your turn now," I replied. "Try *your* hand. If you fail, I promise you I shall not be disappointed."

"But you English sailors," said he, wagging his head and regarding me with a great deal of wildness in his eye, "speak of yourselves as the finest seamen in the world. Justify the maritime reputation of your nation by showing me how we are to escape with the schooner from the ice."

"Mr. Tassard," said I, approaching him and looking him full in the face, "I would advise you to sweeten your temper and change your tone. I have borne myself very moderately towards you, submitted to your insults with patience, and have done you some kindness. I am not afraid of you. On the contrary, I look upon you as a swaggering bully and a hoary villain. Do you understand me? I am a desperate man in a desperate situation. But if I don't fear death, depend upon it, I don't fear *you*—and I take God to witness that if you do not use me with the civility I have a right to expect, I will kill you."

My temper had given way; I meant every word I spoke, and my air and sincerity rendered my speech very formidable. I approached him by another stride; he started up, as I thought, to seize me, but in reality to recoil, and this he did so effectually as to tumble over his bench, and down he fell, striking his bald head so hard that he lay for several minutes motionless.

I stood over him till he chose to sit erect, which he presently did, rubbing his poll and looking at me with an air of mingled bewilderment and fear.

"This is scurvy usage to give a shipmate in distress," said he. " 'Od's life, man! I had thought there was some sense of humour in you. Your hand, Mr. Rodney; I feel dazed."

I helped him to rise, and he then sat down in a somewhat rickety manner, rubbing his eyes. It might have been fancy, it might have been the illusion of the furnace light combined with the venerable appearance his long hair and naked pate gave him, but methought in those few minutes he had grown to look twenty years older.

"Never concern yourself about my humour, Mr. Tassard," said I, preserving my determined air and coming close to him again. "How is it to stand between us? I leave the choice to you. If you will treat me civilly you'll not find me wanting in every disposition to render our miserable state tolerable; but if you insult me, use me injuriously, and act the pirate over me, who am an honest man, by God, Mr. Tassard, I will kill you."

He stooped away from me, and raised his hand in a posture as if to fend me off, and cried in a whining manner, "I lost my head—this gunpowder business hath been a hellish disappointment, look you, Mr. Rodney. Come! We will drink a can to our future amity!"

I answered coldly that I wanted no more wine and bade him beware of me, that he had gone far enough, that our hideous condition had filled my soul with desperation and misery, and that I would not have my life on this frozen schooner made more abominable than it was by his swagger, lies, and insults, and I added in a loud voice and in a menacing manner that death had no terrors for me, and that I would dispatch him with as little fear as I should meet my doom, whatever shape it took.

I marched on deck, not a little astounded by the cowardice of the old rascal, and very well pleased with the marked impression my bearing and language had produced on him. Not that I supposed for a moment that my bold comportment would save me from his knife or his pistol when he should think proper to make away with me. No. All I reckoned upon was cowing him into a civiller posture of mind, and checking his aggressions and insolence. As to his murdering me, I was very sure he would not attempt such an act whilst we remained imprisoned. Loneliness would have more horrors for him than for me; and though my machinery of mines had apparently failed, he was shrewd enough, despite his rage of disappointment, to understand that more was to be done by two men than by one, and that between us something might be attempted which would be impracticable by a simple pair of hands, and particularly old hands, such as his.

I stayed but a minute or two on deck. Such was the cold that I do not know I had ever felt it more biting and bitter. The sound of foaming waters filled the wind, and the wind itself was blowing fairly strong, in gusts that screamed in the frozen rigging or in blasts that had the deep echo of the thunder-claps of the splitting ice. The clouds were numerous and dark with the shadow of the night; and the swiftness of their motion as they sailed up out of the south-west quarter was illustrated by the leaping of the few bright stars from one dusky edge to another.

I returned below and sat down. The Frenchman asked me no questions. He had his can in the oven and his death's head in his great hand, and puffed out clouds of smoke of the colour of his beard, and indeed in the candle and fire light looked like a figure of old Time with his long nose and bald head. I addressed one or two civil remarks to him, which he answered in a subdued manner, discovering no resentment whatever that I could trace in his eyes or the expression of his countenance; and being wishful to show that I bore no malice I talked of pirates and their usages, and asked him if the *Boca del Dragon* fought under the red or black flag.

"Why, the black flag, certainly," said he; "but if we met with resistance, it was our custom to haul it down and hoist the red flag, to let our opponents know we should give no quarter."

"Where is your flag locker?" said I.

"In my berth," he answered.

"I should like to see the black flag," I exclaimed: " 'tis the one piece of bunting, I believe, I have never viewed."

"I'll fetch it," said he, and taking the lanthorn went aft very quietly, but with a certain stagger in his walk, which I should have put down to the wine if it was not that his behaviour was free from all symptoms of inebriation. The change in him surprised me, but not so greatly as you might suppose; indeed, it excited my suspicions rather than my wonder. Fear worked in him unquestionably, but what I seemed to see best was some malignant design which he hoped to conceal by an air of conciliation and a quality of respectful *bonhomie*.

He came back with a flag in his hand, and we spread it between us; it was black, with a yellow skull grinning in the middle, over this an hourglass, and beneath a cross-bones.

"What consternation has this signal caused and does still cause!" said I, surveying it, whilst a hundred fancies of the barbarous scenes it had flown over, the miserable cries for mercy that had swept up past it to the ear of God, crowded into my mind. "I think, Mr. Tassard," said I, "that our first step, should we ever find ourselves afloat in this ship, must be to commit this and all other flags of a like kind on board to the deep. There is evidence in this piece of drapery to hang an angel."

He let fall his ends of the flag and sat down suddenly.

"Yes," he answered, sending a curious rolling glance around the cook-room and at the same time bringing his hand to the back of his head, "this is evidence to dangle even an honester man than you, sir. All flags but the ensign we resolve to sail under must go—all flags, and all the wearing apparel, and—and—but"—here he muttered a curse—"we are fixed—there is to be no sailing."

He shook his head and covered his eyes. His manner was strange, and the stranger for his quietude.

I said to him, "Are you ill?"

He looked up sharply and cried vehemently, "No, no!" then stretched his lips in a very ghastly grin and turned to take the can from the oven, but his hand missed it, and he appeared to grope as if he were blind, though he looked at the can all the time. Then he catched it and brought it to his mouth, but trembled so much that he spilt as much as he drank, and after putting the can back sat shaking his beard and stroking the wet off it, methought, in a very mechanical lunatic way.

I thought to myself, "Is this behaviour some stratagem of his? What device can such a bearing hide? If he is acting, he plays his part well."

I rolled the black flag into a bundle and flung it into a corner, and, resuming my seat and my pipe, continued, more for civility's sake than because of any particular interest I took in the subject, to ask him questions about the customs and habits of pirates.

"I believe," said I, "the buccaneers are so resolute in having clear ships that they have neither beds nor seats on board."

"The English," he answered, speaking slowly and letting his pipe droop whilst he spoke with his eyes fixed on deck, "not the Spanish. 'Tis the custom of most English pirates to eat and sleep upon the decks for the sake of a clear ship, as you say. The Spaniard loves comfort—you may observe his fancy in this ship."

"How is the plunder partitioned?" I asked.

"Everything is put into the common chest, as we call it, and brought to the mast and sold by auction—Strange!" he cried, breaking off and putting his hand to his brow. "I find my speech difficult. Do you notice I halt and utter thickly?"

I replied, No; his voice seemed to be the same as hitherto.

"Yet I feel ill. Holy Mother of God, what is this feeling coming upon me? O Jesus, how faint and dark!"

He half rose from his bench, but sat again, trembling as if the palsy had seized him, and I noticed his head dotted with beads of sweat. He had drunk so much wine and spirits throughout the day that a dram would have been of no use to him.

I said, "I expect it will be the blow on the back of your head, when you fell just now, that has produced this feeling of giddiness. Let me help you to lie down" (for his mattress was on deck); "the sensation will pass, I don't doubt."

If he heard he did not heed me, but fell a-muttering and crying to himself. And now I did certainly remark a quality in his voice that was new to my ear; it was not, as he had said, a labour or thickness of utterance, but a dryness and parchedness of old age, with many breaks from high to low notes, and a lean noise of dribbling threading every word. He sweated and talked and muttered, but this was from sheer terror; he did not swoon, but sat with a stoop, often pressing his brows and gazing about him like one whose senses are all abroad.

"Gracious Mother of all angels!" he exclaimed, crossing himself several times, but with a feeble, most agitated hand, and speaking in French and English, and sometimes interjecting an invocation in Italian or Spanish, though I give you what he said in my own tongue; "surely I am dying. O Lord, how frightful to die! O holy Virgin, be merciful to me. I shall go to hell—O Jesu, I am past forgiveness—for the love of heaven, Mr. Rodney, some brandy! Oh that some saint would interpose for me! Only a few years longer—grant me a few years longer—I beseech for time that I may repent!" and he extended one quivering hand for the brandy (of which a draught stood melted in the oven) and made the sign of the cross upon his breast with the other, whilst he continued to whine out in his cracked pipes the wildest appeals for mercy, saying a vast deal that I durst not venture to set down, so plentiful and awful were his clamours for time that he might repent, though he never lapsed into blasphemy, but on the contrary discovered an agony of religious horror.

I was much astonished and puzzled by this illness that had come upon him, for, though he talked of darkness and faintness and of dying, he continued to sit up on his bench and to take pulls at the can of brandy I had handed to him. It might be, indeed, that a sudden faintness had terrified him nearly out of his senses with a prospect of approaching death; but that would not account for the peculiar note and appearance of age that had entered his figure, face, and voice. Then an extraordinary fancy occurred to me: Had the whole weight of the unhappy wretch's years suddenly descended upon him? Or, if not wholly arrived, might not these indications in him mark the first stages of a gradually increasing pressure? The heat, the vivacity, the fierceness, spirits, and temper of the life I had been instrumental in restoring to him probably illustrated his character as it was eight-and-forty years since; that had flourished artificially from the moment of his awakening down to the present hour; but now the hand of Time was upon this man, whose age was above an hundred. He might be decaying and wasting, even as he sat there, into such an intellectual condition and physical aspect as he would possess and submit had he come without a break into his present age.

I was fascinated by the mystery of his vitality, and breathlessly watched him as if I expected to witness some harlequin change in his face and mark the transformation of his polished brow into the lean austerity of wrinkles. His voice sank into a mere whisper at last, and then, ceasing to speak altogether, he dropped his chin on to his bosom and began to sway from side to side, catching himself from falling with several paralytic starts, but without lifting his head or opening his eyes that I could see, and manifesting every symptom of extreme drowsiness.

I got up and laid my hand on his shoulder, on which he turned his face and viewed me with one eye closed, the other scarce open.

"How are you feeling now?" said I.

"Sleepy, very sleepy," he answered.

"I'll put your mattress into your hammock," said I, "and the best thing you can do is to go and turn in properly and get a long night's rest, and to-morrow morning you'll feel yourself as hearty as ever."

He mumbled some answer which I interpreted to signify "Very well!" so I shouldered his mattress and slung a lanthorn in his cabin, and then returned to help him to bed. He sat reeling on the bench, his chin on his breast, catching himself up as before with little sharp terrified recoveries, and I was forced to put my hand on him again to make him understand I had come back. He then made as if to rise, but trembled so violently that he sank down again with a groan, and I was obliged to put my whole strength to the lifting of him to get him on to his legs. He leaned heavily upon me, breathing hard, stooping very much and trembling. When we got to his cabin I perceived that he would never be able to climb into his hammock, nor had I the power to hoist a man of his bulk so high. To end the perplexity I cut the hammock down and laid it on the deck, and covering him with a heap of clothes, unslung the lanthorn, wished him good-night, closed the door, and returned to the furnace.

Chapter XXIII.
The Ice Breaks Away

IT was not yet eight o'clock. I was restless in my mind, under a great surprise, and was not sleepy. I filled a pipe, made me a little pannikin of punch, and sat down before the fire to think. If ever I had suspected the accuracy of my conjecture that the Frenchman's sudden astonishing indisposition was the effect of his extreme age coming upon him and breaking down the artificial vitality with which he had bristled into life under my hands, I must have found fifty signs to set my misgivings at rest in his drowsiness, nodding, bowed form, weakness, his tottering and trembling, and other features of his latest behaviour. If I was right, then I had reason to be thankful to Almighty God for this unparalleled and most happy dispensation, for now I should have nothing to fear from the old rogue's vindictiveness and horrid greed. Supposing him to be no more than a hundred, the infirmities of five score years would stand between him and me, and protect me as effectually as his death. I had nothing to dread from a man who could scarce stand, whose palsied hand could scarce clasp a knife, whose evil tongue could scarce articulate the terrors of his soul or the horrors of his recollection.

The wonder of it all was so great it filled me with admiration and astonishment. Had he been dead and come to life again, as Lazarus, or one of those bodies which arose during the time our Lord hung upon the cross, then, questionless, he must have picked up the chain of his life at the link which death had broken, and continued his natural walk into age and decay (though interrupted by a thousand years of the sepulchre) as if his life had been without this black hiatus, and he was proceeding steadily and humanly from the cradle. But collecting that the vital spark could never have been extinguished in him, I understood that time, which has absolute control over life, still knew him as its prey during all those forty-eight years in which he had lain frozen; that it had seized him now and suddenly, and pinned upon his back the full burden of his lustres. This I say, I believed; but the morrow, of course, would give me further proof.

Well, 'twas a happy and gracious deliverance for me. He could do me no hurt; the scythe had sheared his talons, and all without occasioning my conscience the least uneasiness whatever: whereas, but for this interposition, I did truly and solemnly believe that it must have come to my having had to slay him that I might preserve my own life.

Thus I sat for an hour smoking and wetting my lips with the punch, whilst the fire burned low, so exulting in the thought of my escape from the treacherous villain I had recovered from the grave, and in the feeling that I might now be able to go to rest, to move here and there, to act as I pleased without being haunted and terrified by the shadow of his foul intent, that I hardly gave my mind for a moment to the situation of the schooner nor to the barren consequences of my fine scheme of mines.

The wind blew strong. I could hear the humming of it in every fibre of the vessel. The bed on which she rested trembled to the blows of the seas upon the rocks. From time to time, in the midst of my musing, I started to the sharp claps of parted ice. Still feeling sleepless, I threw a few coals on the fire, and catching sight of the pirate flag opened it on the deck as wide as the space would permit, and sat down to contemplate the hideous insignia embroidered on it. My mind filled with a hundred fancies as my gaze went from the skull on the black field to the death's-head pipe that had fallen from the grasp of Tassard and lay on the deck, and I was sitting lost in a deep dreamlike contemplation, when I was startled and shocked into instantaneous activity by a blast of noise, louder than any thunder-clap that ever I heard, ringing and booming through the schooner. This was followed by a second and then a third, at intervals during which you might have counted ten, and I became sensible of a strange sickening motion, which lasted about twenty or thirty moments, such as might be experienced by one swiftly descending in a balloon, or in falling from a height whilst pent up in a coach.

For a little while the schooner heeled over so violently that the benches and all things movable in the cook-room slided as far as they could go, and I heard a great clatter and commotion among the freight in the hold. She then came upright again, and simultaneously with this a vast mass of water tumbled on to the deck and washed over my head, and then fell another and then another, all in such a way as to make me know that the ice had broken and slipped the schooner close to the ocean, where she lay exposed to its surges, but not free of the ice, for she did not toss or roll.

I seized the lanthorn and sprang to the cabin, where I hung it up, and mounted the companion-steps. But as I put my hand to the door to thrust it open a sea broke over the side and filled the decks, bubbling and thundering past the companion-hatch in such a way as to advise me that I need but open the door to drown the cabin. I waited, my heart beating very hard, mad to see what had happened, but not daring to trust myself on deck lest I should be immediately swept into the sea. 'Twas the most terrible time I had yet lived through in this experience. To every blow of the billows the schooner trembled fearfully; the crackling noises of the ice was as though I was in the thick of a heavy action. The full weight of the wind seemed to be upon the ship, and the screeching of it in the iron-like shrouds pierced to my ear through the hissing and tearing sounds of the water washing along the decks, and the volcanic notes of the surges breaking over the vessel. I say, to hear all this and not to be able to see, to be ignorant of the situation of the schooner, not to know from one second to another whether she would not be crushed up and crumbled into staves, or be hurled off her bed and be pounded to fragments upon the ice-rocks by the seas, or be dashed by the cannonading of the surge into the water and turned bottom up, made this time out and away more terrible than the collision between the *Laughing Mary* and the iceberg.

I drew my breath with difficulty, and stood upon the companion-ladder hearkening with straining ears, my hand upon the door. I was now sensible of a long-drawn, stately, solemn kind of heaving motion in the schooner, which I put down to the rolling of the ice on which she rested; and this convinced me that the mass in whose hollow she had been fixed had broken away and was afloat and riding upon the swell that under-ran the billows. But I was far too much alarmed to feel any of those transports in which I must have indulged had this issue to my scheme happened in daylight and in smooth water. I was terrified by the apprehensions which had occurred to me even whilst I was at work on the mines; I mean, that if the bed broke away the schooner would make it top-heavy and that it would capsize; and thus I stood in a very agony of expectancy, caged like a rat, and as helpless as the dead.

Half an hour must have passed, during which time the decks were incessantly swept by the seas, insomuch that I never once durst open the door even to look out. But nothing having happened to increase my consternation in this half-hour, though the movement in the schooner was that of a very ponderous and majestical rolling and heaving, showing her bed to be afloat, I began to find my spirits and to listen and wait with some buddings of hope and confidence. At the expiration of this time the seas began to fall less heavily and regularly on to the deck, and presently I could only hear them breaking forward, but without a quarter their former weight, and nothing worse came aft than large brisk showers of spray.

I armed myself with additional clothing for the encounter of the wet, cold, and wind, and then pushed open the door and stepped forth. The sky was dark with rolling clouds, but the ice put its own light into the air, and I could see as plain as if the first of the dawn had broken. It was as I had supposed: the mass of the valley in which the schooner had been sepulchred for eight-and-forty years had come away from the main, and lay floating within a cable's length of the coast. A stranger, wonderfuller picture human eye never beheld. The island shore ran a rampart of faintness along the darkness to where it died out in liquid dusk to right and left. The schooner sat upon a bed of ice that showed a surface of about half an acre; her stern was close to the sea, and about six feet above it. On her larboard quarter the slope or shoulder of the acclivity had been broken by the rupture, and you looked over the side into the clear sea beyond the limit of the ice there; but abreast of the foreshrouds the ice rose in a kind of wall, a great splinter it looked of what was before a small broad-browed hill, and the wind or the sea having caused the body on which the schooner lay to veer, this wall stood as a shield betwixt the vessel and the surges, and was now receiving those blows which had heretofore struck her starboard side amidships and filled her decks.

Oh for a wizard's inkhorn, that I might make you see the picture as I view it now, even with the eye of memory! The posture of the little berg pointed the schooner's head seawards, about west; the ice-terraces of the island lay with the wild strange gleam of their own snow radiance upon them upon the larboard quarter; around the schooner was the whiteness of her frozen seat, and her outline was an inky, exquisitely defined configuration upon it; above the crystal wall on the larboard bow rose the spume of the breaking surge in pallid bodies, glancing for an instant, and sometimes shaking a thunder into the ship when a portion of the seething water was flung by the wind upon the forecastle deck; at moments a larger sea than usual overran the ice on the larboard beam and quarter, and boiled up round about the buttocks of the schooner. To leeward the smooth backs of the billows rolled away in jet, but the fitful throbbings and feeble flashings of froth commingled with the dim shine of the ice were over all, tincturing the darkness with a spectral sheen, giving to everything a quality of unearthliness that was sharpened yet by the sounds of the wind in the gloom on high and the hissing and foaming of waters sending their leagues-distant voices to the ear upon the wings of the icy blast.

The wind, as I have said, blew from the south-west, but the trend of the island-coast was north-east and as the mass of ice I was upon in parting from the main had floated to a cable's length from the cliffs, there was not much danger, whilst the wind and sea held, of the berg (if I may so term it) being thrown upon the island. That the ice under the schooner was moving, and if so, at what rate, it was too dark to enable me to know by observing the marks on the coast. There was to be no sleep for me that night, and knowing this, I stepped below and built up a good fire, and then went with the lanthorn to see how Tassard did and to give him the news; but he was in so deep a sleep, that after pulling him a little without awakening him I let him lie, nothing but the sound of his breathing persuading me that he had not lapsed into his old frozen state again.

Of all long nights this was the longest I ever passed through. I did truly believe that the day was never to break again over the ocean. I must have gone from the fire to the deck thirty or forty times. The schooner continued upright. I had no fear of her oversetting; she sat very low, and the ice also showed but a small head above the water, and as the body of it lay pretty flat, then, even supposing its submerged bulk was small, there was little chance of its capsizing. I also noticed that we were setting seawards—that is to say, to the westward—by a noticeable shrinking of the pallid coast. But I never could stay long enough above to observe with any kind of narrowness, the wind being full of the wet that was flung over the ice-wall and the cold unendurable.

All night I kept the fire going, and on several occasions visited the Frenchman, but found him motionless in sleep. I kept too good a look-out to apprehend any sudden calamity short of capsizal, which I no longer feared, and during the watches of that long night I dreamt a hundred waking dreams of my deliverance, of my share of the treasure, of my arriving in England, quitting the sea for ever, and setting up as a great squire, marrying a nobleman's daughter, driving in a fine coach, and ending with a seat in Parliament and a stout well-sounding handle to my name.

At last the day broke; I went on deck and found the dawn brightening into morning. The wind had fallen and with it the sea; but there still ran a middling strong surge, and the breeze was such as, in sailors' language, you would have shown your top-gallant sails to. I could now take measure of our situation, and was not a little astonished and delighted to observe the island to be at least a mile distant from us, and the north-east end lying very plain, the ocean showing beyond it, though in the south-west the ice died out upon the sea-line. That we had been set away from the main by some current was very certain. There was a westerly tendency in all the bergs which broke from the island, the small ones moving more quickly than the large, for the sea in the north and west was dotted with at least fifty of these white masses, great and little. On the other hand, the wind and seas were answerable for the progress we had made to the north.

The wall of ice (as I call it) that had stood over against the larboard bow was gone, and the seas tumbled with some heaviness of froth and much noise over the ice, past the bows, and washed past the bends on either side in froth rising as high as the channels. I noticed a great quantity of broken ice sinking and rising in the dark green curls of the billows, and big blocks would be hurled on to the schooner's bed and then be swept off, sometimes fetching the bilge such a thump as seemed to swing a bellow through her frame. It was only at intervals, however, that water fell upon the decks, for the ice broke the beat of the moderating surge and forced it to expend its weight in spume, which there was not strength of wind enough to raise and heave. Since the vessel continued to lie head to sea, my passionate hope was that these repeated washings of the waves would in time loosen the ice about her keel, in which case it would not need much of a billow, smiting her full bows fair, to slide her clean down and off her bed and so launch her. There were many clouds in the heavens, but the blue was very pure between. The morning brightening with the rising of the sun, I directed an earnest gaze along the horizon, but there was nothing to see but ice. Some of the bergs, however, and more particularly the distant ones, stole out of the blue atmosphere to the sunshine with so complete a resemblance to the lifting canvas of ships that I would catch myself staring fixedly, my heart beating fast. But there was no dejection in these disappointments; the ecstasy that filled me on beholding the terrible island, the hideous frozen prison whose crystal bars I had again and again believed were never to be broken, now lying at a distance with its northern cape imperceptibly opening to our subtle movement, was so violent that I could not have found my voice for the tears in my heart.

This, then, was the result of my scheme; it was no failure, as Tassard had said; as he owed his life to me, so now did he owe me his liberty. Nay, my transports were so great that I would not suffer myself to feel an instant's anxiety touching the condition of the schooner—I mean whether she would leak or prove sound when she floated—and how we two men were to manage to navigate so large a craft, that was still as much spellbound aloft in her frozen canvas and tackle as ever she had been in the sepulchre in which I discovered her.

I went below, and put the provisions we needed for breakfast into the oven, and entered Tassard's cabin. On bringing the lanthorn to his face as he lay under half a score of coats upon the deck, I perceived that he was awake, and, my heart being full, I cried out cheerily, "Good news! good news! the gunpowder did its work! The ice is ruptured and we are afloat, Mr. Tassard, afloat—and progressing north!"

He looked at me vacantly, and giving his head a shake exclaimed, "How can I crawl from this mound? My strength is gone."

If I was amazed that the joyful intelligence I had delivered produced no other response than this querulous inquiry, I was far more astonished by the sound of his voice. It was the most cracked and venerable pipe that ever tickled the throat of old age, a mingling of wailing falsettos and of hollow gasping growls, the whole very weak. I threw the clothes off him, and said, "Do you wish to rise? I will bring your breakfast here if you wish."

He looked at me, but made no answer. I bawled again, and observed (by the dim lanthorn light) that he watched my lips with an air of attention; and whilst I waited for his reply he said, "I don't hear you."

Anxious to ascertain to what extent his hearing was impaired, I kneeled on the deck, and putting my lips to his ear said, not very loud, "Will you come to the cook-house?" which he did not hear; and then louder, "Will you come to the cook-house?" which he did not hear either. I believed him stone-deaf till, on roaring with all the power of my lungs, he answered "Yes."

I took him by the hands and hauled him gently on to his feet, and had to continue holding him or he must have fallen. Time was beginning with him when he had gone to bed, and the remorseless old soldier had completely finished his work whilst his victim slept. I viewed the Frenchman whilst I grasped his hands, and there stood before me a shrunk, tottering, deaf, bowed, feeble old man. What was yesterday a polished head was now a shrivelled pate, as though the very skull had shrunk and left the skin to ripple into wrinkles and sit loose and puckered. His hands trembled excessively. But his lower jaw was held in its place by his teeth, and this perpetuated in the aged dwindled countenance something of the likeness of the fierce and sinister visage that had confronted me yesterday. I was thunder-struck by the alteration, and stood overwhelmed with awe, confusion, and alarm. Then, re-collecting my spirits, I supported the miserable relic to the fire, putting his bench to the dresser that he might have a back to lean against.

He could scarce feed himself—indeed, he could hardly hold his chin off his breast. He had gone to bed a man, as I might take it, of fifty-six, and during the night the angel of Time had visited him, and there he sat, *a hundred and three years of age*!

He looked it. Ha, thought I, I was dreading your treachery yesterday; there is nothing more to fear. Besides that he was nearly stone deaf, he could hardly see; and I was sure, if he should be able to move at all, he could not stir a leg without the help of sticks. I was going to roar out to him that we were adrift, but he looked so imbecile that I thought, to what purpose? If there be aught of memory in him, let him sit and chew the cud thereof. He cannot last long; the cold must soon stop his heart. And with that I went on eating my breakfast in silence, but greatly affected by this astonishing mark of the hand of Providence, and under a very heavy and constant sense of awe, for the like of such a transformation I am sure had never before encountered mortal eyes, and it was terrifying to be alone with it.

Chapter XXIV.
The Frenchman Dies

HOWEVER, if I expected my Frenchman to sit very long silent, he soon undeceived me by beginning to complain in his tremulous aged voice of his weakness and aching limbs.

" 'Tis the terrible cold that has affected me," said he, whilst his head nodded nervously. "I feel the rheumatism in every bone. There is no weakness like the rheumatic, I have heard, and 'tis true, 'tis true. It may lay me along—yes, by the Virgin, 'tis rheumatism—what else?" Here he was interrupted by a long fit of coughing, and when it was ended he turned to address me again, but looked at the bulkhead on my right, as if his vision could not fix me. "But my capers are not over!" he cried, setting up his rickety shrill throat; "no, no! Vive l'amour! vive la joie! The sun is coming—the sun is the fountain of life—ay, mon brave, there are some shakes in these stout legs yet!" He shook his head with a fine air of cunning and knowingness, grinning very oddly; and then, falling grave with a startling suddenness, he began to dribble out a piratical love-story he had once before favoured me with, describing the charms of the woman with a horrid leer, his head nodding with the nervous affection of age all the time, whilst he looked blindly in my direction—a hideous and yet pitiful object!

I could not say that his mind was gone, but he talked with many breaks for breath, and not very coherently, as though the office of his tongue was performed by habit rather than memory, so that he often went far astray and babbled into sentences that had no reference to what had gone before, though on the whole I managed to collect what he meant. I was sure he had not power enough of vision to observe me in the dim reddish light of the cook-room, and this being so, he could not know I was present, more particularly as he could not hear me, yet he persisted in his poor babble, which was a behaviour in him that, more than even the matter of his speech, persuaded me of his imbecility.

He made no reference to our situation, and in solemn truth I believe his memory retained no more than a few odds and ends of the evil story of his life, like bits of tarnished lace and a rusty button or two lying in the bottom of a dark chest that has long been emptied of the clothes it once held.

But my condition made such heavy demands upon my thoughts that I had very much less attention to give to this surprising phenomenon of senility than its uncommon merits deserved. It has puzzled every member of the faculty that I have mentioned it to, the supposition being that, given the case of suspended animation, there is no waste, and the person would quit his stupor with the same powers and aspect as he possessed when he entered it, though it lasted a thousand years. But granting there is no waste, Time is always present waiting to settle accounts when the sleeper lifts his head. There may be an artificial interval, during which the victim might show as my pirate did, but the poised load of years is severed on a sudden by the scythe and becomes superincumbent, and with the weight comes the transformation; and this theory, as the only eye-witness of the marvellous thing, I will hold and maintain whilst I have breath in my body to support it.

I left him gabbling to himself, sometimes grinning as if greatly diverted, sometimes lifting a trembling hand to help his ghostly recital by an equally ghostly dumb-show, and went on deck, satisfied that he was too weak to get to the fire and meddle with it, but sufficiently invigorated by his long night's rest to sit up without tumbling off the bench.

This time I carried with me an old perspective glass I had noticed in the chest in my cabin—the chest in which were the nautical instruments, charts, and papers—and levelled it along the coast of the island, but it was a poor glass, and I found I could manage nearly as well with the naked eye. There was no change of any kind, only that there was a sensible diminution in the blowing of the wind and a corresponding decrease in the height of the seas. The ice stretched in a considerable bed on either hand the ship and ahead of her; the water frothed freely over it, and there was a great jangling and flashing of broken pieces, but the hull was no longer heavily hit by them.

I got into the main chains to view the body of the vessel, and noticed with satisfaction that the constant pouring of the sea had thinned down the frozen snow to the depth of at least a foot. This encouraged me to hope that the restless tides would sap to her keel at least, and put her into a posture to be easily launched by the blow of a surge upon her bows— that is if fortune continued to keep her head on. But by this time, my transports having moderated, I was grown fully sensible of the extreme peril of our position. Should the sea rise and the ice bring her broadside to it, it was inevitable, it seemed to me, that she must go to pieces. Or if the ice on which she floated, fouled some other berg it might cost us all our spars. Then again occurred the dismal question, Suppose she should launch herself, would she float? For eight-and-forty years she had been high and dry; never a caulker's hammer had rung upon her in all that time. Tassard had spoken of her as a stout ship, and so she was, I did not doubt; but the old rogue talked as if she had been stranded six months only! I had no other hope than that the intense cold had treated her timbers as it had treated the bodies of her people, an expectation not unreasonable when I considered the state of her stores and the manifest substantiality of her inward fabric.

I regained the deck and stepped over to the pumps. There were two of them, but built up in snow. My business was to save my life if I could, and the schooner too, for the sake of the great treasure in her. Nothing must disconcert me I said to myself—I must spare no labour, but act a hearty sailor's part and ask for God's countenance. So I trotted below, and selecting some weapons from the arms-room, such as a tomahawk, a spade-headed spear, a pike and a chopper, I returned to the pumps and fell upon them with a will. The ice flew about me, but I continued to smite, the exercise making me hot and renewing my spirits, and in an hour—but it took me an hour—I had chopped, hacked, and beaten one of the pumps pretty clear of its thick crystal coat. They were what is called brake-pumps—that is to say, pumps which are worked by handles. The ice, of course, held them immovable, but they looked to be perfectly sound, in good working order, though there would be neither chance nor need to test them until the schooner went afloat.

I cleared the other one and was well satisfied with my morning's work. But I did bitterly lament the lack of a little crew. Even the Frenchman as he was yesterday would have served my turn, for between us we might have made shift to clamber aloft, and with hatchets break the sails free of their ice bonds, and so expose canvas enough to hold the wind, which could not have failed to impart a swifter motion to the berg. But with my single pair of hands I could only look up idly at the yards and gaffs standing hard as granite. Still, even such surface as the spars and rigging offered to the breeze helped our progress. We were but a very little berg, nay, not a berg, but rather a sheet of ice lying indifferently flat upon the sea, and, as I believe, without much depth. Our spars and gear were as if the ice itself were rigged as a ship, and then there was the height of the hull besides to offer to the breeze a tolerable resistance for its offices of propulsion. In this way I explain our progress; but whatever the cause, certain it was that our bed of ice was fairly under weigh, and at noon the island of ice bore at least half a league distant from us, and we had opened the sea broadly past its northern cape.

I have often diverted myself with wondering what sort of impression the posture of our schooner would have made on the minds of sailors sighting us from their deck. We looked to be floating out of water, and mariners who regard the devil as a conjuror must have accepted us as one of his pet inventions.

The many icebergs which encumbered the sea filled me with anxiety. We were travelling faster than they, and it seemed impossible that we could miss striking one or another of them. Yet perilous as they were, I could not but admire their beautiful appearance as they floated upon the dark blue of the running waters, flashing out very gloriously to the sun with a sparkling of tints upon their whiteness as if fires of twenty different colours had been kindled upon their craggy steeps, and then fading into a sulky watchet to the dull violet shadowing of the passing clouds. I particularly marked a very brilliant scene on the opening of five or six of them to the sunshine. They lay in such wise that the shadow of the cloud covered them all as with a veil, the skirts of which, trailing, left them to leap one after the other into the noontide dazzle; and as each one shot from the shadow the flash was like a volcanic spouting of white flame enriched with the prismatic dyes of emeralds, rubies, sapphires, and gems of lovely hue.

To determine the hour and our position I fetched a quadrant from my cabin, and was happily just in time to catch the sun crossing the meridian. My watch was half an hour fast, so I had been out of my reckoning to the extent of thirty minutes ever since I had been cast away. I made our latitude to be sixty-four degrees twenty-eight minutes south, and the computation was perhaps near enough.

This business ended, I went to the cook-house to prepare dinner, and the first object I saw was Tassard flat upon his face near the door that opened into the cabin. He groaned when I picked him up, which I managed without much exertion of strength, for so much had he shrunk that I dare say more than half his weight lay in his clothes; and set him upon his bench with his back to the dresser. I put my mouth to his ear and roared, "Are you hurt?" His head nodded as if he understood me, but I question if he did. He was the completest picture of old age that you could imagine. I fetched a couple of spears from the arms-room, and, cutting them to his height, put one in each hand that he might keep himself propped; and whilst my own dinner was broiling I made him a mess of broth with which I fed him, for now that he had the sticks he would not let go of them. But in any case I doubt if his trembling hand could have lifted the spoon to his lips without capsizing the contents down his beard.

With some small idea of rallying the old villain, I mixed him a very stiff bumper of brandy, which he supped down out of my hand with the utmost avidity. The draught soon worked in him, and he began to move his head about, seeking me in his blind way, and then cried in his broken notes, "I have lost the use of my legs and cannot walk. Mother of God, what shall I do! O holy St. Antonio, what is to become of me?"

I guessed from this that, impelled by habit or some small spur of reason, he had risen to go on deck and fallen. He went on vapouring pitifully, gazing with sufficient steadfastness to let me understand that his vision received something of my outline, though he would fix his eyes either to left or right of me, as though he was not able to see if he looked straight; and this and his mournful cackle and his nodding head, bowed form, propped hands, and diminished face made him as distressful and melancholy a picture of Time as ever mortal man viewed. He broke off in his rambling to ask for more brandy, taking it for granted that I was still in the cook-room, for I never spoke, and I filled a can for him and as before held it to his mouth, which he opened wide, a piece of behaviour which went to show that some of his wits still hung loose upon him. This was a strong dose, and co-operating with the other, soon seized hold on his head, and presently he began to laugh to himself and talk, and even broke into a stave or two—some French song which he delivered in a voice like the squeaking of a rat alternating with the growling of a terrier.

I guess his stumbling upon this old French catch (which I took it to be from seeing him feebly flourish one of his sticks as if inviting a chorus) put him upon speaking his own tongue altogether, for though he continued to chatter with all the volubility his breath would permit during the whole time I sat eating, not one word of English did he speak, and not one word therefore did I understand. Seeing how it must be with him presently, I brought his mattress and rugs from his cabin, and had scarce laid them down when he let fall one of his sticks and drooped over. I grasped him, and partly lifting, partly hauling, got him on his back and covered him up. In a few minutes he was asleep.

I trust I shall not be deemed inhuman if I confess that I heartily wished his end would come. If he went on living he promised to be an intolerable burden to me, being quite helpless. Besides, he was much too old for this world, in which a man who reaches the age of ninety is pointed to as a sort of wonder.

As there was nothing to be done on deck, I filled my pipe and made myself comfortable before the furnace, and was speedily sunk in meditation. I reviewed all the circumstances of my case and considered my chances, and the nimble heels of imagination carrying me home with this schooner, I asked myself, suppose I should have the good fortune to convey the treasure in safety to England, how was I to secure it? Let me imagine myself arrived in the Thames. The whole world stares at the strange antique craft sailing up the river; she would be boarded and rummaged by the customs people, who of course would light upon the treasure. What then? I knew nothing of the law; but I reckoned, since I should have to tell the truth, that the money, ore, and jewellery would be claimed as stolen property, and I dismissed with a small reward for bringing it home. There was folly in such contemplation at such a time, when perhaps at this hour to-morrow the chests might be at the bottom of the sea, and myself a drowned sailor floating three hundred fathoms deep. But man is a froward child, who builds mansions out of dreams, and, jockeyed by hope, sets out at a gallop along the visionary road to his desires; and my mind was so much taken up with considering how I should manage when I brought the treasure home, that I spent a couple of hours in a conflict of schemes, during which time it never once occurred to me to reflect that I was a good way from home still, and that much must happen before I need give myself the least concern as to the securing of the treasure.

Nothing worth recording happened that day. The wind slackened, and the ice travelled so slow that at sundown I could not discover that we had made more than a quarter of a mile of progress to the north since noon, though we had settled by half as much again that distance westwards. Whilst I was below I could hear the ice crackling pretty briskly round about the ship, which gave me some comfort; but I could never see any change of consequence when I looked over the side or bows, only that at about four o'clock, whilst I was taking a view from the forecastle, a large block broke away from beyond the starboard bow with the report of a swivel gun.

I had not closed my eyes on the previous night, and was tired out when the evening arrived, and, as no good could come of my keeping a watch, for the simple reason that it was not in my power to avert anything that might happen, I tumbled some further covering over the Frenchman, who had lain on the deck all the afternoon, sometimes dozing, sometimes waking and talking to himself, and appearing on the whole very easy and comfortable, and went to my cabin.

I slept sound the whole night through, and on waking went on deck before going to the cook-house and lighting the furnace (as was my custom), so impatient was I to observe our state and to hear such news as the ocean had for me. It was a very curious day, somewhat darksome, and a dead calm, with a large long swell out of the south-east. The sky was full of clouds, with a stooping appearance in the hang of them that reminded you of the belly of a hammock; they were of a sallow brown, very uncommon; some of them round about sipped the sea-line, and their shadows, obliterating those parts of the cincture which they overhung, broke the continuity of the horizon as though there were valleys in the ocean there. A good part of our bed of ice was gone, at least a fourth of it; but the schooner still lay as strongly fixed as before. I had come to the deck half expecting to find her afloat from the regular manner of her heaving, and was bitterly disappointed to discover her rooted as strongly as ever in the ice, though the irritation softened when I noticed how the bed had diminished. The mass with the ship upon it rose and sank with the sluggish squatting motion of a water-logged vessel. It was an odd sensation to my legs after their long rest from such exercise. The heaving satisfied me that the base of the bed did not go deep, but at the same time it was all too solid for me, I could not doubt, for had the sheet been as thin as I had hoped it, it must have given under the weight of the schooner and released her.

The island lay a league distant on the larboard beam, and looked a wondrous vast field of ice going into the south, and it stared very ghastly upon the dark green sea out of the clouds whose gloom sank behind it. I could not observe that we had drifted anything to the north, whilst our set to the westwards had been steady though snail-like. The sea in the north and north-west swarmed with bergs, like great snowdrops on the green undulating fields of the deep. Now and again the swell, in which fragments of ice floated with the gleam of crystal in liquid glass, would be too quick for our dull rise and overflow the bed, brimming to the channels with much noise of foam and pouring waters, but the interposition of the ice took half its weight out of it, and it never did more than send a tremble through the vessel.

What to make of the weather I knew not. Certainly, of all the caprices of this huge cold sea, its calms are the shortest lived, but this knowledge helped me to no other. The clouds did not stir. In the north-east a beam of sunshine stood like a golden waterspout, its foot in a little flood of glory. It stayed all the while I was on deck, showing that the clouds had scarce any motion, and made the picture of the sea that way beyond nature to my sight, by the contrast of the defined shaft of gold, burning purely, with the dusk of the clouds all about, and of the pool of dazzle at its foot with the ugly green of the water that melted into it.

I went below and got about lighting the fire. The Frenchman lay very quiet, under as many clothes as would fill a half-dozen of sacks. It was bitterly cold, sharper in the cook-house than I had ever remembered it, and I could not conceive why this should be, until I recollected that I had forgotten to close the companion-hatch before going to bed. I prepared some broth for my companion, and dressed some ham for myself, and ate my breakfast, supposing he would meanwhile awake. But after sitting some time and observing that he did not stir, a suspicion flashed into my mind; I kneeled down, and clearing his face, listened. He did not breathe. I brought the lanthorn to him, but his countenance had been so changed by his unparalleled emergence from a state of middle life into extreme old age, he was so puckered, hollowed, gaunt, his features so distorted by the great weight of his years that I was not to know him dead by merely viewing him. I threw the clothes off him, listened at his mouth breathlessly, felt his hands, which were ice-cold. Dead indeed! thought I. Great Father, 'tis Thy will! And I rose very slowly and stood surveying the silent figure with an emotion that owed its inspiration partly to the several miracles of vitality I had beheld in him during our association, and to a bitter feeling of loneliness that swelled up in me.

Yes! I had feared and detested this man, but his quick transformation and silent dark exit affected me, and I looked down upon him sadly. Yet, to be perfectly candid with you, I recollect that, though it occurred to me to test if life was out of him by bringing him close to the fire and chafing him and giving him brandy, I would not stir. No, I would not have moved a finger to recover him, even though I should have been able to do so by merely putting him to the furnace. He was dead, and there was an end; and without further ado I carried him into the forecastle and threw a hammock over him, and left him to lie there till there should come clear water to the ship to serve him for a grave.

Chapter XXV.
The Schooner Frees Herself

ALL day long the weather remained sullen and still, and the swell powerful. I was on deck at noon, looking at an iceberg half a league distant when it overset. It was a small berg, though large compared with most of the others; yet such a mighty volume of foam boiled up as gave me a startling idea of the prodigious weight of the mass. The sight made me very anxious about my own state, and to satisfy my mind I got upon the ice and walked round the vessel, and to get a true view of her posture went to the extreme end of the rocks beyond her bows, and finally came to the conclusion that, supposing the ice should crumble away from her sides so as to cause the weight of the schooner to render it top-heavy, her buoyancy on touching the water would certainly tear her keel out of its frosty setting and leave her floating. Indeed, so sure was I of this that I saw, next to the ice splitting and freeing her in that way, the best thing that could happen would be its capsizal.

I regained the ship, and had paused an instant to look over the side, when I perceived the very block of ice on which I had come to a halt break from the bed with a smart clap of noise, and completely roll over. Only a minute before had I been standing on it, and thus had sixty seconds stood between me and death, for most certainly must I have been drowned or killed by being beaten against the ice by the swell! I fell upon my knees and lifted up my hands in gratitude to God, feeling extraordinarily comforted by this further mark of His care of me, and very strongly persuaded that He designed I should come off with my life after all, since His providence would not work so many miracles for my preservation if I was to perish by this adventure.

These thoughts did more for my spirits than I can well express; and the intolerable sense of loneliness was mitigated by the knowledge that I was watched, and therefore not alone.

The day passed I know not how. The shadow as of tempest hung in the air, but never a cats-paw did I see to blurr the rolling mirror of the ocean. The hidden sun sank out of the breathless sky, tingeing the atmosphere with a faint hectic, which quickly yielded to the deepest shade of blackness. The mysterious desperate silence, however, that on deck weighed oppressively on every sense, as something false, menacing, and malignant in these seas, was qualified below by the peculiar straining noises in the schooner's hold caused by the swinging of the ice upon the swell. I was very uneasy; I dreaded a gale. It was impossible but that the vessel must quickly go to pieces in a heavy sea upon the ice if she did not liberate herself. But though this excited a depression melancholy enough, nothing else that I can recollect contributed to it. When I reviewed the apprehension the Frenchman had raised, and reflected how unsupportable a burden he must have become, I was very well satisfied to be alone. Time had fortified me; I had passed through experiences so surprising, encountered wonders so preternatural, that superstition lay asleep in my soul, and I found nothing to occasion in me the least uneasiness in thinking of the lifeless shrivelled figure of what was just now a fierce, cowardly, untamed villain, lying in the forecastle.

I made a good supper, built up a large fire, and mixed myself a hearty bowl of punch, not with the view of drowning my anxieties—God forbid! I was too grateful for the past, too expectant of the future, to be capable of so brutish a folly—but that I might keep myself in a cheerful posture of mind; and being sick of my own company took the lanthorn to the cabin lately used by the Frenchman, and found in a chest there, among sundry articles of attire, a little parcel of books, some in Dutch and Portuguese, and one in English.

It was a little old volume, the author's name not given, and proved to be a relation of the writer's being taken by pirates, and the many dangers he underwent. There was nothing in it, to be sure, that answered to my own case, yet it interested me mightily as an honest unvarnished narrative of sea perils; and I see myself now in fancy reading it, the lanthorn hanging by a lanyard close beside my head, the book in one hand, my pipe in the other, the furnace roaring pleasantly, my feet close to it, and the atmosphere of the oven fragrant with the punch that I put there to prevent it from freezing. I had come to a certain page and was reading this passage: "*Soon after we were on board we all went into the great cabin, where we found nothing but destruction. Two scrutores I had there were broke to pieces, and all the fine goods and necessaries in them were all gone. Moreover, two large chests that had books in them were empty, and I was afterwards informed they had been all thrown overboard; for one of the pirates on opening them swore there was jaw-work enough (as he called it) to serve a nation, and proposed that they might be cast into the sea, for he feared there might be some books amongst them that might breed mischief enough, and prevent some of their comrades from going on in their voyage to hell, whither they were all bound*"—I say, I was reading this passage, not a little affected by the impiety of the rascal, for whose portrait my dead Frenchman might very well have sat, when I was terrified by an extraordinary loud explosion, that burst so near and rang with such a prodigious clear note of thunder through the schooner that I vow to God I believed the gunpowder below had blown up. And in this suspicion I honestly supposed myself right for a moment, for on running into the cabin I was dazzled by a crimson flame that clothed the whole interior with a wondrous gush of fire; but this being instantly followed by such another clap as the former, I understood a thunderstorm had broken over the schooner.

It was exactly overhead, and that accounted for the violence of the crashes, which were indeed so extreme that they sounded rather like the splitting of enormous bodies of ice close to, than the flight of electric bolts. The hatch lay open; I ran on deck, but scarce had passed my head through the companion when down came a storm of hail, every stone as big as a pigeon's egg, and in all my time I never heard a more hellish clamour. There was not a breath of air. The hail fell in straight lines, which the fierce near lightning flashed up into the appearance of giant harp strings, on which the black hand of the night was playing those heavy notes of thunder. I sat in the shelter of the companion, very anxious and alarmed, for there was powder enough in the hold to blow the ship into atoms; and the lightning played so continuously and piercingly that it was like a hundred darts of fire, violet, crimson, and sun-coloured, in the grasp of spirits who thrust at the sea, all over its face, with swift movement of the arms, as though searching for the schooner to spear her.

The hailstorm ceased as suddenly as it had burst. I stepped on to the deck, and 'twas like treading on shingle. There was not the least motion in the air, and the stagnation gave an almost supernatural character to the thunder and lightning. The ocean was lighted up to its furthest visible confines by the flames in the sky, and the repeated explosions of thunder exceeded the roaring of the ordnance of a dozen squadrons in hot fight. The ice-coast in the east, and the two score bergs in the north and west leapt out of one hue into another; and were my days in this world to exceed those of old Abraham, I should to my last breath remember the solemn and terrible magnificence of that picture of lightning-coloured ice, the sulphur-tinctured shapes of the swollen bodies of clouds bringing their dark electric mines together in a huddle, the answering flash of the face of the deep to the lancing of each spiral dazzling bolt, with the air as still as the atmosphere of a cathedral for the thunder to roll its echoes through.

There was a second furious shower of hail, and when that was over I looked forth, and observed that the storm was settling into the north-east, whence I concluded that what draught there might be up there sat in the south-west. Nor was I mistaken; for half an hour after the first of the outburst, by which time the lightning played weak and at long intervals low down, and the thunder had ceased, I felt a crawling of air coming out of the south-west, which presently briskened into a small steady blowing. But not for long. It freshened yet and yet; the wrinkles crisped into whiteness on the black heavings; they grew into small surges with sharp cubbish snarlings preludious of the lion's voice; and by ten o'clock it was blowing in strong squalls, the seas rising, and the clouds sailing swiftly in smoke-coloured rags under the stars.

The posture of the ice inclined the schooner's starboard bow to the billows; and in a very short time she was trembling in every bone to the blows of the surges which rolled boiling over the ice there and struck her, flinging dim clouds of spume in the air, which soon set the scuppers gushing. My case was that of a stranded ship, with this difference only, that a vessel ashore lies solid to the beating of the waves, whereas the ice was buoyant, it rose and fell, sluggishly it is true, and so somewhat mitigated the severity of the shocks of water. But, spite of this, I was perfectly sure that unless the bed broke under her or she slipped off it, she would be in pieces before the morning. It was not in any hull put together by human hands to resist the pounding of those seas. The weight of the mighty ocean along whose breast they raced was in them, and though the wind was no more than a brisk gale, each billow by its stature showed itself the child of a giantess. The ice-bed was like a whirlpool with the leap and flash and play of the froth upon it. The black air of the night was whitened by the storms of foam-flakes which flew over the vessel. The roaring of the broken waters increased the horrors of the scene. I firmly believed my time was come. God had been merciful, but I was to die now. As to making any shift to keep myself alive after the ship should be broken up, the thought never entered my head. What could I do? There was no boat. I might have contrived some arrangement of booms and casks to serve as a raft, but to what purpose? How long would it take the wind and sea to freeze me?

I crouched in the companion-way hearkening to the uproar around, feeling the convulsions of the schooner, fully prepared for death, dogged and hopeless. No, I was not afraid. Suffering and expectation had brought me to that pass that I did not care. " 'Tis such an end as hundreds and thousands of sailors have met," I remember thinking; "it is the fittest exit for a mariner. I have sinned in my time, but the Almighty God knows my heart." To this tune ran my thoughts. I held my arms tightly folded upon my breast, and with set lips waited for the first of those crashing and rending sounds which would betoken the ruin and destruction of the schooner.

So passed half an hour; then, being half perished with the cold, I went to the furnace, for when the vessel went to pieces it would matter little in what part of her I was, and warmed myself and took a dram as a felon swallows a draught on his way to the scaffold. Were I to attempt to describe the character of the thunderous noises in the ship I should not be believed. The seas raised a most deafening roaring as they boiled over the ice and rolled their volumes against the vessel's sides. Every curl swung a load of broken frozen pieces against the bows and bends, and the shocks resounded through her like blows from cyclopean hammers. It was as if I had been seated in the central stagnant heart of a small revolving hurricane, feeling no faintest sigh of air upon my cheek, whilst close around whirled the hellish tormenting conflict of white waters and yelling blasts.

On a sudden—in a breath—I felt the vessel rise. She was swung up with the giddy velocity of a hunter clearing a tall gate; she sank again, and there was a mighty concussion forward, then a pause of steadiness whilst you might have counted five, then a wild upward heave, a sort of sharp floating fall, a harsh grating along her keel and sides, as though she was being smartly warped over rocks, followed by an unmistakable free pitching and rolling motion.

I had sprung to my feet and stood waiting. But the instant I gathered by the movements of her that she was released I sprang like a madman up the companion-steps. The sea, breaking on her bow, flew in heavy showers along the deck and half blinded me. But I was semi-delirious, and having sat so long with Death's hand in mine was in a passionately defiant mood, with a perfect rage of scorn of peril in me, and I walked right on to the forecastle, giving the flying sheets of water there no heed. In a minute a block of sea tumbled upon me and left me breathless; the iciness of it cooled my mind's heat, but not my resolution. I was determined to judge as best I could by the light of the foam of what had happened, and holding on tenaciously to whatever came to my hand and progressing step by step I got to the forecastle and looked ahead.

Where the ice was the water tumbled in milk; 'twas four or five ship's lengths distant, and I could distinguish no more than that. I peered over the lee bow, but could see no ice. The vessel had gone clear; how, I knew not and can never know, but my own fancy is that she split the bed with her own weight when the sea rose and threw the ice up, for she had floated on a sudden, and the noises which attended her release indicated that she had been forced through a channel.

I returned aft, barely escaping a second deluge, and looked over the quarter; no ice was there visible to me. The vessel rolled horribly, and I perceived that she had a decided list to starboard, the result of the shifting of what was in her when the ice came away from the main with her, and it was this heel that brought the sea washing over the bow. I took hold of the tiller to try it, but either the helm was frozen immovable or the rudder was jammed in its gudgeons or in some other fashion fixed.

Had she been damaged below? was she taking in water? I knew her to be so thickly sheathed with ice that, unless it had been scaled off in places by the breaking of her bed, I had little fear (until this covering melted or dropped off by the working of the frame) of the hull not proving tight. I should have been coated with ice myself had I stayed but a little longer in my wet clothes in that piercing wind, so I ran below, and bringing an armful of clothes from my cabin to the cook-room, was very soon in dry attire, and making an extraordinary figure, I don't question, in the buttons, lace, and fripperies of the old-fashioned garments.

The incident of the schooner's release from the ice had come upon me so suddenly, and at a time too when my mind was terribly disordered, that I scarce realized the full meaning of it until I had shifted myself and fortified my heart with a dram and got warm in the glow of the furnace. By this time she had fallen into the trough and was labouring like a cask; that she would prove a heavy roller in a sea-way a single glance at her fat buttocks and swelling bilge might have persuaded me, but I never could have dreamt she would wallow so monstrously. The oscillation was rendered more formidable by her list, and there were moments when I could not keep my feet. She was shipping water very freely over her starboard rail, but this did not much concern me, for the break of the poop-deck kept the after part of the vessel indifferently dry, and the forecastle and main hatches were well secured. But there was one great peril I knew not how to provide against—I mean the flotilla of icebergs in the north and west. They lay in a long chain upon the sea, and though to be sure there was no doubt a wide channel between each, through which it might have been easy to carry a ship under control, yet there was every probability of a vessel in the defenceless condition of the schooner, without a stitch of sail on her and under no other government of helm than a fixed rudder, being swept against one of those frozen floating hills when indeed it would be good-night to her and to me too, for after such a catastrophe the sun would never rise for me or her again.

Meanwhile I was crazy to ascertain if the schooner was taking in water. If there was a sounding-rod in the ship I did not know where to lay my hands upon it. But he is a poor sailor who is slow at substitutes. There were several spears in the arms-room (piratical plunder, no doubt) with mere spikes for heads, like those weapons used by the Caffres and other tribes in that country; they were formed of a hard heavy wood. I took a length of ratline line and secured it to one of these spears, and carried it on deck with the powder-room bull's-eye lamp; but when I probed the sounding-pipe I found it full of ice, and as it was impossible to draw the pumps, I flung my ingenious sounding-rod down in a passion of grief and mortification.

Yet was I not to be beaten. Such was my temper, had the devil himself confronted me, I should have defied him to do his worst, for I had made up my mind to weather him out. I entered the forecastle, lanthorn in hand, prized open the hatch and dropped into the hold. It needed an experienced ear to detect the sobbing of internal waters amid the yearning gushes, the long gurgling washings, the thunderous blows, and shrewd rain-like hissings of the seas outside. I listened with strained hearing for some minutes, but distinguished no sounds to alarm me with assurance of water in the hold. I could not mistake. I hearkened with all my might, but the noise was outside. I thanked God very heartily, and got out of the hold and put the hatch on. There was no need to go aft and listen. The schooner was by the head, and there could be no water in the run that would not be forward too.

Being reassured in respect of the staunchness of the hull, I returned to the fire and proceeded to equip myself for a prolonged watch on deck. Whilst I was drawing on a great pair of boots I heard a knocking in the after part of the vessel. I supposed she had drifted into a little field of broken ice, and that she would go clear presently, and I finished arming myself for the weather; but the knocking continuing, I went into the cabin where I heard it very plain, and walked as far as the lazarette hatch, where I stood listening. The noises were a kind of irregular thumping accompanied by a peculiar grinding sound. In a moment I guessed the truth, rushed on deck, and by the dim light in the air saw the long tiller mowing to and fro! The beat of the beam seas had unlocked the frozen bonds of the rudder, and there swung the tiller, as though like a dog the ship was wagging her tail for joy!

The vessel lay along, rolling so as to bring her starboard rail to a level with the sea; her main deck was full of water, and the froth of it combined with the ice that glazed her made her look like a fabric of marble as she swung on the black fold ere it broke into snow about her. I seized the tiller and ran it over hard a-starboard, and I had not held it in that posture half a minute when to my inexpressible delight I observed that she was paying off. Her head fell slowly from the sea; she lurched drunkenly, and some tons of black water rolled over the bulwarks; she reeled consumedly to larboard, and rose squarely and ponderously to the height of the surge that was now abaft the beam. In a few moments she was dead before it, the helm amidships, the wind blowing sheer over the stern with half its weight seemingly gone through the vessel running, the tall seas chasing her high stern and floating it upwards, till looking forward was like gazing down the slope of a hill.

My heart was never fuller than then. I was half crazy with the passion of joy that possessed me. Consider the alternations of hope and bitter despair which had been crowded into that night! We may wonder in times of security that life should be sweet, and admit the justice of the arguments which several sorts of writers, and the poets even more than the parsons, use in defence of death. But when it comes to the pinch human nature breaks through. When the old man in Aesop calls upon Death to relieve him, and the skeleton suddenly rises, the old man changes his mind, and thinks he will go on trying for himself a little longer. I liked to live, and had no mind for a wet shroud, and this getting the schooner before the wind, along with the old familiar feeling of the decks reeling and soaring and sinking under my feet, was so cordial an assurance of life that, I tell you, my heart was full to breaking with transport.

However, I was still in a situation that made prodigious demands upon my coolness and wits. The wind was south-west, the schooner was running north-east; the bulk of the icebergs lay on the larboard bow, but there were others right ahead, and to starboard, where also lay the extremity of the island, though I did not fear *that* if I could escape the rest. It was a dark night; methinks there should have been a young moon curled somewhere among the stars, but she was not to be seen. The clouds flew dark and hurriedly, and the frosty orbs between were too few to throw a light. The ocean ahead and around was the duskier for the spectral illumination of the near foam and the glimmer of the ice-coated ship. I tested the vessel with the tiller and found she responded but dully; she would be nimbler under canvas no doubt, but it was enough that she should answer her helm at all. Oh, I say, I was mighty thankful, most humbly grateful. My heart was never more honest to its Maker than then.

She crushed along, pitching pitifully, the dark seas on either hand foaming to her quarters, and her rigging querulous with the wind. Had the Frenchman been alive to steer the ship, I might have found strength enough for my hands in the vigour of my spirit to get the spritsail yard square and chop its canvas loose—nay, I might have achieved more than that even; but I could not quit the tiller now. I reckoned our speed at about four miles an hour, as fast as a hearty man could walk. The high stern, narrow as it was, helped us; it was like a mizzen in its way; and all aloft being stout to start with and greatly thickened yet by ice, the surface up there gave plenty for the gale to catch hold on; and so we drove along.

I could just make out the dim pallid loom of the coast of ice upon the starboard beam, and a blob or two of faintness—most elusive and not to be fixed by the eye staring straight at them—on the larboard bow. But it was not long before these blobs, as I term them, grew plainer, and half a score swam into the dusk over the bowsprit end, and resembled dull small visionary openings in the dark sky there, or like stars magnified and dimmed into the merest spectral light by mist. I passed the first at a distance of a quarter of a mile; it slided by phantasmally, and another stole out right ahead. This I could have gone widely clear of by a little shift of the helm, but whilst I was in the act of starboarding three or four bergs suddenly showed on the larboard bow, and I saw that unless I had a mind to bring the ship into the trough again I must keep straight on. So I steered to bring the berg that was right ahead a little on the bow, with a prayer in my soul that there might be no low-lying block in the road for the schooner to split upon. It went by within a pistol-shot. I was very much accustomed to the sight of ice by this time, yet I found myself glancing at this mass with pretty near as much wonder and awe as if I had never seen such a thing before. It was not above thirty feet high, but its shape was exactly that of a horse's head, the lips sipping the sea, the ears cocked, the neck arching to the water. You would have said it was some vast courser rising out of the deep. The peculiar radiance of ice trembled off it like a luminous mist into the dusk. The water boiled about its nose, and suggested a frothing caused by the monster steed's expelled breath. Let a fire have been kindled to glow red where you looked for the eye, and the illusion would have been frightfully grand.

The poet speaks of the spirits of the vasty deep; if you want to know what exquisite artists they are, enter the frozen silences of the south.

Thus threading my way I drove before the seas and wind, striking a piece of ice but once only, and that a small lump which hit the vessel on the bow and went scraping past, doing the fabric no hurt; but often forced to slide perilously close by the bergs. I needed twenty instead of one pair of eyes. With ice already on either bow, on a sudden it would glimmer out right ahead, and I had to form my resolution on the instant. If ever you have been amid a pack of icebergs on a dark night in a high sea you will understand my case; if not, the pen of a Fielding or a Defoe could not put it before you. For what magic has ink to express the roaring of swollen waters bursting into tall pale clouds against the motionless crystal heights, the mystery of the configuration of the faintness under the swarming shadows of the flying night, the sudden glares of breaking liquid peaks, the palpitating darkness beyond, the plunging and rolling of the ship, making her rigging ring upon the air with the reeling of her masts, the gradual absorption of the solid mass of dim lustre by the gloom astern, the swift spectral dawn of such another light over the bows, with many phantasmal outlines slipping by on either hand, like a procession of giant ocean-spectres, travelling white and secretly towards the silent dominions of the Pole?

Half this ice came from the island, the rest of it was formed of bergs too tall to have ever belonged to the north end of that great stretch. It took three hours to pass clear of them, and then I had to go on clinging to the tiller and steering in a most melancholy famished condition for another long half-hour before I could satisfy myself that the sea was free.

But now I was nearly dead with the cold. I had stood for five hours at the helm, during all which time my mind had been wound up to the fiercest tension of anxiety, and my eyes felt as if they were strained out of their sockets by their searching of the gloom ahead, and nature having done her best gave out suddenly, and not to have saved my life could I have stood at the tiller for another ten minutes.

The gear along the rail was so iron-hard that I could not secure the helm with it, so I softened some lashings by holding them before the fire, and finding the schooner on my return to be coming round to starboard, I helped her by putting the tiller hard a port and securing it. I then went below, built up the fire, lighted my pipe, and sat down for warmth and rest.

Chapter XXVI.
I am Troubled by Thoughts of the Treasure

THE weight of the wind in the rigging steadied the schooner somewhat, and prevented her from rolling too heavily to starboard, whilst her list corrected her larboard rolls. So as I sat below she seemed to me to be making tolerably good weather of it. Not much water came aboard; now and again I would hear the clatter of a fall forwards, but at comfortably long intervals.

I sat against the dresser with my back upon it, and being dead tired must have dropped asleep on a sudden—indeed, before I had half smoked my pipe out, and I do not believe I gave a thought to my situation before I slumbered, so wearied was I. The cold awoke me. The fire was out and so was the candle in the lanthorn, and I was in coffin darkness. This the tinder-box speedily remedied. I looked at my watch—seven o'clock, as I was a sinner! so that my sleep had lasted between three and four hours.

I went on deck and found the night still black upon the sea, the wind the same brisk gale that was blowing when I quitted the helm, the sea no heavier, and the schooner tumbling in true Dutch fashion upon it. I looked very earnestly around but could see no signs of ice. There would be daylight presently, so I went below, lighted the fire, and got my breakfast, and when I returned the sun was up and the sea visible to its furthest reaches.

It was a fine wintry piece; the sea green and running in ridges with frothing heads, the sky very pale among the dark snow-laden clouds, the sun darting a ray now and again, which was swung into the north by the shadows of the clouds until they extinguished it. Remote in the north-west hung the gleam of an iceberg; there was nothing else in sight. Yes—something that comforted me exceedingly, though it was not very many days ago that a like object had heavily scared me—an albatross, a noble bird, sailing on the windward close enough to be shot. The sight of this living thing was inexpressibly cheering; it put into my head a fancy of ships being at hand, thoughts of help and of human companions. In truth, my imagination was willing to accept it as the same bird that I had frightened away when in the boat, now returned to silently reproach me for my treatment of it. Nay, my lonely eye, my subdued and suffering heart might even have witnessed the good angel of my life in that solitary shape of ocean beauty, and have deemed that, though unseen, it had been with me throughout, and was now made visible to my gaze by the light of hope that had broken into the darkness of my adventure.

Well, supposing it so, I should not have been the only man who ever scared his good angel away and found it faithful afterwards.

I unlashed the tiller and got the schooner before the wind and steered until a little before noon, letting her drive dead before the sea, which carried her north-east. Then securing the helm amidships I ran for the quadrant, and whilst waiting for the sun to show himself I observed that the vessel held herself very steadily before the wind, which might have been owing to her high stern and the great swell of her sides and her round bottom; but be the cause what it might, she ran as fairly with her helm amidships as if I had been at the tiller to check her, a most fortunate condition of my navigation, for it privileged me to get about other work, whilst, at the same time, every hour was conveying me nearer to the track of ships and further from the bitter regions of the south.

I got an observation and made out that the vessel had driven about fifteen leagues during the night. She must do better than that, thought I; and when I had eaten some dinner I took a chopper, and, going on to the forecastle, lay out upon the bowsprit, and after beating the spritsail-yard block clear of the ice, cut away the gaskets that confined the sail to the yard, heartily beating the canvas, that was like iron, till a clew of it fell. I then came in and braced the yard square, and the wind, presently catching the exposed part of the sail, blew more of it out, and yet more, until there was a good surface showing; then to a sudden hard blast of wind the whole sail flew open with a mighty crackling, as though indeed it was formed of ice; but to render it useful I had to haul the sheets aft, which I could not manage without the help of the tackles we had used in slinging the powder over the side; so that, what with one hindrance and another, the setting of that sail took me an hour and a half.

But had it occupied me all day it would have been worth doing. Trifling as it was as a cloth, its effect upon the schooner was like that of a cordial upon a fainting man. It was not that she sensibly showed nimbler heels to it; its lifting tendency enabled her to ride the under-running seas more buoyantly, and if it increased her speed by half a knot an hour it was worth a million to me, whose business it was to take the utmost possible advantage of the southerly gale.

I returned to the helm, warm with the exercise, and gazed forward not a little proud of my work. Though the sail was eight-and-forty years old and perhaps older, it offered as tough and stout a surface to the wind as if it was fresh from the sailmaker's hands, so great are the preserving qualities of ice. I looked wistfully at the topsail, but on reflecting that if it should come on to blow hard enough to compel me to heave the brig to she would never hull with that canvas abroad, I resolved to let it lie, for

I could cut away the spritsail if the necessity arose and not greatly regret its loss; but to lose the topsail would be a serious matter, though if I did not cut it adrift it might carry away the mast for me; so, as I say, I would not meddle with it.

Finding that the ship continued to steer herself very well, and the better for the spritsail, I thought I would get the body of the old Frenchman overboard and so obtain a clear hold for myself so far as corpses went. I carried the lanthorn into the forecastle, but when I pulled the hammock off him I confess it was not without a stupid fear that I should find him alive. Recollection of his astounding vitality found something imperishable in that ugly anatomy, and though he lay before me as dead and cold as stone, I yet had a fancy that the seeds of life were still in him, that 'twas only the current of his being that had frozen, that if I were to thaw him afresh he might recover, and that if I buried him I should actually be despatching him.

But though these fancies possessed, they did not control me. I took his watch and whatever else he had in that way, carried him on deck and dropped him over the side, using as little ceremony as he had employed in the disposal of his shipmates, but affected by very different emotions; for there was not only the idea that the vital spark was still in him; I could not but handle with awe the most mysterious corpse the eye had ever viewed, one who had lived through a stupor or death-sleep, for eight-and-forty years, in whom in a few hours Time had compressed the wizardry he stretches in others over half a century; who in a night had shrunk from the aspect of his prime into the lean, puckered, bleared-eyed, deaf, and tottering expression of a hundred years.

But now he was gone! The bubbles which rose to the plunge of his body were his epitaph; had they risen blood-red they would have better symbolized his life. The albatross stooped to the spot where he had vanished with a hoarse salt scream like the laugh of a delirious woman, and the wind, freshening momentarily in a squall, made one think of the spirit of Nature as eager to purify the air of heaven from the taint of the dead pirate's passage from the bulwarks to the water's surface.

All that day and through the night that followed the schooner drove, rolling and plunging before the seas, into the north-east, to the pulling of the spritsail. I made several excursions into the fore-hold, but never could hear the sound of water in the vessel. Her sides in places were still sheathed in ice, but this crystal armour was gradually dropping off her to the working of her frame in the seas, so that, since she was proving herself tight, it was certain her staunchness owed nothing to the glassy plating. I had seen some strange craft in my day; but nothing to beat the appearance this old tub of a hooker submitted to my gaze as I viewed her from the helm. How so uncouth a structure, with her tall stern, flairing bows, fat buttocks, sloping masts, forecastle-well, and massive head-timbers ever managed to pursue and overhaul a chase was only to be unriddled by supposing all that she took to be more unwieldy and clumsy than herself. What would a pirate of these days, in his clean-lined polacca or arrowy schooner, have thought of such an instrument as this for the practice of his pretty trade? The ice aloft still held for her spars and rigging the resemblance of glass, and to every sunbeam that flashed upon her from between the sweeping clouds she would sparkle out into many-coloured twinklings, marvellously delicate in colour, and changing their tints twenty times over in a breath through the swiftness of the reeling of the spars.

I should but fatigue you to follow the several little stories of these hours one by one; how I got my food, snatched at sleep, stood at the helm, gazed around the sea-line and the like. Just before sundown I saw a large iceberg in the north, two leagues distant; no others were in sight, but one was enough to make me uneasy, and I spent a very troubled night, repeatedly coming on deck to look about me. The schooner steered herself as if a man stood at the helm. The spritsail further helped her in this, for, if the curl of a sea under her forefoot brought her to larboard or starboard, the sail forced her back again. Still, it was a very surprising happy quality in her, the next best thing to my having a shipmate, and a wonderful relief to me who must otherwise have brought her to, under a lashed helm, every time I had occasion to leave the deck.

The seaworthiness of the craft, coupled with the reasonable assurance of presently falling in with a ship, rendered me so far easy in my mind as to enable me to think very frequently of the treasure and how I was to secure it. If I fell in with an enemy's cruiser or a privateer I must expect to be stripped. This would be the fortune of war, and I must take my chance. My concern did not lie that way; how was I to protect this property, that was justly mine, against my own countrymen, suppose I had the good fortune to carry the schooner safely into English waters? I had a brother-in-law, Jeremiah Mason, Esq., a Turkey merchant in a small way of business, whose office was in the City of London, and, if I could manage to convey the treasure secretly to him, he would, I knew, find me a handsome account in his settlement of this affair. But it was impossible to strike out a plan. I must wait and attend the course of events. Yet riches being things which fever the coldest imaginations, I could not look ahead without excitement and irritability of fancy, I should reckon it a hard fate indeed after my cruel experiences, my freeing the vessel from the ice, my sailing her through some thousand of miles of perilous seas, and arriving finally in safety, to be dispossessed of what was strictly mine—as much mine as if I had fished it up from the bottom of the sea, where it must otherwise have lain till the crack of doom.

I remember that, among other ideas, it entered my head to tell the master of the first ship I met, if she were British, the whole story of my adventure, to acquaint him with the treasure, to offer to tranship it and myself to his vessel and abandon the schooner, and to propose a handsome reward for his offices. But I could not bring my mind to trust any stranger with so great a secret. The mere circumstance of the treasure not being mine, in the sense of my having earned it, of its being piratical plunder, and as much one's as another's, might dull the edge even of a fair-dealing conscience and expose me to the machinations of a heavily tempted mind.

Therefore, though I had no plan, I was resolved at all hazards to stick to the schooner, and, with a view to providing against the curiosity or rummaging of any persons who should come aboard I fell to the following work after getting my breakfast. I hung lanthorns in the run and hatchways and cabin to enable me to pass easily to and fro; I then emptied one of the chests in my cabin and carried it to where the treasure was. The chest I filled nearly three-parts full with money, jewellery, &c., which sank the contents of the other chests to the depth I wanted. I then fetched a quantity of small arms, such as pistols and hangers and cutlasses, and filled up the chests with them, first placing a thickness of canvas over the money and jewellery, that no glitter might show through. To improve the deception I brought another chest to the run, and wholly filled it with cutlasses, powder-horns, pistols, and the like, and so fixed it that it must be the first to come to hand. My cunning amounted to this: that, suppose the run to be rummaged, the contents of the first chest were sure to be turned out, but, on the other chests being opened, and what they appeared to contain observed, it was as likely as not that the rummagers would be satisfied they were arms-chests, and quit meddling with them.

Herenow might I indulge in a string of reflections on the troubles and anxieties which money brings, quote from Juvenal and other poets, and hold myself up to your merriment by a contemptuous exhibition of myself, a lonely sailor, labouring to conceal his gold from imaginary knaves, toiling in the dark depth of the vessel, and never heeding that, even whilst he so worked, his ship might split upon some half-tide rock of ice, and founder with him and his treasure too, and so on, and so on. But the fact is I was not a fool. Here was money enough to set me up as a fine gentleman for life, and I meant to save it and keep it too, if I could. A man on his deathbed, a man in such peril that his end is certain, can afford to be sentimental. He is going where money is dross indeed, and he is in a posture when to moralize upon human greed and the vanity of wishes and riches becomes him. But would not a man whose health is hearty, and who hopes to save his life, be worse off than a sheep in the matter of brains not to keep a firm grip of Fortune's hand when she extended it? I know I was very well pleased with my morning's work when I had accomplished it, and had no mind to qualify my satisfaction by melancholy and romantic musings on my condition and the uncertainty of the future. This was possibly owing to the fineness of the weather; a heavy black gale from the north would doubtless have given a very different turn to my humours.

The wind at dawn had weakened and come into the west. There was a strong swell—indeed there always is in this ocean—but the seas ran small. The sky looked like marble, with its broad spreadings of high white clouds and the veins of blue sky between. I wished to make all the northing that was possible, but there was nothing to be done in that way with the spritsail alone. Had not the capstan been frozen I should have tried to get the mainsail upon the ship, but without the aid of machinery I was helpless. So, with helm amidships, the schooner drove languidly along with her head due east, lifting as ponderously as a line-of-battle ship to the floating launches of the high swell, and the albatross hung as steadfastly in the wake of my lonely ocean path as though it had been some messenger sent by God to watch me into safety.

Chapter XXVII.
I Encounter a Whaler

I HAD been six days and nights at sea, and the morning of the seventh day had come. With the exception of one day of strong south-westerly winds, which ran me something to the northwards, the weather had been fine, bitterly cold indeed, but bright and clear. In this time I had run a distance of about six hundred and fifty miles to the east, and with no other cloths upon the schooner than her spritsail.

I confess, as the hours passed away and nothing hove into view, I grew dispirited and restless; but, on the other hand, I was comforted by the bright weather and the favourable winds, and particularly by the vessel's steering herself, which enabled me to get rest, to keep myself warm with the fire, and to dress my food, yet ever pushing onwards (however slowly) into the navigated regions of this sea.

On the morning of the seventh day I came on deck, having slept since four o'clock. The wind was icy keen, pretty brisk, about west by south; the movement in the sea was from the south, and rolled very grandly; there was a fog that way, too, that hid the horizon, bringing the ocean-line to within a league of the schooner; but the other quarters swept in a dark, clear, blue line against the sky, and there was such a clarity of atmosphere as made the distances appear infinite.

I went below and lighted the fire and got my breakfast, all very leisurely, and when I was done I sat down and smoked a pipe. It was so keen on deck that I had no mind to leave the fire, and, as all was well, I lounged through the best part of two hours in the cook-house, when, thinking it was now time to take another survey of the scene I went on deck.

On looking over the larboard bulwark rail, the first thing I saw was a ship about two miles off. She was on the larboard tack, under courses, topsails, and main-topgallant sail, heading as if to cross my bows. The sunshine made her canvas look as white as snow against the skirts of the body of vapour that had trailed a little to leeward of her, and her black hull flashed as though she discharged a broadside every time she rose wet to the northern glory out of the hollow of the swell with a curl of silver at her cutwater.

My heart came into my throat; I seemed not to breathe; not to have saved my life could I have uttered a cry, so amazed and transported was I by this unexpected apparition. I stared like one in a dream, and my head felt as if all the blood in my body had surged into it. But then, all on a sudden, there happened a revulsion of feeling. Suppose she should prove a privateer—a French war-vessel—of a nation hostile to my own? Thought so wrought in me that I trembled like an idiot in a fright. The telescope was too weak to resolve her, I could do better with my eyes; and I stood at the bulwarks gazing and gazing as if she were the spectre ship of the Scandinavian legend.

There were flags below and I could have hoisted a signal of distress: but to what purpose? If the appearance of the schooner did not sufficiently illustrate her condition, there was certainly no virtue in the language and declarations of bunting to exceed her own mute assurance. I watched her with a passion of anxiety, never doubting her intention to speak to me, at all events to draw close and look at me, wholly concerning myself with her character. The swell made us both dance, and the blue brows of the rollers would often hide her to the height of her rails; but we were closing each other middling fast she travelling at seven and I at four miles in the hour, and presently I could see that she carried a number of boats.

A whaler, thought I; and after a little I was sure of it by perceiving the rings over her top-gallant rigging for the look-out to stand in.

On being convinced of this, I ran below for a shawl that was in my cabin, and, jumping on to the bulwarks, stood flourishing it for some minutes to let them know that there was a man aboard. She luffed to deaden her way, that I might swim close, and as we approached each other I observed a crowd of heads forward looking at me, and several men aft, all staring intently.

A man scrambled on to the rail, and with an arm clasping a backstay hailed me:

"Schooner ahoy!" he bawled, with a strong nasal twang in his cry. "What ship's that?"

"The *Boca del Dragon*," I shouted back.

"Where are you from, and where are you bound to?"

"I have been locked up in the ice," I cried, "and am in want of help. What ship are you?"

"The *Susan Tucker*, whaler, of New Bedford, twenty-seven months out," he returned. "Where in creation got you that hooker?"

"I'm the only man aboard," I cried, "and have no boat. Send to me, in the name of God, and let the master come!"

He waved his hand, bawling, "Put your helm down—you're forging ahead!" and so saying, dismounted.

I immediately cast the tiller adrift, put it hard over, and secured it, then jumped on to the bulwarks again to watch them. She was Yankee beyond doubt; I had rather met my own countrymen; but, next to a British, I would have chosen an American ship to meet. Somehow, despite the Frenchman, I felt to have been alone throughout my adventure; and so sore was the effect of that solitude upon my spirits that it seemed twenty years since I had seen a ship, and since I had held commune with my own species. I was terribly agitated, and shook in every limb. Life must have been precious always; but never before had it appeared so precious as now, whilst I gazed at that homely ship, with her main-topsail to the mast, swinging stately upon the swell, the faces of the seamen plain, the smoke of her galley-fire breaking from the chimney, the sounds of creaking blocks and groaning parrels stealing from her. Such a fountain of joy broke out of my heart that my whole being was flooded with it, and had that mood lasted I believe I should have exposed the treasure in the run, and invited all the men of the whaler to share in it with me.

They stared fixedly; little wonder that they should be astounded by such an appearance as my ship exhibited. One of the several boats which hung at her davits was lowered, the oars flashed, and presently she was near enough to be hit with a biscuit; but when there the master, as I supposed him to be, who was steering, sung out, " 'Vast rowing!" the boat came to a stand, and her people to a man stared at me with their chins upon their shoulders as if I had been a fiend. It was plain as a pikestaff that they were frightened, and that the superstitions of the forecastle were hard at work in them whilst they viewed me. They looked a queer company: two were negroes, the others pale-faced bearded men, wrapped up in clothes to the aspect of scarecrows. The fellow who steered had a face as long as a wet hammock, and it was lengthened yet to the eye by a beard like a goat's hanging at the extremity of his chin.

He stood up—a tall, lank figure, with legs like a pair of compasses—and hailed me afresh, but the high swell, regular as the swing of a pendulum, interposed its brow between him and me, so that at one moment he was a sharply-lined figure against the sky of the horizon, and the next he and his boat and crew were sheer gone out of sight, and this made an exchange of sentences slow and troublesome.

"Say, master," he sung out, "what d'ye say the schooner's name is?"

"The *Boca del Dragon*," I replied.

"And who are *you*, matey?"

"An English sailor who has been cast away on an island of ice," I answered, talking very shortly that the replies might follow the questions before the swell sank him.

"Ay, ay," says he, "that's very well; but *when* was you cast away, bully?"

I gave him the date.

"That's not a month ago," cried he.

"It's long enough, whatever the time," said I.

Here the crew fell a-talking, turning from one another to stare at me, and the negroes' eyes showed as big as saucers in the dismay of their regard.

"See, here, master," sung out the long man, "if you han't been cast away more than a month, how come you clothed as men went dressed a century sin', hey?"

The reason of their misgivings flashed upon me. It was not so much the schooner as my appearance. The truth was, my clothes having been wetted, I had ever since been wearing such thick garments as I met with in the cabin, keeping my legs warm with jackboots, and I had become so used to the garb that I forgot I had it on. You will judge, then, that I must have presented a figure very nicely calculated to excite the wonder and apprehension of a body of men whose superstitious instincts were already sufficiently fluttered by the appearance of the schooner, when I tell you that, in addition to the jackboots and a great fur cap, my costume was formed of a red plush waistcoat laced with silver, purple breeches, a coat of frieze with yellow braiding and huge cuffs, and the cloak that I had taken from the body of Mendoza.

"Captain," cried I, "if so be you are the captain, in the name of God and humanity come aboard, sir." Here I had to wait till he reappeared. "My story is an extraordinary one. You have nothing to fear. I am a plain English sailor; my ship was the *Laughing Mary*, bound in ballast from Callao to the Cape." Here I had to wait again. "Pray, sir, come aboard. There is nothing to fear. I am alone—in grievous distress, and in want of help. Pray come, sir!"

There was so little of the goblin in this appeal that it resolved him. The crew hung in the wind, but he addressed them peremptorily. I heard him damn them for a set of curs, and tell them that if they put him aboard they might lie off till he was ready to return, where they would be safe, as the devil could not swim; and presently they buckled to their oars again and the boat came alongside. The long man, watching his chance, sprang with great agility into the chains, and stepped on deck. I ran up to him and seized his hand with both mine.

"Sir," cried I, speaking with difficulty, so great was the tumult of my spirits and the joy and gratitude that swelled my heart, "I thank you a thousand times over for this visit. I am in the most helpless condition that can be imagined. I am not astonished that you should have been startled by the appearance of this vessel and by the figure I make in these clothes, but, sir, you will be much more amazed when you have heard my story."

He eyed me steadfastly, examining me very earnestly from my boots to my cap, and then cast a glance around him before he made any reply to my address. He had the gauntness, sallowness of complexion, and deliberateness of manner peculiar to the people of New England. And though he was a very ugly, lank, uncouth man, I protest he was as fair in my sight as if he had been the ambrosial angel described by Milton.

"Well, cook my gizzard," he exclaimed presently, through his nose, and after another good look at me and along the decks and up aloft, "if this ain't mi-raculous, tew. Durned if we didn't take this hooker for some ghost ship riz from the sea, in charge of a merman rigged out to fit her age. Y' are all alone, air you?"

"All alone," said I.

"Broach me every barrel aboard if ever I see sich a vessel," he cried, his astonishment rising with the searching glances he directed aloft and alow. "How old be she?"

"She was cast away in seventeen hundred and fifty-three," said I.

"Well, I'm durned. She's froze hard, sirree; I reckon she'll want a hot sun to thaw her. Split me, mister, if she ain't worth sailing home as a show-box."

I interrupted his ejaculations by asking him to step below, where we could sit warm whilst I related my story, and I asked him to invite his boat's crew into the cabin that I might regale them with a bowl of such liquor as I ventured to say had never passed their lips in this life. On this he went to the side, and, hailing the men, ordered all but one to step aboard and drink to the health of the lonesome sailor they had come across. The word "drink" acted like a charm; they instantly hauled upon the painter and brought the boat to the chains and tumbled over the side, one of the negroes remaining in her. They fell together in a body, and surveyed me and the ship with a hundred marks of astonishment.

"My lads," said I, "my rig is a strange one, but I'll explain all shortly. The clothes I was cast away in are below, and I'll show you them. I'm no spectre, but as real as you; though I have gone through so much that, if I am not a ghost, it is no fault of old ocean, but owing to the mercy of God. My name is Paul Rodney, and I'm a native of London. You, sir," says I, addressing the long man, "are, I presume, the master of the *Susan Tucker*?"

"At your sarvice—Josiah Tucker is my name, and that ship is my wife Susan."

"Captain Tucker, and you, men, will you please step below," says I. "The weather promises fair; I have much to tell, and there is that in the cabin which will give you patience to hear me."

I descended the companion-stairs, and they all followed, making the interior that had been so long silent ring with their heavy tread, whilst from time to time a gruff, hoarse whisper broke from one of them. But superstition lay strong upon their imagination, and they were awed and quiet. The daylight came down the hatch, but for all that the cabin was darksome.

I waited till the last man had entered, and then said, "Before we settle down to a bowl and a yarn, captain, I should like to show you this ship. It'll save me a deal of description and explanation if you will be pleased to take a view."

"Lead on, mister," said he; "but we shall have to snap our eyelids and raise fire in that way, for durned if I, for one, can see in the dark."

I fetched three or four lanthorns, and, lighting the candles, distributed them among the men, and then, in a procession, headed by the captain and me, we made the rounds. I had half-cleared the arms-room, but there were weapons enough left, and they stared at them like yokels in a booth. I showed them the cook-house and the forecastle, where the deck was still littered with clothes, and chests, and hammocks; and, after carrying them aft to the cabins, gave them a sight of the hold. I never saw men more amazed. They filled the vessel with their exclamations. They never offered to touch anything, being too much awed, but stepped about with their heads uncovered, as quietly as they could, as though they had been in a crypt, and the influence of strange and terrifying memorials was upon them. I also showed them the clothes I had come away from the *Laughing Mary* in; and, that I might submit such an aspect to them as should touch their sympathies, I whipped off the cloak and put on my own pilot-cloth coat.

There being nothing more to see, I led them to the cook-room, and there brewed a great hearty bowl of brandy-punch, which I seasoned with lemon, sugar, and spices into as relishable a draught as my knowledge in that way could compass, and, giving every man a pannikin, bade him dip and welcome, myself first drinking to them with a brief speech, yet not so brief but that I broke down towards the close of it, and ended with a dry sob or two.

They would have been unworthy their country and their calling not to have been touched by my natural manifestation of emotion; besides, the brandy was an incomparably fine spirit, and the very perfume of the steaming bowl was sufficient to stimulate the kindly qualities of sailors who had been locked up for months in a greasy old ship, with no diviner smells about than the stink of the try-works. The captain, standing up, called upon his men to drink to me, promising me that he was very glad to have fallen in with my schooner, and then, looking at the others, made a sign, whereupon they all fixed their eyes upon me and drank as one man, every one emptying his pot and inverting it as a proof, and fetching a rousing sigh of satisfaction.

This ceremony ended, I began my story, beginning with the loss of the *Laughing Mary*, and proceeding step by step. I told them of the dead body of Mendoza, but said nothing about the Frenchman and the mate, and the Portugal boatswain, lest I should make them afraid of the vessel, and so get no help to work her. As to acquainting them with my recovery of Tassard, after his stupor of eight-and-forty years, I should have been mute on that head in any case, for so extraordinary a relation could, from such people, have earned me but one of two opinions: either that I was mad and believed in an impossibility, or that I was a rogue and dealt in magic, and to be vehemently shunned. Yet there were wonders enough in my story without this, and I recited it to a running commentary of all sorts of queer Yankee exclamations.

There were seven seamen and the captain and I made nine, and we pretty nearly filled the cook-room. 'Twas a scene to be handled by a Dutch brush. We were a shaggy company, in several kinds of rude attire, and the crimson light of the furnace, whose playing flames darted shadows through the steady light of the lanthorns, caused us to appear very wild. The mariners' eyes gleamed redly as their glances rove round the place, and, had you come suddenly among us, I believe you would have thought this band of pale, fire-touched, hairy men, with the one ebon visage among them, rendered the vessel a vast deal more ghostly than ever she could have shown when sailing along with me alone on board.

They were a good deal puzzled when I told them of the mines I had made and sprung in the ice. They reckoned the notion fine, but could not conceive how I had, single-handed, broken out the powder-barrels, got them over the side, and fixed them.

"Why," said I, " 'twas slow, heavy work, of course; but a man who labours for his life will do marvellous things. It is like the jump of a hunted stag."

"True for you," says the captain. "A swim of two miles spends me in pleasurin'; but I've swum eight mile to save my life, and stranded fresh as a new-hooked cod. What's your intentions, sir?"

"To sail the schooner home," said I, "if I can get help. She's too good to abandon. She'll fetch money in England."

"Ay, as a show."

"Yes, and as a coalman. Rig her modernly, and carry your forecastle deck into the head, captain, and she's a brave ship, fit for a Baltimore eye."

He stroked down the hair upon his chin.

"Dip, captain, dip, my lads; there's enough of this to drown ye in the hold," said I, pointing to the bowl. "Come, this is a happy meeting for me; let it be a merry one. Captain, I drink to the *Susan Tucker*."

"Sir, your servant. Here's to your sweetheart, be she wife or maid. Bill, jump on deck and take a look round. See to the boat."

One of the men went out.

"Captain," said I, "you are a full ship?"

"That's so."

"Bound home?"

"Right away."

"You have men enough and to spare. Lend me three of your hands to help me to the Thames, and I'll repay you thus; there should be near a hundred tons of wine and brandy, of exquisite vintage, and choice with age beyond language in the hold. Take what you will of that freight; there'll be ten times the value of your lay in your pickings, modest as you may prove. Help yourself to the clothes in the cabin and forecastle; they will turn to account. For the men you will spare, and who will volunteer to help me, this will be my undertaking: the ship and all that is in her to be sold on her arrival, and the proceeds equally divided. Shall we call it a thousand pounds apiece? Captain, she's well found: her inventory would make a list as long as you; I'd name a bigger sum, but here she is, you shall overhaul her hold and judge for yourself."

I watched him anxiously. No man spoke, but every eye was upon him. He sat pulling down the hair on his chin, then, jumping up on a sudden and extending his hand, he cried, "Shake! it's a bargain, if the men 'll jine."

"I'll jine!" exclaimed a man.

There was a pause.

"And me," said the negro.

I was glad of this, and looked earnestly at the others.

"Is she tight?" said a man.

"As a bottle," said I.

They fell silent again.

"Joe Wilkinson and Washington Cromwell—them two jines," said the captain. "Bullies, he wants a third. Don't speak all together."

The man named "Bill" at this moment returned to the cook-room, and reported all well above. My offer was repeated to him, but he shook his head.

"This is the Horn, mates," said he. "There's a deal o' water 'tween this and the Thames. How do she sail?—no man knows."

"I want none but willing men," said I. "Americans make as good sailors as the English. What an English seaman can face any of you can. There is another negro in the boat. Will you let him step aboard, captain? He may join."

A man was sent to take his place. Presently he arrived, and I gave him a cup of punch.

" 'Splain the business to him, sir," said the captain, filling his pannikin; "his name's Billy Pitt."

I did so; and when I told him that Washington Cromwell had offered, he instantly said, "All right, massa, I'll be ob yah."

194

This was exactly what I wanted, and had there been a third negro I'd have preferred him to the white man.

"But how are you going to navigate this craft home with three men?" said the man "Bill" to me.

"There'll be four; we shall do. The fewer the more dollars, hey, Wilkinson?"

He grinned, and Cromwell broke into a ventral laugh.

They seemed very well satisfied, and so was I.

Chapter XXVIII.
I Strike a Bargain with the Yankee

THE captain put his cup down; the bowl was empty; I offered to brew another jorum, but he thanked me and said no, adding significantly that he would have no more *here*, by which he meant that he would brew for himself in his own ship anon. The drink had made him cheerful and good-natured. He recommended that we should go on deck and set about transhipping whilst the weather held, for he was an old hand in these seas and never trusted the sky longer than a quarter of an hour.

"This here list," says he, "wants remedying and that'll follow our easin' of the hold."

"Yes," said I, "and I should be mighty thankful if some of your men would see all clear aloft for me, that we might start with running rigging that will travel, capstans that'll revolve, and sails that'll spread."

"Oh, we'll manage that for you," said he. "Tru-ly, she's been bad froze, very bad froze. Durned if ever I see a worse freeze."

So saying he called to "Bill," who seemed the principal man of the boat's crew, and gave him some directions, and immediately afterwards all the men entered the boat and rowed away to the ship.

Whilst they were absent I carried the captain into the hold and left him to overhaul it. I told him that all the spirits, provisions, and the like were in the hold and lazarette, which was true enough, wanting to keep him out of the run, though, thanks to the precaution I had taken, I was in no fear even if he should penetrate so deep aft. Before he came out five-and-twenty stout fellows arrived in four boats from the ship, and when we went on deck, we found them going the rounds of the vessel, scraping the guns to get a view of them, peering down the companion, overhauling the forecastle-well, as I call the hollow beyond the forecastle, and staring aloft with their faces full of grinning wonder. The captain sang out to them and they all mustered aft.

"Now, lads," said he, "there's a big job before you—a big job for Cape Horn, I mean; and you'll have to slip through it as if you was grease. When done there'll be a carouse, and I'll warrant ye all such a sup that the most romantic among ye'll never cast another pining thought in the direction o' your mother's milk."

Having delivered this preface, he divided the men into two gangs; one, under the boatswain, to attend to the rigging, clear the canvas of the ice, get the pumps and the capstans to work, and see all ready for getting sail on the schooner; the other, under the second mate, to get tackles aloft and break out the cargo, taking care to trim ship whilst so doing.

They fell to their several jobs with a will. 'Tis the habit of our countrymen to sneer at the Americans as sailors, affirming that if ever they win a battle at sea it is by the help of British renegades. But this I protest; after witnessing the smartness of those Yankee whalemen, I would sooner charge the English than the Americans with lubberliness came the nautical merits of the two nations ever before me to decide upon. They had the hatches open, tackles aloft, and men at work below whilst the mariners of other countries would have been standing looking on and "jawing" upon the course to be taken. Some overran the fabric aloft, clearing, cutting away, pounding, making the ice fly in storms; others sweated the capstans till they clanked; others fell to the pumps, working with hammers and kettles of boiling water. The wondrous old schooner was never busier, no, not in the heyday of her flag, when her guns were blazing and her people yelling.

I doubt whether even a man-of-war could have given this work the despatch the whaler furnished. She had eight boats and sixty men, and every boat was afloat and alongside us ready to carry what she could to the ship. I wished to help, but the captain would not let me do so; he kept me walking and talking, asking me scores of questions about the schooner, and all so shrewd that, without appearing reserved, I professed to know little. The great show of clothes puzzled him. He also asked if the crucifix in the cabin was silver. I said I believed it was, fetched it, and asked him to accept it, saying if he would give me the smallest of his boats for it I should be very much obliged.

"Oh, yes," says he, "you can have a boat. The men would not sail with you without a boat;" and after weighing the crucifix without the least exhibition of veneration in his manner, he put it in his pocket, saying he knew a man who would give him a couple of hundred dollars for the thing on his telling him that the Pope had blessed it.

"Ay, but," says I, "how do you know the Pope has blessed it?"

"Then *I'll* bless it," cried he; "why, am I a cold Johnny-cake that my blessing ain't as good as another man's?"

I was glad I had hidden the black flag; I mean, that I had stowed it away in the cabin of the Frenchman after he was dead. The Yankee needed but the sight to make his suspicions of the original character of the *Boca del Dragon* flame up; and you may suppose that I was exceedingly anxious he should not be sure that the schooner had been a pirate, lest he might have been tempted to scrutinize her rather more closely than would have been agreeable to me.

He asked me if I had met with any money in her: and I answered evasively that in searching the dead man on the rocks, I had discovered a few pieces in his pocket, but that I had left them, being much too melancholy and convinced of my approaching end to meddle with such a useless commodity. From time to time he would quit me to go to the hatch and sing down orders to the second mate in the hold. How many casks he meant to take I did not know; when he asked me how much I would give, I replied: "Leave me enough to keep me ballasted; that will satisfy me."

The high swell demanded caution, but they managed wonderfully well. They never swung more than three casks into a boat, and with this cargo she would row away to the ship that lay hove-to close, and the men in her hoisted the casks aboard.

The wind remained light till half-past three; it then freshened a bit. Though all hands had knocked off at noon to get dinner—and a fine meal I gave them of ham, tongue, beef, biscuits, wine, and brandy—by half-past three they had eased the hold of ten boatloads of casks, besides clearing out the whole of the clothes from the forecastle along with as much of the bedding as we did not require; and I began to think that my Yankee intended to leave me a clean ship to carry home, though I durst not remonstrate. Yet was my turn handsomely served too. The pumps had been cleared and tried, and found to work well, and—which was glad news to me—the well found dry. The running rigging had been overhauled, and it travelled handsomely. The sails had been loosed and hoisted and lowered again, and the canvas found in good condition. The jibboom had been run out, and the stays set up. The stock of fresh water had been examined and found plentiful, and the casks in the head brought out and secured on the main deck. In short, the American boatswain had worked with the judgment and care of a master-rigger, of a great artist in ropes, booms, and sails, and the schooner was left to my hands as fit for any navigation as the whaler that rose and fell on our quarter.

But, as I have said, at half-past three in the afternoon, the breeze began to sit in dark curls upon the water, and there was evidence enough in the haziness in the west, and in the loom of the shoulders of vapour in the dark-blue obscure there, to warrant a sackful for this capful presently.

"I reckon," says the captain to me, after looking into the west, "that we'd best knock off now. There's snow and wind yonder, and we'd better see all snug while there's time."

He called to one of the men to tell the second mate to come up from below and get the hatches on, and bringing me to the rail, he pointed to a boat, and asked if that would do? I said yes, and thanked him heartily for the gift, which was handsome, I must say, the boat being a very good one, though, to be sure, he had got many times its value out of the schooner; and a party of men were forthwith told off to get the boat hoisted and stowed.

"Now, Mr. Rodney," said the captain, standing in the gangway, "how can I serve you further?"

"Sir," said I, "you are very obliging. Two things I stand sadly in need of: a chart of these waters and a chronometer."

"I'll send you a chart," said he, "that'll carry you as high as San Roque; but I've only got one chronometer, sir, and can't spare him."

"Well then," said I, "if, when you get aboard, you'll give me the time by your chronometer, I'll set my watch by it; but I'll thank you very much for the chart. The tracings below are as shapeless as the moon setting in a fog."

"You shall have the chart," said he, and then called to Wilkinson and the two negroes.

"Lads," said he, "you're quite content, I hope?"

They answered "Yes."

"You've all three a claim upon me for the amount of what's owing ye," said he, "and when you turn up at New Bedford you shall have it—that's square. I see fifteen hundred dollars a man on this job, if so be as ye don't broach too thirstily as you go along. Mr. Rodney, Joe here's a steady, 'spectable man, and'll make you a good mate. Cromwell and Billy Pitt are black only in their hides; all else's as good as white."

He then shook me by the hand, and, calling a farewell to Wilkinson and the negroes, scrambled into the chains and dropped into his boat, very highly satisfied, I make no doubt, with the business he had done that day.

A boat's crew were left behind to help us to make sail. But the weather looking somewhat wild in the west with the red light of the sun among the clouds there, and the dark heave of the swell running into a sickly crimson under the sun and then glowing out dusky again, I got them to treble-reef the mainsail and hoist it, and then thanking them, advised them to be off. Then, putting Cromwell to the tiller, I went forward with the others and set the topsail and forestaysail (the spritsail lying furled), which would be show enough of canvas till I saw what the weather was to be like. I kept the topsail aback, waiting for a boat to arrive with my chart, and in a few minutes the boat we had cheered returned with what I wanted.

Meanwhile they were shortening sail on the whaler, and though she was no beauty, yet, I tell you, I found her as picturesque as any ship I had ever beheld as she lay with her main-topgallant-sail clewed up, her topsail yards on the caps, and the heads of men knotting the reef-points showing black over the white cloths, her hull floating up out of the hollow and flinging a wet orange gleam to the west, a tumble of creamy foam about her to her rolling, shadows like the passage of phantom hands hurrying over her sails to the swaying of her masts, and the swelling sea darkling from her into the east.

I hollowed my hands, and, hailing the captain, who was on the quarter-deck, asked him for the time by his chronometer. He flourished his arm and disappeared and, presently returning, shouted to know if I was ready. I put the key in my watch and answered yes, and then he gave me the time. My watch, though antique, was a noble piece of mechanism, and I have little doubt, as trustworthy as his chronometer. But I was careful to let it lie snug in my hand. I did not want the negro at the tiller nor the others to see it. They would wonder that so fine a jewelled piece as this should be in the possession of the second mate of a little brig, and it was my business to manage that they never should have cause to wonder at anything in that way.

The dusk of the evening came quick out of the east, and the wind freshened with a long cry in our rigging as if the eastern darkness was a foe it was rushing out of the west to meet. I brought the schooner north-north-east by my compass and watched her behaviour anxiously. The swell was on the quarter, and the wind and sea a trifle abaft the larboard beam; she leaned a little to the weight of her clothes, but was surprisingly stiff considering how light she was. Wilkinson and the negro came and stood by my side. The sea broke heavily from the weather bow, and the water roared white under the lee bends and spread astern in a broad wake of foam. The whaler did not brace his yards up till after we had started, and now hung a pale faint mass in the windy darkness on the quarter. A tincture of rusty red hovered like smoke coloured by the furnace that produces it, in the west, but the night had drawn down quick and dark; the washing noise of the water was sharp, the wind piercingly cold; each sweep of the schooner's masts to windward was followed by a dull roaring of the blast rushing out of the hollows of the canvas, and she swung to the seas with wild yaws, but with regularity sufficient to prove the strict government of the helm.

But it was being at sea! homeward bound too! There was no wish of mine, engendered by my hideous loneliness on the ice, by my abhorred association with the Frenchman, that I could not refer to as, down to this moment, gratified. My heart bounded; my spirits could not have been higher had this ocean been the Thames, and yonder dark flowing hills of water the banks of Erith and the Gravesend shore.

I turned to the three men: "My lads," said I, "you prove yourselves fine bold fellows by thus volunteering. Do not fear: if God guides us home—to my home, I mean—you shall find a handsome account in this business."

"Six more chaps would have jined had th'ole man bin willin'," said Wilkinson. "But best as it is, master, though she's a trifle short-handed."

"Why, yes," said I; "but being fore and aft, you know! It isn't as if we'd got courses to hand and topsails to reef."

"Ay, ay, dat's de troof," cried Billy Pitt. "I tort o' dat. Fore an' aft makes de difference. Don't guess I should hab volunteer had she been a brig."

"There are four of us," said I. "You're my chief mate, Wilkinson. Choose your watch."

"I choose Cromwell," said he; "he was in my watch aboard the whaler."

"Very well," I exclaimed; and this being settled, and both negroes declaring themselves good cooks, we arranged that they should alternately have the dressing of our victuals, that Wilkinson should have the cabin next mine, and the negroes the one in which the Frenchman had slept, one taking the other's place as he was relieved.

I asked Wilkinson what he thought of the schooner. He answered that he was watching her.

"There's nothing to find fault with yet," said he; "she's a whale at rolling, sartinly. I guess she walks, though. I reckon she's had enough of the sea, like me, and's got the scent o' the land in her nose. I guess old Noah wasn't far off when her lines was laid. Mebbe his sons had the building of her. There's something scriptural in her cut. How old's she, master?"

"Fifty years and more," said I.

"Dere's nuffin' pertickler in dat," cried Cromwell. "I knows a wessel dat am a hundred an' four year old, s'elp me as I stand."

"I don't know how the whaler's heading," said I, "but this schooner's a canoe if we aren't dropping her!"

Indeed she was scarce visible astern, a mere windy flicker hovering upon the pale flashings of the foam. It might be perhaps that the whaler was making a more northerly course than we, and under very snug canvas, though ours was snug enough, too; but be this as it may, I was mighty pleased with the slipping qualities of the schooner. I never could have dreamt that so odd and ugly a figure of a ship would show such heels. But I think this: we are too prone to view the handiwork of our sires with contempt. I do not know but that their ships were as fast as ours. They made many good passages. They might have proved themselves fleeter navigators had they had the sextant and chronometer to help them along. Fifty years hence perhaps mankind will be laughing at our crudities; at us, by heaven, who flatter ourselves that the art of ship-building and navigation will never be carried higher than the pitch to which we have raised them!

Cromwell being at the tiller, I told Billy Pitt to go below and get supper, instructing him what to dress and how much to melt for a bowl, for as you know there was nothing but spirits and wine to season our repasts with. I saw Cromwell grin widely into the binnacle candle flame when he heard me talk of ham, tongue, sweetmeats, marmalade and the like for supper, together with a can of hot claret, and knowing sailor's nature middling well, I did not doubt that the fare of the schooner would bring the three men more into love with the adventure than even the reward that was to follow it.

I had noticed that the bundles which had been sent from the whaler as belonging to the poor fellows were meagre enough and showed indeed like the end of a long voyage, and I detained Billy Pitt a minute whilst I told them that there was a handsome stock of clothes in the cabins, together with linen, boots, and other articles of that sort; that, though the coats, breeches, and waistcoats were of bright colour and old-fashioned, they would keep them as warm as if they had been cut by a tailor of to-day.

"These things," said I, "you can wear at sea, keeping your own clothes ready to slip on should we be spoken or to wear when we arrive in England. To-morrow they shall be divided among you, and they will become your property. The suit you saw me in to-day is all that I shall need."

Both negroes burst into a most diverting laugh of joy on hearing this. Nothing delights a black man more than coloured apparel. They had seen the clothes in the forecastle and guessed the kind of garments I meant to present them with.

Whilst supper was getting, I walked the deck with Wilkinson, both of us keeping a bright look-out, for it was blowing fresh; the darkness lay thick about us, there might be ice near us, and the schooner was storming under her reefed mainsail, topsail, and staysail through the hollow seas, thundering with a great roaring seething noise into the trough, and lifting to the foaming slope with her masts wildly aslant. I talked to my companion very freely, being anxious to find out what kind of person he was, and I must say that there was something in his conversation that impressed me very favourably. He told me that he had a wife at New Bedford, that he was heartily sick of the sea, and that he hoped the money he would get by this adventure, added to his *lay*, would enable him to set up for himself ashore.

"Well," said I, "we will see to-morrow what cargo Captain Tucker has left us. But that you may be under no misapprehension, Wilkinson, if we are fortunate enough to bring the ship safely to England, I will enter into a bond to pay you five hundred pounds sterling for your share one week after the date of our arrival."

He answered that if he could get that sum he would be a made man for life. "But it's too much to expect, sir," says he.

I told him that he had no idea of the value of the cargo. The wines and spirits were of such a quality I would stake my interest in the schooner in their fetching a large sum of money.

"That'll depend," said he, "on how much the capt'n left us."

"He helped himself freely," I answered, "but we are well off too. You shall judge to-morrow. Then there's the schooner—as she stands: besides a noble stock of stores of all kinds, sails, ropes, tools, ammunition and several chests of small arms. I tell you I will give you five hundred pounds for your share."

His satisfaction was expressed by his silence.

"But," continued I, "we must act with judgment. What we have we must keep. Are the negroes trustworthy men?"

"Yes, they are honest fellows. I wouldn't have shipped with them else."

"We shall not require much for ourselves," said I, "and the rest we'll batten down and keep snug. There'll be some manoeuvring needed in order to come off clear with this booty when we arrive: but there's plenty of time to think that over, and our business till then is to look after the ship and pray for luck to keep clear of anything hostile."

And then we fell to other talk; in the course of which he told me he was an Englishman born, but having been pressed into a man-o-war, deserted her at Halifax and made several voyages in American ships. He was wrecked on the Peruvian coast and became a beachcomber, and then got a berth in a whaler. He married at New Bedford and sailed with Captain Tucker—this was his second whaling trip, he said, and he wanted no more. I told him I was glad to learn that he was a countryman of mine, but not surprised. His speech was well-larded with Americanisms, "but," said I, "the true twang is wanting, and," added I, laughing, "I should know you for Hampshire for all your reckons and guesses if I had to eat you should I be mistaken."

"The press-gang's the best friend the Yankees has," said he a little sheepishly. "Do any man suppose I hadn't sooner hail from my native town Southampton than from New Bedford? Half the American foksles is made up of Yankees who'd prove hearts of oak if it wasn't for the press."

His candour gratified me as showing that he already looked upon me as a shipmate to be trusted, and, as I have said, this first chat with the man left me strongly disposed to consider myself fortunate in having him as an associate.

Chapter XXIX.
I Value the Lading

THE day had been so full of business, there had been so much to engage my mind, that it was not until I was seated at supper in the old cook-room in which I had passed so many melancholy hours, that I found myself able to take a calm survey of my situation, and to compare the various motions of my fortunes. I could scarcely indeed believe that I was not in a dream from which I should awake presently, and discover myself still securely imprisoned in the ice, and all those passages of the powder-blasts, the liberation of the schooner, my lonely days in her afloat, my encounter with the whaler, as visionary and vanishing as those dusky forms of vapour which had swarmed in giant-shape over my little open boat.

But even if confirmation had been wanting in the sable visage of Billy Pitt, who sat near the furnace munching away with prodigious enjoyment of his food and bringing his can of hot spiced wine from his vast blubber lips with a mighty sigh of deep delight, I must have found it in each hissing leap and roaring plunge of the old piratical bucket, so full of the vitality of the wind-swollen canvas, so quick with all the life-instincts of a vessel storming through the deep with buoyant keel and under full control. Oh, heaven! how different from the dull ambling of the morning, the sluggish pitching and rolling to the weak pulling of the spritsail!

Wilkinson and Cromwell kept the deck whilst Billy Pitt and I got our supper, and I had some talk with my negro, who seemed to be a very simple childish fellow, heartily in love with his stomach and very eager to see England. He told me that he had heard it was a fine country, and his wish to see it was one reason of his volunteering.

"Dey say," said he, "dat Lunnon's a very fine place, sah, bigger dan Philadelphy, and dat a man's skin don' tell agin him among de yaller gals dere."

I laughed and said, that in my country people were judged rather by the colour of their hearts than by the hue of their faces.

"But dollars count for something too, sah, I spects?" said he.

"Why, yes," said I, "with dollars enough you can make black white in England."

"Hum!" cried he, scratching his head. "I guess it 'ud take an almighty load of dollars to make me white, massa."

"Put money in your pocket and chink it," said I, "and your face'll be found white enough, I warrant."

"By golly!" cried he, "I'll do it den. S'elp me de Lord, massa, I'd chink twenty year for a white face. Dat comes ob bein' civilized. Tell'ee what dey dew, massa, dey makes you feel like a white man, but dey lets you keep black, blast 'em!"

I checked his excitement by telling him that in my country he would find that the negro was a person held in very high esteem, that the women in particular valued him for that very dinginess which the Americans found distasteful, and told him that I could name several ladies of quality who had married their black servants.

He looked surprised, but not incredulous, and said in his peculiar dialect that he had no doubt I spoke the truth, as he had always heard that England was a fine country to live in. I then led him insensibly from this topic to talk of the sea and his experiences, and found that he had seen a very great deal, having been freed when young, and keeping to the ocean ever since in many different sorts of craft. Indeed, I was as much pleased with him as with Wilkinson, but then I had foreseen a simplicity in both the negroes, and in expectation of finding this quality, so useful to one in my strange position, I was overjoyed when they consented to help me sail the schooner to the Thames.

We went on deck to relieve Wilkinson and Cromwell. Billy Pitt took the tiller and I walked to either rail and stared into the darkness. It was very thick with occasional squalls of snow, which put a screaming as of tortured cats into the wind as they swung through it. The sea was high, but the schooner was making excellent weather of it, whilst she rolled and pitched through the troubled darkness at seven knots in the hour. 'Twas noble useful sailing, yet a speed not to be relished in these waters amid so deep a shadow. Still the temptation to "hold on all," as we say, was very great; every mile carried us by so much nearer to the temperate parallels, and shortened to that extent the long, long passage that lay before us.

I was pacing the deck briskly, for the wind was horribly keen, when Pitt suddenly called out, "I say, massa!"

"Hullo," I replied.

"Sah," he cried, "I smell ice!"

I knew that this was a capacity not uncommon among men who had voyaged much in the frosty regions of the deep, and instantly exclaimed, "Luff, then, luff! shake the way out of her!" sniffing as I spoke, but detecting no added shrewdness in the air that was already freezingly cold. He put the helm down, and I called to the others below to come on deck and flatten in the main sheet. They were up in a trice and tailed on with me, asking no questions, till we had the boom nearly amidships.

I was about to speak when Wilkinson cried out, "I smell ice." He sniffed a moment: "Yes, there's an island aboard. Anybody see it?"

"Ay, dere it am, sure enough!" cried Cromwell. "Dere—on de lee-bow—see it, sah? See it, Billy?"

Yes, I saw it plain enough when I knew where to look for it. 'Twas just such another lump of faintness as had wrecked the *Laughing Mary*, a mass of dull spectral light upon the throbbing blackness, and it lay exactly in a line with the course we had been steering when Pitt first called out, so that assuredly we had not shifted our helm a minute too soon. We chopped and wallowed past it slowly, keeping a sharp look-out for like apparitions in other quarters, and when it had disappeared, I made up my mind to heave the schooner to and keep her in that posture till daylight, unless the night cleared. So we got the mainsail down and stowed it, clewed up the topsail (which I lent a hand to roll up), and let the vessel lie under a reefed foresail with her helm lashed. The weather, however, must have ultimately compelled what the thickness had required; for by ten o'clock it was blowing a hard gale, with a frequent hoariness of clouds of snow upon the blackness, the seas very high and foaming, and the wind crying madly in the rigging.

I let some time go by, and then sounded the well and found no more water than the depth at which the pumps sucked. This did wonders in the way of reassuring the men, who were rendered uneasy by the violent motions of the unwieldy vessel, and by the very harsh straining noises which rose out of the hold, which latter they would naturally attribute to the craziness of the fabric, though the true cause of it lay in the number of loose, movable bulkheads.

"It's amazin' to me that she holds together at all," cried Wilkinson, "so ancient she is!"

"She's only old," said I, "in the sound of the years she's been in existence. The ice has kept her young. Would the hams and tongues we're eating be taken to be half a century old? yet where could you buy sweeter and better meat of the kind ashore? A ship's well is your only honest reporter of her condition. Ours has vouched in a way that should keep you easy."

"Arter de *Soosan Tucker* dis is like bein' hung up to dry," exclaimed one of the negroes. "It war pump, pump dere and no mistake. I call dis a werry beautiful little sheep, massa; yes, s'elp me de Lord, dere's nuffin could persuade me she ain't what I says she am."

However, I was up and down a good deal during the night. But for the treasure I should have been less anxious, I dare say. I had come so successfully to this point that I was resolved, if my hopes were to miscarry, the misfortune should not be owing to want of vigilance on my part; and there happened an incident which inevitably tended to sharpen my watchfulness, though I was perfectly conscious there was a million to one against its occurring a second time. I came on deck to relieve Wilkinson, at midnight, after a half-hour's nodding doze by the furnace below. He went to his cabin; I stood under the lee of a cloth seized in the weather main rigging. Pitt arrived, and I told him he could return to the cook-house and stay there till I called him. The helm being lashed, and the schooner doing very well, nothing wanted watching in particular, yet I would not have the deck abandoned, and meant to keep a look-out, turn and turn about with Pitt, as Wilkinson and Cromwell had. The snow had ceased; but it was very dark and thick, the ocean a roaring shadow, palpitating upon the eyes in rolling folds of blackness, with the quick expiring flash of foam to windward. On a sudden, looking over the weather quarter, methought I discerned a deeper shade in the night there than was elsewhere perceptible. It was like a great blot of ink upon the darkness. Even whilst I speculated, it drew out in the shape of a ship running before the gale. She seemed to be heading directly for us. The roof of my mouth turned dry as desert-sand; my tongue and limbs refused their office; I could neither cry nor stir, being indeed paralyzed by the terrible suddenness of that apparition and the imminence of our peril. It all happened whilst you could have told thirty. The great black mass surged up with the water boiling about the bows; she brought a thunder along with her in her rigging and sails as she soared to the crowns of the seas she was sweeping before. I could not tell what canvas she was under, but her speed was a full ten knots, and as I did not see her till she was close, she looked to come upon us as with a single bound. She passed us to windward within a stone's throw, and vanished like a dark cloud melting into the surrounding blackness. Not a gleam of light broke from her; you heard nothing but the boiling at her bows and the thunderous pealing of the gale in her canvas. A quarter turn of the wheel would have sent us to the bottom, and her, no doubt, on top of us. Whether she was the *Susan Tucker*, or some other whaler, or a big South-Sea-man driven low and getting what easting she could out of the gale, I know not. She was as complete a mystery of the ocean night as any spectral fabric, and a heavier terror to me than a phantasm worked by ghosts could have proved.

I knew such a thing could not happen again, yet when I called Pitt I talked to him about it as though we must certainly be run down if he did not keep a sharp look-out, and when my watch below came round at four o'clock, I was so agitated that I was up and down till daybreak, as though my duty did not end till then.

The gale moderated at sunrise, and, though it was a gloomy, true Cape Horn morning, with dark driving clouds, the sea a dusky olive, very hollow, and frequent small quick squalls of sleet which brought the wind to us in sharp guns, yet as we could see where we were going, I got the schooner before it, heading her east-north-east, and under a reefed topsail, mainsail, and staysail, the old bucket stormed through it with the sputter and rage of a line-of-battle ship. There was a log-reel and line on deck, and I found a sand-glass in the chest in my cabin in which I had met with the quadrants, perspective glass, and the like, and I kept this log regularly going, marking a point of departure on the chart the American captain had given me, which I afterwards found to be within two leagues and a half of the true position. But for three days the weather continued so heavy that there was nothing to be done in the shape of gratifying the men's expectations by overhauling what was left of the cargo. Indeed, we had no leisure for such work; all our waking hours had to be strictly dedicated to the schooner, and in keeping a look-out for ice. But the morning of the fourth day broke with a fine sky and a brisk breeze from a little to the east of south, to which we showed every cloth the schooner had to throw abroad, and being now by dead reckoning within a few leagues of the meridian of sixty degrees, I shaped a course north by east by my compass, with the design of getting a view of Staten Island that I might correct my calculations.

When we had made sail and got our breakfast, I told Wilkinson and Cromwell (Pitt being at the tiller) that now was a good opportunity for inspecting the contents of the hold; and (not to be tedious in this part of my relation, however I may have sinned in this respect elsewhere) we carried lanthorns below, and spent the better part of the forenoon in taking stock. From a copy of the memorandum I made on that occasion (still in my possession), we discovered that the Yankee captain had left us the following: thirty casks of rum, twenty-eight hogsheads of claret, seventy-five casks of brandy, fifty of sherry, and eighteen cases of beer in bottles. In addition to this were the stores in the lazarette (besides a quantity of several kinds of wine in jars, &c.) elsewhere enumerated, besides all the ship's furniture, her guns, powder, small-arms, &c., as well as the ship herself. I took the men into the run and showed them the chests, opening the little one which I had stocked with small-arms, and lifting the lids of two or three of the others. They were perfectly satisfied, fully believing all the chests to be filled with small-arms and nothing else, and so we came away and returned to the cabin, where, to please them, I put down the value of the cargo at a venture, setting figures against each article, and making out a total of two thousand six hundred and forty pounds. This of course included the ship.

"How much'll dat be a man, massa?" asked Cromwell.

"Six hundred and sixty pounds," I answered.

The poor fellow was so transported that, after staring at me in silence with the corners of his mouth stretched to his ears, he tossed up his hands, burst into a roar of laughter, and made several skips about the deck.

"Of course," said I, addressing Wilkinson, "my figures may be ahead or short of the truth. But if you are disposed to take the chance, I'll tell you what I'll do; I'll stand by my figures, accepting the risk of the value of the lading being less than what I say it is, and undertake to give each man of you six hundred and sixty pounds for your share."

"Well, sir," said he, "I don't know that I ought to object. But a few pounds is a matter of great consequence to me, and I reckon if these here goods and the wessel should turn out to be worth more than ye offer, the loss 'ud go agin the grit, ay, if 'twere twenty dollars a man."

I laughed, and told him to let the matter rest, there was plenty of time before us; I should be willing to stand to my offer even if I lost by it, so heartily obliged was I to them for coming to my assistance. And in this I spoke the truth, though, as you will understand who know my position, I had to finesse. It went against my conscience to make out that the chests were full of small-arms, but I should have been mad to tell them the truth, and, perhaps, by the truth made devils of men who were, and promised to remain, steady, temperate, honest fellows. I was not governed by the desire to keep all the treasure to myself; no, I vow to God I should have been glad to give them a moiety of it, had I not apprehended the very gravest consequences if I were candid with them. But this, surely, must be so plain that it is idle to go on insisting on it.

The fine weather, the golden issue that was to attend our successful navigation, the satisfactory behaviour of the schooner, put us into a high good-humour with one another; and when it came to my collecting all the clothes in the after cabins and distributing them among the three men, I thought Billy Pitt and Cromwell would have gone mad with delight. To the best of my recollection the apparel that had been left us by the American captain (who, as you know, had cleared the forecastle of the clothes there) consisted of several coats of cut velvet, trimmed with gold and silver lace, some frocks of white drab with large plate buttons, brocade waistcoats of blue satin and green silk, crimson and other coloured cloth breeches, along with some cloaks, three-corner hats, black and white stockings, a number of ruffled shirts, and other articles, of which I recollect the character, though my ignorance of the costumes of that period prevents me from naming them.

Any one acquainted with the negro's delight in coloured clothes will hardly need to be told of the extravagant joy raised in the black breasts of Cromwell and Pitt by my distribution of this fine attire. The lace, to be sure, was tarnished, and some of the colours faded, but all the same the apparel furnished a brave show; and such was the avidity with which the poor creatures snatched at the garments as I offered them first to one and then another, that I believe they would have been perfectly satisfied with the clothes alone as payment for their services. I made this distribution on the quarter-deck, or little poop, rather, that all might be present: Wilkinson was at the tiller, and appeared highly delighted with the bundle allotted him, saying that he might reckon upon a hearty welcome from his wife when she came to know what was in his chest. The negroes were wild to clothe themselves at once; I advised them to wait for the warm weather, but they were too impatient to put on their fine feathers to heed my advice. They ran below, and were gone half an hour, during which time I have no doubt they put on all they had; and when at last they returned, their appearance was so exquisitely absurd that I laughed till I came near to suffocating. Each negro had tied a silver laced hat on to his woolly head; one wore a pair of crimson, the other a pair of black, velvet breeches; over their cucumber shanks they had drawn white silk stockings, regardless of the cold; their feet were encased in buckled shoes, and their costumes were completed by scarlet and blue waistcoats which fell to their knees, and crimson and blue coats with immense skirts. What struck me as most astonishing was their gravity. Their self-complacency was prodigious; they eyed each other with dignified approbation, and strutted with the air of provincial mayors and aldermen newly arrived from the presence of royalty.

"They're in keepin' with the schooner, any ways," said Wilkinson.

And so perhaps they were. The antique fabric needed the sparkle of those costumes on her deck to make her aspect fit in with the imaginations she bred. But, as I had anticipated, the cold proved too powerful for their conceit, and they were presently glad to ship their more modern trousers, though they clung obstinately to their waistcoats, and could not be persuaded to remove their hats on any account whatever.

Chapter XXX.
Our Progress to the Channel

WHEN I started to relate my adventure I never designed to write an account of the journey home at large. On the contrary, I foresaw that, by the time I had arrived at this part, you would have had enough of the sea. Let me now, then, be as brief as possible.

The melting of the ice and the slowly increasing power of the sun were inexpressibly consoling to me who had had so much of the cold that I do protest if Elysium were bleak, no matter how radiant, and the abode of the fiends as hot as it is pictured, I would choose to turn my back upon the angels. I cannot say, however, that the schooner was properly thawed until we were hard upon the parallels of the Falkland Islands; she then showed her timbers naked to the sun, and exposed a brown solid deck rendered ugly by several dark patches which, scrape as we might, we could not obliterate. We struck the guns into the hold for the better ballasting of the vessel, got studding-sail booms aloft, overhauled her suits of canvas and found a great square sail which proved of inestimable importance in light winds and in running. After the ice was wholly melted out of her frame she made a little water, yet not so much but that half an hour's spell at the pump twice a day easily freed her. But, curiously enough, at the end of a fortnight she became tight again, which I attribute to the swelling of her timbers.

We were a slender company, but we managed extraordinarily well. The men were wonderfully content; I never heard so much as a murmur escape one of them; they never exceeded their rations nor asked for a drop more of liquor than we had agreed among us should be served out. But, as I had anticipated, our security lay in our slenderness. We were too few for disaffection. The negroes were as simple as children, Wilkinson looked to find his account in a happy arrival, and if I was not, strictly speaking, their captain, I was their navigator without whom their case would have been as perilous as mine was on the ice.

Outside the natural dangers of the sea we had but one anxiety, and that concerned our being chased and taken. This fear was heartily shared by my companions, to whom I also represented that it must be our business to give even the ships of our country a wide berth; for, though I had long since flung all the compromising bunting overboard, and destroyed all the papers I could come across, which being written in a language I was ignorant of, might, for all I knew, contain some damning information, a British ship would be sure to board us and I should have to tell the truth or take the risks of prevaricating. If I told the truth, then I should have to admit that the lading of the vessel was piratical plunder; and though I knew not how the law stood with regard to booty rescued from certain destruction after the lapse of hard upon half a century, yet it was a hundred to one that the whole would be claimed in the king's name under a talk of restitution, which signified that we should never hear more of it. On the other hand prevarication would not fail to excite suspicion, and on our not being able to satisfactorily account for our possession of the ship and what was in her, it might end in our actually being seized as pirates and perhaps executed.

This reasoning went very well with the men and filled them with such anxiety that they were for ever on the look-out for a sail. But, as you may guess, my own solicitude sank very much deeper; for, supposing the schooner to be rummaged by an English crew, it was as certain as that my hand was affixed to my arm that the chests of treasure would be transhipped and lost to me by the law's trickery.

Now, till we were to the north of the equator we sighted nothing; no, in all those days not a single sail ever hove into view to break the melancholy continuity of the sea-line. But between the parallels of 12° and 22° N. we met with no less than eight ships, the nearest within a league. We watched them as cats watch mice; making a point to bear away if they were going our road, or, if they were coming towards us, to shift our helm—but never very markedly—so as to let them pass us at the widest possible distance. Some of them showed a colour, but we never answered their signals. That they were all harmless traders I will not affirm; but none of them offered to chase us. Yet could I have been sure of a ship, I should have been glad to speak. My longitude was little more than guesswork; my latitude not very certain; and my compass was out. However, I supported my own and the spirits of my little company by telling them of the early navigators; how Columbus, Candish, Drake, Schouten and other heroic marine worthies of distant times had navigated the globe, discovered new worlds, penetrated into the most secret solitudes of the deep without any notion of longitude and with no better instruments to take the sun's height than the forestaff and astrolabe. We were better off than they, and I had not the least doubt, I told them, of bringing the old schooner to a safe berth off Deal or Gravesend.

But it happened that we were chased when on the polar verge of the North-East Trade-wind. It was blowing brisk, the sea breaking in snow upon the weather bow, the sky overcast with clouds, and the schooner washing through it under a single-reefed mainsail and whole topsail. It was noon: I was taking an observation, when Pitt at the tiller sang out "Sail ho!" and looking, I spied the swelling cloud-like canvas of a vessel on a line with our starboard cathead. I told Pitt to let the schooner fall off three points, and with slackened sheets the old *Boca del Dragon* hummed through it brilliantly, flinging the foam as far aft as the gangway. The strange sail rose rapidly, and the lifting of her hull discovered her to be a line-of-battle ship. We held on as we were, hoping to escape her notice; but whether she did not like our appearance, or that there was something in the figure we cut that excited her curiosity, she, on a sudden, put her helm up and steered a true course for us.

At the first sight of her I had called Wilkinson and Cromwell on deck, and I now cried out, "Lads, d'ye see, she's after us. If she catches us our dream of dollars is over. Lively now, boys, and give her all she can stagger under; and what she can't carry she must drag." And we sprang to make sail, briskly as apes, and every one working with two-man power. I knew the old *Boca's* best point; it was with the wind a point abaft the beam; we put her to that, got the great square-sail on her, shook out all reefs, and gave all she had to the wind. The wake roared away from her like a white torrent that flies from the foot of a foaming cataract. She had the pirate's instincts, and being put to her trumps, was nimble. God! how she did swing through it! Never had I driven the aged bucket before like this, and I understood that speed at sea is not irreconcilable with odd bodies. But the great ship to windward hung steady; a cloud of bland and swelling cloths. When we had set the studding-sail we had nothing more to fly with; and so we stood looking. She slapped six shots at us, one after another, as a haughty hint to us to stop; but we meant to escape, and at last we did, outsailing her by thirteen inches to her foot—one foot to her twelve—though she stuck to our skirts the whole afternoon and kept us in an agony of anxiety.

The sun was setting when she abandoned us: she was then some five or six miles distant on our weather quarter. What her nation was I did not know; but Wilkinson reckoned her French when she gave us up. We rushed steadily along the same course into the darkness of the night and then, shortening sail, brought the schooner to the wind again, after which we drank to the frisky old jade in an honestly-earned bowl.

It was on the 5th of December that we sighted the Scilly Isles. I guessed what that land was, but so vague had been my navigation that I durst not be sure; until, spying a smack with her nets over, I steered for her and got the information I needed from her people. They answered us with an air of fear, and in truth the fellows had reason; for, besides the singular appearance of the ship, the four of us were apparelled in odds and ends of the antique clothes, and I have little doubt they considered us lunatics of another country, who had run away with a ship belonging to parts where the tastes and fashions were behind the age.

Now, as you may suppose, by this time I had settled my plans; and as we sailed up channel, I unfolded them to my companions. I pointed out that before we entered the river it would be necessary to discharge our lading into some little vessel that would smuggle the booty ashore for us. The figure the schooner made was so peculiar she would inevitably attract attention; she would instantly be boarded in the Thames on our coming to anchor, and, if I told the truth, she would be seized as a pirate, and ourselves dismissed with a small reward, and perhaps with nothing.

"My scheme," said I, "is this: I have a relative in London to whom I shall communicate the news of my arrival and tell him my story. You, Wilkinson must be the bearer of this letter. He is a shrewd, active man, and I will leave it to him to engage the help we want. There is no lack of the right kind of serviceable men at Deal, and if they are promised a substantial interest in smuggling our lading ashore, they will run the goods successfully, do not fear. As there is sure to be a man-of-war stationed in the Downs, we must keep clear of that anchorage. I will land you at Lydd, whence you will make your way to Dover and thence to London. Cromwell and Pitt will return and help me to keep cruising. My letter to my relative will tell him where to seek me, and I shall know his boat by her flying a jack. When we have discharged our lading we will sail to the Thames, and then let who will come aboard, for we shall have a clean hold. This," continued I, "is the best scheme I can devise. The risk of smuggling attend it, to be sure; but against those risks we have to put the certainty of our forfeiting our just claims to the property if we carry the schooner to the Thames. Even suppose, when there, that we should not be immediately visited, and so be provided with an opportunity to land our stuff—whom have we to trust? The Thames abounds with river thieves, with lumpers, scuffle-hunters, mud-larks, glutmen, rogues of all sorts, to hire whom would mean to bribe them with the value of half the lading and to risk their stealing the other half. But this is the lesser difficulty; the main one lies in this: there are some sixteen hundred men employed in the London Custom House, most of whom are on river duty as watchmen; thirty of these people are clapped aboard an East Indiaman, five or six on West India ships, and a like proportion in other vessels. So strange a craft as ours would be visited, depend on't, and smartly, too. D'ye see the danger, lads? What do you say, then, to my scheme?"

The negroes immediately answered that they left it to me; I knew best; they would be satisfied with whatever I did.

Wilkinson mused a while and then said, "Smuggling was risky work. How would it be if we represented that we had found the schooner washing about with nobody aboard?"

"The tale wouldn't be credited," said I. "The age of the vessel would tell against such a story, even if you removed all other evidence by throwing the clothes and small-arms overboard and whatever else might go to prove that the schooner must have been floating about abandoned since the year 1750!"

"Musn't lose de clothes, massa, on no account," cried Pitt.

"Well, sir," says Wilkinson, after another spell of reflection, "I reckon you're right. If so be the law would seize the vessel and goods on the grounds that she had been a pirate and all that's in her was plunder, why, then, certainly, I don't see nothin' else but to make a smuggling job of it, as you say, sir."

This being settled (Wilkinson's concurrence being rendered the easier by my telling him that, providing the lading was safely run, I would adhere to my undertaking to give them six hundred and sixty pounds each for their share), I went below and spent half an hour over a letter to Mr. Jeremiah Mason. There was no ink, but I found a pencil, and for paper I used the fly-leaves of the books in my cabin. I opened with a sketch of my adventures, and then went on to relate that the *Boca* was a *rich ship*; that as she had been a pirate, I risked her seizure by carrying her to London; that I stood grievously in need of his counsel and help, and begged him not to lose a moment in returning with the messenger to Deal, and there hiring a boat and coming to me, whom he would find cruising off Beachy Head. That I might know his boat, I bade him fly a jack a little below the masthead. "As for the *Boca del Dragon*," I added, "Wilkinson would recognize her if she were in the middle of a thousand sail, and indeed a farmer's boy would be able to distinguish her for her uncommon oddness of figure." I was satisfied to underscore the words "a rich ship," quite certain his imagination would be sufficiently fired by the expression. At anything further I durst not hint, as the letter would be open for Wilkinson to read.

When I had finished, I took a lanthorn and the keys of the chest and went very secretly and expeditiously to the run, and removing the layers of small-arms from the top of the case that held the money, I picked out some English pieces, quickly returned the small-arms, locked the chest, and returned.

All this time we were running up Channel before a fresh westerly wind. It was true December weather, very raw, and the horizon thick, but I knew my road well, and whilst the loom of the land showed, I desired nothing better than this thickness.

But wary sailing delayed us; and it was not till ten o'clock on the night of the seventh that we hove the schooner to off the shingly beach of Lydd within sound of the wash of the sea upon it. The bay sheltered us; we got the boat over; I gave Wilkinson the letter and ten guineas, bidding him keep them hidden and to use them cautiously with the silver change he would receive, for they were all guineas of the first George and might excite comment if he, a poor sailor, ill-clad, should pull them out and exhibit them. Happily, in the hurry of the time, he did not think to ask me how I had come by them. He thrust them into his pocket, shook my hand and dropped into the boat, and the negroes immediately rowed him ashore.

I stood holding a lanthorn upon the rail to serve them as a guide, waiting for the boat to return, and never breathed more freely in my life than when I heard the sound of oars. The two negroes came alongside, and, clapping the tackles on to the boat, we hoisted her with the capstan, and then under very small canvas stood out to sea again.

Chapter XXXI.
The End

I SHOULD require to write to the length of this book over again to do full justice by description to the difficulties and anxieties of the days that now followed. If it had not been thick weather all the time, I do not know how I should have fared, I am sure. I was between two fires, so to say; on the one side the French cruisers and privateers, and on the other side the ships of my own country, and particularly the revenue cutters and the sloops and the like cruising after the smugglers. As I knew that my relative could not be with me under four days, I steered out of sight of land into the middle of the Channel, betwixt Beachy Head and the Seine coast, and there dodged about under very small canvas, heartily grateful for the haze that shrouded the sea to within a mile of me. I scarcely closed my eyes in sleep, and though my worries were now of a very different kind from those which had racked me on the ice, they were, in their way, to the full as tormenting. Every sail that loomed in the dinginess filled me with alarm. Several ships passed me close, and I could scarce breathe till they were out of sight. Indeed, I lay skulking out upon that sea as if I was some common thief broken loose from jail. However, it pleased heaven that I should manage to keep out of sight of those whom I most strenuously desired not to see; and the afternoon of the fourth day found the *Boca* lying off Beachy Head, and I peering over the rail, with a haggard face, at the dark shadow of the land.

It had been blowing and snowing all day. The seas ran short and spitefully. It was a dismal December afternoon, and the more sensibly disgusting to us who were fresh from several weeks of the balm and glory of the tropics. And yet I would not have exchanged it for a clear fine day for all that I was like to be worth.

It was the most reasonable thing in the world that a vessel should be hove-to in such sombre weather, and so I was under no concern that our posture in this respect would excite suspicion, should we be descried. The hours stole away one by one. Now and again a little coaster would pass, some hoy bound west, a sloop for the Thames, a lugger on some unguessable mission: all small ships, oozing dark and damp out of the snow and mist and passing silently. I kept the land close aboard to be out of the way of the bigger craft, and held the vessel in the wind till it was necessary to reach to our station. The three of us were mighty pensive and eager, staring incessantly with all our eyes; but it looked as if we were not to expect anything that day when the night put its darkness into the weather. Then, as I foresaw a serious danger if the wind shifted into the south, and as I could not obtain a glimpse of a shore-light, I resolved to bring up and ride till dawn. Long ago we had got the schooner's old anchors at the catheads and the cables bent, so, lowering the mainsail and hauling down the stay foresail, we let fall the starboard anchor, and the ship came to a stand. I put the lead over the side that we might know if she dragged, hung a lantern on the forestay and one on either quarter that our presence might be marked by my relative should he be out in quest of us, and went below, leaving Cromwell to keep the look-out.

I was extremely fretful and anxious and had no patience to talk with Billy Pitt. There were too many risks, too many vague chances in this exploit to render contemplation of it tolerable. Suppose my relative should be dead? Suppose Wilkinson should be robbed of his money? fall to the cutting of capers, as a sailor newly delivered to the pleasures of the land with ten guineas in his pocket? Get locked up for breaking the peace? Blab of us in his cups and start the Customs on our trail? There was no end to such conjectures, and I made myself so melancholy that I was fool enough to think that the treasure was no better than a curse, and that on the whole I was better off on the ice than here with the anchor in English ground and my native soil within gunshot.

I was up and about till midnight, and then, being in the cabin and exhausted, I fell asleep across the table, and in that posture lay as one dead. Some one dragging at my arm, with very little tenderness, awoke me. I was in the midst of a dream of the schooner having been boarded by a party of French privateersmen, with Tassard at their head, and the roughness with which I was aroused was exactly calculated to extend into my waking the horror and grief of my sleep.

I instantly sprang to my feet and saw Washington Cromwell.

"Massa Rodney," he bawled, "Massa Rodney, de gent's 'longside—him an' Wilkinson—yaas, by de good Lord—dey'se both dere! Dey hail me an' I answer and say who are you, and dey say are you de *Boca*? We am, I say, and dey say——"

I had stood stupidly staring at him, but my full understanding coming to me on a sudden, I jumped to the ladder and darted on deck. I heard voices over the starboard side and ran there. It was not so dark but that I could see the outline of a Deal lugger. Whilst I was peering, the voice of my man Wilkinson cried out, "On deck, there! Cromwell—Billy—where's Mr. Rodney?"

"Here I am!" cried I.

"My God, Paul!" exclaimed the voice of Mr. Mason, "this encounter is fortunate indeed."

I shouted to the negroes to show a light, and in a few minutes Mr. Mason, Wilkinson, and a couple of Deal boatmen came over the side. I grasped my relative by both hands. I had not seen him for four years.

"This is good of you, indeed!" I cried. "But you must be perished with the cold of that open boat. Come below at once—come Wilkinson, and you men—there's a fire in the cook-room and drink to warm us;" and down I bundled in the wildest condition of excitement, followed by Mason and the others.

My relative was warmly clad and did not seem to suffer from the cold. He took me by the hand and brought me to the lanthorn-light, and stood viewing me.

"Ay," said he, "you are your old self: a bit worried looking, but that'll pass. Stout and burnt. Odd's heart! Paul, if you have passed through the experiences Wilkinson has given me a sketch of, we must have your life, man, we must have your life—for the booksellers."

Well, I need not detain you by reciting all the civilities and congratulations which he and I exchanged. He and Wilkinson had arrived at Deal at three o'clock that afternoon, and, after a hurried meal, had hired a lugger and started at once for Beachy Head. It was now three o'clock in the morning; and what I may consider a truly extraordinary circumstance is, that they had sailed as true a course for the schooner as if she had lain plain to the gaze at the very start; that since the night had drawn down they had met no vessel of any kind or description, until they came up to us; that in all probability they would have run stem on into us if they had not seen our lights, and that their seeing our lights had caused them to hail us, their "ship ahoy!" being instantly answered by Cromwell.

"Well," said I, "there are stranger things to tell of than this, even. Now, Wilkinson, and you Billy, and Cromwell, get us a good supper and mix a proper bowl. How many more of you are in the lugger?"

"Four, sir," says one of the boatmen.

"Then fetch as many as may safely leave the boat," said I. "Billy, get candles and make a good light here. Throw on coal, boys; there's enough to carry us home."

I saw Mason gazing curiously about him.

" 'Tis like a tale out of the Arabian Nights, Paul," he exclaimed.

"Ay," said I, "but written in bitter prose, and no hint of enchantment anywhere. But, thank God, you are come! I have passed a dismal time of expectation, I promise you." I added softly, "I have something secret—we will sup first, man—I shall amaze you! We must talk apart presently."

He bowed his head.

Three more boatmen arrived, giving us the company of five of them. Soon there was a hearty sound of frying and a smell of good things upon the air. Pitt put plates and glasses upon the cabin table, two great bowls of punch were brewed, and in a little time we had all fallen to. I whispered Wilkinson, who sat next me, "These boatmen know nothing of our business; I shall have to take Mr. Mason apart and arrange with him. These fellows may not be fit for our service. Let no hint escape you."

"Right, sir," said he.

This I said to disarm his suspicions should he see me talking alone with Mr. Mason. He entertained us with an account of his excursion to London; and then, partly to appease the profound curiosity of the boatmen and partly to save time when I should come to confer with my relative, I gave them the story of my shipwreck, and told how I had met with the schooner and how I had managed to escape with her.

"And now, Mason," said I, "whilst our friends here empty these bowls, come you with me to the cook-room." And with that we quitted the cabin.

"D'ye mean to tell me, Paul," was the first question my relative asked, "that this vessel was on the ice eight-and-forty years?"

"Yes," I replied.

"Surely you dream?"

"I think not."

"What we have been eating and drinking—is that forty-eight years old, too?"

"Ay, and older."

"Well, such a thing shall make me credulous enough to duck old women for witches. But what brandy—what brandy! Never had spirit such a bouquet. Every pint is worth its weight in guineas to a rich man. To think of Deal boatmen and negroes swilling such nectar!"

"Mason," said I, speaking low, "give me now your attention. In the run of this schooner are ten chests loaded with money, bars of silver and gold, and jewellery. This vessel was a pirate, and her people valued their booty at ninety to a hundred thousand pounds."

His jaw fell; he stared as if he knew not whether it was he or I that was mad.

"Here is evidence that I speak the truth," said I. "A little sample only—but look at it!" And I put the pirate captain's watch into his hand.

He eyed it as though he discredited the intelligence of his sight, turned it about, and returned it to me with a faint "Heaven preserve me!" Then said he, still faintly, "You found some of the pirates alive?"

"No."

"Who told you that the people of the vessel valued their plunder at that amount?"

I answered by giving him the story of the recovery of the Frenchman.

He listened with a gaze of consternation: I saw how it was; he believed my sufferings had affected my reason. There was only one way to settle his mind; I took a lanthorn, and asked him to follow me. As we passed through the cabin I whispered Wilkinson that I meant to show my relative the lading below, and bade him keep the Deal men about him. I had the keys of the chests in my pocket: lifting the after-hatch, we entered the lazarette, and Mason gazed about him with astonishment. But I was in too great a hurry to return to suffer him to idly stand and stare. I opened the second hatch and descended into the run, and crawling to the jewel chest opened it, removed a few of the small-arms, and bade him look for himself.

"Incredible! incredible!" he cried. "Is it possible! is it possible! Well, to be sure!" And for some moments he could find no more to say, so amazed and confounded was he.

I quickly showed him the gold and silver ingots and then returned the firearms and locked the chests.

"*These*," said I emphatically, pointing to the cases, "have been my difficulty; not the lading, though there is value there too. My crew know nothing of these chests: of their value, I mean; they believe them cases of small-arms. How am I to get them ashore? If I tell the truth, they will be seized as piratical plunder. If I equivocate, I may tumble into a pit of difficulties. I durst not carry them to the Thames, the river swarms with thieves and Custom House people. I am terrified to linger here, lest I be boarded and the booty discovered. There is but one plan, I think: we must hire some Deal smugglers to run these chests and the cargo for us. The boat now alongside might serve, and I don't doubt the men are to be had at their own price."

My relative had regained his wits, which the sight of the treasure had temporarily scattered, and surveyed me thoughtfully whilst I spoke; and then said, "Let us return to the fire; I think I have a better scheme than yours."

The men still sat around the table talking. Some liquor yet lay in one of the bowls, and the fellows were happy enough. I smiled at Wilkinson as I passed, that he might suppose our inspection below very satisfactory, and I saw him look meaningly and pleasantly at Washington Cromwell, who sat with a laced hat on his head.

"Paul," said Mason, sitting down and folding his arms, "your smuggling plan will not do. It would be the height of madness to trust those chests to the risks of running and to the honesty of the rogues engaged in that business."

"What is to be done?"

"Tell me your lading," said he.

I gave it to him as accurately as I could.

"Why," he exclaimed, "a single boat would take a long time to discharge ye—observe the perils—several boats would mean a large number of men; they would eat you up; they would demand so much, you would have nothing left. And suppose they opened the chests! No, your scheme is worthless."

"What's to do, then, in God's name?"

"I'll tell you!" he exclaimed, smiling with the complacency of a man who is master of a great fancy. "I shall sail to Dover at once. 'Tis now a quarter past four. Give me twelve hours to make Dover: I shall post straight to London and be there by early morning. Now, Paul, attend you to this. To-day is Wednesday; by to-morrow night you must contrive to bring your ship to an anchor off Barking Level."

"The Thames!" I cried.

He nodded.

I looked at him anxiously. He leaned to me, putting his hand on my leg.

"I own a lighter," said he: "she will be alongside of you at dusk. I have people of my own whom I can trust. The lighter will empty your hold and convey the lading to a ship chartered by me, arrived from the Black Sea on Sunday and lying in the Pool. The stuff can be sold from that ship as it is—"

"But the chests—the chests, Mason!"

"They shall be lowered into another boat, and taken ashore and put into a waggon that will be in waiting—I in it—and driven to my home."

I clapped him on the shoulder in a transport.

"Nobly schemed indeed!" I cried; "but have we nothing to fear from the Customs people?"

"No, not low down the river and at dark. You bring up for convenience, d'ye see. Mind it is dark when you anchor. A lighter and boat shall be awaiting you. It is down the river, you know, that all the lumpers drop with the lighters they go adrift in from ships' sides. There's more safety in smuggling over Thames mud than on this coast shingle. One thought more: you say that Wilkinson believes the chests hold small-arms?"

"Yes."

"Then account to him for sending the chests away separately by saying that I have found a purchaser, and that they are going to him direct. You have your cue—you see all!"

"All."

"Let me hurry, then, Paul; that brandy should fetch you half a guinea a pint. You are in luck's way, Paul. See that you bring your ship along safely. Till to-morrow night!"

He clasped and wrung my hand and ran into the cabin.

"Now, lads, off with us!" he cried. "Off to Dover! Put me ashore there smartly and you shall find your account. Off now—time presses."

Five minutes afterwards the boat was gone.

When fortune falls in love with a man she makes him a bounteous mistress. Everything fell out as I could have desired. We got our anchor at five, and by daybreak were off Hastings jogging quietly along towards London river, the weather conveniently obscure, the wind south, and forty hours before us to do the run in. I exactly explained my relative's scheme to Wilkinson and the others, who declared themselves perfectly satisfied, Wilkinson adding that though he had not objected to the Deal smuggling project he throughout considered the risk too heavy to adventure. I told them that Mr. Mason believed he could immediately find a purchaser for the small-arms, in which case they would have to be sent privately ashore; and to give a proper colour to this ruse I made them pack away all the remaining weapons in the arms-room and carry them to the run, ready to be taken with the other chests.

Once fairly round the Forelands half my anxieties fell from me. There was no longer the French cruiser or privateer to be feared, and however wonderingly the people of my own country's vessels might stare at the uncommon figure of my schooner, they could find no excuse to board us. Besides, as I have said, I was greatly helped by the weather, which continuing hazy, though happily never so thick as to oblige me to stop, delivered me to the sight only of such vessels as passed close, and offered me as a mere smudge to the shore.

We arrived off Barking Level on the Thursday night, and dropped anchor close to a lighter that lay there with a large boat hanging by her. It was then very dark. The first person to come on board was Mason. He was followed by several men, one of whom he introduced to me as his head clerk, who would see to the unloading of the schooner and to the transhipment of the goods to the ship in the Pool. He informed me that there was a covered van waiting on shore; and telling Wilkinson that the small-arms had been disposed of, and that Mr. Mason would hand over the proceeds on our calling at his office, I went with a party of my relative's men into the run and presently had the whole of the chests in the boat. Mason went with her.

Then, as she disappeared in the darkness, but not till then, did I draw the first easy breath I had fetched since the hour of the collision of the *Laughing Mary* with the iceberg. A sob shook me: I had gone through much: many wonderful things had happened to me: I had been delivered from such perils that the mere recollection of them will stir my hair, though it is years since; my duty I knew, and I discharged it by withdrawing to my cabin and kneeling with humble and grateful heart before the throne of that Being to whom I owed everything.

Postscript

Here concludes the remarkable narrative of Mr. Paul Rodney. It is to be wished that he had found the patience to tell us a little more. The circumstance of his dying in 1823, worth 31,000*l*., leads me to suspect that his associate Tassard greatly exaggerated the value of the treasure. I am assured that he lived very quietly, and that the lady he married, who bore him two children, both of whom died young, was of a nunlike simplicity of character and loved show and extravagance as little as her husband. Hence there is no reason to suppose that he squandered any portion of the fortune that had in the most extraordinary manner ever heard of fallen into his hands. I have ascertained that he very substantially discharged the great obligation that his relative Mason laid him under, and that his three men received a thousand pounds apiece. It is possible, then, that the pirates were themselves deceived, that what they had taken to be gold or silver ingots were not all so; or it might be that the case of jewellery was less valuable than the admiring and astonished eyes of a plain sailor, who admits that he had never before seen such a sight, figured it. Be this, however, as it may, it is nevertheless certain, as proved by Mr. Rodney's last will and testament, that he did uncommonly well out of his adventure on the ice.

Whatever may be thought of his story of the Frenchman's restoration to life, in other directions Mr. Rodney's accuracy seems unimpeachable. It is quite conceivable that a stoutly-built vessel locked up in the ice and thickly glazed, should continue in an excellent state of preservation for years. The confession of his superstitious fears exhibits honesty and candour. It is related that a Captain Warren, master of an English merchant-ship, found a derelict (in August, 1775) that had long been ice-bound, with her cabins filled with the bodies of the frozen crew. "His own sailors, however, would not suffer him to search the vessel thoroughly, through superstition, and wished to leave her immediately." A pity they did not try their hands at thawing one of the poor fellows: the result might have kept Mr. Rodney's strange experience in countenance!

Accounts of vast bodies of ice, such as that which Mr. Rodney fell in with, will be found in the South Atlantic Directory. For instance:

"Sir James C. Ross crossed Weddel's track in Lat. 65°S., and where he had found an open sea, Ross found an ice-pack of an impassable character, along which he sailed for 160 miles; and again, when only one degree beyond the track of Cook, who had no occasion to enter the pack, Ross was navigating among it for fifty-six days.

"But these appear insignificant when compared with a body of ice reputed to have been passed by twenty-one ships during the months of December, 1854, and January, February, March, and April, 1855, floating in the South Atlantic from Lat 44°S., Long. 28°W., to Lat. 40°S., Long. 20°W. Its elevation in no case exceeded 300 feet. The first account of it was received from the *Great Britain*, which in December, 1854, was reported to have steamed 50 miles along the outer side of the longer shank." One ship was lost upon it: others embayed.

THE END

About the Author

WILLIAM CLARK RUSSELL (1844–1911) was born in New York to English parents. Both his mother, Isobel, through her family connection to poet Charles Lloyd, and his father, Henry, a musician and composer best known for writing such stirring anthems as "Life on the Ocean Wave" and "Cheer, Boys, Cheer", had artistic leanings.

Young William himself appears to have had a taste for adventure. It was reported that while at school he and a classmate, one of Charles Dickens's sons, had planned to run away.

William aged 5 years old.

At the age of 13 William became a midshipman in the British Merchant Service and his experience of sea life came from his eight years of service.

226

Midshipman Russell aged about 17 years old.

After leaving the sea, Russell worked as a stockbroker but decided he wanted to be a writer. His first work, a play, "Fra Angelo" was performed at London's Haymarket Theatre in 1865 but was a flop. He continued with his writing and often used his seafaring experience.

Russell's second seafaring novel, *The Wreck of the Grosvenor*, published in 1877, took two months to write and was sold to a publisher for £50 (the equivalent of the annual salary of a shop worker). The novel was an outstanding success and started a career in writing sea stories.

As an indication of the popularity of Russell's novels, Arthur Conan Doyle mentioned him in one of the Sherlock Holmes's stories, *The Five Orange Pips*, where Dr Watson is described as being "deep in one of Clark Russell's fine sea-stories until the howl of the gale from without seemed to blend with the text, and the splash of the rain to lengthen out into the long swash of the sea waves".

According to John Sutherland, Emeritus Professor of Modern English Literature at University College London, *The Wreck of the Grosvenor* was "the most popular mid-Victorian melodrama of adventure and heroism at sea". It was a bestselling book well into the first half of the twentieth century.

William Clark Russell, successful novelist, aged about 49 years old.

Reanimation: An Age-old Obsession?

George Cavendish

CLARK Russell's *The Frozen Pirate* was published in 1877 and it is said to have been the first example of cryogenic suspension being used in an English-language novel (Dodds, 2002).

A contemporary reviewer (*New York Tribune*, 1887) pointed out that Clark Russell might owe a debt to Edmond About for his *The Man With the Broken Ear*, which was published in French as *L'homme à l'oreille cassée* in 1862. In this novel the idea of dehydrating and then reanimating someone is featured. It appears that there was an English translation of the novel published in the USA in 1867.

Clark Russell's cryogenic idea is perhaps a more plausible reanimation technique as there have been many reports of animals being brought "back to life" out of a frozen state. To be fair to Clark Russell, he may have come up with the idea of reanimation from a frozen state from the scientific press and not About's book. The *Scientific American* (1852) journal carried one such article:

> We have received a great many communications on this subject [the resuscitation of frozen fish], all of them corroborating the statement, "frozen fish will come alive again when placed in a tub of water."
>
> Quarterman & Son, this city [New York], informs us that the fish in the streams of Westchester Co., N.Y., are frequently caught, thrown out, left to freeze, and are resuscitated when thawed.
>
> Mr. Cumings Martin, of Taftsville, Vt., caught suckers out of White River, Vt., flung them on the ice, allowed them to be there for hours until they were apparently frozen through, and would rattle in the basket like pine knots. When thawed out in cold water, they would wriggle and move about as good as new.
>
> J.H. Bacon, of Westchester, Mass., says he has taken Tom Cod out of the river, allowed them to freeze, carried them to Boston and has seen them come alive when thawed.
>
> William Rummel, of Jersey City, N.J., caught a some perch in the Hackensack river, in 1836, which froze quickly, he carried them to market which was very dull, he then packed them in snow for three weeks, and after this, when applying pump water to them, every twenty-five in thirty

swam about in the tub. He says if fish be frozen in moderate weather, and take a long time to do so, they will not return to life.

Robert Pike, of Wakefield, N.H., says he has caught brook trout in January, which froze through in a few minutes, and which, after five hours, when he took them home and put them in a tub of cold water, swam around quite lively.

Thomas Power, of Hudson, N.Y., says he has seen fish which were frozen as hard as rock come to life when thawed in cold water. The fish were yellow perch found in the Hudson river.

D.H. Quail, of Philadelphia, noticing the statement of Prof. Lathrop, says he has caught fish in N.J. near Fortescue's Beach, in Delaware Bay, in winter, in the following manner, which is interesting; he says, "having procured a small boat, we dragged it into the ponds that were formed on the marsh by high tides, and which were frozen over nearly hard enough to bear the boat; then commenced the sport; one would stand in front to break the way, another push the boat along, the third with a small crab net would scoop up the fish which could be seen upon the bottom frozen as stiff as bones—they were all large perch. I caught half a bushel, which, when taken home and put into a tub of cold water from the well, in a short time were swimming about quite lively."

Mr. B.M. Douglass, of East Springfield, Conn., says he has caught perch, pickerel, trout, and carp, in winter, allowed them to freeze, carried them for miles, and when thawed out in well water, not one in six but would come to life. He adds, they can be carried to any distance if kept frozen, but if not frozen quickly after being caught "they will not come too," this he has always noticed. By this, it appears, that if a considerable time elapses between the period when the fish is taken out of the river and thawed they cannot be resuscitated.

Ransom Cook, of Saratoga, N.Y., a very observing man, adds a new fact to this store of information on the subject. He says, that all fish which have been frozen and resuscitated, have their sense of sight destroyed—they all become blind.

The *New York Tribune* (1887) reviewer also reminded his or her readers of the reanimation of the "Famous Fakir of Lahore". The *New York Times* (1880) contained the following interesting article taken from the *Daily Telegraph*, a London newspaper. ("Runjeet Singh" would appear to be Maharaja Ranjit Singh, 1780–1839, the founder of the Sikh Empire that exited in the Punjab region of India from 1799 to 1849).

Runjeet Singh had heard from a Seyd or Fakir, who lived in the mountains, that the latter could allow himself to be buried when in a condition of apparent death, without really ceasing to live, seeing that he understood the art of being brought back to life on being exhumed after several months had passed. To the Maharajah this appeared to be a rank impossibility. In order, however, that he should he convinced one way or the other, he ordered the Fakir to be summoned to the Court, and caused him to undertake the singular experiment, under a threat that no means of precaution would be wanting toward the discovery of fraud. The Fakir consequently caused himself to appear in a state of apparent death. When every spark of life had seemingly vanished, he was, in the presence of the Maharajah and the nobles who surrounded him, wrapped up in the linen on which he had been sitting, and on which the seal of Runjeet Singh was placed. The body was then deposited in a chest, on which Runjeet Singh, with his own hand, fixed at heavy padlock.

The chest was carried outside the town and buried in a garden belonging to the Minister; barley was sown over the spot, a wall was erected around it, and sentinels posted. On the fortieth day, when the chest containing the Fakir was dug up and opened the man was found cold and stark in precisely the same condition as that in which he had been left. With much trouble he was restored to life by means of heat applied to the head, afflation [breathing or blowing] in the ears and mouth, rubbing the body, &c. The Minister, Rajah Dhyan-Singh, assured a friend that he had this Fakir, whose name was Haridas, for a period of four months under the earth at Jummoo in the mountains. On the day of his burial he had caused his beard to be shaved off, and when he was taken up again his chin was just as smooth as on the day when he was consigned to the earth—a proof, as would seem, of suspended animation. It is related that the Fakir in question took a purgative some time before the burial display, and for several days afterward lived only on a scanty milk diet. On the day of the interment it is said that, instead of taking any nourishment, he swallowed 30 yards of a strip of linen of the breadth of three fingers, which he immediately drew up again, his object being to clean the stomach. However wonderful and perhaps laughable these operations appear to many, it is plain that these people must have a singular control over the different organs of their bodies, and more especially over their muscular contractions. When all the necessary preparations have been accomplished, the Fakir closes all the openings of his body with stoppers made of aromatic wax, lays his tongue far back in his throat, crosses his hands on his breast, and suspends animation by means of holding his breath. On his being brought back to life one of the first operations is by means of the fingers, to draw the tongue away from the back of the throat; a warm and aromatic paste made of meal is then placed on his head, and air is blown into his lungs and into the ear-holes, from which the wax stoppers have been removed, the stoppers in the nostrils being presently forced out with an explosive noise. This is said to be the first sign of a return to life. He then gradually commences to breathe, opens the eyes, and recovers consciousness, continuous friction of the body being carried on all the time.

Here is a further curious statement of opinion on the subject of the Indian stories from an equally rare source, the little pamphlet of Sir Claude Wade, published in 1837. "I was present," he writes, "at the Court of Runjeet Singh when the Fakir, mentioned by the Hon. Capt. Osborne, was buried alive for six weeks; and, although I arrived at few hours after his actual internment; and did not, consequently, witness that part of the phenomenon, I had the testimony of Runjeet Singh himself, and others of the most credible witnesses of his Court, to the truth of the Fakir having been buried before them; and, from my having been myself present when he was disinterred, and restored to a state of perfect vitality in a position so close to him as to render any deception impossible, it is my firm belief that there was no collusion in producing the extraordinary sight which I have to relate. I will briefly state what I saw, to enable others to judge of the weight due to my evidence, and whether my proof of collusion can, in their opinion, be detected. On the approach of the appointed time, according to invitation, I accompanied Runjeet Singh to the spot where the Fakir had been buried. It was in a square building, called a *barra durra*, in the middle of one of the gardens adjoining the Palace at Lahore, with an open veranda all round, having an enclosed room in the center. On arriving there, Runjeet Singh, who was attended on the occasion by the whole of his Court, dismounted from his elephant, asked me to join him in examining the building to satisfy himself that it was closed as he had left it. After our examination we seated ourselves in the veranda opposite the door, while some of Runjeet Singh's people dug away the mud wall, and one of his officers broke the seal and opened the padlock. When the door was thrown open nothing but a dark room was to be seen. Runjeet Singh and myself then entered it, in company with the servant of the Fakir, and, a light being brought, we descended about three feet below the floor of the room, into a sort of cell, where a wooden box about 4 feet long by 3 feet broad, with a sloping roof, contained the Fakir, the door of which had also a padlock and seal similar to that on the outside. On opening it we saw a figure enclosed in a bag of white linen, fastened by a string over the head, on the exposure of which at grand salute was fired, and the surrounding multitude came crowding to the door to see the spectacle. After they had gratified their curiosity, the Fakir's servant putting his arms into the box, took the figure out, and, closing the door, placed it with its back against it, exactly as the Fakir had been squatting (like a Hindu idol) in the box itself. Runjeet Singh and myself descended into the cell, which was so small we were only able to sit on the ground in front of the body, and so close to it as to touch it with our hands and knees. The servant then began pouring warm water over the figure, but as my object was to see if any fraudulent practices could be detected, I proposed to Runjeet Singh to tear open the bag and have a perfect view of the body before any means of resuscitation were employed. I accordingly did so; and may here remark that the bag when first seen by us looked mildewed, as if it had been buried some time. The legs and arms of the body were shriveled and stiff, the face full, the head reclined on the shoulder like that of a corpse. I then called to the medical gentleman who was attending me to come down and inspect the body, which he did, but could discover no pulsation in the heart, the temples, or the arms. There was, however a heat about the region of the brain which no other part exhibited. The servant then commenced bathing him with hot water, and gradually relaxing his arms and legs from the rigid state in which they were contracted, Ranjeet Singh taking his right and I his left leg, to aid by friction in restoring them to their proper action, during which time the servant placed at hot wheaten cake, about an inch thick, on the top of the head—a process which he twice or thrice repeated. He then pulled out of his nostrils and ears the wax and cotton with which they had been stopped, and after great exertion opened his mouth by inserting the point of a knife between his teeth, and while holding his jaw open with his left hand drew the tongue forward with his right, in the course of which the tongue flew back several times to its curved position upward, in which it had been, so as to close the gullet. He then rubbed his eyes with ghee (or clarified butter) for some seconds, till he succeeded in opening them, when the eyes appeared quite motionless and glazed. After the cake had been applied for the third time to the top of the head the body was violently convulsed, the nostrils became inflated, when respiration ensured, and the limbs began to assume a nature of fullness; but the pulsation was still faintly perceptible. The servant then put some of the ghee on his tongue and made him swallow it. A few minutes afterward the eyeballs became dilated, and recovered their natural color, when the Fakir recognized Runjeet Singh sitting close to him, and articulated in a low sepulchral tone, scarcely audible. 'Do you believe me now?' Runjeet Singh replied in the affirmative, and invested the Fakir with a pearl necklace and a superb pair of gold bracelets, and pieces of silk and muslin, and shawls, forming what is called a *khelat*, such as is usually conferred by the Princes of India on persons of distinction. I share entirely in the apparent incredibility of the fact of a man being buried alive and surviving the trial without food or drink for various periods of duration; but, however incompatible with our knowledge of physiology, in the absence of any visible proof to the contrary, I am bound to declare my belief in the facts winch I have represented, however impossible their existence may appear to others."

Scientific research continues to this day and an article by McIntyre and Fahy (2015) describes the preservation and recovery of frozen rabbit and pig brains. The scientists used a novel technique to preserve the brains which were then frozen to −135°C. The brains were later thawed and it was found that the neurons and synapses "displayed ultrastructural preservation indistinguishable from that of controls".

Cryonics of people started in the 1960s and today there are several thousand dead bodies frozen in vaults of commercial companies hoping for future science to be able to bring them back to life, or perhaps to have their brains "digitally resurrected" (Day, 2015).

References

Day, E., 2015. "Dying is the last thing anyone wants to do – so keep cool and carry on", *The Observer*, 11 October 2015. www.theguardian.com/science/2015/oct/11/cryonics-booms-in-us (accessed 11 February 2015).

Dodds, George T., 2002. A review of *The Frozen Pirate*. www.sfsite.com/07a/fp131.htm (accessed 11 February 2016).

McIntyre, R.L. and Fahy, G.M., 2015. "Aldehyde-stabilized cryopreservation", *Cryobiology*, Volume 71, pages 448–58.

New York Times, 1880. "Buried For Forty Days; Wonderful Performances of the Indian Fakirs", 22 August 1880, page 2.

New York Tribune, 1887. Book reviews, 25 November 1887, page 6.

Scientific American, 1852. "Resuscitation of Frozen Fish", Volume VII, No. 22, 14 February 1852, page 171.

Printed in Great Britain
by Amazon